The Skeleton Man

Jim Kelly is a journalist. He lives in Ely in Cambridgeshire with the writer Midge Gillies and their young daughter. *The Skeleton Man* is his fifth novel, following *The Coldest Blood*, *The Moon Tunnel*, *The Fire Baby* and *The Water Clock*, which was shortlisted for the CWA John Creasey Award for best first novel of 2002. He is currently at work on his new mystery, *Death Wore White*, featuring DI Peter Shaw (who is introduced in *The Skeleton Man*).

In 2006 Jim Kelly was awarded the Dagger in the Library by the Crime Writers' Association for a body of work 'giving greatest enjoyment to crime fiction readers'.

To find out more about Jim Kelly and other Penguin crime writers, go to www.penguinmostwanted.co.uk

The Skeleton Man

JIM KELLY

MICHAEL JOSEPH
an imprint of
PENGUIN BOOKS

MICHAEL JOSEPH

Published by the Penguin Group
Penguin Books Ltd, 80 Strand, London WC2R ORL, England
Penguin Group (USA) Inc., 375 Hudson Street, New York, New York 10014, USA
Penguin Group (Canada), 90 Eglinton Avenue East, Suite 700, Toronto, Ontario, Canada M4P 2Y3
(a division of Pearson Penguin Canada Inc.)
Penguin Ireland, 25 St Stephen's Green, Dublin 2, Ireland
(a division of Penguin Books Ltd)
Penguin Group (Australia), 250 Camberwell Road,
Camberwell, Victoria 3124, Australia (a division of Pearson Australia Group Pty Ltd)
Penguin Books India Pvt Ltd, 11 Community Centre,
Panchsheel Park, New Delhi – 110 017, India
Penguin Group (NZ), 67 Apollo Drive, Rosedale, North Shore 0632, New Zealand
(a division of Pearson New Zealand Ltd)
Penguin Books (South Africa) (Pty) Ltd, 24 Sturdee Avenue,
Rosebank, Johannesburg 2196, South Africa

Penguin Books Ltd, Registered Offices: 80 Strand, London WC2R ORL, England

www.penguin.com

First published 2007
1

Set in 13.5/16 pt Monotype Garamond
by Palimpsest Book Production Limited, Grangemouth, Stirlingshire
Printed in England by Clays Ltd, St Ives plc

A CIP catalogue record for this book is available from the British Library

ISBN: 978-0-718-14949-9

In memory of
Robert J. M. Gillies
MBE, MRCVS
1921–2006

A proud son of the Rock, and a great reader of books

Acknowledgements

I owe a debt to many in the writing of *The Skeleton Man*. The village of Jude's Ferry is a fiction but its story was inspired by that of a real-life community. I must therefore thank Rex Sawyer for his affectionate history, *Little Imber on the Down: Salisbury Plain's Ghost Village*. My lost village is a patchwork of many places real and imaginary. I stole the name from the Jude's Ferry Inn at West Row, near Mildenhall, and anyone wishing to drink in the true atmosphere of the watery fens can do no better than to stop a while at this inn on the site of a Roman port. The Five Miles from Anywhere pub I describe doesn't exist, although the name was once popular in the Fens.

The live Peytons in my story are also fictitious, though the Peyton family tombs are real enough; they lie in the church at Isleham, near Ely, and are well worth a visit.

In my career as a provincial journalist I have on several occasions been the guest of the Territorial Army – particularly during Operation Lionheart, the largest troop exercise in Europe since D-Day. I would like to thank the TA for their welcome in the past and for providing valuable background information. All my military characters are fictional, but their diligence and courage are real.

My thanks to Paul Horrell for lending me his expertise on cars generally over the years and particularly for offering an insight into the left-hand-drive market.

One of the most bizarrely named institutions I have ever

described is the Oliver Zangwill Centre for Neuropsychological Rehabilitation in Ely, but it is most certainly real and does a wonderful job. Of course, all characters and episodes related to it here are fictional.

Dr Andrew Balmford of the University of Cambridge provided some jargon-free advice on DNA identification within families; Jane Kennedy, Surveyor of Fabric at Ely cathedral, delivered an invaluable primer in medieval tombs; and Roger Steward, of Anglian Water Services, took the time to show me round the magnificent Soham water tower.

As always, this book would not have appeared without the support of the team which has so far ensured the publication of five Philip Dryden mysteries. Beverley Cousins, my editor, Faith Evans, my agent, and Midge Gillies, my wife, are a triumvirate without whom I would be lost. Trevor Horwood, my copy-editor, and Jenny Burgoyne, who read the manuscript, allow us all to sleep easier at nights.

Lastly, the landscape. Anyone trying to follow the plot using an Ordnance Survey map will go mad in the attempt. I have shuffled the real world to make the most of the wonderful treasure house of Fen nomenclature, and to keep one step ahead of the libel lawyers.

St Swithun's Day
Sunday, 15 July 1990

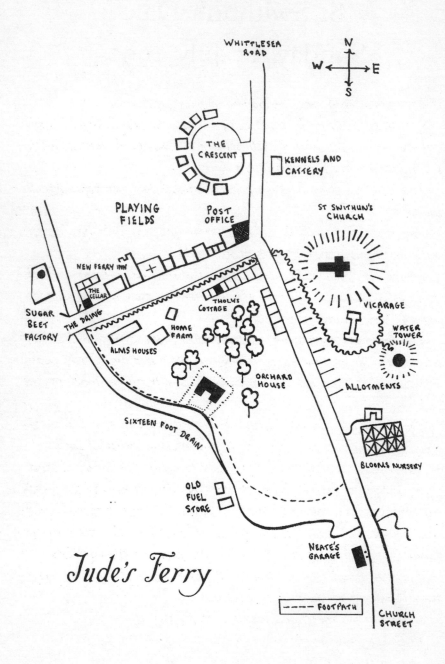

Jude's Ferry

It was a child's high stool, commandeered for the execution.

I stood with my back to the wall, part of the crowd, not the mob, but even then I knew that such a line could not be drawn: a line to separate the guilty from the innocent.

Twelve of us then, and the accused on the stool, the rope tight to the neck.

Again the question. 'Why?' Each time marked by a blow to the naked ribs, blood welling up beneath the skin.

I could have answered, ended it then. But instead I pressed my back against the cool wall, wondering why there were no more denials, wondering why life had been given up.

The victim's knees shook, and the legs of the stool grated on the cellar's brick floor. Outside in the night there was a dog's bark, heard through the trapdoor above, and twelve chimes from the church on the hill.

Then the ringleader did it, because he had the right that was in his blood. Stepping forward he swung a foot, kicking the stool away.

The body, a dead weight, fell; but not to earth. The plastic click of the neck breaking marked the extent of the rope, followed by the grinding of shattered vertebra as the body turned, its legs running on air. The moment of death stretched out, calibrated by the rattle in the throat. Urine trickled from the bare feet, yellow in the torchlight.

I fainted, standing, for a heartbeat. When I looked again the arms, bound and ugly in death, were lifeless.

It was justice, they said, licking parted lips.

Justice in Jude's Ferry.

3

Seventeen years later

St Swithun's Day
Sunday, 15 July 2007
Whittlesea Mere

I

The Capri shook to the sound of snoring, and through the fly-spattered windscreen of the mini-cab Philip Dryden contemplated the Fen horizon. Humph, the driver, slept peacefully, his lips brought together in a small bow, his sixteen stone compressing the seat beneath him. Around them the drained wasteland that had once been Whittlesea Mere, an inland lake the size of a small English county, stretched beyond sight. Overhead a cloud the size of a battleship sailed across an unblemished sky.

The cab was parked in the cool shadow of a hawthorn, the only tree visible to the naked eye. They'd presented themselves at 9.00am precisely that morning at the checkpoint to Whittlesea Mere Military Firing Range, and been directed down a potholed drove to the assembly point: the wreck of a wartime tank, ferns hanging from the dark observation slit. They hadn't seen another human being since they'd been waved through the gates, which had not stopped Dryden imagining they were being watched.

The reporter smoothed down his camouflage tunic and felt the familiar anxieties crowding round. This isn't a war zone, he told himself, it's a military exercise. And I'm not a soldier, I'm a reporter. I'm here to write about it, not take part. But the sight of a line of soldiers marching towards them, raising a cloud of desert-red peat dust, made his heartbeat pick up. A trickle of sweat set out from the edge of his thick jet-black hair, down towards his eye. He brushed it aside, aware that another one would quickly take its place.

Dryden checked his watch: 10.15am. The time had come. He fingered the webbing inside the blue combat helmet he was holding. The neat carved features of his medieval face remained static. He got out, the Capri's rusted door hinges screaming, and circled the cab to Humph's open side window.

'You can go,' he said, waking the cabbie, watching as he struggled to remember where he was and what he was doing.

'Really . . .' said Humph, wiping his nose with a small pillowcase. 'Can't I stick around until they start trying to kill people?'

Dryden tried to smile. 'Just remember. Same place, five pm. And for Christ's sake don't leave me here.' Boudicca, Humph's greyhound, dozing on a tartan rug in the back seat, yawned in the heat, trapping a bluebottle. Humph turned the ignition key, the engine coughed once and started, and he pulled away at speed, leaving an amber-red cloud as he raced towards the safety of the distant checkpoint. Dryden, alone, felt the hairs on his neck bristle.

The soldiers approached the tank and at a word from an officer made temporary camp. They sat, feet in the ditch, and broke out water bottles while a billycan was set up on a portable gas ring. Winding chimneys of white smoke rose from cigarettes in the still, hot air. Dryden sensed their collective antagonism to the presence of the press, and watched, oddly fascinated, as one soldier dismantled and oiled an automatic rifle. Another stood, walked a few yards downwind and urinated into a ditch.

Sensing the calculated insult Dryden looked away and heard laughter at his back, then footsteps approaching. He turned to face a heavy man with three pips on his jacket. The officer made his way through the gorse, picking up his legs and arms as he walked, a self-conscious compensation

8

perhaps for the onset of middle age. Dryden guessed he was in his late thirties, but a military uniform had never made anyone look any younger. The major's hair was boot-polish black and shone unnaturally, but his complexion was poor, blotched as if his face had been scrubbed with a nail-brush. Cross-checking his position on a hand-held GPS with a map in a plastic see-through wallet he noticed Dryden, and was unable to hide a frisson of annoyance.

'Dryden?' he asked. 'Philip Dryden – from *The Crow*?' They shook hands, the soldier's grip was surprisingly weak, the voice higher than he'd expected but holding some warmth, despite the clipped tones. 'Broderick. Major John Broderick.' He seemed embarrassed by the informality of the first name and turned to scan the horizon. 'You've signed the blood sheet?' he asked.

Dryden nodded. At the gate he'd been presented with an official form for signature which effectively removed his right to claim compensation if some idiot with a long-range peashooter turned him into a human jigsaw.

The major smiled, taking five years off his age: 'Just routine. Only with live firing we insist. Regulations. You lot in the press would be the first to get on our case if we broke the rules.'

Laughter rolled along the line of men by the ditch, and Dryden wondered what was funny. Excluded, he looked towards the north where the guns must be, hidden beyond the horizon.

'So they'll fire over our heads, right?' he asked, realizing immediately that there was little alternative. 'Sorry. Stupid question.'

The major nodded.

'When does the shelling start?' Dryden asked.

'Maroon – that's the signal flare – goes up 10.50am. They'll hit it on the pip. Ten minutes later they open fire with an eight-minute bombardment, then we go into the first line of attack and stop. Then, 11.20, another maroon, followed by a further five-minute bombardment at 11.30. Then we move forward to the targets.' Broderick rubbed his hands together. 'Pictures?'

Dryden swung round a digital camera. 'I'm a one-man band.'

'Great.' The major smiled. That was all the military was ever interested in, thought Dryden – pictures to send home, pictures for the scrapbook, pictures for the mess wall, pictures in the local paper, pictures for the MoD. Sod the words.

Broderick looked up at the sky. 'St Swithun's Day,' he said. 'Looks like we could have a good month.' The battleship cloud was a distant smudge to the east, and the rising sun was already compressing their shadows around their boots.

Dryden slapped a mosquito against the back of his hand. 'You Territorial Army too?' he asked, keen to talk about something other than the weather.

'Sure, sure. These are my men,' he said, managing not to make it sound proprietorial.

'So what do you do in Civvy Street?'

The major looked him in the face. 'Business,' he said, ducking the question.

A maroon thudded from the direction of the checkpoint, the signal that they had ten minutes before the bombardment began. The dull percussion in the sky was marked by a purple blotch and matched by a solid jolt through the earth.

The men stood and gathered round, following Broderick up onto the top of the old tank. The billycan was passed around, the tea inside reeked of tannin, had been sweetened with Carnation milk, and was the colour of liquid cattle manure. Dryden took a gulp, casually, knowing he was being watched.

Broderick sat on the turret, spreading out a map for the men. 'Right. Listen up. Today's exercise is live firing. This range was requisitioned in 1907. That's a century. So far the number of soldiers who have left Whittlesea Mere in a body bag is four. There is absolutely no law of nature which says one of you can't make it five, so listen.'

Dryden imagined the crumpled body bag, his own hand peeping from the folds of black plastic, blood under the fingernails. 'War games,' he thought, realizing what an obscene juxtaposition of words it was.

The major's briefing was brutally short. The Royal Artillery would bomb the two targets – twice – then the company would move in, conduct house-to-house searches, flush out insurgents, secure the target and replace the red target flags with blue. All shells would be live, all personal ammunition blank. Blue helmets denoted Blue Force – those attacking. Red Force, the enemy, was in position. Its soldiers, wooden cutout targets with concentric rings running out from the heart, wore red hats; a helpful designation Dryden could not help feeling undermined the integrity of the exercise. His own yellow armband proclaimed him a non-combatant.

'And this is our target,' said Broderick, stabbing a finger at the heart of the Fen wasteland shown on the map. 'The lost village of Jude's Ferry.'

2

When the first shell ripped overhead Dryden threw himself into the peaty soil, unable to stop his fingers digging down. He knew now why so many corpses in pictures of the carnage that was the trenches of the First World War seemed to be trying to bury themselves, clawing a way down, seeking the only route of escape. Dryden had no illusions about his reserves of courage. He was running on an empty tank and always had been. He was scared of loud noises, scared of pain, scared of dogs to the point of petrification, scared of heights, scared of small spaces and, crucially, scared of looking scared – a final twist which had ironically secured him a reputation for courage.

Sweating silently into his unfamiliar kit he could smell the fear, a pungent aroma normally associated with a loose drain cover. As each volley of shells wailed overhead he hugged the earth, drinking in the smell of warm grass and cow parsley.

The first salvo complete, Broderick got his men to their feet and they moved forward a mile over rough country, taking cover along a dyke dotted with Flanders poppies.

The second maroon sounded and Dryden counted the minutes, lying on his back, watching swallows overhead. He wiped his forehead with the back of his hand and smelt the salt. Broderick made a makeshift pillow with his hands behind his head.

Dryden broke the tension with a question. 'How can you be sure there's no one in the village?'

Broderick brought his hands round and held them up against the sky. 'Well, strictly speaking, we can't. There's a perimeter fence, and the MoD's spent a lot of money in the last few days catching up on repairs, but animals get through, so I guess people could too. There are regular warning boards on the fence, and the old roads are all gated with signs. Quite a bit of the perimeter is bordered with open water – there's the Sixteen Foot Drain, Whittlesea Drain and Popham's Eau. Red flags fly at various points on the fence and there are several over today's targets in the village. Frankly, you'd have to wilfully ignore all that to get into danger.'

The shells began again and Dryden flipped over onto his stomach, his eyes closed, counting, until finally there was silence, and for the first time the distant hiss of a wind over Whittlesea Mere. When he opened his eyes he found Broderick still beside him, making some wild heather into a small bouquet using silver cigarette paper, and trying to fasten it to his tunic with a pin. Dryden could imagine the major chasing butterflies along the trenches of the Great War.

For the first time Dryden looked ahead, south, towards a low hill crowned by a medieval church. Beyond it a cluster of rooftops and the pencil-thin chimney of a long-abandoned sugar beet factory marked the site of the old village. And to the east another low hill, this one dominated by a Victorian water tower in brick with a black metal tank crowned by a whitewood dovecote. The village of Jude's Ferry: a community of not much more than a hundred souls, abandoned seventeen years earlier to accommodate the army and its allies, keen to train for foreign wars.

Artillery had rained down on the targets ahead and smoke rose from a point west of the village itself, while occasional fire flickered amongst the ruins of a house about a hundred yards east of the church, which Dryden took to be the old vicarage. Somewhere automatic gunfire crackled like a party-popper.

'OK?' said Broderick.

Dryden nodded, lifting himself up on his elbows. 'I'm always surprised there's so much left,' he said. 'I guess . . . ,' he shrugged. 'I don't know. You'd think after ten years it would be like Baghdad. Looks more like Camberwick Green.'

'Yup. That's what we need. It's about skills for urban warfare,' said Broderick, and Dryden sensed that this was a subject that failed to make the major's heart sing as sweetly as the wild heather.

'You might as well have one of these,' said the soldier, handing him a map.

It was a large-scale plan of Jude's Ferry, each building etched in, complete with ground-floor windows, doors, yards and gates.

'Only you and I have one of these today. The red dots show the exact positions of the defending targets – the cutout soldiers. That way, hopefully, you can see if these guys can do their job. The dotted lines mark cellars, and they'll need to flush out targets during house-to-house searches. Clearing, entering and making safe, that kind of thing – all vital skills.'

He scanned the horizon ahead with binoculars. 'So you can see that the last thing we want is to flatten the place. Artillery targets today are the old vicarage and the factory: not for the first time. Ordnance is light, even if they hit they won't wipe anything out. Plus the engineers go in every few months and replace basic structures – nothing fancy, just so the cover is there. And there's a network of water pipes which were fed from that water tower, so we've always been able to fight fires.' He licked his upper lip. 'We've got a new pump now, by the river, so the water tower's redundant – which is a good job coz the water stank. The rats up there are the size of dogs.'

He scanned the village with the glasses again. 'When you get up close you'll see that the years have taken their toll all right. It ain't Merrie England, believe me.' He turned aside, adding quietly. 'Never was.'

A radio operator ran up, bent double. A request had been made for permission for another bombardment. Broderick surveyed the line of men along the dyke and the village ahead before giving his OK and sending a command along the ditch to sit tight until the signal to advance was given by word. Then he knelt down in the grass and gave Dryden his field glasses.

'Try looking – the shells can spook people out, but watching helps.'

Dryden smiled, accepting, studying the outline of the village church, the distant rooftops beyond down by the river. Above them the maroon thudded a third time. Broderick rolled over and lay on his back, checking his watch, a pair of swifts engaged in a dogfight high above them.

'So,' he said, finally. 'This is big news, is it?'

'Jude's Ferry?' said Dryden. 'Sure. It's been a big story since the start. When the villagers were shifted out in 1990 they were told they might be back in a year – not just for the annual church service on St Swithun's Day, but back for good. They moved out in the July and the Gulf War started in August – so that was the end of that optimistic scenario. It was never going to happen. They tried everything they could to get back. Now the legal action in the High Court's been thrown out it's finally over. Frankly, I'm amazed the courts stopped the shelling while the case was still live . . . how long's it been?'

Broderick twiddled a fen violet: 'Must be eighteen months since we've been on the range – perhaps more.'

Dryden nodded. 'You know the rest. The MoD's announced there'll be no return to Jude's Ferry – not even for the annual service. But they rang us, wanted to know if we'd like to interview the top brass – why the village was a vital resource for training in the modern army – the familiar pitch. Charm offensive. Least they could do was let us go in one last time. So here I am.'

Broderick laughed. 'We've been using a range up near Lincoln, so the lads are pleased to be back – most of 'em are local and this way they get home for tea.'

'Yeah,' said Dryden, failing to smile.

'You think it was rough justice?' asked Broderick.

'At the time, a lot of people didn't see why the army couldn't go back to using the range half a dozen times a year like they had done since – what did you say? – 1907. The village was never a target. They'd always made sure the damage to agricultural land was minimal – most of the big exercises were timed for after the harvest. They'd close the road in for a day, clear livestock, but otherwise it didn't make much odds to the village.'

Broderick sighed. 'I'll think you'll find that no definite promises were made, you know, when we moved them out . . .'

'I was there,' said Dryden, cutting in.

The major's eyes, watery brown, failed to hold Dryden's. He bit his lip and, flipping over on to his stomach, checked his watch again. 'Thirty seconds,' he said.

'I was there the day of the evacuation,' Dryden repeated. 'My first paper was over at Bedford, it was a big story so I went in to do a colour piece. There were promises made all right, otherwise they wouldn't have got some of them

16

out. Nothing in writing, of course. White lies. Khaki lies.'

The major stayed silent, outranked by an eyewitness.

'Anyway, that's history now,' continued Dryden. 'Nine/eleven, Madrid, London, the wars in Afghanistan and Iraq, who knows where next . . . ? They need the village. And the Americans want to join the party too. So game, set and match. Like you said, urban warfare. Jude's Ferry's too valuable to give back.'

Before the major could reply another gout of flame erupted briefly at the edge of the churchyard, and then they heard the scream of the shell overhead.

'Shite,' said Broderick, waving up the company radio operator. 'Tell 'em they're fifty yards off the vicarage to the west. Tell 'em quick.'

Dryden used the digital camera and a telephoto to get some snaps. He had the church in centre focus when the final volley came in, and he saw clearly the moment when a shell punched a hole through the roof before exploding in the nave; a window of multicoloured glass bursting out into the churchyard, a flame glimpsed within.

Broderick was standing: 'Last sodding shell. Typical.' He glanced at the reporter and Dryden guessed he was weighing up the possibility of sending him back. But Dryden, they both knew, had seen enough.

'Right. Radio Red Centre, tell 'em the urban phase is off. We'll assess the damage, report back.' He stood, produced an umpire's whistle and blew it. Along the line of the dyke the men stood, stretching, and a few removed their tin hats. Dryden half expected them to start playing football in no-man's-land. Broderick jogged down the dyke bank and vaulted the drain below, leading the way across a field pitted with old shell holes and thorn bushes.

It took them twenty minutes to reach the church. As the

village unfolded itself to Dryden he kept expecting to see movement: washing perhaps, flapping on a line, a stooped figure hoeing in a garden, a trundling tractor encircled by seagulls. But except for the rooks over the water tower and the limp target flags the village was lifeless, the shadows untroubled.

At the graveyard wall the major split the company, sending half on to make sure that at least the second target – the old sugar beet factory – had been hit according to plan. The rest were told to check out the graveyard and the exterior of the church and then assemble at the church doors to gauge the damage inside.

Dryden retrieved the digital camera from the webbing inside his tunic and moved amongst the headstones. The stray shell which had punched out the window had sent glass and stone fragments spraying out. He noticed graffiti on some of the reverse faces of the stones, including two sets of 'TROOPS OUT' and one reading 'GIVE OUR VILLAGE BACK'. A snake of grey smoke rose from the roof of St Swithun's. Oak doors in the porch stood at an angle, their locks ruptured by the blast, and Dryden squeezed through.

Outside he could hear the soldiers moving through the long grass around the building. But in the nave he was alone, and for the first time he felt the presence of the ghosts of the past, crowding into the pews which had long gone. It was cool in here, surrounded by stone, shielded from the sun, and he felt the sudden iciness of the sweat on his neck. He moved down one of the side aisles to a Gothic door which he tried, but found it locked. Turning towards the main body of the church he watched as a shaft of sunlight fell to the bare stone floor of the nave. The shell had pitted the stone like the impact of a meteor on the moon. The only fire was in the roof beams, which spluttered blue flames. The sound of falling glass filled the ringing silence. As he walked forward he felt exposed, the subject of watchful eyes, and it made his skin creep.

He stood in the jagged pool of light and looked up into the blue sky above, then down at his boots. A finger, porcelain white, lay on the flagged stone floor. For a moment his stomach turned, he was unable to be sure it was what it must be, a shattered fragment of statuary. But the tomb stood close by, a reclining crusader in stone on the top, the hands once held in prayer reduced to two stumps of chipped marble by the explosion.

The oak doors behind him crashed open and Broderick pushed his way into the church, followed by a dozen more of his men. They fanned out, silent now they could see the damage to the roof, sharing some of the gunner's guilt.

Dryden touched the cool stone tomb. Shrapnel had damaged the top of the funeral chest on which the knight lay – the corner of the stone lid had broken away and lay shattered on the floor. He edged closer to the hole, trying not to block any light which might show the contents within, but he could only glimpse cold stone, just on the margin of vision. Closer, he sniffed the fetid air, laced now with the acrid edge of scorched stone.

He walked behind the chest, recognizing the crusader's tomb from a picture *The Crow* had run the previous week when he'd written a feature hooked on the decision by campaigners to abandon their legal fight, and previewing the return of live firing to the range.

The centuries had worn the name on the side of the tomb but it was still legible: PEYTON.

As he rounded the stone box Dryden glimpsed a spade leaning against the nave's outer wall, and black peaty earth scattered over the cool grey stones of the floor. He froze, suddenly feeling that despite the voices of the soldiers near by he was still alone in the church. He could see that one of the large gravestones set into the floor had been lifted to reveal a hole, most of the earth from which lay in a neat pyramid hidden from wider view by the funeral casket of the Peytons. The grave was just three feet deep and empty, a few damp pebbles reflecting the light from the rich coffee-black soil.

The gravestone removed stood on end, leaning by the spade, and showed a heraldic device like a sunflower with the clear etched letters spelling the name again: PEYTON.

The crackle of a radio startled him and he saw Broderick directly below the hole in the roof with his radio operator.

'Mr Dryden . . . We're moving on into the village. There's nothing we can do here now. I need you close to hand. My men have to run a hose in here – they don't want you in the way.'

Dryden looked around the church and noted signs of earlier damage. One window was boarded up, and parts of the triple-tiered wooden pulpit were charred by a fire long cold. But why the opened grave?

'You should see this . . .' he said. 'St Swithun's has had visitors.'

Broderick shrugged. 'First things first, if you please. I presume they're not here now. We need to check the second target, another wayward shell, I'm afraid.'

Dryden knelt by the pile of soil and ran some of it through his hands. Despite the heavy heat of the summer's day it still felt cool so he plunged his hand in, pulled it back, and examined the moisture visible on his skin.

'Recent visitors,' he said, knowing there was no one to hear.

But he felt the hairs on his arm prickle and, standing, fought against the irrational conviction that he was being watched. Then he ran a finger in the dust along the edge of the tomb and along the ten-inch-high letters etched in its side, wondering why the name was familiar, pushing aside the creeping anxiety that he should know the answer.

3

From the church porch Dryden looked down on Jude's Ferry. St Swithun's stood on a hill thirty feet high, a peak in the billiard-table landscape of the Fens, the highest point on a low island of clay which had been inhabited for more than 1,000 years. He realized with a shock that he had stood on this precise point seventeen years earlier, the day of the evacuation, looking down on a village bustling with removal vans, army trucks, cars, livestock, the press, radio and TV cameras and a small but vocal band of children. Flags had flown from the army tents set up on the old recreation ground, and along the old Whittlesea Road the last of the sheep were herded, their bleating insistent and alarmed.

It had been an unforgettable assignment. Initially the army's PR men had tried to keep all contact between the villagers and media to a mid-morning press conference in the Methodist Hall. The print media had agreed to stay away on the Sunday, the feast of St Swithun, to let the villagers enjoy the last saint's day in privacy. But that Monday morning a bus had taken the press and TV crews from Ely in through the firing-range gates and straight to the Methodist Hall – packed with most of the surviving villagers. It had been a stilted affair dominated by one old soldier who'd clearly been encouraged to stand up and announce that he was proud the village was going to play its part in fighting for freedom. He'd got his medals on for the occasion so the TV boys had fêted him, happy they'd secured their picture story in time for the lunchtime news bulletins. A couple of women, both widows, said they would always remember what the village had done in two world wars – a statement which prompted another photocall at the war memorial at the top of The Dring, the little high street which ran beside an open ditch clogged with tall reeds.

Dryden had gone along to watch, and had noticed a man he presumed was the landlord of the New Ferry Inn, sitting on his doorstep drinking tea, watching with tired eyes, rimmed red. A young man with thick brown hair in a lopsided agricultural cut, shoulders slumped in defeat. Beside him sat a woman, legs bare and folded under her, hair brushed back from a pale face, T-shirt crumpled. She rubbed the heel of her hand into an eye socket, trying to drive away the tiredness, or a memory. He caught her eye and smiled but she fled, the open pub door revealing packing crates on the quarry tiled floor of the bar.

The man let her go, spilling his tea out in the dust.

The rest of the villagers, sullen and wary, watched the half-hearted little theatre put on for the media: the old soldier arranged before the memorial like a living prop, flanked by the widows. Opposite the inn was a terrace of four stone almshouses, little Victorian castles complete with stone windows and Gothic ironwork. The residents, four elderly men and a woman, sat on a bench outside, stoic in the face of an unseemly invasion of their village. Then a shout went up, from down The Dring, where two soldiers were trying to get an old woman through her cottage door, failing to disguise the fact she didn't want to leave.

The woman was crying, unsteady on her feet. 'Please,' she kept saying, 'Please, no.' Her features had dissolved into a mask of anxiety, like a child's.

The crowd, milling, began to boo and someone lobbed a brick towards one of the army Land Rovers, where it landed on the bonnet. Pebbles and dirt began to fly in the air and the TV camera lights thudded into full action. The elderly woman had fainted and had to be half carried to a waiting ambulance, but behind her the front door of her home was already being boarded up. Further along The Dring an army detail was moving past the old cottages, padlocking doors and closing windows. Glass shattered, prompting more boos from the crowd.

'You might have the decency to fucking wait,' shouted a man, his face red and damp with alcohol.

'Come on, boys,' said another voice, and the crowd visibly shrank back. 'Beer's free – don't waste it.' It was the young man from the doorstep of the pub, his tea mug still in hand. 'It's too late for trouble – it's over.'

Dryden tried to judge his age – mid-twenties perhaps, but with a kind of world-weary authority which made him seem older. He led them away, down by the inn where the army had provided lunch in boxes on trestle tables and a last barrel stood out in the shade on blocks. There was a bit more shouting but it was clear now that they didn't have the heart for a real fight. It was their pride which was at stake, not their homes. They were gone.

The soldiers, sensing the mood, regrouped and slipped away to the tents, neat rows of bleached white, like a Boy Scout camp. Dryden tried to gather some quotes from the men by the inn but most shook their heads, ashamed of their impotence now that the end had come.

Lunch for the press was laid out in the orchard below the church, in the shadow of a foursquare Georgian mansion surrounded by a gravel drive. The words 'Orchard House' were carved into the stone pillars which guarded the gates. The window tax had robbed the building of some of its grandeur but it was still a cut above, the upper floor looking out over trimmed hedges at the village beyond. Lawns ran down to the river, across which a deep ditch ran parallel with the towpath, the remnants of an old moat. Dryden had spread himself out on the grass checking his notes, passing time before the bus was due to take them back to Ely, trying to imagine what the village had been like in its heyday in the 1800s, when the wharf had been busy with sugar beet, the factory belching acrid smoke from the pencil-thin chimney.

The rest of the press were clustered near where the army was serving drinks so he'd been the only one to hear the creak of the shutter, and looking up had seen a young man at an upstairs window of the mansion, surveying the orchard below. A hand on the windowsill, the other shading the light from his eyes, he had the languid movements of the rich. Then he'd retreated into the shadows and Dryden wondered what final act of farewell had taken place within. He heard voices then, a light had come on, and another man had hurriedly closed the shutters. He'd been shocked to recognize the landlord again, talking over his shoulder to those unseen within.

Then they'd heard the clanking gears of the council bus, and the press corps had stood silently to watch the last villagers leave, many of them turning their heads away from the windows as it drove past on Church Street, an amber dustcloud marking its progress out onto Whittlesea Mere. A few minutes later three army trucks rolled into the village from the west carrying the troops who would search the houses, survey the infrastructure and prepare the targets for the first live firing.

Dryden looked down on the scene as it was today, the old allotments engulfed in late-summer raspberries, the ruined sheds just breaking the surface like flotsam on a green sea. Across the village the only sounds were inhuman: rooks called from a line of poplars by the river and somewhere the warm breeze rattled a garden gate on rusted hinges. The hum of bees was like the bass note of a soundtrack.

He looked across into the orchard in which they'd had lunch that day. The fruit trees, unpruned for nearly two decades, were heavy with buds, the old moat a waterlogged ditch. The old shuttered mansion was still standing, but the roof had holes and was sagging in the middle, a chimney stack leaning perilously. At one of the windows the wood of the shutter had rotted and Dryden's heart contracted as he saw something move on the sill, something black which caught the light. But as he watched a rook struggled out through the gap, shaking its feathers. It flew low over the garden wall and down to the river.

He ran ahead to join Major Broderick and his platoon as they moved into the village, the road patched in tarmac by army sappers who'd filled shell holes over the years. A row of Victorian cottages had been propped up with brutal concrete frames. Several buildings here had been completely replaced with breeze-block boxes, punched through with crude holes for windows and doors. Dryden reflected that the villagers' annual return to St Swithun's must have been a sad experience, presenting ample evidence that as the years passed there was increasingly less for them to return to. As he walked forward Dryden tried to stop himself scanning the black, empty holes where the windows had once been, sensing that somewhere in the village he'd glimpse a face, waiting just for him.

They moved north, over a hump-backed bridge, to a T-junction where they turned west into what had been the main street. Dominating the turning was an ugly 1950s two-storey building, its windows boarded, but a painted fascia proclaimed 'Palmer's Store'. The red logo of the post office was still visible, and on the second floor a derelict neon sign hung which read 'Mere Taxis' and was dotted with bullet holes. Somewhere inside the building a door creaked rhythmically in the breeze.

Ahead they could see the slight rise of the main bridge over the Sixteen Foot, a drain which carried water off the reclaimed mere and sent it seawards – all that was left of the original 'river' over which Jude's Ferry had crossed. Beyond, on the far bank, the old sugar beet factory burned. But in the foreground another column of smoke rose, tinged with acrid black, with flashes of livid red running through it like lightning.

Broderick stopped to take a radio message from the men he'd sent ahead to recce the village. 'Right,' he said, thrusting the receiver back at the radio operator: 'Not a good day for the Royal Artillery. They've hit some outbuildings down by the New Ferry Inn. A fire too.'

The company moved forward in neat formation, a young soldier no more than eighteen in pole position. Dryden glimpsed from side to side the wooden cutout targets of Red Force in the shadows of derelict houses and shops. In one, behind a perspex window, a soldier in a combat hat stood transfixed beside a marble table, all that was left of the village butcher's. Dryden caught his own reflection, the austere symmetrical face as immobile as that of the knight on the tomb in the church.

A line of rats dashed across the sunlight in single file, swallowed by the shadows of a well-worn doorstep.

The Dring had buildings on its north side, but along the south side a deep ditch ran, water sluggish at the bottom and overgrown with reeds. This brook acted as a culvert, taking water away from the high ground by the church and the water tower. As they walked the street the silky 'plop' of vermin retreating into the stream accompanied them. On the far side a tumbledown line of medieval cottages sagged, a way across the ditch provided by a series of makeshift bridges made of railway sleepers or corrugated iron. Dryden noted that one of the cottages still had its original front door, oak dotted with flaking red paint, a knocker in the shape of a leaping fox. The row was broken by a large gap, an open farmyard in which a rusted plough stood with the burnt-out frame of a tractor. On the side of the barn Dryden recognized the slogan he'd seen on that last day, sprayed by a vandal in letters three feet high: SQUADDIES FUCK OFF. Now the sentiment was almost illegible, the paint faded, but a line of dead crows hung on a wire looked like a more recent warning, a further sign that when the army wasn't firing on Jude's Ferry the village still had its own secret life.

'Poachers,' said Broderick at his shoulder. 'We know they get in, but we patch up the holes, send in the occasional patrol at night, keep them guessing.'

Above them the sunlight died and, looking up, Dryden watched as a dark bank of cloud, fringed with grey falling rain, slid over Jude's Ferry like a coffin lid. The first drops, as fat as grapes, made the dust jump at their feet. They were just thirty feet from the bridge now and they could see where the stray shell had gone. Past the simple façade of the New Ferry Inn was a yard surrounded by outbuildings. One, more substantial than the rest, had taken a direct hit, a hole punched through the low roof, the jagged edges still smoking. Outside in the street three soldiers worked at a manhole cover, from which they had already run a hosepipe across into the ruins of the building. Inside a soldier stood amongst the shadowy rubble, a lit torch turned down to his boots.

He signalled to Broderick. As they picked their way over the strewn bricks and splintered wood the rain began to fall, hissing amongst the smouldering debris. The explosion had blown away the doors and destroyed the ground-floor flight of a wooden staircase which had led up to a loft, revealing a letter-box black hole and a set of steps leading down into a cellar. Dryden could see torches beneath, sweeping the darkness.

At a shout, water gushed into the flames, cascading back down the steps.

Broderick nodded. 'OK. Good stuff. Where's our problem then?' The major looked nervous, suddenly less assured when faced with the unexpected.

One of the soldiers directed a torch beam down the steps.

'You might want to go down alone, sir,' suggested the squaddie.

Broderick thought about it for a second, then a few more.

The major took off his combat helmet, a strange gesture, and led the way. 'Who's been down?' he asked.

'Corporal's down sir; half of A-platoon.'

Broderick looked at Dryden. 'No point being coy now – come on.'

They dropped down the cellar steps and Dryden felt the temperature fall as they left behind the humidity of the day. His eyes switched to night vision and the scene was revealed: the floor already an unbroken glass-like sheet of water just a few centimetres deep. The cellar was large, an underground store in brick, and around the walls stood five of Broderick's men, torches trained to the centre of the room, each immobile, stilled.

Before them, illuminated, a body twisted slowly on a rope. The sudden rainstorm had disturbed the stale air and so the shrouded shape turned, the rope and beam creaking. The face, or what had been the face, swung towards Dryden and he saw the gleam of the lipless mouth, dull teeth and a bone-white skull. Across one cheekbone he glimpsed the mummified remains of a tendon. Clothes, perished beyond shape or colour, floated out like cobwebs.

Outside the rain intensified and turned to hail, falling like gravel, and the wind it brought turned the hanging bones one last time in a graceful arc before the rust-weakened hook finally gave up its prisoner and the body fell to the floor.

4

The cellar, uncorked like a buried bottle, gave off the stale breath of the years. While a military radio crackled with traffic they stood silently in a circle and Dryden tried to make himself memorize the scene, stilling the urge to ascend into the light.

The floor and three walls were old brick and lime, the fourth obscured by stacks of bottle crates. In one corner was a packing case of pint glasses, the top layer lying on newspaper, damp and yellow. By the far wall, opposite the stone steps, was a cupboard, doorless, the shelves within stacked with paint tins, tubes of various DIY kit, brushes stiff with dried turps sticking out of jam jars. Cobwebs hung in tresses to the floor and from the rough brickwork of the walls. The webs shimmered slightly, catching the light, as spiders dashed for the safety of the shadows in the rafters above.

Close to the centre of the room were the shattered remains of a child's high stool, one leg broken away, small pale-yellow teddy bears still just visible painted on the wood. Stacked with the beer crates were some other cast-offs from a child's nursery: a changing mat in plastic almost completely rotted, a wicker Moses basket, a set of wooden bowling pins, a small child's dresser, painted to match the broken high stool.

The corpse sat now, the descent to ground having driven the shattered spine down into the rest of the bones like a javelin so that the torso remained vertical, the head back, revealing the bones of the neck and the hollow underside of the jaw. Defying gravity, the skeleton seemed to demand one last chance to bear witness. Dryden could see now that the corpse had been reduced almost completely to bone, just a few shreds of tendon and cartilage remaining, and that the threadbare clothes had been all that had held it together in the still air of the cellar. Dryden tried to imagine the years of darkness it had spent in the breathless tomb.

But now light filtered and spilled in from above as the sound of the hail subsided. Reflections of the skeleton filled the black water.

Broderick stepped forward and examined the twine that had tied the wrists together in front of the body.

'I wouldn't touch anything,' said Dryden.

Broderick stood, thinking. 'OK,' he said. 'Let's leave it. The Military police will be here soon enough.' The soldiers filed up the stairs towards the light.

Dryden circled the skeleton before leaving, noting the legs splayed within the rotting cloth. The rags gave no clue to the sex; the build was perhaps slight for a man, average for a woman, but it was difficult to judge from the jumble of bones.

'Looks like a woman,' said Broderick, reading his mind from the top of the steps.

Something stirred in Dryden's memory. 'Wasn't there a woman who went missing after the evacuation? Didn't she keep the shop and the post office – Palmer's, along The Dring?'

Broderick sat on the step. 'Yup. Magda Hollingsworth. She'd have been sixty-three in 1990. It could be her. She'd been depressed, but there was no note, no last goodbye. She just wasn't there any more.'

'That's a good memory . . .'

Broderick dusted his palms together. 'Press office at the Army Desk sent me the cuttings on the evacuation – just in case you asked any awkward questions. The story was in there. They searched the village a couple of times – delayed the first shelling by a week or more. But they never found the body and she never turned up, no sightings at all. And she was not the kind of woman who'd have blended in. Romany family; Hungarian, I think. Not exactly a conformist by all accounts . . .'

'Although she was the postmistress, that's hardly eccentric.'

Broderick shrugged. 'Anyway, some people suggested she'd cracked up under the strain of the evacuation and had gone back on the road. Joined the travellers. It kinda makes sense, or at least it did at the time.'

Dryden followed him up into the abandoned bar of the New Ferry Inn. The story of Magda Hollingsworth was a sad coda to the drama of those last days in Jude's Ferry. Her family hadn't reported her missing until after the evacuation and by then the media circus had moved on. There was little interest in the fate of the missing woman even locally, especially as the presumption was she'd taken her own life after a bout of depression, suicide note or no suicide note.

The bar was cool and smelled of rotting wood. A large frosted window, engraved with the words 'The New Ferry Inn' had remarkably survived the years and the army's wayward shells. Beyond it the village filled with the sound of running water. The room itself was half panelled in wood to a height of about five feet. Someone had sprayed TROOPS OUT with a can on one wall – further evidence that Jude's Ferry had been visited over the years since the evacuation by more than troops in training. Movable furniture had been shipped out but a built-in settle ran round the room. A large brick fireplace was empty except for the featherweight corpse of a rook. On the wall the only picture left was of the England football team covered in mimeographed signatures. Dryden noted the date: January 1990. In the dartboard a single dart stuck out of double-tops, and a tin ashtray on the mantelpiece held a single piece of chalk and what looked like rat droppings. The scorer's blackboard held two words, scrawled in chalk: GAME OVER.

If you strained against the silence, Dryden thought, you could almost hear it: the sound of that last night; the last bell, an ironic cheer perhaps, the drunken voices, hoarse with drink and nicotine. And tears in a corner, ignored.

'Military police will be here in twenty minutes,' said Broderick. 'There's a chopper coming in – God knows why, but if you've got a big toy why not play with it? They're off to Basra next month, so I guess they need the practice, poor bastards. CID at Lynn's been notified,' he said.

With the police notified Dryden knew now that the story was only his for a few hours before the rest of the media picked it up. His own paper didn't come out for another two days and he'd been forced to leave his mobile at the firing-range gatehouse. It looked like he'd got a scoop, but no paper to run it in. Not for the first time he cursed the frustrations of working on weekly newspapers.

'When they get here you should mention the church. Someone's been in recently – a hole's been dug by one of the tombs.'

'Grave robbers?' asked Broderick.

'Perhaps. Everyone knew that there was no shelling while the court case was being heard. So it wasn't a bad time to make a visit – there was a good chance the villagers weren't coming back, so perhaps they thought no one would care.

But it's not the first time — there are signs of vandalism. You must have seen them too?

'I need to get to a phone,' he said when the major didn't answer. 'Any chance?'

'I can patch in a call to your mate in the cab — get him back early.'

'Thanks. That's a big help.' Dryden planned to call the local radio station and see if he could get on air with the story, making sure his paper got credit, and promising a full version in the Tuesday edition. It was the only way he was going to get anything out of the story before it broke for the competition.

He took a deep breath, wishing he had a pint in his hand. 'So what do you think?' he said. 'Suicide, right?'

Broderick's soft face creased in a frown. 'I guess. Hands are bound, but in front, which she could have done herself to prevent a reflex attempt to loosen the noose. Feet are unbound, so she could have just stood on the stool, and then stepped off and kicked it away.'

'She? No doubts about that?'

Broderick shrugged. 'Well, we know there was a missing woman. You can't tell much from the bones until they get them in the lab, but anything's better than calling her *it* . . .' He'd removed the heather from his tunic and turned the silver-paper bouquet in his hand, placing it carefully on the map.

'That call?' prompted Dryden.

'Sure,' said Broderick, turning away to use a mobile.

Dryden took out the map Broderick had given him and spread it on the bar top. When the major returned he tapped his finger on the outhouses next to the New Ferry Inn.

'There's no cellar shown,' he said.

Broderick studied the plan carefully. 'Well that can't be

35

right – a lot of time and effort went into making these things. They're based on a series of surveys taken in the three months after the final evacuation – and on questionnaires the villagers had to fill in.'

'So that's kind of weird, isn't it?' said Dryden. 'Not only did the cellar not crop up on the questionnaire, the engineers missed it when the surveys were done after the evacuation. Whereas the cellar under the pub is clearly marked,' he said, stamping his foot on the bare floorboards.

Dryden looked at the key to the map and the legend which carried the name Col. Flanders May.

'Who's Flanders May?' he asked.

'CO for the engineers, the map-makers. That's why it was a work of art. Perfectionist – but then even they make mistakes, right?'

They heard the thwup-thwup of the approaching helicopter and stepped outside.

Dryden looked up into the falling rain, watching the black underbelly of the helicopter emerge from the grey cloud base.

'The questionnaires – they still in the records?' asked Dryden.

But Broderick pointed at his ears as the rotors screamed over their heads.

5

'This is BBC Radio Cambridgeshire bringing you all the news at 6.00pm. This is Mark Edwards in the studio.'

Dryden leant forward and edged the volume up on the Capri's radio; the headlines were dominated again by the mounting death toll in Iraq. Humph flipped down the glove compartment and retrieved two miniature bottles of Bell's whisky, part of the haul he regularly replenished on trips to Stansted Airport.

They cracked the bottle tops open in perfect harmony. The cab stood beside the single-bar gate to the firing range, the landscape beyond reduced to a smudge of bog-green seen through the condensation running down the windows. Rain clattered on the cab roof.

Parked up next to them was the BBC radio car, its tele-scopic mast now fully extended. Dryden swigged the whisky, shuddered and pushed the passenger door open, rust screaming from the hinges. The door of the radio car was open for him by the time he reached it, and he settled into the seat, folding his six-foot-two-inch frame as neatly as a deckchair. The radio reporter was sucking the life out of the butt end of a cigarette before crunching it quickly into an overflowing ashtray.

'And now we go live to Whittlesea Mere Firing Range south of Peterborough where Jason Diprose has a break-ing story . . .'

'Indeed, Mark . . .'

Dryden felt his guts tighten at the prospect of the live

interview. He tried a smile in the rear-view mirror to boost his confidence but his green eyes, wary now, betrayed his anxiety at the prospect of a public performance.

But Diprose was in full flight. '. . . I'm at the gates to the range right now and we have initial reports that during routine training an army patrol has made a gruesome discovery in the village of Jude's Ferry – listeners will recall the village was evacuated by the army nearly twenty years ago to make way for military exercises. I'm joined by *The Crow*'s chief reporter, Philip Dryden, who was with the soldiers of the Ely-based TA unit when they went in this morning. What did you find, Philip?'

Through the window Dryden could see Humph, head thrown back in an attempt to enter deep sleep.

'It was very dramatic, Jason. We found a body, well – just a skeleton really, hanging in a cellar near the village pub, the New Ferry Inn. It's pretty clear it had been there many years – perhaps since the evacuation in 1990. The wrists were tied – but in front of the victim. It was a sad sight, and there is speculation of course that it may have been suicide, but at this stage they can't rule out murder.'

'Any idea yet who the victim was?'

'Too early, Jason. The military police have secured the scene and all firing has been suspended – initially for a week. I understand CID from King's Lynn will be visiting the scene later today. The pub was the centre of village life, and most of the residents who had hung on to the bitter end were there on the last night. At the moment there's a presumption the victim was a woman – but that's all it is. The clothes have just about disintegrated, so they're not much help. At this stage there are very few facts. I'd hope to have a lot more to say in the *Ely Express* on Tuesday, and of course in Friday's *Crow*.'

'And not the only drama today?'

'That's right,' said Dryden, relaxing now that he'd found a spot to slip in his free advertising plug. 'Before we went in there was an artillery bombardment of two targets on the edge of the village. There were two stray shells – one hit the church, and one the outbuildings next to the pub. That's how we found the victim in the cellar. The damage to St Swithun's was extensive, I'm afraid.' Dryden had decided not to mention the opened grave in the church for two reasons: one, it complicated the story which was strong enough already, and two, it left him something to work on for the paper that probably wouldn't get released by the police in the next twenty-four hours. He'd also decided to keep to himself speculation the victim could be Magda Hollingsworth; there was always a chance he could follow the lead up himself and get a new line for the *Express*.

'What will be the reaction from the villagers – there's an association, isn't there – a campaign group?'

'Sure. Friends of the Ferry. There'll be some bitterness. They were angry anyway. This year was the first year in which they were not allowed to return to Jude's Ferry on St Swithun's Day. The MoD announced only last week that there will be no annual pilgrimages back to the village, and the courts have failed to back the villagers' case that they have a right of return. What with the war in Iraq, the chances of getting back are fading fast – and I think they know that now. But the army did promise back in 1990 – in writing – to make sure the church survived. It's still a Grade I listed building. I think this will be seen as a further signal that, as lost villages go, Jude's Ferry is lost for ever.'

'Thanks, Philip. Stick with us for a minute and we'll talk some more after the rest of the local news. I'm sure there are some listeners out there who remember Jude's Ferry and would like to share those memories with us. Do ring us or e-mail. But in the meantime . . .'

The live feed switched back to the studio. 'Quiet day?' said Dryden when he knew they were off air.

'Like a graveyard,' said Diprose. 'We led the lunchtime on twenty-five deaths in Iraq – outside a police station in Baghdad – so that's how thin the news is. Most days its fifty and it's the last item. Good job this turned up. Bloody rain on the roof doesn't help – I better check they want a second slot. Do you mind sticking around?'

They listened to the rest of the bulletin in silence, the radio reporter jotting down questions on a foolscap pad. Dryden fished in his trouser pocket and found a wine gum which he sucked noisily. The studio gave the go-ahead for a second slot on the story, largely because it was indeed a quiet news day both locally and nationally.

The studio finished up the bulletin and came back to the radio car.

'Welcome back,' said Diprose. 'I'm here on the edge of Whittlesea Mere, a few miles south of Peterborough. Earlier today a group of soldiers on exercise in the army's firing range discovered a skeleton – thought to be that of a woman – hanging in a cellar in the abandoned village of Jude's Ferry. I'm joined again by Philip Dryden, chief reporter on *The Crow*, who was with the platoon which made the discovery. Philip, you were in the village seventeen years ago on that last day. Can you describe what it was like?'

Dryden felt the almost visceral thud of the memory.

'It was a very emotional day for some of the villagers, of course. I saw one elderly woman literally carried from her home. She'd been born in the house, her husband was buried in the churchyard, her children had all moved on . . . the village was all she had.

'But, even then, I think many of the villagers knew that Jude's Ferry didn't have a future. The school had long closed and most of the youngsters had left. The beet factory shut down in '89, I think . . . a real blow. And whatever you want to say about the village it isn't the kind of place that would have thrived as a dormitory for commuters. It's not thatched-cottage country at all and Peterborough's still a good drive away, while there are other villages much nearer, much more chocolate-box. So the writing had been on the wall for some time.'

'Right. But it seems incredible now, doesn't it, that these people were moved, just thrown out of their homes. I guess public opinion has shifted since the attacks on New York, Madrid, London – but back in 1990 it must have caused an uproar, surely? It seems sort of medieval – how could the army do that in the twentieth century?'

'Well, the fact is it was, you know, partly the villagers' own fault. The MoD had always used the mere for exercises but in the eighties, when farmers in places like Jude's Ferry were really struggling to stay in business, the government offered to buy the land. They put up a good price and an under-taking to rent back the property to the original owners at low rents, peppercorn actually. And it wasn't just the agri-cultural land – they bought the cottages in the village, the shop, the pub, the lot. Once the big landowners had sold there was a rush to take the money because people feared that anyone who hung out would get caught by a compul-sory purchase order. They said, the army, that the idea was to increase the number of days on which they could use the range for firing, but leave the village as a going concern. But when it came to the crunch, and the crunch was the Middle East, of course, and Saddam Hussein, they had the right to terminate the leases with just twelve weeks' notice.

I guess that's the lesson, you know – it was always there in black and white, why write that into the lease if there wasn't a chance they'd use it? So these people had less than a hundred days to say goodbye to everything, and in some cases each other.'

'But there was some money too, wasn't there?'

'Sure. Compensation was paid for loss of earnings and some removal costs – that was all in the lease agreement as well. And there was this unwritten promise that the villagers would be allowed back, one day.'

'Right. And we've had plenty of e-mails about that – and we've got someone on the line, I believe. A Mrs Drew, is it? Elizabeth Drew – from Peterborough. Hello Mrs Drew, what's your point?'

'Hello. Yes. I just wanted to say, you know, that Mr Dryden makes it sound like Jude's Ferry was dying on its feet, but I don't agree.'

'You were a villager?' cut in Diprose.

'No. I was a rural officer for the county council, and it was my job to keep communities like this alive. So,' she laughed, 'I know I may be biased. I'm not saying it wasn't a struggle and the beet factory closing was a dreadful blow but there were plans for the future – growing flowers was a develop-ing local niche market, and the RSPB was interested in a reserve, the river could have been dredged for pleasure boats, the shop was thriving really. We had this group, which I ran, which tried to encourage enterprise – we got all the school leavers together, for example; there were start-up funds for small businesses, free skills training, a mentoring scheme. I know it wasn't an idyllic thatched village, but what you couldn't see was really special, you know – there was a community there, and I said then that once you cut the ties between the people and the place where they'd lived all their lives, then those networks, those ties, would be gone, gone for ever; and that's what's happened, hasn't it? And now they've found this poor woman. And what's it all been for? I –?'

'I guess some people would say we can all sleep easier in our beds knowing the army's well trained,' offered Diprose, cutting in.

'Well I can't,' she said bluntly. 'What's the point of going half-way round the world to defend freedom when we do this kind of thing on our own doorstep?'

Diprose moved quickly on, reading out a few e-mails, most in support of the army. Finally he wrapped Dryden back into the item. 'So what was Jude's Ferry really like, Philip? Paint us a picture.'

Dryden hugged his knees, beginning to feel the cramped space in the passenger seat. 'Jude's Ferry? You could argue the Fens are full of places like it. Lonely, forgotten, one-horse towns. That last day there were just fifty people left – something like that anyway. A pub, a shop and post office, a garage, a taxi firm, a redundant factory, a wharf that hadn't seen a cargo in sixty years. And a church, of course. It was fifteen miles to anywhere else, and there was hardly any through traffic.'

Diprose cut an imaginary line across his throat with his pen.

'But it was famous for two things, Jason,' said Dryden, expertly taking his cue to wrap up. 'Your listeners will no doubt correct me but . . . I think you'll find the village was originally called Nornea. The name changed sometime in the sixteenth century to Jude's Ferry – a reference to the man who bought the ferry over the new drain and started charging villagers a stiff price for the crossing. Jude's a deriv-ation of Judas, of course – so it was all about betrayal. That's the story anyway.'

They laughed. 'And the other thing it's famous for?' asked Diprose.

'The claim was made – and it's difficult to test this one out – but the claim was made that in its thousand-year history the village boasted not a single recorded crime. But that may change, of course.'

'Sounds idyllic,' said Diprose.

'Sounds like they never got caught,' said Dryden.

6

When the rain cleared, the landscape was crisp and clear, the distant silhouette of Ely cathedral a pin-sharp medieval model on a toy horizon. They drove towards it through a mathematical landscape of right angles, ditches, drove roads and flood banks, intersecting with unnatural precision. The Capri echoed to the sound of Faroese, Humph's latest eccentric choice of European language tape; a Nordic tongue which offered the comforting certainty of being totally redundant in the middle of the English Fens.

Dryden wound down the window and took in the intoxicating freshness of the black peat, soaked with the sudden downpour. He considered the hanging skeleton in the cellar. An impromptu radio interview had not been the place to mention Flanders May's map and the implication that whoever had owned the outbuildings next to the New Ferry Inn in 1990 had failed to indicate that the building had a cellar. It suggested, at the very least, the possibility of premeditation, and even collusion. Dryden presumed that the outbuildings were part of the complex of buildings linked to the village pub – and he wondered how long it would take CID to track down the licensee, presumably the young man Dryden had seen on the doorstep that last morning in the village.

And then there was that partly open grave . . .

The drove road brought them into town through a line of pre-war semis and a play park, the sun glinting now off the water pooled under the swings and slide, a woman smoking on a bench as a single child clambered over a wooden fire engine. Half a mile later they were in the town centre, the sudden sunshine throwing the shadow of the cathedral half-way across Market Square. A pair of seagulls splashed in a wide puddle, rocking a floating ice lolly wrapper.

They dropped down Fore Hill, Dryden drinking in the distant view across the lazy river to a blue horizon as straight as a spirit level. On Waterside holidaymakers were beginning to appear on the decks of the white boats moored by the bank. Wine bottles long uncorked, they emerged blinking into the late-afternoon sunlight.

Humph dropped him by the town bridge and drove off without a word, concentrating with unnatural excitement on repeating the Faroese for a wide range of chocolate puddings.

Dryden began to walk the towpath south. He flicked open his mobile and did a quick round of calls, the schedule of numbers already logged into the phone's memory. His position as chief reporter brought with it a modest set of duties, in return for which he received an even more modest salary, currently one sixth of that he'd drawn during a Fleet Street career which had spanned a decade. So, twice a day, every day, and three times on press days, Dryden made the ritual round of telephone calls: county police, local police, county fire brigade, local fire brigade, ambulance control – then repeated it for West Norfolk and Peterborough. In return for such extra duties the editor had agreed a small guaranteed weekly expense account which Dryden diverted exclusively to Humph, whose role as the reporter's unofficial chauffeur was punctuated with more lucrative contracts ferrying school children in the mornings and nightclub bouncers after midnight. The Capri's meter was stuck permanently reading £2.95, the wires hanging loose and disconnected beneath the dashboard.

46

West Norfolk police confirmed that the body discovered at Jude's Ferry had been transferred from the jurisdiction of the Royal Military Police to King's Lynn CID. A pathologist would undertake an initial examination at 10.00am the following morning. Inquiries had begun in an attempt to trace the identity of the victim, and Lynn CID appealed for anyone with information helpful to the police to come forward. A number was provided for the purpose, and an assurance given that all communications were in strictest confidence. Dryden noted that, while a brief statement confirmed the circumstances of the discovery of the body, there was no mention of possible causes of death, or the sex or age of the victim.

Dryden stopped walking and climbed the flood bank to look south. Ahead the river met Barham's Dock, a 100-yard cut-off channel once used to load vegetables and salad crops direct from the fields into barges for the London markets. *PK 129*, Dryden's floating home, was moored just off the main river. A former inshore naval patrol boat, which had played a small part in the great events of the last century, it had retained its camouflage grey, distinguishing it from the ubiquitous white hulls of the floating gin palaces of the holiday trade. On deck Dryden could just see Laura sitting in the shade of the tarpaulin which he'd rigged over the boat's cockpit.

She raised a hand in welcome, and Dryden was thrilled by the unfamiliarity of the gesture. His wife had suffered severe injuries in a car crash seven years earlier and been left in a coma from which she was only now slowly recovering. Dryden had left his Fleet Street job to be near her, while her own career as a TV soap opera actress had become a briefly celebrated tabloid newspaper tragedy, now long forgotten.

Dryden vaulted the space between the bank and the boat and, kneeling, took his wife's head in his hands. He'd fixed up a spot on the wooden decking where he could secure her wheelchair, a symbol of her slow recovery. But for his wife the chair provided a vital system of support, being fitted with a swing-across desk where she kept her laptop, connected by a wireless link to the internet. Beneath the seat she kept a mobile phone, books, an iPod and drinks and snacks so that she could feed herself. With the crutches she'd begun to master she could get to the galley and bathroom below, although the journey back up the boat's steep ladder-like stair was still a struggle which could leave her exhausted.

Dryden felt again the novelty of her physical reaction to his touch, a hand grasping his hair at the nape of his neck. Her emergence from the coma had been glacial but the summer had seen a series of breakthroughs, her limbs at last freed from the rictus which had blighted the years since the crash.

'Coffee,' said Dryden, throwing open the doors to the galley below. Before he dropped down the ladder he ran his fingers over the brass plaque set above the wheel which read, simply: DUNKIRK 1940.

'Did you hear on the radio?' he shouted up.

She made the sound that they recognized now for yes; a sound that neatly delineated the different ways in which they had come to terms with Laura's accident. He saw it as the first articulation of the voice that she had once had, the voice he wanted to hear again. She saw it as a triumph in itself, and if it had to be, an end in itself.

'It was bizarre,' he said, setting the coffee, with two ice cubes, down beside her with a straw.

He looked at his wife, realizing that her face was recapturing the beauty it had once had. The eyes open fully now, the mouth beginning to recover from the ugly jaggedness it had held since she'd been injured. And her skin, in the sun at last, had regained the rich olive tones which betrayed her Italian ancestry. Her hair, auburn and full, had lost the stagey lifelessness of a shop-window mannequin's.

'You look great,' he said, touching her cheek.

She raised an eyebrow. 'Bizarre?' she asked, the consonants slurred.

'Right, sorry. Yeah. I just stood there in this cellar watching this skeleton turn in the breeze. They think it's suicide – I guess that's the easy bit. The trick'll be finding out who he or she was. Seventeen years is a long time to be missing without anyone noticing. There is a woman who ran the village shop, she went missing at the time of the evacuation, but I don't know, I just don't think it's her, it just doesn't ring true. For a start the cellar wasn't marked on the plans villagers had to submit to the army – which is an odd oversight, and hardly one a potential suicide victim would take the time to arrange.'

Laura turned her head towards him and he saw the excitement in her eyes. 'I'm sorry. Jesus,' said Dryden. He stood looking down at the laptop she had perched almost constantly on her lap. When he'd left that morning she was expecting an e-mail from her agent. The message stood open:

Laura. It's good news. The part in *The Silent Daughter* is yours if you want it. I enclose script. 23 words in all – I've told them, no last minute changes. It's those 23 words. Well done – we're all proud of you. The schedule has you over in Leeds the week beginning 12 August. Car will pick you up in Ely. Talk soon. Love. R.

Dryden kissed her on the neck, but he knew she'd detected the hesitation.

'I'm happy,' she said. 'You should be too.' The words were indistinct, but audible nonetheless. The part was in a play for Granada TV in which Laura would play a woman recovering from an horrific car crash. The audition had taken place in Cambridge earlier that year, her first journey away from Ely since the accident. It would be her only work in seven years. She saw it as a triumph, the beginning of a new career. Dryden felt the role was demeaning, a very public statement that this was now the limit of their ambitions.

'Let's celebrate,' he said, trying too hard. 'I'm proud of you too.' He went below, put two bottles of champagne in the icebox and texted Humph to pick up a Chinese takeaway. Then he put chairs out on the bank and built a fire, breaking up the wooden crates they had their food delivered in, direct from the farm up the lane where Dryden paid the mooring fee.

Humph, who had been sleeping in a lay-by when the summons came, arrived at high speed in the cab, the dog sitting up with excitement in the passenger seat. The cabbie parked up, the two doors open, and switched the radio to a local channel which specialized in 70s and 80s music at that hour, knowing it was Laura's favourite.

They ate by the light of the fire as the sun set, watching Boudicca run along the riverbank after the lurid green balls Humph fired – from a sitting position – using the tennis machine Dryden had given him one Christmas. It had been a truly unselfish present. The reporter harboured a deep-seated fear of dogs, which could stun his nervous system in the shape of a snarling Alsatian. But the greyhound's good nature had disarmed him, and familiarity had softened his fears. It was a small consolation, but a consolation nonetheless, to know that he now had a pathological fear of every dog in the world except one. They ate, Humph producing a small bone for the greyhound. Finished, they burned most of the takeaway packaging on the fire.

'Wait,' said Dryden before Humph could contrive an early exit. He went below to the forward cabin where he had stored his records from nearly twenty years in journalism. All reporters are told to keep their notebooks in case of legal action, a piece of advice widely honoured in the breach. A barely legible scribble is unlikely to be of great use a decade after it was first written, so Dryden usually dumped them after a year. The cabin was a chaotic archive of cuttings, pictures he'd printed up from his more illustrious stories, books, a few microtapes from celebrity or political interviews, and a case of videotaped TV programmes he'd amassed at the *News* when he'd been the stand-in critic. The walls boasted two framed awards for reporting – one in his specialist area of crime, another for feature writing when he was starting out in newspapers after university. And there was a picture from his first evening newspaper of a young reporter accepting an award. The intervening years had taken their toll but there was no mistaking the shock of black hair cut short, the narrow gangly frame and the handsome but immobile face.

Outside he could still hear the Capri's sound system and the murmur of Humph's voice – no doubt re-enacting for Laura her husband's comic appearance in combat uniform. He heard laughter and was thrilled to hear his wife's once familiar giggle.

He sat in his captain's chair and tried to remember where he had last seen the tape he was looking for. There were two ideas wrapped up in the concept of 'filing system' and both were strangers to Dryden's innate sense of informality. He'd always told himself that if he couldn't remember something there was probably a good reason, and that every forgotten fact made way for a memorable one. There was absolutely no chance he still had his notebooks from July 1990 when he'd covered the evacuation of Jude's Ferry. He doubted he even had the cutting from the resulting feature he'd written on the village's last day. But over the years he was sure he'd bundled together stuff which had appeared in the media on the village – keeping a watching brief in case the story reignited.

He knelt down and shifted a pile of books, revealing a little avalanche of paper which had slewed across the deck. He pushed a hand in amongst the notebooks and foxed cuttings. It took a minute of sustained gleaning before his fingers closed on the tape cassette.

'The Village that Died for Us,' he read. The front showed a telephoto shot of St Swithun's seen across the mere from the east, the beet factory chimney in the background.

Humph was pouring Laura wine when Dryden reappeared with the tape and a portable cassette player. He waited for the commentary to begin before adjusting the volume so they could all hear. The evening was quiet now except for the flutter of marine engines on the main river as an armada of pleasure boats slid past heading south for moorings and a pub dinner.

The tape was a history in voices recorded in the summer of 1990 by the local history unit at Cambridge University and released commercially a year after the evacuation. The title was taken from a quote from the then minister of defence who had defended the decision to evacuate the village as vital to national security and the proper training of a modern army. Dryden had bought the tape on a whim and then stashed it, unheard, with other memorabilia.

'This was 1990, in the run-up to the evacuation,' he said,

adding more wood to the fire. The sky was still blue despite a misty sunset, but studded now with emerging stars. A vast flock of birds rose from the reserve at Wicken, beyond the river, and wheeled over them, caught against the backdrop of the moon.

The sound of wind filled the air, buffeting a microphone, and then came the church bells.

'My name is Fred Lake, and I guess I may be the last vicar of St Swithun's here at Jude's Ferry.'

'I met this guy,' said Dryden. 'He was OK. First parish I think, and a bit lost, but he tried to hold it together.'

The sound of bells swelled, then faded, to be replaced by the crunch of footsteps on gravel. Reverend Lake walked round his church accompanied by the sound of swifts flying from the eaves, then came the sound of a key turning in an ancient, oiled, lock.

'We've got loads to do before the final service on St Swithun's Day,' he said, the words echoing slightly in the stone interior, and Dryden noted the voice was unstuffy, laced with the remnants of a South African accent. He imagined the wide skies of the High Veldt and wondered if Lake had felt at home on Whittlesea Mere.

'The MoD tells us the church is not a target and isn't in danger. But they can't make any promises. The graveyard, the vicarage, who knows? We all make mistakes, it's part of being human, so I'm expecting the worst. Everything we can move we will move, to St Anthony's at Whittlesea, our sister church. They've been great about it, so who knows, we may be back in a year and all this will just be behind us like a bad dream.'

A sigh. 'And perhaps we shouldn't be too concerned with material loss. I've been telling everyone who'll listen the story of St Swithun . . .'

Another door creaked and steps echoed, climbing the tower of the church. A gust of wind hit the microphone as they emerged at the top, a seagull screeching overhead.

'It'll be my last sermon – but they know it well. My wife says I bang on about it, but it's relevant, even now, and these days if you want to get something across to people, past the distractions of the TV, and video games, and the rest, well you've got to bang on. So – St Swithun, the great bishop of Winchester, said he wanted to be buried out of doors so that, he said, the "sweet rain of heaven" could fall on his grave. There was a deeper message, a political message really . . .' Dryden noted how strong the accent had suddenly become, the guttural nasal vowels distinct in the word 'political'.

'He was saying that he didn't want to be buried alongside the great and the good inside the cathedral, all the posh people. He wanted to be outside with us, the also-rans.'

He laughed and Dryden thought how little bitterness there was in the voice. 'But then of course the people who came after him thought they knew better. They decided to dig up his bones and put them in a fancy tomb inside. And that, of course, is when it rained, ruining their plans, filling the grave as they dug it. For forty days and forty nights it rained, a mark of just how disappointed God was with their atti-tude, the way they'd forgotten this wonderful lesson they'd been given by Swithun, this great example.'

A cough, a fresh gust of wind . . . 'OK. I think the ringers are ready for us.' The deep note of a tenor bell sounded, being rung down.

'Bubbly?' asked Humph, firing another green tennis ball despite the gathering darkness. They watched as Boudicca moved like a shadow over the field, and the cabbie refilled their glasses. To the north, over the cathedral, a brace of

US fighters wheeled, the roar of the engines swelling suddenly, rattling the boat's portholes.

Laura looked towards them, shielding her eyes awkwardly with her hand. 'Much more now,' she said, and Dryden understood her. Since the invasion of Iraq the US air bases at Mildenhall and Lakenheath were busier; a steady stream of transport planes bringing in fuel and stores for shipment on to the Middle East, while the fighter pilots trained before being posted to the skies over the Gulf.

The tape moved on, through the voices in the belfry to an elderly farm labourer who recalled, beside the slow-crackling peat fire in his cottage, the day the beet factory opened – the steam whistle which marked the shifts salvaged from a transatlantic liner. Then came the village baker, long retired to a cottage over The Dring – the village's narrow high street flanked on one side by a culvert – where he tended an allotment of berries, the gentle clip of the pruning shears marking his progress along a hedge.

Then the tape filled with static, the irritating clatter of a taxi firm's radio network.

'OK, Sam. You picked up yet?'

'Two minutes. Two minutes.'

'OK. Next, can you pick up from Peterborough railway station? That's forecourt Peterborough. Back to the New Ferry, Sam. Back to the New Ferry.'

The static faded. The woman's voice was throaty and scarred by cigarettes.

'My name's Jan Cobley. We've run the firm now for twenty-six years, Sam and me. I do control, here, and he's out in the cab. We've got two, and our son's in the other. He's worked hard, but these days they expect more, don't they? We think we've done all right, really – there's a roof over our heads and we get a holiday, that's more than some here. People said we'd fold, of course. But Jude's Ferry's miles from anywhere and when the factory was running we was off our feet. And the bus don't run at all now, so that's more trade when it's about. And we have to do the school runs – primary and for the college in Whittlesea.'

A kettle whistled and there was the sound of a teapot filling. 'And you'd be surprised where you can get trade,' she said. Humph blew air out of the tiny bow of his mouth. 'Take the army. They might get marched out to the gate posts on the range but they don't mind a lift home.'

She laughed then and Dryden imagined a mouth with wrecked teeth, and cellulite arms.

'We'll keep going, move the business, Sam's got some ideas. We'll be all right, the two of us.' Dryden noted that the Cobleys' son was not included in their plans. Clearly running a mini-cab wasn't top of his career ladder.

Humph left, kissing Laura and ignoring Dryden, gathering the dog into the Capri and swinging it out along the road to Barham's Farm and the A10.

'I wonder who she was,' said Dryden to Laura as he stood on the riverbank watching the tail-lights dim. 'The woman we found in the cellar.'

The swinging skeleton held the focus of his memory, and he was struggling to erase its image. He thought of the cellar now, as night fell, and the cruel hook driven into the beam to take the rope.

From the tape came the unmistakable mewl of a kitten, and distantly, the bark of a dog. Metal cage doors were shut and opened and there was the sound of a bucket on a stone floor.

'My name's Jennifer Smith and I work here at the boarding kennels in Jude's Ferry.' There was another pause for an edited-out question.

'Yeah. There's no problem having dogs and cats together. They have separate compounds and they never see each other. I like the cats best, yes ...' The sound of purring suddenly filled the soundtrack.

'We're full tonight – that's nearly thirty cats and twenty-five dogs – plus two kittens in the house. It's been here – the business – for nearly forty years, so I guess it's the reputation that brings people. Mrs Verity, that's the owner, she says it's because we're so far away from towns and noise and things.

'I'm not clever enough to be a vet but Mrs Verity has a friend, Mrs Royle, who runs a cattery the other side of Peterborough – so I might go there. My brothers are leaving home, and Dad died last year – so Mum said she'd come too. There's some money, from Dad's insurance, so the twins might set up a business of their own, building like Dad, but they can't make up their minds. Brothers, right?'

She laughed, covering something else that she wanted to hide. 'It's a new start, isn't it, and I'm looking forward to the animals. It'll be good, it will.'

The wind buffeted the microphone again and Dryden could hear the sound of a dog straining at a leash. 'I love walkin' them. That's Ely cathedral over there, do you see? That's twenty-two miles – and you don't see it that often. And that's the power station at Flag Fen – that's just eighteen. There's nothing else, just space I guess, and sky.'

Seagulls calling swelled before fading out as the tape moved on to its final talking head. Dryden's fire crackled, dying down to the last orange embers.

The sound of a tractor clattered close, then died. 'My name is George Tudor and I work on Home Farm here in the village, or out in the flower fields.' The voice was light and young, heard against the backdrop of the seagulls which

57

had trailed the plough. 'They say we'll be back here in a year but that's too long for me, too long for a lot of us. I can't live on their promises. I know they need the village and we shouldn't fight it. So I ain't fighting it . . . I'm leaving. Western Australia – they need people out there on the land and I've got my exams. So I've filled out all the forms, and people have said the right things about me, that I work hard and that. Fred, the vicar, he's put his name down for us. So we're off. For good.'

A fighter plane suddenly exploded over their heads, low, screaming east to west.

As the engines faded they listened for the tape again, and the faint sound of a lid being popped off a lunchbox. 'I won't miss it, no,' he said. 'It's a hard place to make a living, Jude's Ferry, and it's a lonely place too, despite the people. Sometimes, because of the people.'

The tape hissed to an end and in the silence an owl flew through the light of the fire.

The first thing I remember about myself is being amongst the reeds. They crowded round, like witnesses, where I lay.

I knew nothing at that moment. I had no name, I had no loves. I just was. Of the life I remember it is the happiest moment.

I didn't panic. I had been here before in another life, in those few seconds after waking when identity eludes us. Where was I? Who was I? I could wait for the answers. They would float up amongst the reeds.

Then the rain fell and I knew I was in the river; the drops splashing around me, my back resting on the mud, my legs, buoyant, in the side stream. And time marked out by the thudding mechanical drum of boat engines going past, the wash rocking me gently.

And still I didn't know my name.

Only the pain was real. It cut down along my arm and across the knuckles of my fingers. So I raised my right hand to the grey sky and saw that the top of each finger had been sliced off. Skin hung from one exposed bone, the fingers white and bloodless.

I felt some disgust then, but distantly, as if on behalf of someone else.

And then I knew two things. I knew I was dying there in the water. And I remembered a voice I'd once known telling me something I'd always feared to hear.

'They've found the cellar. Ring me.'

Tuesday, 17 July

7

It had been two days since that wayward shell had crashed beside the New Ferry Inn but Dryden knew less now about the skeleton in the cellar than he had in those first minutes before its bones had finally fallen to the floor. Which was not a good position for any reporter to be in two hours before his final deadline. *The Crow*'s downmarket tabloid sister paper the *Ely Express* went to bed that morning. Most of the nationals and all the regional evening newspapers had carried the bare details of the story already. He needed a new line, and he needed it fast.

Dryden sat at his desk in the newsroom. He'd opened the central sash in the bay window. Outside he could hear the bustle of Market Street; a dog tied up outside the post office yelped rhythmically while a bell tinkled as customers came and went at the haberdasher's opposite *The Crow*'s offices.

He forced himself to look at his PC screen. He'd knocked out his eyewitness account of the events at Jude's Ferry, but that was already old news and strictly inside-page material. That left him with the opened grave in the church, details of which the police had not released, but had now confirmed in response to his inquiry.

What he needed on the grave-robbers story was some background, some colour to flesh out what little he knew. He went online and called up Google, putting 'Peyton' and 'Jude's Ferry' in the search window. He clicked on peytonfamily.com, a US website, and his screen began to fill with coats of arms and an elaborate family tree, as well as links to chatrooms, an annual convention home page, and a visitors' site.

Dryden read the welcome note: 'Thank you for logging on to the home page for the Peyton family here in the United States. We are one of the nation's oldest families, tracing our roots back to the Pilgrim Fathers and the founding of the Republic. If you are a Peyton, or just interested in one of the country's noble "first families", please read on, or e-mail our online editor, John Peyton Speed, who will deal with your questions. We hope you are as fascinated as we are by the story of one of America's great dynasties.'

Dryden skimmed the history page, finding a society dedicated exclusively to the genealogy of the family and, in particular, its origins in the east of England. Annual trips were organized to visit significant sites in the UK – Battle (apparently the point of arrival for the Peytons with William the Conqueror), the Tower of London and the three parish churches holding the remains of the Peyton ancestors – St Winifred's, Lincoln; St John's, Boston; and St Swithun's at Jude's Ferry. Dryden hit the link for Jude's Ferry and swore . . .

SITE UNDER CONSTRUCTION

So he hit the e-mail link for John Peyton Speed and set out briefly the events at Jude's Ferry, including the damage to the church and the evidence of grave robbery. He explained who he was and asked for a prompt reply, but with the time difference it would have to be a storyline he'd develop later in the week.

Which just about took him back to square one. Compared to what had been dubbed the 'Skeleton Woman' by the tabloids, a bit of grave robbing was a sideshow, especially as there was no evidence it was linked directly with the corpse found hanging in the cellar.

He needed a new line on the main story and his one hope appeared to be Magda Hollingsworth, the missing shop-keeper. None of the other papers had yet mentioned her, and the police seemed to be keeping that line of inquiry discreet, presumably to help shield the family from having to relive their grief. Dryden had done some research in *The Crow*'s archives on her case, which had been briefly covered in the nationals but had then been relegated to a local cause célèbre, warranting only a brief mention on the first anniversary of the evacuation of the village.

Magda Hollingsworth had last been seen alive, without any doubt, at 4.00pm on the day before the final evacuation. Her son, Jacob, had shut up the business for the final time and they'd spent an hour putting stock from the post office in crates before he'd driven into Whittlesea with the last cash box of takings. All the foodstuffs and perishables had been phased off the shelves in the weeks leading up to the final day. According to *The Crow*, Magda had then gone up to her bedroom to write her diary – apparently a daily event – and been heard taking a bath later in the evening. She had plans, according to the diary, to visit one of the villagers that evening and they'd confirmed they'd seen her about 7.30 to 7.45. One of the youngsters who had attended the dance in the Methodist Hall told police he was pretty sure he'd caught sight of her walking out along the road by the allotments at around 8.30pm. While he had not seen her face, her clothes were a distinctive trademark: a multi-coloured pleated dress and a leather waistcoat and bag in harlequin patches of yellow and red.

Mrs Hollingsworth's children, who worked in the shop but had already moved out of the village, did not discover her disappearance until the next morning when they returned to help her pack the last of her belongings into the family car. She had been planning to retire to a bungalow at Wells-next-the-Sea on the north Norfolk coast. But she was nowhere to be found that morning. The family reported her missing at noon to army officials in charge of the final stages of evacuation. Military police, on the scene anyway, took a statement and contacted the control room at Lynn and a general description was circulated. The army conducted a thorough search of the village that evening after the villagers had left. No trace of her body was ever found, her bank account remained untouched, but a police spokesman did say that, having been given access to her diary, they were concerned for her safety and that she may have tried to take her own life. They declined to give further details, except to say that she had been suffering from depression.

Dryden leant back in his chair and studied the stained ceiling of the office, from which hung a single wisp of cobweb. 'I need more,' he said.

He needed to find her children. He tried Google for both and found a Jacob Hollingsworth listed as a lecturer at Stoke University, in the Department of Eastern European Languages. Calling the number given he ran into an answerphone – Dr Hollingsworth was in Budapest and would be for a further ten days. Urgent messages by e-mail. Dryden tapped one out and dispatched it with little hope of getting an answer. Ruth Hollingsworth did not appear online, but she was described in one of the subsequent articles in *The Crow* on her mother's disappearance as working at Littleport Library. Dryden rang, discovered she was now married and had taken the surname Lisle, and was last heard of working for the Fenland Mobile Library Service. They had a website listing the villages to be visited by the fleet of eight mobiles – each one with a librarian. Mrs R. Lisle was given as attending for the service that day in Coveney, just west of Ely.

Dryden checked his watch. He had time for the round trip but he left the news editor an e-mail explaining where he was, and when he'd be back. He grabbed his mobile phone, summoned Humph and met him by the war memorial at the bottom of Market Street. The rain had fallen steadily overnight, soaking the distant landscape into winter colours, illuminated now by a milky sun. They left the cathedral and zigzagged over West Fen towards the low hill that had once been the island of Coveney. En route Dryden phoned his press contact for the Friends of the Ferry to see if the shelling of the church had changed their decision to drop all attempts to win the right of return to the village. There was an answerphone, so he left a message.

The mobile library, decked out in 1950s cream and blue, sat in a lay-by at the village's central T-junction. A Methodist chapel was the only building of any size, leaving the village green to be dominated by a netball court and social club with four ugly halogen floodlights. There was a children's playground, empty at this hour except for an elderly man whistling tunelessly. Somewhere a hammer struck wood rhythmically, but nobody else was in sight. The village's principal asset was the distant view of Ely cathedral, like a battleship steaming head-on, flag flying.

Ruth Lisle was stamping a small pile of large-print books for a woman with grey hair and a stiff back who held a polished stick. Dryden hung back, flicking through some pamphlets on local history, wondering if places like Coveney had a trove of secrets to match that of Jude's Ferry. Humph, bored with the cab, appeared at the door, considering the flight of four metal steps. He took the banister and the whole vehicle tilted a foot, the woman with the stick seeking safety by gripping the counter. Once on board the cabbie tiptoed down to the travel section and began, Dryden guessed, to search for a book on the Faroe Islands to complement his language tape.

Dryden leaped forward to help the elderly reader down the steps and noticed with a flood of relief that Ruth Lisle was wearing a round green badge with white letters proclaiming: Friends of the Ferry.

Alone, except for the snuffling figure of Humph, Dryden decided to try absolute honesty for a change.

'My name's Philip Dryden, from *The Crow*. I'm sorry to bother you – perhaps the police have been in touch already – it's about Jude's Ferry.' He nodded at the badge.

'You mean it's about my mother.' She didn't say it unkindly, and she offered Dryden a seat in the small reading area by the counter.

The mobile library squeaked on its hinges as Humph edged along the travel section.

'I'm so –' Dryden tried to say, but she cut in.

'No. It's OK. They seem to think they might have found her, in this cellar near the inn. I told them I think they're wrong, Mr Dryden. I just don't see her there, not like that. I've never believed that she killed herself. But they'll do some tests, and then we'll know. I'm prepared to be wrong, and in some ways it would be a relief. I gave them a, what do you call it? A swab – yes, a swab of cells from inside my cheek. It's a miracle really, isn't it, DNA? Twenty years ago we'd have never known.'

'I'm sorry,' said Dryden. He paused, forcing himself to keep the pace of the interview languid and informal. 'Magda – it's an unusual name.'

'Hungarian gypsies,' she said quickly, smiling almost wickedly. 'Not a popular ancestry in the Fens, as I'm sure you may know.'

Dryden nodded, trying to suppress the clichéd image of the roadside caravans, the rusted gas bottles and the half-hearted washing lines. Every year saw a fresh outbreak of hostilities between travellers and Fen farmers. The open, fenceless Fens provided an ideal landscape for the itinerant. And each summer saw a fresh influx of Irish travellers, modern-day tinkers, equipped with the local knowledge and the cash to buy up land before moving the rest of the caravans into view. Several long-running planning disputes were wending their way towards the High Court while villagers seethed, watching house prices stagnate, then fall.

'Mum's father, my grandfather, was in a concentration camp at Terezin in Bohemia before the war; we were active, you see – politically. We'd got out of Hungary when it was obvious what was coming – but Czechoslovakia was worse. The Nazis started with the Roma, a fact that's sometimes forgotten. A million died in the camps before '45. Mother got out in '38; they sold everything they had for her train ticket.'

Dryden laughed, unable to comprehend the sacrifice.

'My grandmother died within a few months. They say heartbroken, don't they, and I never believe that, but she was only fifty.'

Dryden thought what an extraordinary looking woman she was – perhaps six foot, in her late thirties, with large long bones and a broad face out of which the skull seemed to press, the cheekbones stretching the leathery skin. She'd moved easily but with a slight effort, as if her body was a burden to her, but now, seated, she seemed to relish the stillness.

'Mum was always very careful to say that it was the family decision for her to leave – that she didn't flee, or seek refuge. The idea that the Nazis had succeeded in forcing her out of her home, even if it was a caravan, made her very angry, but of course it was the truth. She stayed with an uncle in the suburbs – Croydon – but they got bombed out when they attacked the airport in the Blitz, so they moved out to Harlow in Essex. It was just villages then, of course. That's where she met Dad, he was a farmer, although I think that's actually a bit grand. A smallholder perhaps, with pigs. I always think that was so important for Mum – that he was of the land, as it were, something she'd never had. He belonged, didn't he? In a way she never could. Jacob, my brother, was born in the farmhouse – a cottage really, but very idyllic.'

She stopped herself, suddenly worried. 'You can't have something that's just a bit idyllic, can you?'

'I guess not.'

She patted her knee. 'So. Idyllic then. But Dad died in 1970 after a long illness, which was not the kindest of deaths.'

Dryden wondered how much suffering was salted away in that casual phrase. A breeze blew open the door of the mobile library and they could see that the rain was falling steadily now, the playground deserted.

'No one will come now,' she said. 'Would you like a coffee?' There was an automatic cuppa-machine behind the counter and Humph accepted one too, retreating with it to the cab.

She sat eventually, one of her large hands almost encircling the plastic cup, and looked Dryden flatly in the eye.

'I was there when they found the skeleton – she was a slight woman, your mother?' said Dryden.

Ruth laughed. 'I take after my father, Mr Dryden – the Hollingsworths are all country stock, big boned. Although

70

I'm relying on mother's descriptions and the photographs of course. I was born at the Ferry six months after he died. We never met – like Posthumous in the Greek story.'

'I'm sorry,' said Dryden, trying to think of something else to say.

'So am I,' she said, smiling and tilting her chin. Dryden could see how strong she was, how she never used the past as an excuse for weakness.

'Mother,' she said with emphasis, 'was petite by comparison. She was also very depressed about losing her home again. Such an irony, to be driven out by the fascists, then the Luftwaffe, and then the MoD. She was quite calm about it, quite accepting, and devastated in a way. She'd found a place for herself at the Ferry. People liked her – well, most people liked her. And she hadn't compromised much at all. My mother was a flamboyant character, Mr Dryden, not a trait much prized in the Fens. But we were certainly part of the community – Jake and I. So I think that after all that anguish – the flight to England, the bombing, Dad's death – she had this notion that she'd found a place that belonged to her. And then they took it away. It was profoundly depressing for her and I think the idea of starting again really frightened her. After all, she didn't want us around, she wanted us to use our educations and get on. But what was she to do?'

'Do you mind if I quote you in the paper? I don't have to,' asked Dryden, unsettled by her frankness.

'It's kind of you to ask but it's OK. The library service sent me on a course, on how to deal with the press. So I know that if I don't want it in the paper I should just not say it. But I'm proud of Mum, what she achieved, and what she left behind.'

Dryden tilted his chin by way of a question, sipping the gritty coffee.

'The diary,' she said, something like arrogance in the square set of her shoulders. 'When Dad died she took the store at Jude's Ferry. Grief led to depression even then and she needed something to focus on, something that wasn't inside her. I think what she really wanted was to go back on the road, to take the comfort of motion, which I can really understand,' she added, looking fondly around the mobile library. 'The comfort of just being on the way some-where, without the disappointment of ever arriving. But she stayed for us. Have you heard of an organization called Mass-Observation, Mr Dryden?'

Thunder rolled out on the Fen and the rain came in gusts, rocking the suspension under them and clattering on the metal roof.

'Sort of. Wasn't that during the war – people kept diaries of everyday life and then sent them in to a government department as part of a sort of national chronicle? Morale, crime, sex, families, grief, all of human life.'

'Indeed. Well, it wasn't a government department actually. It's all held at the University of Surrey now and they started again in the eighties. Mum applied to be a correspondent and they accepted her. She wrote well, with a real eye for detail. So every day she chronicled village life – no names, just initials for all the characters. They insist on that because they want the entries to be as candid as possible. Then she'd make a copy and send it in.'

Dryden finished the coffee, crunched the cup and checked his watch.

'Have you read the diary?'

'Bits of it. In fact, I'm working my way through the whole thing right now. The police asked if I would read it and see if there might be anything which would help explain what happened in the cellar.'

She waited for him to ask. 'And is there?'

'Nothing and everything. The diary is full of tales of the kind of petty maliciousness which marks out a small community – little feuds, stifling marriages, secrets which are interesting only because they're secrets. And the prejudice against us, against the family, which was always there but which faded I think, as the years went by.'

'But no names,' said Dryden.

'No. Just initials. And this is all – the bits I've read so far – back in the early eighties, so I can't even guess the real identities. I was a teenager, all I was interested in was other teenagers.'

She closed her eyes for a second. 'It's very good, the quality of her description. I thought I might put it all together as a book, and the people at Mass-Observation are ready to release the material for publication. So who knows.'

She raised her cup to her dry lips and let her eyes run along the bookshelves. Dryden wondered if that had been what had drawn her to the library – the prospect of writing a book herself.

'She loved books?' asked Dryden.

'It was the only thing she brought to this country – that and the clothes she stood up in. A Magyar Bible, some poetry and a blank notebook from her father. Books were almost sacred.'

'And she filled in her diary . . . well, religiously?'

They laughed together.

Dryden watched the rain bouncing on the tarmac outside. 'The police looked at the diaries when she disappeared, didn't they?'

'Yes. Mum didn't send everything she wrote to MO, the stuff about her own thoughts and the family she kept separately. The police did look briefly and I think she'd been

73

honest about how she felt, how the prospect of leaving was like a kind of death approaching – but they had to admit she never mentions harming herself. Not once.'

Dryden stood and climbed down the metal steps, letting the cool rain wash against his face. He took out his card and handed it over. 'If you do find something of interest you might call? I know there'd be no names, but let me know if you can.'

She nodded, reading the card, and Dryden thought she'd never ring. He imagined her mother, working diligently at her diary in the bedroom above the shop, listening perhaps to the life of Jude's Ferry outside – a dog barking, a voice raised in anger, feet running home.

'Did anyone know she kept this diary while she was alive?'

'No. It was a secret, and that was certainly the rule. But then . . .'

Dryden waited.

'But then, she knew *their* secrets, didn't she?'

8

He stood on the doorstep of Ely police station, the automatic doors of which refused to open, and looking up watched the drops plunging from a low grey cloud, falling into his eyes. A police communications mast rose into the low cloud, held in position by a series of steel hawsers – home to a flock of chattering starlings. Otherwise the squat two-storey 1970s building appeared to be devoid of life – uniformed or plain clothed. Five squad cars were parked up, smartly washed and waxed, like exhibits in a museum of the motor car. There was a persistent rumour in the town that the station was often completely empty – all semblance of activity being created by a series of time-switch lights. It was where the sleeping policemen worked.

Dryden tried another charge at the immobile doors and, bizarrely, this time they swished open. A police constable appeared at the counter window, recognized Dryden and unclipped his radio from his tunic to access a sheaf of papers in an outside pocket. He thrust a piece of neatly folded A4 into Dryden's hand: 'Jude's Ferry? There's a statement, but it's not much. It's all being run from Lynn, if you want more I'd ring them. Detective Inspector Peter Shaw's your man.'

'Shaw,' said Dryden. He'd already tried CID at Lynn and been told Shaw was running the inquiry. The switchboard had refused to put him through and redirected him to the press office, so he'd hung up. The West Norfolk Constabulary's website was of little more help. Detective

75

Inspector Peter Shaw was listed as head of the Lynn anti-burglary unit, under a helpline number which took messages when Dryden tried it. He'd searched the website for other mentions of Shaw and found nothing except a reference under the force's social club to Detective Chief Inspector Jack Shaw, which rang a distant bell, like the sound of a police car on the bypass. Dryden checked *The Crow*'s library and found a cutting from September 1997. DCI Shaw had taken early retirement after being severely criticized by the judge at Cambridge Crown Court in the trial of a Lynn man for the murder of a six-year-old child. The case had ended in an acquittal amid accusations that the police had fabricated evidence. The Police Complaints Authority had been notified. Father and son? Possibly.

Dryden entered DI Peter Shaw in Google and was directed to the website of Lincoln University. Shaw was listed as a visiting lecturer in forensic science. 'Nobody likes a smart arse' thought Dryden. He'd left a message for Peter Shaw but had heard nothing back.

The PC retreated into the bowels of the station leaving his radio on the counter. A buzz of static suddenly filled the laminated lobby . . .

'Assistance please. Assistance. This is 155 at Ely Riverside. Ely Riverside. Junction of Waterside and Ship Lane. Assistance. Over.'

The PC was back quickly to reclaim his radio, but Dryden was gone.

Humph put the Capri into reverse outside, leaving a comforting double line of burnt rubber on the tarmac.

'Perhaps it's the phantom duck killer back again,' said Dryden, enjoying the sudden burst of action. A boy racer in a souped-up Corsa had been spotted mowing down a line of chicks crossing the road that spring, leading to a local outcry, and to Dryden's eternal disappointment the only upward blip in *The Crow*'s circulation in a decade. The council was being urged to install a special crossing for ducks between the riverside and the cathedral park, although Dryden doubted they'd be able to reach the buttons.

The Capri hit sixty as Humph swerved past the cathedral's Galilee porch and then down Back Hill towards the river. The morning's persistent rain ran in a stream in the gutters. As Humph produced the required screech of tyres, taking the corner by the bottom of Back Hill, Dryden read the one-paragraph police statement:

The human remains removed by the police pathologist from Jude's Ferry are under examination. Detectives from King's Lynn are interviewing several former villagers and are confident that an identification can be made soon. In the meantime members of the public who may have information useful to the inquiry should ring freephone 0700 800 600. All calls will be kept in strictest confidence.

'Well, that tells us less than we know,' said Dryden, balling the paper up in his fist. 'This better be something good or we'll be leading the front page with the price of potatoes in the market.' Humph brought the Capri to a halt outside the Maltings, the fluffy dice hanging from his rear-view mirror gyrating wildly.

'We can presume that's PC 155,' said Dryden, jumping out and grabbing Boudicca's lead. He didn't like dogs, and he didn't like people who liked dogs, but since Humph's inadvertent adoption of the greyhound he had discovered that people were much more likely to talk to a man *with* a dog.

The policeman's uniform set him apart from a gaggle of

77

fishermen in regulation waterproofs. He was trying to keep the small crowd back, repeating his call for assistance by radio. Kit was strewn along the towpath; keep nets, rods, buckets, stools, picnic boxes, tackle boxes, bait boxes, night lights and lanterns; the paraphernalia of the true fishing fanatic.

'What's up?' Dryden asked one of the fishermen, a teenager with hooks stuck in his canvas hat.

At that moment a siren blurted into action as a police squad car pulled up beside Humph's cab. The crowd drew back and Dryden took his chance, pushing his way through until he found himself looking down at a large cylindrical net, laid flat and turned out to reveal the catch.

Dryden saw a zander gasping for air, the teeth slightly coloured with cold blood, some riverweed, and two small eels entwined together. Beside the net an open box of maggots heaved with life.

'Oh God,' said one of the PCs who'd just arrived and joined him at the front.

There was something else in the net, something very dead: the top of two human fingers, as white as pork fat, the stumps clean and showing the sliced bone beneath.

9

The Crow's offices reverberated to the sound of computer keys being struck. Below, through the open bay window, umbrellas jostled. A bus reversed, grinding gears, while two shops along a parrot screeched from the covered cage hung outside a barber's shop. The aroma of freshly ground coffee slipped into the room like a burglar.

Charlie Bracken, the paper's news editor, sat behind a desk by the window exhibiting several signs of alcohol deprivation. A splodge of sweat marred his unironed blue shirt and his eyes occasionally flitted towards the window and the comforting sight of The Fenman bar opposite.

'You all right for time?' he asked Dryden, wasting more of it.

'Sure. I'm nearly there. I need to make a couple of last calls.'

Charlie nodded, running copy up and down his PC screen without reading a word.

Dryden considered the intro for the last time, knowing it was the front-page splash for the *Express*. The paper's circulation was limited to Ely and the villages of the isle, and was a step downmarket of *The Crow*'s county readership. The Jude's Ferry story would go at the foot of the tabloid front, with another story inside on the wayward bombardment of the village, with Dryden's pictures from Whittlesea Mere.

Dryden sipped coffee and tried to concentrate.

By Philip Dryden

Two severed human fingers were found in a fisherman's net on Ely's riverside this morning (Tuesday).

A police diving team arrived at the scene within minutes of the grisly discovery to search upstream.

'Clearly there's a possibility we are dealing with a fatal accident here. We're assuming the injuries were caused by a propeller. We need to find the victim quickly,' said Sgt John Porter, of the county underwater search and rescue unit.

Local postman Andrew Paddock was fishing upstream of the railway bridge when he felt something on the line.

'I got a bite and started to reel it in – it was a zander, a big fish too, so I waded into the reeds to get it. When I got the net on the bank I found a load of weed and the fingers. I was pretty upset, but the other fishermen on the bank helped me call the police and take the net along to the Maltings.

'I should have stayed where I was and used the mobile but I just didn't think,' added Mr Paddock, of Teal Rise, Littleport. 'I've taken the week off to join in the association's competition – but frankly I'm going to give it a miss now. Let's hope whoever it is is still alive.'

This summer has seen several police warnings issued to swimmers in the river at Ely. One man who refused to get out of the water was forcibly removed and later charged with being drunk and disorderly.

A sponsored swimming race past the marina was cancelled owing to concerns over loose fishing lines, river cruiser traffic and the dangerous condition of some of the banks.

Dryden, floundering for more information, checked the word count. 'That's 250 – enough?'

Mack, the chief sub, obscured by a bank of electronic

make-up screens, stood up: 'Do me fifty more please – anything, just tack it on.'

Dryden ran through the stories provided online by the Press Association and found a discarded two-paragraph item about a fire on a houseboat in Cambridge and, adding the word 'meanwhile' tacked it on to the end of the story to make up the length, and then filed the story straight through to the subs.

Then his mobile rang, vibrating in an insistent circle on the Formica desktop.

'Hi. Dryden,' he said, aware that his voice had picked up the general atmosphere of stress. It was the press officer for the Friends of the Ferry returning his earlier call. And there were no surprises; the group had met again briefly to consider their position after the shelling of the church and the discovery of the skeleton. There was little appetite for a new campaign, the older members were now resigned to never going back, and the younger ones had always been more interested in the principle involved rather than actually living in the old village. The group had agreed to disband after nearly eighteen years.

Dryden added a line to the main Jude's Ferry story and re-filed to the sub-editor's basket.

They heard footsteps thumping up the wooden steps from reception and Mitch Mackintosh, *The Crow*'s photographer, barged into the newsroom fresh from the riverside. They all crowded behind the photographer's shoulder to see the shots come up on the digital display of the camera.

The Crow's cub reporter Garry Pymoor was double-checking wedding reports, a tedious chore reserved for the office junior. Dryden got his attention: 'Garry. Ring King's Lynn CID – see if there's anything more on Jude's Ferry. Chop chop.'

The pictures were lurid, the best unusable. 'Henry's not gonna like that . . .' said Charlie, of a crisp shot of the severed fingers in a bed of weeds. Henry Septimus Kew, venerable editor of both *The Crow* and the *Ely Express*, would make a ritual appearance just before the final deadline to check the paper's contents. Charlie's job boiled down to guessing what Henry wanted before the editor knew it himself.

'This one then,' said Dryden, nodding as Mitch paused on a picture of the crowd on the riverbank and one of the police divers slipping into the water. Mitch, a monosyllabic Scot with a strong line in cynicism, grunted and set off back to the darkroom where he lived.

Garry was waving his arms in semaphore thanks to telephone headphones. He pointed at the earpiece and put his thumbs up.

'I'll hold,' he said, then knocked the microphone away from his mouth. 'They say your skeleton is a bloke.'

'What? Bloody hell.'

Garry was nodding. Incompetent in many ways in daily life, *The Crow*'s junior reporter was sharp and reliable with facts if there was a story involved.

'No doubt. Build was slight for sure – dental work might be traceable apparently. Height was average, even if he was a bit thin-boned. They reckon five-ten, eleven.' He looked down at his notebook: 'Age somewhere between twenty and thirty-five – although the build makes those numbers just a guideline, could be a coupla years either way. Date of death somewhere between 1975 and five years ago. They need to examine the scene to get a closer fix. Talk about covering your arse, eh?'

Dryden nodded, calling up the Jude's Ferry story he'd already written on-screen to make the last-minute changes.

Garry talked some more and then hung up. 'Bit more. The

wrist bones were bound with garden wire – the plastic coated stuff. Pathologist believes the victim could have tied them up himself. The knots are loose, but would be – hold on, better get this dead right – "sufficient to prevent a reflex" attempt to save himself. There's some flesh left on the torso – tendons and stuff – and what he called "atrophied" organs. They're all being analysed but at the moment there's nothing sinister showing up. No poisons. Stomach contents long gone. Some indications of rodent activity along the bones. And some-thing else on dating: old newspapers in the cellar used to wrap beer glasses were mostly dated July 1990 – the most recent was the 12th, three days before the evacuation. *Daily Mail.*'

'I need that story,' said Charlie, feeling free to break the office's no smoking policy for the third time in an hour. 'I need it now, Dryden.'

'Well if you have it now it's fucking wrong . . .' said Dryden, stabbing the keys. 'So wait.' Dryden's junior role relative to Charlie was largely nominal. His Fleet Street track record outranked the news editor's formal authority. An embarrassed hush fell over the office while Garry grinned hugely.

'And one other oddity,' said the junior reporter. 'Clothing is in shreds, OK, but there were several layers still on the arms and beneath those, on the left arm, was the remains of what appears to be a piece of surgical gauze.'

'What?' said Dryden, looking up.

'Surgical gauze. Don't ask me. That's what he said.'

Dryden skimmed the Jude's Ferry piece and rewrote the intro . . .

By Philip Dryden

Forensic experts today (Tuesday) identified a skeleton found hanging in a cellar in the abandoned fen village of Jude's

Ferry as the bones of a young man who may have taken his own life.

He dropped down through a description of how the discovery was made to add in the new detail from the CID, and the pathologist's judgement on the knots at the wrist. Then he dropped down further and amended three pars on Magda Hollingsworth, making it clear the police would now be able to exclude her from their inquiries and leaving in the quotes from her daughter.

'Looks like suicide now,' he said when he'd filed it back to Charlie.

'Good job it's down page,' said the news editor, enjoying nothing more than vindication.

Dryden's mobile trilled. It was Humph, and for a second Dryden could hear the heavy breathing of the greyhound as the cabbie fumbled with his handsfree. 'Could be nothing,' said Humph, his voice light, almost weightless. 'Up by Cuckoo Bridge. I've just come along the back road and there's an ambulance and a search and rescue vehicle parked up. I'll try and get a pic.' Dryden heard the sound of Humph extricating himself from the Capri, like a cork from a bottle.

The reporter grabbed his jacket and headed for the door. 'We may have the owner of the fingers,' he said. 'I'll phone.'

10

Cuckoo Bridge crossed the river a mile north of the town, a wooden arch built in the fifties to link Quanea Fen with the towpath. Its pitch-soaked timbers had warped over the decades so that its once graceful lines were tortured now, a miniature nightmare of twisted boards over the wide expanse of the grey river, its surface pockmarked with the falling rain. The river ran through thickets of thorn here, and the only sign of humanity was the distant cathedral tower, just visible over the flood bank. It was here, more than a thousand years before, that the monks had come ashore with the body of St Etheldreda. Dryden always imagined the scene – the mist cloaking the little procession as it dragged the coffin on a cart along the old green lane by the river.

Dryden had hauled Mitch out of the darkroom and commandeered his van for the brief journey. They parked at the river authority depot and walked the last hundred yards along the narrow, single-track drove. Humph was alone on the bridge, the Capri beyond on the other bank beside the emergency vehicles, the cabbie's weight prompting creaks from the woodwork. The safety rail on the down-river side was broken at its central section, the snapped timber ends raw and pale.

The main river pooled here in a wide reed marsh, a clear channel for the tourist boats cut through the middle. The search and rescue team were twenty yards from them on the east bank. A whining inflatable dinghy nosed its way forward through the rushes while four divers squirmed in the shallows like tadpoles.

Humph handed Dryden a set of field glasses, stowing the camera now that the professional had arrived. Mitch, manically equipped for all eventualities, had retrieved waders from the back of his van and was making his way along the opposite bank to get a shot of the action. Dryden could see the victim now, spreadeagled in the reeds, a lifeless starfish. Up close through the field glasses the man's face looked impossibly pale, and his body entirely motionless. One of the divers was trying to bag his right hand, securing a watertight knot at the wrist.

'Looks bad,' said Dryden, trying to feel something for a nameless victim, aware that his profession could produce a disfiguring cynicism.

The dinghy was alongside now and a metal stretcher was manoeuvred under the body. As Dryden watched he saw the victim lift an arm so that he could cover his eyes with his uninjured hand.

'Hold on. Bloody hell. It's a live one,' said Dryden, flicking open the mobile. He got through to Jean – *The Crow*'s half-deaf receptionist and copy-taker. He gave her a three-line paragraph and told her to pass it straight to the editor's screen as a suggested fudge box – an item of late-breaking news which could be added to the back page after the presses had started to run. Then he got her to read it back and corrected the six errors which had crept into less than fifty words.

'Looks like he fell in here,' said Dryden to Humph, edging towards the gap in the safety rail. 'Hard to believe he got caught by a boat – unless it was night time. Surely you'd see him, or hear him. Mind you, half the skippers on the white ships are pissed by ten.' Dryden thought about it – the drifting gin palaces tinkling with wine bottles.

86

Humph took a step towards the edge and they both felt the planks twist under their feet. 'He might have hit those,' said the cabbie, pointing down. Directly below the missing safety rail the bridge's central support was buttressed with timbers. 'That would have knocked him out; he could have drifted into the slipstream and then . . .' He used one hand like a cleaver to cut down on the fingers of the other.

They walked over towards the ambulance and stood a respectful distance away as they slid the stretcher on board. The victim's hair was black, cut stylishly short at the back, the jawline military-straight, hinting at a good diet and inherited wealth, a solid build without being athletic, and despite the pallor – a tan which hadn't come out of a bottle. His clothes were casual but expensive – an olive-green linen shirt, moleskin trousers and one remaining brown leather shoe. Dryden could see a watch and what looked like the trailing lead of a mobile phone's handsfree set entangled with the arm. The sock on the shoeless foot hung loose, the exposed skin ribbed from the long immersion in the river water. He looked away, disturbed by the intimacy and vulnerability of a semi-naked foot.

The stretcher was half-way in when he turned his head towards them, and as the sun broke through the clouds Dryden glimpsed the eyes: pale green against the skin, and in the blast of light he was sure that, while water trickled down from the hairline, tears fell as well. As they slid him into the rear of the ambulance the man grabbed one of the paramedics by his fluorescent jacket and Dryden heard him choke and then the voice, forced out, ragged with stress.

'Don't leave me alone.'

Dryden waited for them to go, light blinking silently, before approaching the diving team, who stood now in a circle inhaling ritual cigarettes. The *Express*'s last edition was long gone so there was no need to push for more information, a luxury which ironically made his job that much easier. Boudicca padded up with him and lay at his feet like a croissant.

Two of the divers were sharing a cigarette, their wetsuits unzipped to the waist and turned back and out of the arms, revealing pallid white muscle and damp hair. One was tall, his long arms painfully pale and hairless, the other squat and tanned, with black curly hair over much of his torso. The support team were smoking too, diligently checking equipment as they repacked it into the unit van. Dryden felt excluded from this aggressively male club and fiddled ineffectually with the top button of his white shirt.

The sudden sunlight had transformed the landscape and revealed a wide sky of chef's-hat clouds. 'You boys got here quick,' said Dryden, making sure they saw him pocket his notebook. 'We got some pix, so if you want copies shout.'

'Eel catcher spotted him,' said the tall diver, speaking expertly while holding the cigarette between his jaws. Ely still boasted a council waterman, and Dryden had often seen him moving stealthily on the river at dawn by Barham's Dock in a low-sided fowlers' punt.

'How long you reckon he's been in there?' said Dryden, waving as Mitch drove off.

The tanned diver shrugged, squeezing water from his hair. 'With a bit of luck, just overnight. There's some hypothermia, any longer than that and he may have trouble recovering. Plus there's a bump on the head – it's a three-inch gash and it'll need stitches. Guess he tumbled in off the bridge. We're gonna close it, by the way, at least until they repair and strengthen the rails. It's in a pretty dangerous state.'

'Nobody noticed the broken handrail then? Not yesterday, not this morning?'

A shrug again. 'It's a lonely spot.'

They tried to turn away, cutting short the interview, but Dryden took a half step in. 'Did he say much? He looked upset – distraught really. Does he remember what happened? Think he jumped?'

An exchange of glances: 'We don't want to see any quotes in the paper, OK?' said the tall one. Dryden nodded. 'At the moment he can't remember his own name.'

Dryden thought about that. 'Amnesia? Believe him?'

They both nodded, but it was the tanned one, squatting down now to remove his leggings who added: 'Sure. Mostly. But he must remember something because that's not just pain in his eyes. He's terrified of something.' They turned then to go. 'Or he's terrified of someone. Nightmare is he can't remember who.'

II

Dryden checked with the news desk that the paper had gone and then walked back into town in the sun, tourists beginning to appear as he walked the towpath south. The Isle of Ely rose up from the fens ahead, the cathedral trailing a pennant of low cloud, all that remained of the morning's leaden sky.

He wondered what it was like not to have a memory. A blessing, perhaps. Laura's coma had been marked by a complete absence of any recall of their accident. The hours spent trapped in the lightless car beneath the winter water was literally a black box; a memory too terrifying to allow a replay. His wife's recovery had been marked by many advances. But not a single shaft of light had fallen into that lost world.

Ely, bathed in sunshine now, had come to life. In Market Square he spotted that one newspaper vendor was already on his pitch. The *Express* and *The Crow* were printed a mile out of town, and the editor had recently introduced an early print run for both in order to catch sales before the shops closed. The seller was a man known as Skeg, thirty perhaps, his face punctured with a single cheek stud, the hair cut savagely short, emphasizing a small triangle of dyed red stubble below his lip, but above his chin. Skeg's job was on the bottom rung of the employment ladder, a career normally reserved for a band of outcasts.

Dryden had to admit that Skeg was not quite so easy to pigeonhole. He lived on one of the dilapidated river boats which took up cheap moorings in the town's clay pits, and he'd come across him several times working at Wicken Fen nature reserve, clearing weed from the waterways, tagging and counting birds. And always, at his heels, the half-drowned short-haired terrier, tugged along on a blue rope. Sometimes Skeg would disappear from his pitch for months, trying another job, but he always reappeared.

Dryden bought a paper, even though he could have waited and got a free one back at the office, and flicking it open at the fold enjoyed the sight of his double front-page bylines. The thrill, even after twenty years on newspapers, was palpable.

Skeg had sensed the inner smile: 'Done all right then,' he said, and Dryden remembered instantly why he didn't like him as much as he normally liked outcasts. There was sarcasm beneath the conviviality, and something cruel about the eyes. At his feet the dog lay curled, ribs showing. Skeg had his own copy open to the feature on Jude's Ferry, and the picture Dryden had taken inside St Swithun's, the now shattered crusader's tomb beside an inset of what it had looked like before the wayward shelling.

'Yeah,' said Dryden. 'Decent day's work.'

Skeg took his pound coin and rummaged for the change in a wooden tray. The dog edged forward to snuffle at Dryden's feet and he felt the first wave of panic as it bared its teeth. He drew in breath, fighting the impulses which were coursing through his nervous system.

'Wow,' said Skeg, bending down and pulling the dog back. 'You're not a big fan of dogs, are ya?'

Dryden tried a smile that failed, aware that his phobia was painfully apparent.

'Think of something else,' he told himself. So he checked the space on the back page where his fudge box on the man in the river should have been and found it blank: either he'd bought one of the earliest copies off the run or they'd failed to get it in at all.

Dryden scanned the badges on Skeg's quilted poacher's jacket as he took his change: Troops Out of Iraq, Shelter, RSPCA, a sticker which proclaimed Green Planet, and another in support of a campaign to stop Cambridge University building a laboratory for animal testing of new drugs.

'Just found the bloke in the river without the fingers,' said Dryden, trying to mask his dislike of someone less fortunate than himself, and edging back still further from the dog.

Skeg nodded. 'That's good. That'll keep the story going then.' That smile again: mocking.

In The Fenman bar he found the entire newspaper staff – minus the editor and Jean from reception – engaged in the ritual press-day binge. Garry was counting peanuts on a tabletop while Charlie Bracken was retelling an anecdote about a riverbank flasher, complete with hand movements. Dryden was unable to catch the mood of timeless celebration. He was bothered by a bizarre double image: the marble broken finger on the stone floor of St Swithun's and the pale stumps of human flesh and bone in the fisherman's net.

He challenged Garry to a game of pool, beat him twice, and then slipped away. Zigzagging across town he reached an acre of empty tarmac now baking in hot afternoon sun, a mirage contorting the image of a cat tip-toeing towards the shadows. On one side stood an ugly red-brick Victorian barracks. Gold letters over a tall pointed doorway read: 36th (Eastern) Signal Regiment. The interior was cool and clinical, walls whitewashed, and the drill-hall floor waxed to a military shine. A raised stage at one end had a crude proscenium arch carrying a regimental crest and the words 'The Territorial Army in East Anglia'. Dryden examined the silence and could almost hear the precise thud of boots coming to attention.

The drill hall had been radically reduced in size to accommodate a suite of offices on one side, glass partitions shielding an array of high-tech computers. Dryden had his nose pressed against the glass when a cough made him jump.

It was Major John Broderick.

'Hi,' said Dryden. 'What's all the gear?'

'This stuff? Signals. It's what the TA's got to offer these days – qualifications. IT, computer maintenance, communications. Popular stuff. And the army needs it; we've got people out in Iraq now on active service. People from here.'

They went into Broderick's office: a sad room, cold despite the sun and dominated by an oak desk which looked too important for the building. Attached to the blotter was a small silver photo frame containing three shots: wife, wife and son, wife and daughter. On one wall was a framed sepia portrait of a soldier in the Indian Army. Dryden touched the frame: 'And this . . . ?'

'It's my father; 1944.'

Dryden declined a seat. 'The evacuation of Jude's Ferry. The army organized everything, yes? You said there were records. Those questionnaires the villagers had to fill in?'

Broderick closed a book on his desk in which Dryden glimpsed a line drawing of an orchid. 'I had a visit yesterday. CID from Lynn. DI Peter Shaw. Same question. Which is good news for you because I think he did most of the work.'

The major led the way along a painted brick corridor to a staircase. At the bottom was an iron door with a double lock. Inside they were blinded by an array of hanging, naked light bulbs illuminating half a dozen metal bookcases packed with box files. The room smelled of old newspapers and something stringent, possibly rat poison or disinfectant.

'Regimental records,' said Broderick. 'The 36th took the key security role for the 1990 operation, organized the evacuation, the final convoy out and then a complete search, for obvious reasons.'

Dryden recalled reports at the time that opponents of the evacuation were threatening to get through the wire and hide in the village, a human shield against bombardment.

'Then the Royal Engineers got stuck in, mapped the place, ran up an inventory of what was there in terms of the built environment: homes, commercial premises, cellars, drains, electrics. That was Colonel Flanders May and his men.'

'You in the TA then?' asked Dryden.

'Yup. Cadet. We did the transport on the day – big job actually, nightmare to organize, especially when dealing with civilians. That wasn't in the village though, it was my job to help run the depot here in Ely. You can tell a soldier where to go but these people had to be eased out in front of the press with cameras everywhere. Up until the passing of the deadline we had very little actual jurisdiction. Persuasion, not force. As I say, bloody good training.'

Dryden saw again the old woman being dragged from her home on The Dring.

'There was trouble on the day,' said Dryden.

Broderick nodded, but made no response.

At the end of the room a trestle table held a few spilled box files.

The major picked up one of the sheets of paper, covered with the archaic jumble of a manual typewriter's letters.

'This is the stuff on Jude's Ferry?' asked Dryden.

'Yup. The CID man – Shaw – brought a warrant but I told him he'd wasted his time. What with freedom of information and everything we'd have to allow public access – hardly needed the power of the courts behind him. Thorough kind of policeman. Anyway, nice bloke. Bit odd – dyed hair. Blond.'

'Good God,' said Dryden, trying for irony, and reflecting that a career as a part-time soldier seemed to have aged Broderick well beyond his thirty-something generation.

Broderick bristled. 'Still. Seemed to know what he was up to. No tie, mind you, which was a bit sloppy. I bet he makes his DS wear one.'

There was a long silence into which a kettle whistled somewhere on the ground floor above.

'I'll leave you to it,' said the major. 'Clearly, you can't take anything away, and I'd ask you to use a pencil to take notes. Sounds like my corporal is making tea – I'll get him to bring you some.'

Dryden wondered if he was being nice to head off a bad press over the Jude's Ferry bombing.

'The paper's out,' he said, handing him the copy he'd bought from Skeg.

Broderick took it, snapping the front page flat. 'Right. I'd better sit down and read this.'

'Help yourself.'

The major closed the door crisply behind him and Dryden settled at the table with his back to it and the rest of the room. The hair on his neck bristled and he kept hearing the tiny shuffle of paper creaking in the box files, so he pulled out the table and took a seat on the far side. Under the crude, unshaded lights dust drifted like blossom in May.

DI Shaw had indeed made his job simple. The documents had been sorted into four separate sets, the first being the questionnaires the villagers had filled in to assist the engineers in mapping Jude's Ferry. Dryden flipped through until he found the New Ferry Inn, Woodruffe, Ellen – Licensee. Tick-boxes and sketches indicated the position of rooms, attic spaces, main services, building materials and, finally, cellars. Those beneath the inn were clearly shown, three rooms, with electric and water supplies. No cellars were marked for the outbuildings. The signature was Ellen Woodruffe's, although the hand was shaky and irregular.

The principal set of documents was a census of Jude's Ferry taken after the MoD gave the villagers notice to quit three months before the evacuation. The announcement was made on Friday 20 April – each household receiving a letter that day. A copy was on the file. Dryden took a shorthand note of the key line:

While there is a pressing military need for the village to be evacuated to allow unhindered use of the surrounding firing range there is every expectation that the international situation will allow a return of the civilian population in due course.

Dryden's tea arrived, a half pint in a tin mug, ferried down by a sullen corporal.

Alone again he considered the details of the first census. The number of inhabitants was listed as 112, including forty-six women and eight children. These were distributed in fifty-one households – including the four single-occupancy almshouses on The Dring. There were sixteen commercial properties, including the then defunct beet factory, which still had a watchman/caretaker on site. It took Dryden only a few minutes to work out that there were just twenty-one men aged between twenty and thirty-five in the village at that point – early May 1990. Any one of them could have ended up on the end of a rope in the cellar.

The second census narrowed the search. It had been taken six days before the final evacuation. It listed all those people from the first document, but most had left by that point and were marked as NON RESIDENT. The total population was given as just forty-three – of which only seven were men in that age bracket. Dryden took the names down:

Paul Cobley, Mere Taxis, Bridge Street
Jason Imber, Orchard House, Church Street
James Neate, Neate's Garage, Church Street
Mark Smith, 14 The Crescent
Matthew Smith, 14 The Crescent
Peter Tholy, 3 The Dring.
Ken Woodruffe, New Ferry Inn

Seven names, a few quick phone calls and, with luck, he could have an ID for the victim. But it was hardly ever that easy, and Dryden suspected that this time would be no exception.

The police had said the estimation of age could be stretched, either way, due to the state of the remains. He checked the file again and found one other to add to the list.

George Tudor, 8 St Swithun's Cottages, Church Street

His age was listed as thirty-six.

So, a list of eight potential victims, as long as they were all of average height – and he couldn't tell that until he tracked them down. He jotted down the names and addresses. Four of the names he recognized immediately. On the tape they'd listened to on the riverbank they'd heard

Jan Cobley talking about the taxi business she ran with her husband. So Paul was presumably the reluctant son who didn't fancy taking the business on to a new village. And George Tudor was on the tape too – talking about his preparations to emigrate to Western Australia with the help of a testimonial from the vicar, Fred Lake. And there were the Smiths; The Crescent was a small council estate on the edge of the village to the north. The brothers' ages were both given as twenty-three. There'd been a Jennifer Smith on the tape and she'd mentioned that her brothers were thinking of setting up a new building business after the evacuation, so they should be easy to trace. And there was Ken Woodruffe, of the New Ferry Inn. If he was the young man Dryden had seen on the doorstep of the pub that last morning then there seemed every chance he was not the victim, and if he'd stayed in the pub trade he should be easy to find as well.

Was the Skeleton Man one of those on his list? It was only an assumption, but there seemed little point in considering the other option – that the victim was an outsider. If he was then they might never know his name. And it was a well-founded assumption, for if the Skeleton Man was a victim of murder then surely his death would have been best timed to coincide with the evacuation of the village – the perfect moment in which to remove someone from the daily pattern of village life, when family and friends were on the brink of a diaspora – thrown out to new jobs, new homes and new futures. No doubt DI Shaw would be thorough, but Dryden needed to concentrate on the eight. It was the only way he could get results.

And if it was suicide? Well, then it made sense again to look amongst the likely candidates in the final census. The moment of leaving would have been an emotional one.

Perhaps the pain of going had pushed the Skeleton Man towards his own death. The newspapers found at the scene made it likely that he had met his death in the final days of the village. There was only one other scenario – that the death in the cellar had come during the long years the village had lain deserted, an option Dryden suspected the pathologist would soon largely discount.

So he needed to track down the eight quickly. He had good leads on four, but the others were unknown to him. So he turned to the third set of documents DI Shaw had left on the table with the two census books. This was a large ledger listing claims for expenses from residents, and compensation for loss of earnings. Dryden leafed through them, each one given a separate page.

It took just ten minutes to reach the form for Neate's Garage – the listed address of James Neate, one of his eight potential victims. Dryden remembered the building, set back from the road in from the south, a foursquare Victorian villa with a single pump on the roadside and a wooden lean-to workshop at the side. Walter R. Neate, proprietor of the business and listed as a widower, had claimed £2,600 in lost earnings and removal costs of £800, plus personal costs of £200 for himself, son and daughter. The new business address was listed as the Stopover Garage, Duckett's Cross. The claims were backed up with an envelope of bills, estimates and a Xeroxed copy of the previous year's accounts. Dryden noted that both claims had been met in full and guessed that in the glare of publicity surrounding the evacuation the MoD had erred on the side of generosity in their dealings with the residents of Jude's Ferry.

He worked through the entries diligently until he reached the New Ferry Inn. Ellen Mabel Woodruffe was listed as licensee and she had claimed £1,200 in lost earnings and removal expenses for stock and household goods of £600, and personal costs for both herself and her son Ken, who was described as the manager. There was no mention of a wife, children, or other dependants. Again there was an envelope of documents to back up the claims, including a letter from the Royal Esplanade nursing home, Lowestoft, accepting Ellen Woodruffe and giving the expected date of arrival as 15 July 1990 – the date of the evacuation of Jude's Ferry. Fittings from the pub – including tables, chairs and kitchen equipment – were also shipped by the army. The address given for removal was the Five Miles from Anywhere, a pub on the river near Ely.

He tracked down claims for the other names on the list. George Tudor and Peter Tholy both entered similar amounts for loss of earnings as general farm labourers. Neither gave a forwarding address or made any attempt to get compensation – except a joint request for £360 for storage of household goods and furniture. Lastly, Dryden found Jason Imber, listed as the sole occupant of Orchard House. His profession was not listed. Removal costs to an address on the edge of Ely were given as £1,300, and there was no claim for compensation. Imber was not a common name, so perhaps he might be found quickly too.

There was a special entry for the old sugar beet factory which had closed in 1988. On site there was still a watchman – Trevor Anthony Armstrong – with the address given as The Lodge. He, his wife June and their son Martyn were shown as residents in those last few weeks, but their forwarding address was marked 'unknown'. For the first time Dryden understood that, for many residents, holding out to the final day at Jude's Ferry had not been a choice: people like Trevor Armstrong didn't have anywhere else to go. Removal costs were a paltry £58, the address for shipping the TA barracks in Ely – no doubt a temporary measure to keep families like the Armstrongs off the streets.

Back with the list a name caught Dryden's eye. On the edge of the village a nursery had been included, the business description being retail cut flowers. Lost earnings were a hefty £14,000 – due to lost sales from flowers which would be ready for market in the late summer. Personal removal costs were given as £360. The company was called Blooms and business removal costs were £3,500, the new address given as Ten Acre House, near Diss in Norfolk. The proprietor, and the only occupant of the house – The Pines – was given as Colonel (Retired) Edmund John Broderick. Dryden heard a footstep above on the drill-hall floor and thought of the picture on the major's desk; the professional soldier standing proudly for the camera in the last year of the war. Dryden respected privacy, understood its humane values, but he wondered if there could be another reason the young Major Broderick appeared to have kept his links with Jude's Ferry to himself.

12

Humph was waiting in the car park, the Capri broadcasting the final notes of a Faroese folk song. The cabbie had a brochure on his lap outlining the attractions of Tórshavn, the capital. After the song came a recitation of endangered fish which inhabit the waters around the islands, to which Humph listened while consuming double cod and chips. A warm wrapped packet lay on the passenger seat, and Dryden unfurled the paper to eat the steak and kidney pie within. They sat watching the sun slowly reduce the puddles of rainwater still lying on the tarmac. Dryden considered the cathedral's Octagon Tower, and wondered what chance there was he could whittle his list of eight down to one by the time he next went to press.

'Slim,' he said, and Humph ignored him, thinking it might be an instruction.

The cathedral bells chimed the hour.

'We should pick Laura up,' said Dryden, balling up the greasy paper.

Humph swung the Capri in a languid arc and set off towards the town centre. Shops were dropping shutters and taking up awnings, a tradition of early closing having survived the influx of household names along the high street. A sunlit siesta was descending, and the rooks clamoured to roost.

A mile and a half north on the old main road to the coast stood the Princess of Wales Hospital, its buildings crowded around a Victorian water tower. The hospital, originally run by the RAF, had specialized in the treatment of burns victims during the Second World War, serving the pilots who flew bombing raids from the airstrips of the Isle of Ely. Now it was a general hospital, with one specialist unit: the Oliver Zangwill Centre for Neuropsychological Re-habilitation. Laura Dryden was a regular outpatient, and received private additional sessions paid for by the Mid-Anglian Mutual Insurance Company, which had agreed a schedule of care for Dryden's wife after her accident.

The unit was in one of the old convalescence wings at the back of the hospital, an elegant two-storey 1930s art deco building with views over neat lawns still tended by the RAF Association. Dryden always imagined the wartime pilots within, swaddled in bandages, listening as their comrades flew overhead towards Germany.

He could see Laura at one of the metal-framed picture windows now, on the second floor, resting after her regular session of physiotherapy. The difference in her posture in the last few months was startling. In the years after the accident she had been held in her wheelchair by supports, her limbs at ugly angles. Now she sat elegantly, her neck held straight, one ankle hitched over the other, her tanned legs stretched out in the sun, her feet bare on the window ledge.

Once inside the unit Dryden was struck again by the quality of the light. The windows at ground level fell full-length to the floor. This far from town the sun's rays were unimpeded and flooded in, glancing off the polished linoleum and the white walls. Dryden considered again the irony that the architects had designed the building as a receptacle for light, while so many of the patients in those early years had sat, their heads swathed, denied the joys of sight.

He climbed the stairs and passed a group of young men and women in white coats accompanying a surgeon, bow tie just visible beneath a grey jumper. On the top floor several patients sat in wicker chairs, an echo of the building's original thirties decor. He walked towards Laura from behind but she recognized his steps, accepting his head as he stooped to kiss her neck. Her right hand tapped at the laptop.

The screen lit, revealing her message. LOOK. ROOM 118.

'A story,' she said, the voice nasal and still sluggish.

He squeezed her shoulders and walked the length of the observation gallery to a door at the end. Laura had been married to Dryden throughout his ten years on Fleet Street, a decade in which she had developed as acute a news sense as her husband's. Many able-bodied nurses and doctors made a serious mistake in her company, which was to presume that the lingering symptoms of coma extended to a poor grasp of her immediate environment. In fact she was hyper-alert, and attuned to the subtle euphemisms of gossip and scandal. Since she had become a regular at the unit she had tipped Dryden off on several good tales – most of which had found their way into the nationals. All had reflected positively on the unit, and he'd actively stifled a couple of less wholesome exclusives, a luxury which had not been available to him during his years on the *News*.

Laura had briefly been admitted to the Zangwill for appraisal when she'd transferred to the NHS from private care a year before. She'd been in Room 106. So Dryden found his way to the corridor quickly and at the door of Room 118 glanced in through the porthole provided.

'Well, well,' he said, and jumped as a hand touched his shoulder. 'Jesus. Don't do that, Desmond.'

Desmond Samjee was the senior unit physiotherapist. He was close to Dryden's height, with the unhurried movements which inspire confidence, and a voice entirely free of the inflexions of his Kenyan-Asian heritage. Dryden's impassive face creased slightly in a smile: 'Caught me,' he said. 'What ya gonna do?'

'Firing squad,' said Desmond, leaning in to take a look himself.

Sitting with her back to the porthole window was a female PC, while in the bed was the man the police divers had pulled from the reeds by the river that morning. His arm lay on the counterpane, the hand bandaged. A drip fed into his arm and his head was as immobile as his pillow, and just as pale. His hair flopped over his eyes. For the first time Dryden noticed a ring, a single gold band on the wedding finger of the uninjured hand.

'Why's he here?' asked Dryden.

Desmond took his arm. 'All I know is he was brought over straight from A&E once they'd dealt with his hand and given him a blood transfusion. He'd got hypothermia but he's recovered well, he's pretty fit, and he's asked for police protection. We're not involved so I don't know the real details, which I wouldn't give you anyway.'

As they watched the man woke and started, rising into a sitting position. His head jerked around the room, checking the view through the two windows, and finally he grasped the hand of the PC, who had stepped forward. Comforted, he subsided back on to the pillows, his eyes pressed closed as if trying to shut out the world.

Desmond looked into Dryden's eyes. 'Desperately sad. Can't remember anything, they say. Just imagine that, Philip, waking up with no past.'

Dryden thought about it again and wondered if it would be so bad.

His friend knew him well enough to guess his thoughts. 'But imagine wanting that past. And it's there, just out of reach. Now that's a nightmare.'

They retraced Dryden's steps back to the observation gallery. Laura was alone in her wicker seat. Desmond walked round to face her. 'Good work today, Laura, you know that, don't you? That neck's supporting your head beautifully now. Let's keep up the hard work.'

Dryden pulled up a stool and sat, letting the sunlight fall on the side of his face. 'So he's said nothing, the guy from the river? He can't recall a single thing?' asked Dryden. They looked out over the sunlit fen to the west, the horizon pin-sharp at twenty miles.

'Didn't say that.' Desmond sighed, acutely aware of Dryden's profession, and dropped his voice. 'I had tea with the A&E nurses coming off shift. It's a perk of their job, hot gossip, but it doesn't mean they get it right, OK – just remember that. Anyway, they had him under observation for the first few hours and he said quite a lot, even if it didn't make much sense. But there were fragments. And a name – Jude's Ferry. He thinks that's where he might have come from.'

Dryden let the words sweep over him. A coincidence? Dryden distrusted the word, seeing by instinct a world in which events were interwoven, like the threads of the hangman's rope. The discovery of the skeleton in the cellar at Jude's Ferry had clearly set in motion a series of events. Violent events. Dryden shuddered as he failed to suppress a single Gothic image. A man, head and arms emerging first, struggling free through the shattered stone lid of a funeral chest.

13

Humph drove away from the sun. Dryden watched it touch the fen horizon in the rear-view mirror, bleeding into the earth. They crossed the river at Ely, a convoy of holiday boats beneath breasting waves raised by the evening breeze. On Bridge Fen a herd of cattle stood as still as a child's toys on a tabletop, casting shadows half a field long. They drove in silence, Dryden still trying to fit the sad figure in Room 118 into the emerging jigsaw that was Jude's Ferry. His appearance, forty-eight hours after the gruesome discovery of the skeleton beneath the storeroom beside the New Ferry Inn, was profoundly unsettling.

But for now Dryden had to leave him to struggle with the past alone in his hospital room. He must return to his list of potential victims and the task of putting a name to the Skeleton Man. The Five Miles From Anywhere stood between the Ouse and the Cam on a lonely peninsula between the two rivers, at the point were they ran forward on a broad sinuous path towards Ely, the cathedral standing clear above its own reflection. Picnic tables crowded the grass down to the riverbank, and in the pub's small marina white boats jostled for a mooring. Dryden preferred the spot in the winter, when the river could freeze if they closed the sluices to the sea at Denver, leaving the pub trapped in ice on three sides. But today the scene was given grandeur by the sky. North towards the sea clouds were building a mythical landscape of mountains tinged with evening colours.

Humph extruded himself from the cab and set off for a

table. Balanced on surprisingly nimble feet he was a human gyroscope, desperately seeking a seat before toppling to the ground. They found a spot at the point where the rivers met: the view before them, all the people behind them. Dryden left his friend with his Faroese phrasebook, announcing a wide range of alcoholic beverages to no one.

In the bar a small scrum had formed waiting for drinks, a lone barman working efficiently to meet the rush. As soon as Dryden saw the face he knew it was Woodruffe: the shock of brown hair had gone but the slump of the shoulders and the narrowly set eyes marked him out as the young man he'd seen on the step of the New Ferry Inn that last morning. Judging the moment, he decided to leave the questions for later. Instead, waiting his turn, he studied the bar. One wall was decorated with a collection of flamenco fans and on a notice board by the food hatch there were pictures of various sunburnt faces sitting outside a bar, the façade draped in Union Flags.

Above the pub's french windows out to the riverbank was a framed picture: the New Ferry Inn at Jude's Ferry, a group of villagers before it in two ranks like a football team, beside them a 1950s motor coach. Dryden squinted at some words scratched on a chalkboard held by a boy with unruly hair in the middle of the front row: Lowestoft, 1973. Behind the boy a man stood, rigid in a suit, one hand on the youngster's shoulder. At an upstairs window a woman's face, a pale oval, was half hidden, a hand raised to brush back her hair. And one other picture, in pride of place over the brick fireplace: the New Ferry Inn again, in black and white, a woman in her fifties snapped pruning a rose beneath the bar window, the smile genuine enough, suffused with affection for whoever was behind the camera.

He took two pints of bitter and a large G&T out to

Humph, an assortment of bar snacks tucked under his arm and in his pockets.

The sun died and customers began to trickle away, back to the boats from which the smells of cooking were drifting downstream. Humph, distracted by the view, delicately broke open a crisp packet and began to cherry-pick the contents. Dryden sipped the beer, trying to imagine the New Ferry Inn on that last night in 1990. The newspapers had been asked to leave the villagers alone, in return receiving an open invitation instead to a press conference the next morning and the promise of a tour of Jude's Ferry. But they'd been told, in retrospect, the lengths to which the army had gone to try and soften the blow which had fallen on these people. There'd been a dance in the Methodist Hall, free drinks and food at the inn – all paid for by the MoD, and fireworks set up on the town bridge. But even the army spokesman had been forced to admit that not all the villagers had been up for a celebration. Many had stayed at home, boycotting the festivities, quietly packing away their things in the tea-crates provided.

And beneath perhaps, in the cellar, the Skeleton Man.

'Let's eat,' said Dryden suddenly, standing. 'Properly. My shout.'

Humph was silent, his cheeks full of pork scratchings. 'What?' he asked. 'On a plate?'

The bar was packed now, almost exclusively with a coach party of OAPs. They sat at two long tables set with glasses and cutlery, a middle-aged woman with a clipboard moving amongst them checking choices pre-ordered for dinner. A group of young waitresses fluttered around them like sparrows around a garden feeder. Dryden noticed that all the girls were dark-haired and pretty, and wondered if it was a qualification for employment at the pub. He recalled seeing

Woodruffe on that final morning in Jude's Ferry, sitting in the sun with the girl in the crumpled T-shirt. Tonight the publican was on the customers' side of the bar, drinking from a pottery mug, and reading the *Ely Express*.

Dryden ordered food and included Woodruffe in the round. He offered his hand: 'Philip Dryden. I wrote that . . .' he said, tapping the front-page story on Jude's Ferry. 'You're Ken Woodruffe? Your mother was the licensee of the New Ferry Inn?'

Up close Dryden could see that Woodruffe was younger than he first looked but the hair was thinning fast, revealing a high, frail skull, the thin neck rising out of a brutally white shirt buttoned up to take a sober blue tie. His skin was pale, as if he'd spent a lifetime under the bar's neon strip light, thin wrinkles grey with other people's cigarette smoke.

'Sorry, sorry,' he said, holding up his hands. 'Today, you know. I've had enough. It's all been very difficult and I've answered the police questions. I'll bring your food out, OK? But I really don't want to talk.'

He stood suddenly, his hands readjusting the bar mats, ashtray and a newspaper. Dryden could see that the mug held an amber liquid rather than tea or coffee and he guessed it was whisky. Even here, on the right side of the bar, Woodruffe seemed anxious to preserve some distance from strangers, stepping back from his seat and taking the mug with him.

Dryden nodded, backing off and giving him room. 'No problem. I was just interested. I was there, like I said in that piece, in the cellar when they found him.'

He retreated with the drinks and they waited in the dusk, watching the river turn violet under the first stars.

'Are they catching that fish?' asked Humph. 'We could have had chips in town by now.'

Woodruffe brought the food on a tray and set it out, then retreated without a word only to return a minute later with the pottery mug. He sat, placing a large packet of chewing gum on the table, which he began to rotate in 45-degree instalments.

'Bar staff are on now – it's eight. I can talk, for a bit.'

Dryden pushed a plate of chips towards him, noticing the sheen of sweat on his forehead even in the cool night air. He wondered what had changed his mind. 'Help yourself,' said Dryden.

Woodruffe shook his head. 'Off me food.'

'Big party in?'

Woodruffe's shoulders sagged. 'Every Tuesday. We do a cut-price meal for OAPs; it's all linked to the heart unit at the West Suffolk. I did their Christmas bar last year, girls came too. They looked after Mum – the West Suffolk – did a great job so it's the least we can do.'

A hand strayed across the table and rearranged the ketchup and salt.

Dryden nodded, thinking about the woman in the picture in the bar. Looking round he saw that a couple of children were still playing on a climbing frame set back from the riverbank.

'Your kids?'

'No. No.' He flipped the gum packet and took some and Dryden guessed he was trying not to think of a cigarette, the moment when the nicotine hits the nervous system a second after the first deep breath.

'Sorry,' said Dryden, knowing he was about to push his luck, delving into someone else's past. 'I thought you were married – there was a woman with you on that last morning, outside the inn, and we found kids' stuff in the cellar.'

'You were there? What – back in 1990?'

Dryden nodded. 'Like I said, it was one of my first decent assignments so I'm not likely to forget.'

Woodruffe watched a pleasure boat slip past, the portholes lit. 'Jill Palmer – we weren't married. A lot of things didn't survive the move, you know – that was one of them. She went north – Lincoln, I think. A new life. Haven't seen her since we left.'

One of the waitresses came out with a ham sandwich and salad and put it in front of Woodruffe. He watched her leave and then tossed the lettuce into the reeds, biting without enthusiasm into the white processed bread.

'I didn't ask for this. They think I need mothering,' he said. Then, almost without a beat, he went on, 'So you were there when they found him. Anything else . . . ? The police don't seem to know what it was all about . . . this bloke's skeleton just hanging there all those years. I mean, that's fucking weird.'

The children sniggered at the language. Woodruffe dropped his head, sipping from the mug. The scent of the whisky hung about them now in the evening air and Humph sniffed loudly.

'I think it's all in the paper,' said Dryden, nodding at the rolled-up copy. 'All that they know.'

Woodruffe unfurled the *Express* but didn't even try to read it, and Dryden guessed he'd been through it several times.

'So the police have been round?' Dryden asked.

'Could say that. Two hours this morning. I had to go in this afternoon, all the way to soddin' Lynn. I've got a business to run.'

'You can see why they're worried,' said Dryden carefully. 'He was hanging in your cellar. A cellar you hadn't registered with the army. I've seen the questionnaire – nothing's listed. It's your mother's signature, right? But I guess they think you would have checked the place out. What are they supposed to think?'

Woodruffe nodded. 'I don't want this in the paper,' he said.

Dryden held his hands up as if that constituted a promise, wondering again why Woodruffe had agreed to talk, what was in it for him.

'We never used that cellar, it floods in winter. I told 'em. When the form came round there was loads to do – it just slipped by. I've told 'em I'm sorry. And then they didn't find it after anyway, did they? When they did a survey. It's not all my fault.'

Dryden let the answer peter out. 'So, who do you think he is, our Skeleton Man?'

Woodruffe pushed the gum packet away, turning the now-empty sandwich plate with his other hand.

'God knows,' he said, and Dryden found he wanted to believe him. But the landlord's hand shook slightly as he sketched a line on the rough wooden tabletop.

'But it was your cellar. There was stuff down there. You must have used it.'

'Must I?' Dryden saw a flash of anger in the eyes and watched as the muscles on Woodruffe's arm bunched, adrenaline pumping round his blood system.

He pushed himself back from the table, creating more distance again between them.

He ripped open a piece of chewing gum and his jaw began to work at it manically. 'Like I said, it flooded most winters. We used the bottle store above, but the cellar was useless. Everyone knew it was there – back in the eighties they tried running a folk club in it in the summer. Some kids formed a group and hired it for practice. It was no secret. There was no key, and you didn't need to be the Pink Panther to get into the bottle store upstairs. Mum had put some things down there from when I was a kid because she didn't want to chuck them, but that was it. That and some old bottles.'

'Why d'you think the army never found it then?'

Woodruffe stretched his arms above his head, the joints clicking.

'We stored stuff over the trapdoor, timber, logs for the inn. I guess they didn't look very hard,' he said, avoiding Dryden's eyes.

'When d'you go down last?'

He shrugged again, running a hand through the thinning hair. 'Last day, perhaps second to last, to make sure there was nothing worth taking away with us. There were some glasses I think – but we left most of them because they were old-fashioned straights. Worth a fortune now,' he laughed. 'And Mum wanted some kids' books, a few wooden toys.' Dryden looked him in the eyes, which were small but calculating. So he'd remembered to check the cellar out. He could see why the police wanted another word.

'That last night in the pub. It must have been extraordinary, knowing that you might not come back. Any of you. What was it like – party or wake?'

'Bit of both,' said Woodruffe, tipping the mug back. 'There was certainly a party on by the time I closed the place, no point in leaving half-filled barrels, was there? We'd saved one for the next morning but they drank the rest and I wasn't charging. MoD had put enough cash behind the bar to keep them happy for a week. A few lads had too much, and we had the old boys from the almshouses in – kinda guests of honour, if you like, and they can put it away. But then they didn't have far to stagger home.'

'No trouble? No scores settled?'

'I've told the police everything, OK?' Dryden noticed he hadn't answered the question.

'Punch-up?'

'Nothing that wouldn't have been out of place in most pubs on a Saturday night. A family dispute, there's nothing like brothers for falling out.'

Dryden was mildly drunk, the effects of the third pint multiplying his natural intuition. With fifty people left in the village there can't have been that many siblings in the bar that night. 'Twin brothers?' he asked, remembering the list he'd compiled from the TA records.

Woodruffe watched a couple kiss at a table in the shadows. 'Like I said, the police are on to it.'

Dryden decided not to push; he could track down the Smith brothers soon enough, although he suspected DI Shaw would have got there first.

On the river a boat went past, its engine spluttering, the portholes lit.

'That last morning there was some trouble, when one of the old women was dragged out of her home. But you helped calm everybody down, didn't you? People seemed to respect you.'

Woodruffe held his face in a mask.

'I've always wondered why,' said Dryden, allowing the ambiguity to remain unclarified.

'What was the bloody point?' he said. 'We'd sold up, taken their money, and now they wanted us out. If there's one thing running a boozer teaches you it's to give up on anything if you think you're coming second.'

Dryden opened his notebook at the page where he'd listed his eight potential victims, turning it so that Woodruffe could read. 'We know the victim was average height – five-ten, eleven – something like that. Any of these a lot bigger, or a lot smaller?'

Woodruffe read the list too quickly. 'Nah. Paul Cobley

wasn't a big lad – but, it's difficult to tell. And Jimmy Neate looked six foot.'

Dryden closed the notebook. 'Ellen Woodruffe, your mother. Did I speak to her that last day? Is that possible?'

He stood. 'Doubt it. Mum didn't want to go and she didn't make a secret of it, but she was very ill that summer, and she wasn't stupid. She knew the army would do what it wanted to do. She'd had a coupla strokes the year before, paralysed her left side, so she knew she was on borrowed time. She wanted to die in Jude's Ferry; in fact that's all she wanted. But she didn't die, that took longer, a lot longer than she wanted. Anyway, she left quietly enough. She'd given up the fight.'

'I'm sorry – what happened to her?'

'I got her into a nursing home on the coast. Lowestoft. Cost a fortune, of course, but we'd banked the money when we sold the pub to the army back in the nineties. The price was good, very good. We know why now, of course – so they could chuck us out for good.'

The landlord pulled out a wallet and flicked it open. It was her again, a hand held to ward off the sun, the arcaded front of a Victorian seaside villa behind. In discreet letters above the bay window a sign read 'Royal Esplanade'.

'She died in '97, that winter. But she did come home in a way. I scattered her ashes at St Swithun's – on the feast day. I didn't ask. I just did it. So she came home in the end.'

They've told me to write a letter, every day, setting down what I have remembered.

But a letter to whom? I know I loved someone once, because I can feel the ring now, cool, solid, and gold, but I've forgotten her with almost everything else.

So this is for nobody. A message on a computer screen, tapped out with the fingers of my one good hand, for no one to read.

And this is what I have remembered.

At first there was a place, Jude's Ferry, lying beneath the two hills, the spotless Georgian windows of a house looking out towards the single brick chimney of an old factory. On one hill the church, on the other a water tower with a wooden painted dovecote.

I was a child then, thrilled by the sight of the two hills glimpsed through the windscreen of a car, bumping along a road without a single turn.

And then, like a gift, there was another name.

Kathryn.

I knew something about Kathryn. I knew she didn't give me the ring that I wear.

Where do I see her? I see her first sitting with the others at the back of a classroom. No proper wooden desks, just those plastic seats with the flip-over rest. She's what? Sixteen perhaps, maybe not. There are no uniforms, no clues. Outside a vast concrete playground disfigured by puddles. I see her hair, lustrous black, under the neon light, and the small ripe mouth partly hidden by the hand.

And although I can't see it I know her body beneath; the long limbs curled effortlessly in mine, the thin white neck arched with pleasure.

What am I to her? I'm outside looking in, a porthole meshed with wire, and then the door opens and I find the desk at the front, sitting on the edge, a lesson begun, while I watch her with peripheral vision.

So we know now what I did. And was this what was wrong?

Now the nurse comes with the painkillers. I can see her through the porthole window, like the one in the classroom door, checking, just as the others have done, waiting for me to finish. To rest.

But there is too much fear for sleep. And I still have work. I must set down what I know now to be true, even as I write it: that Kathryn is dead and guilt, like the dusk, fills my room.

Wednesday, 18 July

14

He took the call on the deck of *PK 129* in the early morning rain, his voicemail ringing him back with a message left
overnight. The river, cratered with big fat storm drops, gave
off the exhilarating aroma of dawn.

A voice echoing in an enclosed space, cars swishing past,
a whisper close up. 'Listen.' The menace in the word, the
cruelty, made his heart freeze for a beat. 'Jude's Ferry, you
were there. We were there too. We opened the tomb, at St
Swithun's. We've taken her bones. If Peyton doesn't shut
down Sealodes Farm – stop the breeding – he'll never get
them back . . .'

There was the rustling of paper and, approaching, the
sound of a light aircraft.

'Our aim is to inflict economic damage on those who
profit from the misery and exploitation of innocent animals
. . .' he read on, another voice cajoling in the background.
A prepared statement, larded with the stilted language of
the true fanatic. Then he said it again: if they didn't shut
down Sealodes Farm, announce it in the press, then they'd
ditch the bones down a sewer. There was a brief silence in
which Dryden could hear the light aircraft returning. 'We've
told them. Now we're telling you. We want it in the paper
that they're closing down the business. Otherwise this is just
the start. We gave them a little visit a couple of weeks ago.
This time no police, until it's in the paper. Tell 'em that.'

Dryden timed it – less than thirty seconds. A public call
box. He got a notebook and took the call down verbatim

in case he lost it from the mobile's memory. Then he listened to it five times, noting the double return of the aircraft, and the jittery voice, the strain of disguise audible. He wondered what they'd done on their visit to Sealodes Farm, and why they felt they needed to fool him about the voice. Did he know him – or did they think they'd trace a recording? At least he now knew why he should have recognized the name on the tomb. Henry Peyton was a well known local farmer and owner of a highly controversial business: breeding animals for laboratory experiments.

Humph appeared out of the rain at 8.00am with two fried-egg sandwiches wrapped in foil. Dryden took out the coffees and they watched the dog run through the wet grass. Laura had got herself in her shower seat and dressed by the time they went down for her, lifting her just as far as she couldn't go herself, into the waiting wheelchair on the deck. The ambulance would call at 10.00am to take her for the regular sessions: physiotherapy, hydrotherapy and speech therapy. Dryden arranged the tarpaulin cover so that she was dry and made sure the laptop and the mobile were within reach.

'What yer gonna do?' he said, curling a loop of hair off the nape of her neck.

'Lines to learn – twenty-three words,' she said, the tongue still lazy as if she was recovering from a dentist's needle. Dryden kissed her and refilled the coffee cup at her elbow. Then, making an effort, he knelt by the chair. 'You can do a reading for me tonight – OK? I'll play the rest of the cast, you do your stuff.'

He kissed her again and got into the Capri, Humph pulling away immediately, hooting the horn twice before they swung out of sight.

'Take the Manea road, over the Levels at Welney,' said Dryden, then he left a message on the news desk answerphone asking Charlie to send Garry to the magistrates' court in his place. He had a story, a good one, and he'd be back by lunch with it in the bag. It was the kind of message he loved to leave.

He'd never been to Sealodes Farm. It wasn't the kind of place that welcomed publicity. It was poor land, below the dyke which kept the tidal water out of the richer peat fen. Over the years, in the dry summers, the water had welled up in the fields, leaving behind a deadly rime of salt. Sealodes was good only for turnips and beet, not the cash crops which underpinned the fortunes of the big corporate-owned farms of the Black Fen. So twenty-five years ago Sealodes had turned to a less conventional crop: breeding guinea pigs and rats for big companies and universities.

The farm looked like a battery-hen unit. The old farm-house, a Victorian London-brick cube, had been abandoned and cracks veined its façade, the roof sagging like a hammock strung between the chimneys. Next to it stood a tasteless Southfork-style bungalow with four garages and a bristling mast of TV dishes and aerials. An ugly brick wall encircled a garden crowded with pots, a water feature and a line of palm trees in containers. Against the ugly brick wall was a line of three ugly brick kennels, but there was no sign of the ugly dogs within.

Dryden got out of the Capri, slammed the door and listened to the echo bouncing off the distant bank of the dyke. The rain had stopped but the cloud was low and oppressive, a grey lid on a grey landscape. A large corporate flag hung limp from a flagpole, but Dryden could just discern the logo of a pale sunflower. A man in a one-piece green overall appeared from one of the battery sheds with a pet carrier in his hand. He stood his ground, waiting for Dryden to close the space between them. Up close he still had a farmer's face despite the green wellington boots and a Mediterranean tan. He said nothing so Dryden introduced himself, squatting down to get a closer look at the black guinea pig in the carrier.

The man was nodding as he removed a newspaper cutting from a zip-up pocket. It was Dryden's feature piece on Jude's Ferry written ahead of his return to the village with the TA, illustrated by the picture taken from files of the nave of the church, dominated by the crusader's tomb.

'So I have you to thank for this, do I?' He held it up, his thumb on the picture. 'The name's Peyton. Henry Peyton.'

'Right.' said Dryden. 'OK. So you got the call too.'

'Indeed. Last night actually. They saw the picture in last week's paper, knew the range was still closed until firing started again on St Swithun's Day, that the church was wide open, so they went in and took what they wanted from the tomb.'

Dryden made a point of never apologizing for anything he'd written unless it was inaccurate. 'Look. I'm sorry this has happened but . . .' He held out his hands, palm up. 'If these people want to make life difficult they will.'

'Let's talk,' said Peyton, walking away before he got an answer.

Dryden followed him towards a distant hut, distrusting the invitation to chat. Up close the huts were bigger than he'd imagined, crisply painted, exterior heating- and water-pipes gleaming aluminium. When he stepped inside the heat and smell made him choke. It wasn't unpleasant, just too close, like pushing your face into cat's fur.

The guinea pigs covered the floor area, with a few patches of exposed sawdust. A network of pipes ran water to small troughs and automatic feeders. Dryden realized there was a noise, a multi-note high-pitched squeal.

''s OK,' said Peyton. 'They don't like strangers. They'll calm down.' As they moved down a central corridor fenced off from the animals the noise died down to be replaced by a gentle cooing.

'How many are there?' asked Dryden.

Peyton stopped, surveying the hut with proprietorial pride. 'About three thousand in here. There's eleven huts. Work it out. Then two huts for the rats, two thousand in total.'

At the far end there was an office with glass panels down to floor level to give an uninterrupted view of the animals. Peyton made coffee in a cafetière.

The guinea pigs cooed more insistently, some of them gurgling with pleasure as the feeders automatically released pellets of food. The seething mass of twitching fur seemed to vibrate at a common frequency.

'See how we torture them,' said Peyton, smiling again. Dryden didn't smile, aware that the artificial lighting and the gentle hum of institutional happiness were his idea of hell.

'Who do you sell them to?' asked Dryden, tired of being patronized. 'Aren't they the ones that do the torturing?'

Peyton shrugged, ignoring the bait. 'Biggest customer prefers to remain anonymous. Commercial drugs developer. But there's universities too, plenty, that's why we started up, to meet the academic demand.'

Dryden got out a notebook but left it on his knee unopened. 'So they rang?'

On the desk a mobile phone buzzed, but Peyton pressed a button quickly to silence it. Outside the animals, startled, chattered their teeth.

'Yes. Some lunatic extremist faction of the animal rights movement. I am to expect a campaign of terror unless I use your newspaper to announce the closure of the business.' He laughed, handing Dryden a mug. 'They haven't made a good start. They seem to be under the impression they've got some bones for which I will consider giving up this business, a business I have fought hard to establish over a quarter of a century. Well, they're a bit wide of the mark. First. We are a minor branch of the Peyton family. I wish it was otherwise. The money went to America shortly after the Pilgrim Fathers. If I was one of *the* Peytons I might be worried, but then I'd be rich, so not a bad trade off, eh? We use the family crest – the Jerusalem artichoke . . .'

Dryden pointed outside. 'On the flag. The sunflower?'

'Indeed. Same biological family. But as I say, the link is tenuous, we've got nothing to do with the American Peytons. Suffice to say any bones they've plundered from this tomb are more likely to be carrying your DNA than mine. My first wife died in 1983, clearly something these idiots did know, because they think it's her bones. Fact is, when Sandra died she was cremated.'

He put his boots up on the desk. 'So they can turn their precious bones into cuppa soup if they like. They might get a few bob off the Yanks, but they won't get Sealodes Farm closed.'

'When they called me, the animal rights people, they said they'd given you a warning, a couple of weeks ago?'

Peyton's eyes glazed, the bluster frozen out in an instant. 'They took our dogs. Sorry. Liberated is the term used. We called the police. They got nowhere and we heard nothing from . . .' He drank his coffee, which seemed to add to the bitterness in his voice. 'From these people. I guess they wanted us to stew in our own juices.'

'Dogs. Family pets or security?'

'My wife is a breeder of Alsatians. I am, actually, very keen to get the dogs back, as is she. But not keen enough to close the business down.' Peyton nodded rhythmically, thinking about what he wanted to say. 'Which I think confirms two things. That while we are dealing with nasty bastards, we are also dealing with amateur nasty bastards. This business means more to me – and incidentally to the fourteen staff here at Sealodes – than three pedigree Alsatians and a pile of old bones.'

'How'd they get the dogs? Doesn't sound like an amateur operation to me.'

Peyton met his gaze. 'No. That is worrying. The dogs are controlled by key words – it doesn't matter who says them. We did that so that Rosie, my wife, could be away. So – "Saverne" ensures docility. It's a small town in Alsace. My guess is they knew the word, which means they've talked to someone who works here.'

'Or they work here.'

Peyton ignored him. 'And they took some stock when they took the dogs.'

'Stock? You mean animals?'

'About a hundred of the rats from one of the outside sheds.'

'And nobody heard anything, saw anything?'

'I was away on a sales trip. Security staff found a hole in the fence in the morning and the door on the animal shed forced.'

Dryden stood. 'So what should I say, then – what's the official line from Sealodes Farm Ltd?'

'Why would you need a line from me?' He put the pet carrier on his desk and looked balefully at the ball of fur within.

'For the paper. It'll make the front of *The Crow*. The nationals will pick it up. They may be a bunch of amateurs but they've raided a medieval tomb in the middle of a military firing range. They're news.'

Peyton stood too. 'Do you really think I'd be sat here

talking to you like this if I thought all this was going in the paper?' He fished in his pocket and found a card, tossing it down on the desktop. Dryden recognized the raised crest of the West Norfolk Constabulary above the name Detective Inspector Peter Shaw.

'They told me no police,' said Dryden.

'Forgive me, I have a mind of my own. Take that with you. Ring him. I'm afraid your little scoop is going to have to wait, Mr Dryden. The inspector's instructions were quite clear. A news blackout. I understand your editor has already agreed.'

Peyton's voice had risen, fuelled by anger, and the guinea pigs responded, their squeals rising an octave, swept by fear and anxiety.

By the time Dryden had got DI Shaw on the phone he was angry too, angry enough to make a hash of the conversation.

'Shaw,' he said, not bothering with his rank or a welcome. 'Give me one good reason why I should sit on the story,' was Dryden's opening gambit.

Humph had parked the Capri up on a low bank by the Hundred Foot River. The rain clouds were clearing and a watery sun was just visible, like a gold coin in the bottom of a dirty fountain.

Shaw was driving, presumably talking on a handsfree mobile. In the background Dryden could hear something country and western, Johnny Cash perhaps, the bass turned up to maximum.

The engine died and Dryden heard a handbrake being applied. In the background seagulls called and Dryden was sure he could hear the crash of waves on a beach.

Twenty seconds of silence passed before Shaw spoke. 'Look, I'm sorry, Mr Dryden, but I need your help in this. A crime's been committed and I'd very much like to catch the people responsible.'

Dryden cut in. 'Yeah, I know that . . .'

'No you don't. Not *that* crime.'

Shaw had his attention, and Dryden bristled at the detective's expert use of information as bait.

'And not *that* story. I think you'll find this is a much better one, and one I can share. But we do need an embargo to be respected. I'd have talked to you direct about that but there wasn't time so I went straight to your editor. I'm sorry it happened like that.'

The voice intrigued Dryden, light and youthful, but modulated, with the confidence not to rush.

Dryden kicked open the glove compartment in front of him to reveal a tumbled store of miniature bottles. He took two at random, gave one to Humph and, twisting the cap off his own, swallowed half in one gulp. It was tequila and he choked asthmatically.

'I think judging a good story is my line,' he said, tears rolling down his cheeks.

'I know. And I understand that I need your cooperation,' said Shaw. It was a statement of fact, and they both knew it was true. If Dryden rushed out a few paragraphs he could flog them to the local evening papers before Shaw could stop them – and local radio stations would snap it up too. News blackouts only really worked if the police were the ones with the information to start with. Dryden had the upper hand, his problem was dealing with the fallout once he'd scooped his own paper.

'Look, I'm at home now,' said Shaw, and Dryden heard it again, the hiss, like a whisper, of a wave breaking along a beach. 'I'm on my way to Jude's Ferry. We've got less than forty-eight hours to finish up with the forensics in the cellar because the army boys want back in. There's a big offensive on in Iraq, and they're sending more troops, and the least they deserve is, I guess, twenty-four hours training in house clearance before they say goodbye. Anyway, not my call. So my orders, from the top, are to get in, wrap up the scene of crime, and get out. We've set up an incident room at the site to make the most of the time we've got.'

Shaw ignited the engine and Dryden heard the crunch of

sand under the wheels. 'How about you come out too? We could talk there,' said Shaw.

Dryden finished the tequila. They both knew it was an offer he couldn't refuse, a guided tour of the crime scene by the detective in charge of the inquiry.

But self-respect made him push harder. 'If I get anything extra on the Skeleton Man, can I use that?'

'We can discuss that. But in principle, yes. All I want is a few days in which to operate freely. You need to know the background and who we're dealing with on this. These are not nice people, in fact they are seriously not nice people. So – I'll see you at the gatehouse at Whittlesea range at 11.30. OK?'

Dryden killed the mobile and chucked it over his shoulder, where it hit the dog. A decade of bitter experience told him that holding a story that was ready to print almost always ended in tears. His. He thought about ringing *The Crow*'s editor Septimus Henry Kew and arguing the point but his boss's attachment to the Establishment was sealed in Masonic blood – he was a former Special Constable himself and a regular dinner guest at the Chief Constable's monthly soirées for the media. If they gave him an honorary uniform he'd never take it off.

Dryden pressed his forehead against the cold glass of the passenger-side window. Getting back into Jude's Ferry was a trade-off of sorts. DI Shaw had two cases under his belt: the Skeleton Man and Peyton's farm. If Dryden could get enough leverage on the detective for agreeing to the embargo on the animal rights story there might be an upside to the situation, although he very much doubted it. When it came to it he knew he had little choice. Flogging the story would earn him a couple of hundred quid and result in endless aggravation, and Shaw was right, he didn't know the full facts. And he'd made no promises. He could hear Shaw out and then go back to Plan A – flogging the story.

'We've got two hours,' he said to Humph, rummaging under Boudicca's tartan blanket to find his notebook. He checked the eight names he'd dug out of the TA records Broderick had shown him; the eight men of the right age who might have ended up on the end of a hangman's rope at Jude's Ferry. 'It's got to be one of them,' he said.

He knew DI Shaw had, like Dryden himself, interviewed Ken Woodruffe, whose mother had run the New Ferry Inn, and that there had been a fight that night between the twin brothers Mark and Matthew Smith; but he knew the police would have got to them quickly if there was anything like a clear trail.

Dryden needed to focus on the rest of the list. There was Paul Cobley, for example, whose parents might well still be running a cab firm, although Dryden guessed that healthy old age and sitting in a taxi office for twelve hours a day were not always compatible.

He leant forward and cut the power to the tape deck, bringing a Faroese lesson to an abrupt halt.

'Sorry. Know of a taxi firm run by people called Cobley? It was mentioned on that tape we listened to on the river-bank, the one about Jude's Ferry.'

Humph puckered his lips into a small bow. 'Nope.'

'If you get a chance, can you ask around?' asked Dryden, flicking the tape back on.

After Cobley his best bet was James Neate, the son of the garage owner Walter, who had made a claim for compensation which included a forwarding address: the Stopover Garage, Duckett's Cross.

They were there in twenty minutes, time in which Dryden got through to the rural affairs department at the county

132

council on his mobile. Elizabeth Drew, the woman responsible for Jude's Ferry who'd phoned in when Dryden was on
the radio, had left her job in 1998. No, there was no forwarding address, no telephone number. Dryden hung on, asking
if the secretary could find a friend who could talk; it was
important, he said, something she'd be sorry to miss. The
phone was dropped with a thud on a desktop and he heard
voices off, then a man answered. 'Sorry. But Elizabeth left
nearly ten years ago now. Who is this?'

'A friend,' said Dryden. 'It's personal really.' Dryden hesitated for effect. 'It's just that my wife and I have lost contact
and we're in the area for a few days.'

'Right. Well – you could ask at Richardson's – the big cash
'n' carry store, outside Ely. Know it?'

'Sure.'

'Ask there. But please, just say you'd heard from a friend,
OK? We're not supposed to give out contact details.'

Dryden went back to the list, rang 118 118 and asked if
there was a Jason Imber, one of his eight possible victims,
in the Ely area: nothing, but a J. H. Imber was listed in
Upwell, a village out on the Fens towards Peterborough. Ex-
directory.

'Shit,' said Dryden, killing the phone and letting it slide
to the floor.

The Stopover Garage lay on a straight stretch of
unclassified back road – one of the many 'fen motorways'
which locals used to criss-cross the landscape. They could
see a clear two or three miles in either direction along the
arrow-straight carriageway. Mid-morning there was no traffic
but come the rush hour Dryden knew the road would be a
moving ribbon of commuters trailing home, avoiding the
jams on the overloaded A and B roads.

The four pumps stood at a spot where two drove roads

turned off from the straight, one east, one west, running into the black peatfields like lost causes. A modern canopy had been slung over the pumps but, battered and dirty, it was a symbol of hard times, not modern times. A farmhouse stood on one side, abandoned now, the windows full of shadows and shattered glass. Back from the forecourt was a stand of pine trees sheltering a small bungalow and to one side a large engine shed built of corrugated asbestos. Once crisply whitewashed it was now peeling, but the giant letters STOPOVER were still legible in black enamel.

Beside the pumps there was a wooden kitchen chair, set outside the shadow of the old canopy, on which sat a man in blue overalls drinking from a tin mug. He wore a peaked cap and held his free hand loosely in his lap. It could have been an everyday scene anywhere on the Great Plains.

The route to the Stopover had taken them around the perimeter of Whittlesea Mere Firing Range and the security fence could be seen beyond the garage, through the trees. It was eight feet tall, topped with razor wire and as welcoming as a warning shot from a 12-bore shotgun.

As Humph trundled the Capri off the tarmac and onto the gravel of the forecourt the man's head came round, but he didn't stand. Humph killed the engine and began to unfold a greaseproof paper package on his lap which concealed a Cornish pasty, a Scotch egg, a Yorkie bar and a single grape.

Dryden kicked open the stiff passenger-side door with his boot. It was quiet now the cab's engine was still, the hot metal ticking as it cooled. From the engine shed a radio played loud enough for the petrol-pump attendant to hear.

The man in the overalls stood, one hand to a sore back. His hair was black, as oily as the rag in his hands, his age mid to late thirties, the eyes an emotionless blue against an outdoor tan. He was powerfully built, with a compact muscular frame, but he moved his limbs with exaggerated ease, as if concealing a tension within. His face was almost handsome, but the miss was as good as a mile. The features were too heavy, the brow Celtic and bony, the chin too weak by comparison – an ensemble which mocked the subtle beauty of the eyes.

'James Neate?' asked Dryden.

His hand held the tin mug lightly, but the muscles on the arm were knotted under the skin.

'Jimmy.' The nod was cocky, a screen for insecurity, the smile boyish if not childish.

'I can take it you're not dead then.'

'Yes you can,' said Neate, tossing the straggly black hair out of his eyes.

'Sorry. I work for *The Crow* at Ely. It's about the skeleton they found at Jude's Ferry.'

Neate didn't move his face, but he withdrew his leading foot an inch. 'You probably heard about it on the radio,' said Dryden. 'I'm just checking on anyone who was in the village in those last days who would fit the age of the victim. Police called already?'

'Phone,' said Neate, drinking from the mug. Dryden noticed that Neate's ring finger was bare.

Dryden nodded. 'What about your dad; Walter, wasn't it?'

'Dad's fine, he's still a partner in the business. We look after him.' He slopped the dregs of the tea in the dust.

Dryden could feel the interview dying on its feet. He wondered why Walter needed looking after but felt his witness had become hostile. From the Capri came the sound of Humph biting clean through the Cornish pasty, the upper set of teeth meeting the lower set with an enamel click. 'You don't sell food, do you?' asked Dryden.

Neate nodded and walked off towards the engine shed. A

small office had been built inside to house the till. The place was deserted except for a brown-sugar Labrador which lay, as fat as a pig, on the cool concrete. There was a cold unit with a few pre-packed sandwiches, rolls, pies, biscuits, crisps and sweets. Dryden bought something he didn't want and looked around as Neate got the change. A Ford van was up on a ramp for service, the entrails of the engine spilling out, dangling down like severed arteries. At one end of the shed logs were piled for sale, and down the side charcoal bags for barbecues.

'How's business?'

Neate smiled, indulging Dryden's attempt to keep the interview going. 'No worse than it was at Jude's Ferry.'

He threw the rag onto a workbench. 'In fact it's better – we specialize.' He nodded to one wall of the old shed which was covered with a board from which hung various car parts in cellophane wrappers. An advertising banner read FIRE-STONE AUTO TIRES.

'Left-hand drives,' said Neate. 'We do repairs, spares, the lot. Good market with the US air bases – they all get a car, pick-up, whatever, shipped when they're posted. They need the indicators changed, the dip altered, that kind of stuff. It's a tidy business.'

Dryden nodded, freshly amazed at how little interest he had in motor cars.

'Sorry about the questions,' he said, turning back towards the cab, where he could see Humph had finished his lunch and was preparing for a siesta.

Dryden got out in the sun then stopped and swung round so that Neate was closer than either of them had planned. 'Who'd you reckon it is? The man in the cellar? On my reckoning there are only half a dozen possibilities . . . you must have known them all.'

'If he's from the village,' Neate said, rocking back on his heels.

'I hadn't thought of that,' said Dryden, lying.

'We went back one year for the service, coupla years after Dad's health started to slide. There was graffiti and stuff in the church, and a campfire down by the river. The army can't keep people out. There's a fence here, behind the pines, and there's a hole – they don't check as often as they say. OK they've patched it up, but there are others along the boundary. I've seen people on the far side, dusk, with guns, out for the rabbits and pheasants. I don't think you'll ever find out who it is. That's why he chose Jude's Ferry, he doesn't want you or anyone else to know who he is, or why he died.'

Dryden nodded, thinking it had been quite a speech off the cuff. 'Don't suppose you remember Colonel Broderick? He ran the cut-flower business by the allotments. Blooms – that the name?'

Neate was looking at the wreck that was Humph's beloved cab. He squatted down, looking under the rear bumper, examining a dent in the boot.

'Everybody knew everybody in the Ferry,' he said. 'But it's not gonna be him, is it? He must have been – what – seventy?'

'I was just interested. I know his son.'

Neate straightened up. 'The colonel lived alone and grew his flowers. The son visited, holidays and stuff. Didn't seem especially close, you know. Dutiful I guess. By the end the old man was in a wheelchair, so he had help, but we didn't see much more of the son, less if anything. Anyway, the Brodericks had money so they didn't talk to people like us except when they wanted their four-wheel drives filled up.'

'The son's a major in the TA, in fact he was with us when

we found chummy in the cellar,' said Dryden, wondering again about Broderick's motives.

A car swung in off the road and skidded on the gravel, small stones pinging off Humph's Capri. It was an American pick-up with giant wheels and a picture paint job of a Red Indian on the driver's door.

Neate looked at his watch, a flash of anger disfiguring the carefully neutral features. A woman got out, long blonde hair black at the roots, jeans and T-shirt leaving three inches of flesh exposed at the waist.

As she walked up she threw Neate a bunch of keys. 'He's calling later to get her,' she said, the accent more mid-Fen than Midwest.

'Hi. I'm Philip Dryden. *The Crow* at Ely.'

She came up close, her breasts moving easily under a loose shirt. Her eyes, brown and frank, lingered on his. 'I'm Julie Watts. What's this about then, Jimmy?' she asked, not looking at him. 'It's the Ferry, isn't it? Dump of a place. Best thing about it was the road out.'

'You were there?'

'Sure. We lived on The Dring. Jim didn't talk to people like us then.' She laughed, running a hand round Neate's waist.

'I was asking about Broderick – the cut-flower business.'

'Him!' She patted Neate's stomach as he tried to wriggle free. 'Well we all knew about him.'

She took out a packet of cigarettes from her jeans and lit up, offering one out. Dryden shook his head, and so did Neate, but he rolled his tongue along his bottom lip.

'That's just gossip,' said Neate, trying to stop her hands worming inside his overalls, unable to hide his embarrassment.

'Well, well,' she said. 'Since when did you not enjoy badmouthing someone from the Ferry?'

She grabbed the hair at the nape of his neck. 'You're right,' she said, turning back towards Dryden. 'It probably was just talk. That's all we had at the Ferry – talk. It was the village where nothing happened.'

'Except something happened in the end,' said Dryden.

'We can't help,' said Neate. 'I need to get started on the Yank's engine,' he said, walking away.

She looked for a long moment into Dryden's eyes. 'Don't mind Jimmy, he's not the sociable type. But the best mechanic in the Fens according to his dad – very proud of him, is Walter. In fact that's all Jimmy really cares about, making sure Dad's still proud of him. He comes out sometimes from the home, sits in a chair and watches the traffic go by. That's what counts as fun for the Neates.'

Dryden looked around. 'So Walter's never lived out here?'

She shook her head, coiling the hair behind one ear. 'A few years. A home now, council geriatric unit at Ely. Not much of a memory our Walter, lucky if he can get the season right. He's sixty-six, looks a decade older, mind. Jimmy visits and they talk about cars, that's the kind of family it is, you see, close – but superficial. As long as Jimmy thinks Walter's proud of him he's happy.'

She smiled, and Dryden tried to guess how quickly the good looks would fade to match the cynicism.

'So what did they say about Colonel Broderick?' said Dryden.

'Like Jimmy says, villages are all about gossip. Colonel Broderick lived alone; charming, polite, with an interest in flowers. He employed young men to work his fields. What d'you think they said about him? Ask me, I don't think the old bloke had it in him. Doesn't mean to say it didn't go on – you'd be surprised, a little place like the Ferry.'

They watched as Neate threw up the hood on the pickup and began noisily to examine the engine within.

Dryden tried another line. 'You there the last night – at the village?'

She gave him a sideways look. The lower lip, as full as the top, jutted out.

'Wouldn't have missed it for the world. I was fifteen so we got to dance in the Methodist Hall, what more could a young girl want? Orange squash all round and choccy biccies for the neat and tidy. Good job they didn't smell the cigarettes we were smoking round the back. Most of the lads were allowed in the pub, but not the girls. That's the crappy bit about living in a small place, you can't lie about your age. Place was medieval.'

'Jimmy take you to the dance?'

She laughed. 'Nope. I was chasing him. In fact I chased him all night.'

'Catch him?'

'Not that night. He had other things on his mind. Took me ten years to corner him, but I got my man. Lucky me.' She bit her lip.

Dryden would have asked the next question but Neate was walking back, kicking up the red dust with his boots. He went to the back of the cab and, down on one knee, looked under the wheel arch.

'The exhaust is hanging loose, I could see from over there. It'll be off soon. I could do that for you – and fill the dent.'

Dryden nodded, opening the passenger side door. 'Thanks. But I think he likes it that way.'

Humph woke.

'The man wants to fix the car,' said Dryden. 'The exhaust is gonna drop off.'

'Let it,' said the cabbie, firing up the engine.

As they drove off Dryden watched them in the rear-view

mirror. Jimmy Neate broke away quickly, his head and shoulders back beneath the hood of the pick-up. But Julie Watts watched them go, her weight on one leg, a hand shading her eyes from the sun.

16

DI Shaw spread the pictures on the wooden trestle table, which was the only furniture in the detective's office – the old bottle store behind the bar of the New Ferry Inn. Each print was set precisely and neatly apart, a gallery of disfigurement. Dryden sipped bitumen-strong coffee from a mug that Shaw had given him marked THE TEAM. At the firing-range gate he'd got a lift in Shaw's car, an immaculate black Land Rover with the multicoloured sail of a windsurf board and a beach-kite furled on the roof like emerging butterflies. The interior had been unnervingly neat and well ordered, a characteristic which made Dryden anxious. The pictures made him anxious too, calling up an unspecific sense of guilt. He didn't lean forward but his eye was drawn to that first print, which Shaw was tapping rhythmically with a ballpoint.

'Daughter of the company's on-site assistant chemist,' he said. Shaw was early-thirties, white open-necked shirt and an outdoor tan, the skin like slightly creased quality leather.

'Mary Christine's the name. The company, Lincoln Life Sciences, tests cosmetics for the big corporates, using rabbits, guinea pigs, rats and dogs. It's been the subject of low-level animal rights interest for some years. We knew that extremists based in the East Midlands had become interested and so security at the site was increased.'

He tapped the picture again. 'Unfortunately that wasn't where they struck. Mary Christine opens the post at home just one day a week – Saturday. Rest of the time she's at boarding school. She's thirteen years old, thirteen years and two months. So that morning there was a parcel with her name on it with the rest of the letters on the mat. A thin parcel, just the right size for the letterbox. No stamp, delivered by hand, but there's no CCTV.

'She sits on the doormat to open it up. She's excited because she doesn't get post often and when she does it's usually a present from her gran. It's June, but it's Christmas for Mary Christine, until she gets the bubble wrap off. Then it explodes in her face.'

The burn covered the forehead and left cheek, the ear on the left side reduced to a trace of crackling, the upper eyelid raw.

Dryden felt sick and looked around for a chair but the room was otherwise empty.

'Sorry,' said Shaw. He seemed genuinely flustered. 'I don't seem to use chairs,' he laughed. 'I can get you one from the incident room?'

Dryden shook his head. 'What was in it? The package.'

'The chemical was phosphorus,' said Shaw, looking at Dryden, not the picture. 'It was mixed with various other common ingredients to create an effective incendiary. I can give you the exact chemical composition if you want. The company's based in Sleaford, forty miles up the road.'

Shaw's eyes were an extraordinary light blue, like falling water, creating the illusion for Dryden that he was looking through him. He had the impression he was dealing with someone with a well-ordered mind, and it was spooking him out. So far he hadn't asked a question to which the detective inspector had not been able to give a precise answer.

And Major Broderick had been wrong about the hair; it was cut short and blond, but Dryden guessed it had been dyed by immersion in the salt of the sea. He'd been right about the tie, though, which was missing from the immaculately white shirt. Shaw's face was broad and open, and Dryden could imagine him looking out to sea. It was the kind of face that's always searching a horizon. Above the trestle table was a notice board with rotas and pictures taken in the cellar and at St Swithun's. There was one personal note, a snapshot of a beach, a single empty chair by the water's edge, a sea rod beside it. Perhaps it was the one chair he did use.

The detective's mobile rang and he snapped it open quickly. 'Shaw,' he said. 'Of course I've checked,' he said quickly, laughing as if the reverse was an impossibility.

Dryden stepped out of the office into the public bar of the New Ferry Inn, which had been commandeered as an operations room and was almost unrecognizable from the one in which he and Broderick had talked just three days earlier. Shaw had explained that the scene of crime forensics team had swept the upstairs rooms in the pub on the first night of the investigation and found nothing of significance. An industrial sized coffee maker gurgled on the bar, and six new darts stuck out of the old board. A wad of insulated cables had been fed in through the front window and provided telephone links and a broadband connection running to a radio car parked up on the town bridge. At a desk two plain-clothed detectives were on phones, tapping at laptops. Plastic sheeting had been draped over the door to the snug bar, beyond which Dryden could see two white-coated scene-of-crime officers working at a trestle table. Box files ran the length of the bar top. It was exactly the kind of operation you didn't set up to deal with a decade-old suicide victim, and now Dryden knew why. DI Shaw's interest was in animal rights extremists, and it was pretty clear he was under pressure to catch them quickly before they decided to send another deadly surprise by post.

The detective followed Dryden out of his office and ended the call. He took a couple of paces away before turning on his heel to return. Shaw was still holding the picture of Mary Christine.

Dryden sighed. 'Look, can we skip this stuff? I've seen enough pictures. You want me to sit on this story. The question is, why – it's a simple one and I think I deserve an answer which is a little more sophisticated than trading on any sympathy I might have for a damaged child.'

A rook called from somewhere in the village and Dryden was aware of the deserted buildings which surrounded them, the empty street outside, and the just audible trickling of water down the ditch beside The Dring. Something rat-like scuffled over their heads in the room above.

Shaw said the forensic team had slept overnight at the inn to get an early start, a night's rest Dryden couldn't imagine attempting.

The detective leant against the wall, one knee bent up so that he could place a foot flat against the flaking plaster.

'All right. An answer then.' He looked at a point on the ceiling where the wires of the light fitting still hung loose and Dryden guessed he was framing the answer, ordering his thoughts. He recalled the reference he'd found online to Shaw's role as a visiting lecturer in forensics. He could imagine him pacing a stage, deftly holding an audience with the authority in his voice.

'My job,' said Shaw, 'initially, at least, was to clear up the case of the Skeleton Man. Chances are it was suicide. Chances are we'll never know who did it. Chances are very few people care.'

He pushed himself away from the wall and went to the bar to look again at the picture of Mary Christine.

'Then Henry Peyton gets his call from the animal rights extremists and we find that the tomb here at St Swithun's has been emptied. There's a unit at King's Lynn – made up of personnel from across the East of England forces – which is about tracking down the leadership of these groups. It's a big deal, Dryden, a lot bigger than sweetie snatching from a corner shop, which was my last major arrest of any note. This unit's job is to track down the people who cooked Mary Christine's face.

'And now that's my job too because I've been seconded in to that unit as I'm on the spot – thanks to our friend in the cellar. The line from the team in Lynn is that it looks like this local cell of activists, the one that's contacted you, is indeed a renegade band. That's why none of the CID team is here in person – although they've sent down their forensics people. No. They've got bigger fish to fry keeping an eye on the really nasty bastards. But it is just possible the people who contacted you may lead us to the same people.'

Dryden didn't understand. 'So we're saying these people are taking orders from someone smart? You reckon? They've kidnapped some dogs, a herd of rats, and they've mustered enough loose change for two telephone calls. It's not al-Qaeda, is it?'

The heat in the room was fetid, a layer of dust drifting in a box of sunlight which fell through the frosted glass of the bar windows. Shaw produced a cold box from behind the bar and extracted a can of sparkling mineral water. Dryden accepted another coffee. The can finished, Shaw lobbed it perfectly through a toy basketball hoop which had been fixed to the wall above an oil-drum dustbin. An electric gizmo in the hoop produced the sound of a crowd cheering.

'I agree. But despite being inadequate, and possibly violent, they are also clearly ambitious. They're trying to get noticed, Dryden. They wouldn't have phoned you otherwise. But they don't just want to be famous in the local paper, or even the national papers. I think they want to be admired by the nasty bastards, the leadership. Yes, they're out of their depth, and they've already made a string of mistakes, but it would actually be in our interests if they did attract the attention of the people we're really after. And they'll do that if they succeed, or at least think they're going to succeed. Which is where you come in.'

Dryden held up both palms by way of surrender.

'So this is the deal. They have your mobile number. They told Peyton they would ring you for his decision and expect a story in *The Crow*. We want you to tell them Henry Peyton will shut Sealodes Farm down, and go into early retirement, but only if he gets back the bones of his beloved wife first, or more accurately the old bones they think are his wife's. He also wants the dogs – up front and unharmed – before he makes any irreversible decisions about Sealodes Farm. Peyton's in his late sixties, there's been talk of him retiring anyway. Tell 'em he's had an offer for the land and he's going to take it. In effect they've struck gold, they hit him just at the moment he was at his weakest.'

'And we expect them to swallow that, do we? They can't really be *that* stupid,' said Dryden.

'Well, I wouldn't count on it. I'll talk you through the forensics on the Peyton tomb later but I think we can say that we're dealing with some consummate idiots here; they're only still at large thanks to beginners' luck. But as I say, there's evidence they are not just a renegade group – there are links up the chain. And that's where we need to get, Dryden, up the chain.'

'Evidence?'

'Phone taps. There was some local radio coverage of the

first raid on Sealodes Farm, a bit in the evening papers. One of the men in the East Midlands the central unit is tracking was followed shortly afterwards to Ely. Our guess is he was checking the locals out, trying to get a handle. Either they'd contacted him or he'd seen the story.'

'Where'd he go?'

Shaw's blue water eyes were unblinking. 'Local surveillance lost him.' The detective brought his hands together in a church.

'Anyway, our friends want an answer. And they want you to give it to them. They told Peyton they'd ring you tonight – before *The Crow*'s Thursday deadline. They'll use a call box again. If you give me your details we'll try to get it traced – presuming they're still under the impression you haven't talked to the police. I think we're pretty safe here.' He smiled, and Dryden found it difficult not to respond.

'When they call I'd like you to tell them there's nothing going in the paper about the closure until they hand over the bones. I'd like you to ask to meet them to hand over the goods. Perhaps you could tell them you want a brief interview – that it isn't much of a story without it, just try and make it clear that if they want publicity you want to meet. We have local ALF sympathizers under surveillance, all run from here. If one of them is involved we'll get the lot, and the bones, and you get the story.'

Dryden tried to think it through, knowing something was wrong. 'But why would Henry Peyton play ball? You catch 'em and there's a court case, then every animal rights nutter in the country will be heading for Sealodes Farm. They haven't got his wife's bones, just the dogs. Why not call their bluff?'

Shaw got himself another mineral water. 'Well, firstly because that might not work. Does he really want a long slow war of attrition? He's no spring chicken but he'd like to leave the business to his son, or possibly sell it as a going concern to one of his big customers, and neither of those options is that attractive if the farm is an ongoing target. He'd like to solve the problem. We've offered him a solution.'

'Which is?'

'Well, think about it. Getting the local people into court will serve little long-term good. The idea is to trade them in for information. They walk if we get the names, and the evidence, we need to move against the leadership in the East Midlands. We get one of them to start talking then we can crack the lot, including the people who did this.'

He held the picture up so Dryden could see it again. 'We think they'll have more to worry about than tracking the trail back to Ely. When it comes to court there'll be no mention of Scalodes Farm. Peyton's willing to take the chance, he's smart enough to know it may be the only chance he's got if he wants a happy, and wealthy, old age. So that's our game.'

'Yours. Or the people running this unit back in Lynn?' asked Dryden.

'That's the plan,' said Shaw, not answering, lacing his fingers across his eyes and rubbing the sockets.

'But if it works we might see a timely promotion for DI Peter Shaw, a few less burglaries in future, right?'

Those water blue eyes again, giving nothing away.

Dryden stood. 'OK. And if they don't call?'

'You can run the story – but no names. The farm is just that – a farm, somewhere near Ely. The story's good enough without the detail.'

Dryden ran a hand along the files, fighting an urge to tell Shaw to stuff his plan. But there was always the other story. 'And matey in the cellar? It still looks like a suicide, surely? There's no link with animal rights there?'

Shaw smiled, and again it was difficult not to join in. 'Take a look at this,' he said. The childlike enthusiasm was infectious, and they hunched over a plan drawn on graph paper – about three foot by four foot. There was an etched outline of a room, expertly drawn.

'It's the cellar,' said Shaw.

'So you *don't* think it's suicide?'

Shaw shrugged. 'Who cares what I think? I need to be sure it isn't murder. My job's to catch people who break the law. It's pretty black and white. On this case I have two problems. Identifying the victim, and then working out if there's any chance they were strung up by a person or persons unknown.'

'What about the Smith twins?'

Shaw smiled. 'Bravo. Indeed.' The detective's shoulders relaxed visibly. 'Research of your own?'

'Maybe,' said Dryden, determined to gather information, not give it away.

Shaw pressed on. 'Yup. It's a good question. They went for each other's throats that last night, out in the yard of the inn apparently, thirty yards from the trapdoor down to the cellar. Woodruffe, the landlord, has given us a blow-by-blow account – but then he's keen to divert attention from the fact that we found the skeleton in his cellar.'

'Brothers fall out all the time – why should this end in murder?'

'Standard version of events says it's money – isn't it always? At least that's what Mark Smith says – he ended up working for one of the big national builders, based out near Thetford. He's a bitter man. He says the two brothers had a great opportunity to relocate their own business – the father was a builder, and they'd been brought up in the trade. The old man died in 1989 and there was some insurance money, plus a lump sum off the MoD for compensation. Mark reckons something like £45,000 in total. It was their mother's really, but she said she'd back whatever they agreed to do – if they agreed. But Matthew said no – he had his own ideas, a new life. Sounds like he was smarter, wanted to start up a design business with a friend customizing websites. So they came to blows, like brothers do, and stumbled out into the dark. That's the last time anyone seems to have seen Matthew outside the family. None of the witnesses we know were in the inn that night say they followed them outside, a lack of curiosity which borders on the unnatural, I think. That was just after eleven o'clock. Mark claims the fight petered out and they walked home twenty yards apart. Next morning there was a silent breakfast, punctuated by an announcement from Matthew that he'd been offered a job in computers in North Wales and he was going to take it. A story which is corroborated by the sister – Jennifer. Mark says his brother phoned home a couple of times to talk to his mother, and there was a telephone number where they could call him, but they never did. Apparently the mother felt he'd deserted them when they needed him most. She'd taken the death of her husband very badly. As far as she was concerned Matthew was a non-person, a view which turns out to be uncannily close to the truth.'

'Which is?'

'Matthew doesn't appear to exist. We've tried Swansea, Inland Revenue, trades unions, credit companies, banks, but so far there's no record of a Matthew James Smith.'

'The mother – where's she?'

'Dead within eighteen months of the move.'

'And Mark got all the money?'

'Yup. She'd changed her will to cut out Matthew from inheriting half the estate, but there was a small bequest which was never claimed. Mark says that his brother phoned soon after the death and was devastated to find he'd missed the funeral. Why hadn't they called? A good question, to which they don't have much of an answer. Anyway, Mark says his brother's view was that if they really wanted him out of their lives he'd oblige. They'd never see him again, and if they were that ashamed of him he'd change his name. A convenient detail, which doesn't mean it's not true, although there's no official record of a change of name by deed poll.'

Dryden thought about the Skeleton Man, turning slowly on the rusted hook. 'But Mark couldn't have done it alone – strung him up like that. And it would mean the sister was in it too – or at least in covering up. If the victim was conscious he'd have kicked out, the hands were only loosely tied so he could have done some damage with his arms as well. There's no way one man could get him up onto that stool unless he went willingly, and I don't think that's likely, do you?'

Shaw nodded. 'If it is murder, it's a lynch mob.'

Dryden had thought of that but it was the first time anyone had said it out loud. It was an ugly term, even uglier than the thought of the yellow bones hanging silently in the cellar for seventeen years.

'Mark Smith has given us a DNA sample to cross-check with the skeleton. We'll know in two to three days if there's a family link. I have to say he looks pretty relaxed about that, but you never know.'

The detective smoothed out the plan of the cellar. 'Which brings us back to the forensics. We needed the best examination possible of the cellar floor – the best in the circumstances, given the time limits – and luckily the animal rights SOCO team is first class, so when they'd finished with Peyton's tomb they did some overtime for us.

'One of the problems here is that with over a decade separating us and the crime in question any successful prosecution will demand material evidence that puts our villain, or villains, in the cellar. The problem is contamination of the scene. Half the British army had been through it by the time we got here, led by Major Broderick himself. In fact if someone had set out to contaminate a crime scene they couldn't have done it better. Size 12 boots everywhere. Then there was the water from the hoses they used to put the fires out. We put in some hot-air blowers but it took us twenty-four hours to dry the place out. Then they combed it, every centimetre, starting here at the foot of the stairs and working outwards. We're nearly done now.'

'And?'

'These,' said Shaw, unlocking a small cash box. He took out a plastic envelope with three or four pieces of gravel inside. 'Shropshire pea,' he said. 'Ornamental gravel. Looks like it fell out of the tread of someone's shoes. We've checked the squaddies' boots – nothing.'

'So, is there a match in the village?'

'Several. But it's not a standard gravel size. It's much smaller than the commercial brands we've located so far. So we're having samples from the village analysed upstairs. We might get a match, who knows.'

Dryden held the small packet as if it might bite. 'Where'd you get the degree in forensics then?'

Shaw looked at the gravel in the bag. 'Cambridge.'

'Couldn't you get in anywhere else?'

Shaw laughed.

'So what else did you find?'

The next packet held three cigarette ends, reduced to shreds barely held together by thin cylinders of paper. 'Standard brands. All date to mid to late eighties, early nineties

– except for one, a single Ducados stub. Common Spanish brand – we're having the company take a look in case there's something – anything – unusual.'

'Spanish?'

'Yes. But we're not that excited. It's the kind of brand holidaymakers used to pick up through duty free. There's no genetic material on any of these stubs – the soaking didn't help – but I'd be delighted if you forgot to mention that in your story. The Ducados is significant in a way, but I'll get to that later.'

Dryden wondered if Shaw realized the depth of the parochialism of the Fens. A Spanish cigarette was about as exotic as a snow leopard.

Shaw shook another evidence bag. 'There was one crisp new Marlboro dog-end, but Major Broderick informs me one of his men is on a charge as a result. Got bored on guard duty, apparently.'

Putting it aside he brought out a fourth envelope. 'There was this,' said Shaw. It held a small curl of plastic, a bit like one half of a DNA helix. 'Fibreglass shaving, machine tooled.'

They both shrugged, but Dryden suspected Shaw was holding back, giving him just enough for a decent story which would unnerve the culprit, or culprits, if they were still alive, and still local. He noted that he hadn't mentioned any progress on the surgical gauze found under the victim's sleeve.

Dryden peered at the helix through the evidence bag. 'It could be good,' he said.

Shaw smiled again, the teeth as white as chalk cliffs. 'Not as good as what we found under the floor.'

17

Plastic sheeting covered the well of the stairs down to the cellar and Shaw had to lift two folds to descend, holding one back for Dryden to duck under. Dryden stepped down, acutely aware that his pulse rate had picked up. Below, the brick floor glistened with moisture, lit by the halogen lamp which burned in the far corner, where a woman in wrap-around scene-of-crime overalls worked on her knees with pincers. A small video camera stood on a tripod, its nose dipped down at 90 degrees to the floor, behind a sheet of reflective foil.

The hook which had held the Skeleton Man had fallen to the floor with his bones, but the broken screw end was still embedded in the overhead timber. They stood beneath it.

Shaw took a breath and Dryden sensed again that he was framing what he would say next.

'We noticed as we worked our way across the floor that the bricks over here, in this far corner, were loosely laid down without cement, just bedded in the clay beneath. So we took up the bricks, as you can see.'

On the floor a white line edged a rectangular shape set into the cellar corner, the bricks that had been removed being piled in a neat heap to one side.

'We dug them up and dug down. We dug down six feet – into the clay subsoil. Then we put it all back.'

The hair on the back of Dryden's neck prickled and he felt sure the temperature had dropped.

'What was in the hole?'

'Nothing. The point is that the hole had been dug before, and then filled in. The stuff we took out was jumbled up peat, topsoil and some building hardcore. We've taken a look down elsewhere using an auger and the soil profiles are undisturbed. You'll know yourself that if you've ever dug a hole the big problem is that there is always more to put back than you took out. And we found the excess; in the crates up against the far wall which we've moved out. So. It's pretty clear that someone dug the hole, then filled it in, replacing the bricks.'

'It is a grave, isn't it?'

Shaw shrugged. 'It's difficult to come up with another sensible suggestion. It's about five foot six long — which is a bit short — and five feet deep, which is a bit shallow, and two foot wide, which is narrow. A chest maybe? But I doubt it. No. A grave has to be the working hypothesis. Which prompts two questions. Who was it dug for, and why aren't they in it?'

Dryden laughed, shaking his head. The officer working in the corner sat back on a small stool, massaging her hands.

'The Skeleton Man, surely,' said Dryden.

'But then why leave him hanging?'

'Perhaps there wasn't time,' suggested Dryden.

'They had time to fill it in, put the bricks back. It was neat work. So either they abandoned a plan to bury some- one in the grave, or — outside chance — they buried someone and then dug them up. It's possible the infill has been used twice — there's no real way of telling, although the experts seem to think its unlikely as the material is still roughly stratified, whereas if they'd done it twice it would be more mixed up. Make sense?'

Dryden nodded. 'And there's something else,' said Shaw, nodding to the SOCO before leading Dryden back upstairs into a splash of sun. In a dry corner of the storehouse above plastic sheeting had been wrapped round various bits of timber and brick.

'When the shell exploded it blew bits of the cellar roof out into the street. We've found these pieces, bits of the jigsaw. We found this too.'

Shaw drew back some sheeting. It was a trapdoor, about three foot square, made of wood.

'This would have been at the top of the steps down to the cellar?' asked Dryden.

'Indeed. But look at the other side.' He flipped it over and what would have been the top side was covered in small floor tiles – many of them shattered, but which matched those on the storehouse floor. In one was a small slot, cut through to the other side.

'I don't get it,' said Dryden.

'I can't pretend we do either. It's not that unusual – but it might be significant. The trapdoor has been concealed by blending it with the rest of the floor – the hole is for a crude key, you just drop it down through the slit, turn it, and pull up.'

'Which is why it was never found during the military exercises?'

'Right – plus the fact that the people running the exercises thought there was nothing here to find, so I doubt the squaddies were given much time to search the building anyway – certainly not long enough to find a door like this, and Woodruffe says the storeroom was full of packing cases and there's still loads of them around.'

'And what's the explanation for the trapdoor being concealed?' asked Dryden.

'He says it was like that for as long as he can remember. He was brought up at the inn – his mother was the licensee, the father before that. He says he thinks the building might have been a shop at one time – hence the tiles, which are Victorian. In that context, tiling over the trap isn't that bizarre.'

They walked out into the street.

'But it adds to the picture, doesn't it?' asked Dryden. 'The Skeleton Man, an empty grave, a hidden door.'

'Yes,' said Shaw.

'I said the grave was empty,' said Shaw. 'But that's not quite true. We found this.' Another evidence bag, a cigarette butt inside. 'Ducados,' said Shaw. 'Our exotic friend again – and because the water hadn't soaked down that far there's some DNA material this time, enough for an ID if we're lucky.'

Shaw smiled. 'And I feel lucky.'

18

The rain was setting in, falling in curtains of newsprint-black from a low grey sky. They walked up the street towards the hump-backed bridge over The Dring which trickled now with water from the hill. A rat scuttled in the gutter beside them, slipping effortlessly down a drain with a languid splosh. Birds' wings fluttered amongst the exposed roof beams of Palmer's Store, where Magda Hollingsworth had so painstakingly written her diary.

Dryden caught his own reflection in the broken window of a house by the bridge. Startled, he jumped visibly, and Shaw stopped. 'There always seems to be something moving in the shadows in this village,' said Dryden, and a sparrow-hawk took up position high above their heads, as if listening.

They turned south towards Neate's Garage as Magda had done that last evening seventeen years earlier, but then cut up through the allotments to the church. A single uniformed PC stood guard at the oak doors of St Swithun's, a radio set on the graveyard wall helping to break the suffocating silence.

The shattered stained-glass window had been boarded up and the hole the shell had ripped through the roof had been patched. But somewhere water fell, plashing on stone, reviving the smell of winter's damp and on the altar steps a crow lay dead, a wing sticking up like an arrow. In the draught from the door the feathers twitched, making Dryden's stomach tighten.

They walked to the Peyton tomb, which lay now in the

depressing shadow of the boarded window. Dryden took a torch and tried again to peer inside the shattered top of the burial chest – which brought his own face close to the mutil- ated cheek of the reclining crusader. Up close the genius of the medieval sculptor made the alabaster face almost human, and Dryden had to suppress the uncanny fear that it was about to move.

'So what was in here?' he asked.

'Nothing. Memorial funeral chests like this are always empty – I'm an expert now, believe me. Just a bit of conspic- uous consumption after death apparently, something for the neighbours to gape at. The body is usually buried beneath or near the tomb, or there's a crypt underneath for multiple burials.'

Shaw went behind the monument, to the space between the stone chest and the nave wall. The neat pyramid of sand, soil and loose stones Dryden had found on the day the church had been hit by Broderick's wayward bombardment seemed larger, and had been moved to one side.

'We had a look at this right at the start, of course – after you'd found it. But it didn't seem to mean much more than a bit of gruesome vandalism until our friends made their telephone calls.'

The two large stones which had been taken up from the floor were now laid neatly on wooden pallets. The inscrip- tion of P above an etched sunflower had been washed clean to reveal the precision of the original workmanship. The hole itself seemed deeper, cutting down through the foun- dations into grey, damp clay; the shadow at the bottom impenetrable.

'They had to work for it then?' said Dryden, kneeling at the stone edge.

'We dug down a bit further – just to check it out, and

we've tidied up the spoil. They broke one of the covering stones, in fact they made a right bodge-up of the whole job. We've sieved the soil and there's little to report, some splinters of wood, a churchwarden clay pipe fragment. But, our grave robbers did leave this . . .'

It was an entrenching tool, bagged in cellophane. 'Isn't that army issue?' said Dryden.

'Originally yes. But you can get them anywhere. This one's got a truly staggering six sets of fingerprints on it. My guess is they lacked a bit of muscle and needed to do the job in shifts. We've put all the prints on the national computer but there're no matches, which may explain their carefree methods.'

Dryden imagined them, working by night, the light of a lantern splayed across the medieval vaulting above. They might lack the cool intelligence of the real extremists, he thought, but there was no doubt they had guts.

'And all that confirms they're amateurs on a first job?' said Dryden.

'Possibly.'

Shaw squatted by the open grave and picked up a handful of soil. 'They must have taken some coffin wood too – if there was any left. We could be talking several centuries since the last burial – so I doubt there was much to get hold of but some thigh bones and a skull.'

But Shaw looked worried.

'What's wrong?' asked Dryden.

'Probably nothing. The Peytons were rich – you'd expect a few bits of metalwork off a coffin – nails, screws, handles, that kind of thing.'

Dryden nodded. 'Perhaps they took them.' But he didn't believe that either, so he checked his watch. 'Look, I need to get back. So if they ring, they'll ring tonight? My mobile?'

Shaw smiled, and Dryden realized that the question implied he'd agreed to the detective's plan. 'Yup. Then you ring me. Like I said, if we're lucky they'll go for a meeting rather than just dumping the bones somewhere. I don't think they'll be able to resist trying to talk to you in person. Publicity again, and they're after thrills. That's if they fall for it, of course – but they've got very little to lose if they believe you haven't been to the police and the prospect of it working for them would be a triumph. They'd make national news and they know it. Clearly, if they say no, that they just want to dump them, don't push them too hard. There's always a chance we'll get them anyway – so back off if they insist.'

Outside the rain still fell softly, leaving Shaw's black Land Rover covered in jewels of water. Dryden again felt uneasy in the ordered interior, the footwells litter-free, an air freshener hanging from the rear-view mirror where Humph's fluffy dice should be.

Shaw got in and, hitting the ignition, set Johnny Cash in motion as well, the sound system making Dryden's inner ear buzz.

'Sorry,' said Shaw, killing the CD.

Dryden, unthinking, flipped down the glove compartment and found a collection of shells within – a bone-white nautilus and several studded sea urchins. And a packet of Silk Cut, unopened.

'My DS,' said Shaw. 'She has to smoke outside.'

They bumped down the track off Church Hill towards the open mere, the rain cutting visibility to a few hundred yards, a line of distant poplars reduced to grey silhouettes. Dryden watched the outline of the village fade in the side mirror, the crescent of council houses where the Smiths had lived the last to dissolve into the mist.

As they drove the breeze made the fabric of the wind-surfer on the roof flutter. 'Yours?' said Dryden, nodding up.

Shaw shook his head, 'Wife's business, our business. We live on the coast, run a water sports academy, rent out huts and stuff.'

'Where?'

'Old Hunstanton, in the dunes; there's a house too.' He retrieved a snapshot from the sun visor in front of him. A clapboard house set amongst marram grass and sand, the distant lighthouse at Hunstanton in the background. A woman on the beach with long legs as brown as the sand. Dryden guessed the chair and the rod were there, unseen, down by the distant water's edge.

'Wow,' said Dryden, genuinely envious. Hunstanton's principal claim to fame was that it was the only west-facing east coast resort – giving it a monopoly on holiday sunsets. 'Great in summer,' he added.

'Great anytime,' said Shaw, looking at it once before he put it back.

Dryden nodded. 'So, Jack Shaw, any relation? DCI, right?'

Shaw gave him a long look, as cold as one of St Swithun's showers. 'Yes. My father, he died in 2000.'

'Sorry. You on the force when he retired?'

Shaw nodded. 'Yup. Youngest DS in the county, which everyone said was down to him, of course, not me. You can't win with these people. And he didn't retire, they forced him out.'

'Fabricating evidence, wasn't it? A child murder case – what was the boy's name?'

'Tessier. Jonathan Tessier. He was six.'

'Guess there's a lot of pressure in cases like that, to get a conviction.'

Shaw swung the Land Rover through the gates of the

range. 'Dad always said he hadn't done it, hadn't planted the evidence. That was good enough for me. Good enough for everyone who knew him – it just wasn't good enough for him. He was a good copper, an honest copper.'

Dryden nodded. 'But it's given you something to prove,' he said, not unkindly.

Humph pulled up in the Capri, fluffy dice gyrating from the rear-view.

'I've got lots of things to prove,' said Shaw, flicking Johnny Cash back on.

19

Dryden stood in front of Curry's window looking at the faces. He counted them: he could see twenty-six, but he knew there were more because of the reflections bouncing off the white goods at the rear of the shop. Every TV screen held the same image, the man's face pale against the luxuriant black hair, framed by hospital pillows. Overlaid was Dryden's own reflection, and beyond it the Capri, parked up for lunch with Humph partly obscured by a baker's bap. Dryden walked in through the open doors to get close enough to hear the commentary from the local BBC news team.

'. . . and police are hopeful that releasing the man's picture will lead quickly to his identification. As we reported earlier this week he was fished from the River Ouse near Ely on Tuesday after what looks like an accident involving a pleasure boat on the river. His right hand was badly injured after becoming entangled in machinery, possibly a propeller. Police say he is suffering from amnesia and is unable to recall his name or address. Anyone with information which may lead to his early identification should ring Ely police on 01353 555321. And now, the local weather . . .'

High Street was damp, steam rising from puddled pavements as the sun broke through. Dryden cut down Chequer Lane, around the back of the Indian takeaway, and out into Market Street. *The Crow*'s reception was crowded with people placing late adverts in the paper. Jean, the paper's long-serving front office dogsbody, caught his eye as he slipped through and up the bare wood stairs to the newsroom.

165

Splash, the office cat, ran a figure of eight round his legs as he climbed.

Other than a trapped wasp lying dead on Dryden's keyboard, the room was empty. He felt a pang of loss for the *News*, his Fleet Street home for more than a decade. Its newsroom had held 200, and was wired by adrenaline. *The Crow*'s newsroom rarely held double figures and had been on Valium since the death of Queen Victoria. Dryden checked his watch: 2.35pm. He'd put money on Charlie Bracken being in The Fenman with the rest of the production team, and checking the diary he saw that Garry Pymoor was still in court, marked down for the committal hearing for a fraud trial involving a local accountant. Embracing the rare silence Dryden got a coffee from the machine by the news desk and sat at his PC, trying to think. The attempt failed and instead he booted up the screen and began tapping his thoughts out as copy, a favourite ploy which seemed to work.

> *What have I got?*
> *Two stories.*
> *The Skeleton Man and the grave robbers.*
> *Three stories – the man in the river.*
> *What do they all have in common? Jude's Ferry.*
> *Are they linked?*
> *We know the link between the Skeleton Man and the grave robbers because they saw the picture with my story about the village and spotted the Peyton tomb – an opportunity they felt they couldn't miss. But the man in the river. Coincidence? Hardly.*

Dryden drank some more coffee and read what he'd got. Then he deleted the lot and started again.

Where next?

The grave robbers. I wait for the call.

The man in the river. We check to see if the TV appeal works.

The Skeleton Man.

Who is the Skeleton Man? I started with eight possible victims. Jimmy Neate is still alive. Ken Woodruffe is still alive. Shaw is on the case of the Smith brothers – one of whom may be our man. I can use that, but I'd have to be careful. I could probably contact another two at least before deadline tomorrow. George Tudor, the farm labourer, said on the tape he'd got the vicar to sign his emigration request. Then there's Peter Tholy. Not that common a name – I'll hit the directories just in case he's back. And I'll nag Humph to track down the Cobleys – if they're still in the taxi business they can't be that hard to find.

Dryden stopped typing and, standing, stretched. The plastic click in his back brought relief and he walked over to the shelf behind the subs' bench and retrieved a copy of *Crockford's Clerical Directory*. He sat on the bay window seat and flicked through until he found the 'L's.

Frederick Rhodes Lake. Rev. St Bartholomew's, Fleetside, King's Lynn.

'Right. So that's where you've gone. Very downmarket.' He made a note of the telephone number and returned the book.

He read what he'd written on screen and remembered someone else who could help him write about the Skeleton Man: Elizabeth Drew. She was a valuable witness to the death of Jude's Ferry because she wasn't an insider, but stood outside the close network of family and friendship which seemed to wrap the village in a cocoon. Her workmates had said to try the cash 'n' carry on the edge of town – an MFI-style double box the size of an airport terminal.

Dryden checked his watch: he had time to try and find

167

Elizabeth Drew, a ticking miniature eternity of time before he could expect a call from the animal rights extremists. On his desk his mobile sat waiting for the incoming call. Typically, as the moment drew nearer his fears grew more acute. They'd meet after dark, some godforsaken stretch of fen, delivering grey bones. Picturing cruel teeth, seen through the slash of a balaclava, his guts tightened. He'd keep Humph near by, he promised himself that, Humph and his four-wheeled security blanket.

He grabbed the mobile, stuffed it deep in a pocket and left the office.

By the time he got downstairs the phone had rung, so he ducked into one of the small interview cubicles the sales staff used for taking adverts and answered the mobile.

It was Ruth Lisle, Magda's daughter. 'Mr Dryden?'

He wondered if she was calling from the mobile library but somewhere in the background a clock chimed and whirred in its casement and so Dryden imagined a very English Victorian hallway, and the tall, cool figure of Magda Hollingsworth's daughter standing in the splash of coloured light from the fanlight over the door.

'I promised, and you were kind. I've found something in the diaries. I made some photocopies and dropped them in at the police station here at Ely and they said they'd pass them on to the right people, although they didn't see them as relevant. In fact they were a bit dismissive actually, which made me quite angry. So, I certainly don't see why I shouldn't share this with you. Do you have a moment?'

'Please,' said Dryden.

'Well, on top of my mother's diary, which she filled out each day, Mass-Observation asked its correspondents to write on specific subjects. During the winter of 1989 they requested contributions on the subject of women and depression.

Mother talked privately to many of her friends about this and the entry is copious, a very important document in itself, I would say. There was one girl in particular, a teenager, and she was very depressed during a pregnancy – an unwanted pregnancy. She'd turned to an aunt for help, and Mum had found out about it that way – indirectly, I suppose. The aunt was ill herself and Mum visited, it was the sort of thing she was good at. This girl said, apparently, that she'd thought about killing the child when it was born. Dreadful, isn't it? Yes,' she added, answering herself. 'Anyway, later in the diaries she says that the child did die, a few days after a premature birth, and she wonders if the girl had carried out her threat. At first she talks about going to the police but puts that aside, and concludes – characteristically – that she should think the best of her, especially as there was a post mortem which found the death was due to natural causes.

'But then in the next entry the tone changes. I think she felt she couldn't leave the village without discharging her responsibilities. She says that she feels she must say something after all, confront the mother I suppose, or the family, and perhaps report the matter to the authorities. That's the meaning I took from it anyway, although it's not completely clear. That bit wasn't in the official MO document, you see, but in her private diaries – and they're written in a much more subjective and emotional style.

'But what is clear is that she suddenly saw the child's death as partly her own fault. It's awful to see this guilt surfacing on the page. And to that she had to add this dilemma; that she'd been entrusted with this confidence, but felt a duty to the child that had died. I think it was entirely personal for Mother, I think she felt burdened with this secret and she wanted to either pass it on, or throw it back so that the mother could deny it if she could. I think she hoped passionately that it would be denied, because of course that would alleviate her guilt as well.'

She paused, breathing deeply.

'Do you know who this young woman was, Mrs Lisle?' asked Dryden.

'Well. The initials in the text are L.O., but I'm afraid that means nothing. And the private diary follows the same notation. But yes, I do know, I think, and I contacted the university – there's an advice desk there – to ask what I should do. They seemed to think I should tell the police but ask them to respect the confidence as far as is possible, so I've put a note with the photocopies.'

Dryden tried to break in but she spoke over him. 'The skeleton in the cellar is that of a man, isn't it? So I don't think we'll ever find my mother.'

'I'm sorry,' said Dryden, aware that part of her had wanted her mother to find peace at last.

'Mrs Lisle, if I asked you to tell me . . .'

'I'd have to say nothing, Mr Dryden. The young woman would be – what – in her mid-thirties now. I don't think it's any time for the press to be asking questions again. The rules laid down by MO are quite clear – there must be no general identification. The police are an exception, and although I suppose technically I'm not bound by the rules, I think Mother would have wanted me to respect them. So I'm sorry.'

'That's fine,' said Dryden, lying. 'But can you tell me what day this was, when she talks about confronting the mother of the child? About going to the family?'

'It's the last entry, the night before the evacuation, the night she went missing.'

20

The car park of Richardson's cash 'n' carry held three large Volvo estates, three super-size abandoned trolleys, a forklift truck and a squashed hedgehog. Dryden pushed open a large metal swing door and found himself in the swaddled hush of the vast store, the silence polluted only by the tinny, bass-less crackle of muzak. There was one woman in a cubicle till waiting for a customer to appear. She had red hair piled high and held in place by clips and she was reading some-thing just below the counter. Dryden's footsteps made her look up through myopic eyes, her squint drawing together the wrinkles in her face. She shuffled the book sideways and Dryden saw it was a romance, a heroine fleeing a house with battlements.

'Hi. Sorry – I'm looking for someone.'

'Only trade customers. I'm sorry – you know, you have to have a card,' she smiled. She flicked a finger across a pile of forms. 'You can fill one in now if you like, but we need the VAT number of the business.'

'My name's Philip,' he said, 'Philip Dryden.'

'I'm Ena, but you still need a card.'

'I don't want to shop.'

Ena looked sideways like she was planning something. At the far end of the aisle of empty till boxes was a glass office, and within that the cone of light from a desk lamp point-ing down.

'Mr Newall's doing the books,' she said.

'It's Elizabeth, Elizabeth Drew. I wanted to talk to her.'

Ena pulled the wrinkles together again, the short-sighted eyes searching his face for a clue. 'She's in charge at the back – Goods In – through the store. I shouldn't let you really.'

She retrieved a pair of spectacles from around her neck and began to shuffle with the forms.

'Thanks,' said Dryden, setting off down an aisle flanked by metal shelving twenty feet high loaded with catering packs of soup, tinned vegetables and beans. At the end there was a crossroads where one aisle cut the store in two – a clear vista 150 yards long. In the distance a shelf stacker in khaki overalls was drop-kicking empty boxes over the top of the shelving. As Dryden watched a shopper crossed the aisle pushing a large flatbed trolley piled with boxes, cans and film-wrapped packs. Something flapped over Dryden's head and looking up he saw a pigeon in the metal rafters of the roof, shaking free a fall of dust. The tannoy system bing-bonged and Dryden recognized Ena's pinched voice: 'Can I have a stacker at the tills, please. A stacker at the tills.' Stress made her lengthen the final word into a small cry.

The shop worker stopped his game and headed for the tills, pausing to stoop down and pick up the shredded remains of one of the boxes he'd been kicking. Dryden set off again for the back of the warehouse, the air heavy with the smell of broken soap-powder boxes and the papery scent of several thousand toilet rolls stacked in towers along the rear wall.

Goods In was shielded by stacks of wooden pallets and a steel wall. A juggernaut was parked through a bay in the rear partition, the doors folded like a concertina, the engine and onboard refrigeration unit silent. There was another small glass-walled office dominated by a large colour calendar of Wicken Fen nature reserve, a wedge of swans caught at sunset replacing the usual splayed limbs of the Playmate of the Month.

A woman with round shoulders was leaning over the desk checking a document, a large lunchbox open beside her revealing a neat stack of sandwiches and what looked like a pastry. Dryden leant against the door jamb.

'Mrs Drew?'

She looked up, the face without make-up, pale white Fen complexion, the brown wispy hair tucked back into an ethnic headscarf of chaotic Caribbean colours. Dryden guessed that food was a substitute for her, and wondered how long she'd been overweight.

'How can I help?' The voice was lighter than he expected, a decade younger than the fifty years he would have guessed from her face. 'I'm interested in Jude's Ferry – you rang in when I was on the radio. I work for *The Crow*.'

She smiled. 'How'd you find me?'

Dryden looked around, avoiding the question. Through the HGV's offside mirror, he could see the driver asleep in his cab. 'Chummy on break?'

She nodded. 'Tachograph. He needs to stop still for an hour. So . . . late lunch break.'

Dryden thought about his first question, balancing the phrases to avoid antagonizing his witness, taking time to get it right. 'You were a rural officer for the county council. I don't know much about the job, but it must have been a tall order keeping places like Jude's Ferry going, getting everyone to work together. I was just trying to get a feel for the place, a picture in my head.'

'I got sacked,' she said, answering the question he hadn't asked. 'They probably said.' Dryden shook his head. 'My David died and I couldn't really take it any more.'

Dryden took a step back, embarrassed by the personal detail.

'They were right, I wasn't pulling my weight. David had

been the manager here, so they got me in. It was good of them, it's a family firm.'

She stood, a kettle beginning to boil on the ground by the plug, and took two crockery mugs out of a small sink. She made Dryden tea without asking, and they didn't say a word while she completed the little ceremony.

'It's a bit soulless,' said Dryden, nodding towards the empty aisles and the stacks of packed food hidden by the steel wall.

'Yes,' she said, and for a moment Dryden thought she was going to cry. 'It's better here.'

'So. Jude's Ferry, what was it like? Soulless too?'

'Good God no,' she said, hitching her feet expertly up on to the first open drawer of the desk. 'People don't understand about communities like that. Everyone was part of a network, you see, part of the place, and it held them together, the village, and it held them apart, far enough apart that they could live with people they sometimes didn't like, people they might even have hated. In small communities that's what they learn – how close to get.'

'And then they had to leave,' he said.

'Yes – so all those networks fell apart. I'm not surprised someone died. It was a trigger – the evacuation. I could feel the tension in those last few weeks.'

'Did you know any of the villagers well?'

She shook her head, tapping a finger on the desktop. 'Not really. Once they all sold up in the eighties to the MoD it was almost impossible to get new investment to come in for any project.'

She leant back, covering her eyes with the hand that didn't hold her cup. 'I tried to get some development fund money behind a project to put start-up units in the old beet factory, small manufacturing enterprises. I know one of the micro-brewers was interested. But you couldn't take it forward because there was always that question: what if the Army cuts the lease? So you couldn't blame the banks, although we did, of course.'

Dryden nodded, setting the cup down on a coaster with a picture of a barn owl.

She looked towards the internal window and Dryden guessed she was looking at her own reflection. 'My only real contact with the village was through SEN.'

'Special needs?'

'Yes. That was part of my remit. I had to make sure any children in the village who needed support got it. So we had to coordinate social services, education, transport, the lot. You'd be surprised at the kind of problems you find in a place like Jude's Ferry.'

Dryden looked her in the eyes. 'I was born on Burnt Fen,' he said. 'We had a farm.'

She had the good grace to look down. 'Sorry. I guess you wouldn't be surprised then. I took the accent for London.'

Dryden, sensing he had the advantage, pressed forward. 'In those last few months a baby died in the village, do you remember that?'

She shook her head. 'If it was natural causes that's not our bag, the health trust in Whittlesea might have a record.'

Dryden made a note. 'So, SEN kids – how many were there at the end?'

She buried her face in her hands trying to remember. 'Two I think. There was Peter Tholy of course . . .'

'Right,' said Dryden, recalling his list of eight potential identities for the Skeleton Man.

'He went to Australia after the evacuation,' she said.

'Are you sure? I thought George Tudor was the one who emigrated.'

'Both of them, friends of course, so it was a joint project. We helped with Peter's application because there were obvious difficulties. He had quite severe learning difficulties, dyslexia, and some communication problems, some dysfunctional speech patterns, although his IQ was actually very high. Didn't stop everyone treating him like the village idiot, of course – that's a rural tradition I've never tried to protect. The only friends he had were amongst the girls, who mothered him, and George.'

'Why were they friends?'

She shrugged. 'Workmates, I guess; landwork and the flower fields. They both got decent references from the vicar, and from Blooms, the wholesale nursery business.'

'So you knew Colonel Broderick then?'

'Yes. One of the few local businesses with any kind of potential. Broderick generated a lot of local employment, it was a good thing it was there in those last years.'

'What was he like – Peter?' Dryden thought of the Skeleton Man, wondering if Peter Tholy had ever really left the village in which he was born.

'I met him once, twice perhaps, most of the hands-on stuff was done by social services. But, you know, cute I guess. He wasn't your typical farmhand – strong in the arm, thick in the head. He'd taken some hard knocks growing up in the village, but he'd come through.'

Looking through him she remembered another face. 'And there was Martyn Armstrong. He'd have been about fifteen when the family finally left – well, I say family, there was the father, the watchman at the beet works. The mother was still officially resident but in fact she'd walked out. Which was one of Martyn's problems. They had a house in the middle of the factory, it was a bit creepy actually, just the two of them, surrounded by all those empty buildings.'

'And Martyn needed help?'

'Yeah. He wasn't cute. I'm not an expert in educational needs but he definitely needed help. I interviewed the father – briefly – just to see where we could find him a place.'

'So, nasty, violent?'

She nodded. 'He came to our attention – isn't that a dreadful euphemism – thanks to the police in Whittlesea. There'd been nothing in the village, or at least they said there'd been no complaints, but you can never tell with a place as close as Jude's Ferry. But he was one of the kids we taxied over to the college, and that's when the problems started. His dad kept dogs on the factory site and Martyn had cats, mice, a ferret, you name it. Bit of an animal nutter. Vegetarian too, which you know, for the Fens, is like as weird as it gets.'

'So what did he do – steal a goldfish, couple of pound of curly kale?'

'Not quite. There was a pet shop in the town and apparently Martyn went in and complained about the conditions, said it was cruel the way they kept the rabbits in small cages. He'd turn up most afternoons and berate the owner in front of the customers. Then the police got called and they chucked him out, told him to keep clear of the shop.'

The hair on the back of Dryden's neck had begun to bristle. 'What'd he do?'

'One night he got himself a milk bottle and a tin of paraffin and made a Molotov cocktail, which he lit and lobbed through the window of the owner's flat above the shop. When he ran out Martyn sprayed floor polish in his eyes.'

'Jesus. So then what happened?'

They heard a groan from the driver's cab as a small alarm pulsed, and a round, bald head appeared with sleep lines in red running across one cheek.

'Juvenile court and a spell in a secure unit. That's the last I heard of him, I'm afraid. There were psychiatric reports too. They didn't throw the key away or anything, people wanted to help. But in terms of life chances I think Martyn's were running out fast. I don't think a happy ending was on the cards, do you?'

She ushered Dryden out of the door as the driver ran the back of the container up to reveal a row of butchered sides of beef hanging from hooks, the meat red and bloody where the circular saw had split the bodies open, the bones caressed by the ice which hung in the refrigerated air.

21

The first time he saw them together it felt like a dislocation; bones parting in the socket. Laura hadn't been on the gallery in the sun, enjoying solitude in a wicker chair. Instead he'd been directed down through one of the wards to the unit where the patients were taken for physiotherapy. She was on a weights machine, lying flat, trying to raise the bar hung with circular lead cogs which crossed her feet.

And he was beside her, the man they'd fished out of the river, the man who didn't have a past. He was talking into her ear, his wheelchair pulled up and braked, the wounded hand held on his lap like a parcel, the fingers swaddled to form a mitt. Even in a dressing gown he looked elegant, the arms drooping languidly from the rests of the chair. The kind of man, Dryden imagined, who would shoot the cuffs on a suit.

Something about the attitude of his neck, the slightly bowed head, suggested confession.

It was the first time since the accident he'd seen her talking to someone he didn't know, someone who wasn't from his world. A good sign, he reasoned; she was getting better, putting together an independent life, building her own world as best she could.

Laura said, 'Hi,' the syllable clearer, sharper than he'd heard since the speech therapy had begun just six months earlier.

'Hi,' said Dryden, fighting an urge to apologize for the intrusion. 'Humph and I are off to the coast,' he said. 'We could do the beach – I've got an interview in Lynn. We thought you'd come.'

The man released the brake on the chair and a uniformed PC whom Dryden had not noticed stood, ready to escort him back to his room. But Laura raised her hand, struggling to control her face. 'This . . .' she said, and then they laughed. 'This is the man who does not know his name,' she said, each word contorting her face with effort, but each sound now distinct, articulated.

They all laughed this time, but Dryden thought he was somehow outside the joke. Laura's face was flushed with effort and something else, something close to joy.

'I know,' he said. 'I was there when they got you out of the river. My name's Dryden. Philip Dryden.' He took the proffered good hand, noting again the handsome face, the crisp line of the jaw, and the complexion Dryden always associated with money. 'I work for *The Crow* – that's the local paper. Remember much?'

He shrugged, laughing, the green eyes searching Dryden's. 'Not really – just fragments and they seem to belong to someone else, someone who isn't me, at least not yet. It's a really bizarre experience. I can remember everything about life – you know, how to operate a coffee machine, or send a text message, or find Radio Four – but nothing about *my* life.'

'How'd you feel, inside – emotionally?'

The man looked at Laura. 'Scared, to be frank. Anxious. I don't know what happened at the bridge. I can't be sure someone didn't throw me in – so, yeah, scared. How would you feel? If they're out there, this person, these people, then they might try again. So I feel a bit hunted, a target.'

The voice was modulated, unhurried, with the self-possession of a BBC newsreader.

'Anything . . . do you not remember anything?'

'I'm writing it all down in a diary, but it's just feelings really. And some inconsequential fragments from a childhood, the childhood of this other me I suppose. I can see a garden with all these exotic plants – palms, not spindly Cornish ones, hundred-foot ones. And I can see an ocean, with boats on it, thousands of them, and this incredible lawn, like a cool green carpet, between the flowering shrubs. God knows what all that's about.'

'A holiday?' suggested Dryden.

He shook his head, but didn't answer. 'And rugby posts. This is a different place because there are low hills in the background dusted with snow. There must be six pitches, more, and round every one is arranged a thin crowd. I think my parents are there, in that memory somewhere. But I don't know, I don't see them.'

He laughed. 'So, stuff like that. Not very useful. Laura's said I could send her what I write. There's nobody else, and the doctors said it might help. She says she'll write back. I'm really grateful. There's something about words that's comforting, something really fundamental.' He picked a magazine from the metal folder attached to the side of his chair. 'Something about the black letters arranged on the white paper. It's just important, but I don't know why. They make me happy, I guess; happier, anyway.'

Dryden nodded, trying to look pleased, irritated by the note of self-pity.

'Does Jude's Ferry mean anything?'

He edged his chair towards the machine next to Laura and swung himself easily into the seat. Dryden thought he was making the time to think through an answer. 'Sure. I think I was born there; like I say, bits of childhood have come back. But this is just a name – there's not much to go with it.'

'It's not much of a place.'

'There's this street with a ditch full of reeds on one side. Is that right?'

Dryden nodded. 'Sure. That's The Dring – the main street.'

'And bells ringing over my head, and the smell of wax on the ropes, the scent of a guttering candle. Peacocks on a lawn – not the exotic green one, this one's covered in leaves at autumn, and it's patchy. And a post office. I can remember the smell of it, and bells again, the little bells when the door opened, and one of those trays of sweets just right for my height. It's just the echo of a memory.'

Dryden shrugged, wondering where he'd learned to use words like that, the sophistication of the imagery.

'But nothing about falling in the river? The handrail was broken, that took some force . . .'

Laura pulled herself upright, cutting in. 'Philip. Give him time.' Dryden knew what she'd said, but he could see the other man struggling to unpick the sentence.

'We should give you a name,' said Dryden, knowing the thought was callous. Outside, through a picture window, he could see the Capri idling, the boot up ready to stow the wheelchair.

'The coast?' he said.

She shook her head. 'I'll do the weights,' she said, making a mess of the last word. 'I must. See you at the boat. Tonight.'

They kissed, but as he walked away he felt uneasy, as if his back was being watched. Then his mobile rang.

22

By the time he'd reached the Capri the call was over. It was the same man, unable to disguise the voice or the triumph within it, once he heard that Henry Peyton didn't want a fight, that he'd shut down Sealodes Farm and retire quietly with the fortune he'd already made. Then the suspicions had kicked in: had Dryden called the police? Had Peyton? One blue uniform, he said, and they'd dump the bones in a ditch and Peyton would never see the dogs again. And then they'd be back: they'd be back every day of every week of every month of every year until his business was ruined and his life was a living nightmare. Dryden imagined the face on the other end of the line, a glove over the mouthpiece, spit in the wool.

They fixed a point to pick up the bones and the dogs. Thieves Bridge, Ten Mile Bank, at dusk – 9.45pm that evening. He was to come alone, leave the cab in the village, and walk out to the river. Dryden didn't have time to say no. He rang DI Shaw with the details and the detective outlined his plans. He'd put a team on the river in a boat, and a helicopter would be ready on the ground at Downham ten miles to the north, where they had a helipad for the holiday traffic snarl-ups on the A10. Shaw and the team would maintain a cordon half a mile from the bridge. They were a professional unit, he said, and no one would spot them. He promised it would be all right; in the way that people always do when they think it might not.

Dryden cut the call and tried a big smile. 'Shit,' he said,

feeling his guts tighten. 'Tonight, Ten Mile Bank,' he said to Humph. He covered his face with his hands and wished he wasn't such a coward as to always agree to anything that proved he wasn't. Now he had hours to contemplate his fear before his appointment with the balaclavas.

'Where's Laura?' said Humph.

'She's got to work out. We do the coast another day – the Reverend Lake's not going anywhere fast.'

Humph, sensing an unhealthy silence, took control. He swung the cab out onto the old A10 and headed north. 'I've got someone you should meet,' he said by way of explanation.

At Southery they pulled off the road and into the village. The high street was blocked by two tractors, travelling in opposite directions, which had stopped to allow the drivers to enjoy a chat. Humph deftly mounted the pavement, crossed a grass verge, and left them to it.

Clear of the last house they burst out onto a wide fen flattened by a vast sky. This was Methwold Severals, a tract of peat distinguished by nothing but a single sugar beet factory, a plume of smoke from its giant modern chimney trailing across the late afternoon sky. They zigzagged towards it using a maze of drove roads, navigating by sight, leaving in their wake the abandoned farmsteads which had given way to the big commercial farming companies which dominated the whole of the Black Fen.

They inched closer, impeded by a series of right-angle bends, until they came to the factory gates. This was a modern industrial site, a 1960s beet plant, as removed from the small-scale operation in Jude's Ferry as Stephenson's *Rocket* is from an Inter-City 125. Four towering silos blocked the view north towards the sea, each linked to its partners by an overground complex of pipes, cables and conveyor belts. Steam leaked from various valves and Dryden could feel the hum of the machinery vibrating through the cab once Humph had parked up by the entrance.

The factory had replaced an older one on the same site, the only remnant of which was a pair of two-up, two-down brick cottages to one side of the new plate-glass reception and security building. Across the façade of both was a neon sign which read TAXIS.

Humph adjusted his headphones and flicked on his language tape. 'This is it. You did ask – the Cobley family? Used to run the cab firm in Jude's Ferry. This is them.' He closed his eyes, job done.

Dryden got out and considered the inappropriate extravagance of the neon, which flickered slightly, emitting a trembling buzz. One door was bricked up, the other was half glass, reinforced with wire, and had been slammed shut a million times by people who didn't care. Inside was a waiting room, with three armchairs of tattered leather and a wall map of the Black Fen.

Behind the glass sat a woman smoking a cigarette, her flesh piled on itself to produce a torso the shape of a Walnut Whip. Beside her was an old TV showing a video of *Shrek 2*. Shelves held the black cartridges of hundreds of others.

'Mrs Cobley?' asked Dryden, inadvertently drawing in a lungful of smoke.

'If you want a car it's a wait. The shift's just finished and we're ferrying the regulars home.'

Dryden nodded: 'Sure. How many work here now?' The sugar works was the biggest employer within thirty miles.

She killed the sound on the video. 'Two hundred, in the season it's nearly three. A lot of 'em live out nowhere. Shall I book you one? It'll be an hour now.' As she said it she looked in a mirror up by a security camera and saw Humph's Capri idling at the kerb.

'Oh. What is it then?'

'My name's Dryden – from *The Crow*. I'm writing something about Jude's Ferry – you've probably heard?'

She flicked off the microphone in front of her. 'Sure. That skeleton they found. The police have been anyway. You've wasted a trip.' Dryden thought that must be the ultimate crime in the taxi trade.

Behind her on the wall was a notice board with snapshots pinned up over a rota. Several showed a teenager with thick black hair and adolescent lips, plus a fringe which had been out of fashion for more than a decade.

Dryden looked at her face, a study in neutrality. 'It's your son,' he said. 'I know it sounds daft but I'm just tracking down all the lads from the village whose age would fit the body they found. Sorry. I know it sounds ghoulish – but I guess he's OK, yeah? Police probably asked the same question.'

But he knew then, because all the snapshots were of the same age.

She took her time lighting a fresh Silk Cut, half of which she appeared to inhale in one draw, the ash falling unnoticed on her bare arm.

A light flickered on her console. She flipped the button on the microphone. 'OK, Sam. Sam. Picked up?' He recognized her voice now from the tape they'd listened to on the riverbank. The intervening years had simply shredded it some more, nicotine smoking the vocal cords.

Static filled the room, a burst of sound as raw as whale song. She listened and seemed to get the sense. 'Number, 134. That's one, three, four, Sam. Customer still waiting.' She killed the noise and began to fiddle with an electric kettle on a table beside her.

'Paul was the name, wasn't it?' asked Dryden carefully.

'It's not him,' she said, dropping her chin into the folds of fat around her throat. 'I told the police the same. Told them not to bother. They thought it might be but I'd know. I know I'd know.' She held her hand to her chest where Dryden guessed the pain was sharpest.

He studied the snapshots. 'But you haven't seen him since – when?'

They watched the video in silence as Shrek talked to a giant gingerbread man. 'He had an argument with his father, it's a long time ago now. He hated the cabs, the late nights. Computers was his thing, design and that. We didn't know what he was talking about. So he left.'

'Right. But when?'

'When we left the Ferry. We stuck around – there was loads of business, carting everyone about, taking the soldiers around too. Then we'd moved in 'ere. He had a room and everything but he had this friend, he said, a boy.' She blew a smoke ring with exaggerated finesse. 'That was the final straw really. They were more than friends – you know,' she laughed bitterly. 'We didn't understand. And Sam wouldn't have it. He was angry, really angry.' She caught Dryden's eye and remembered to add something. 'We both were.'

Dryden could see why the police were interested in the whereabouts of Paul Cobley, and he didn't believe they'd taken mother's intuition as evidence he was still alive.

She looked at him then, unable to sustain the lack of emotion in her face, and Dryden could see what the years between had done to her. 'We didn't bring him up like that,' she said, but it sounded like a formula she'd used before.

'You must wonder, you know – how he is, where he is? It's seventeen years – more.'

'Thanks. I can count.' She nodded, looking at the

winking lights on her console. 'If you don't want a cab . . .'

'Sorry.' But he held his ground, remembering his motto – there's always time for one more question.

'There was a death in the village in those last months, a baby. I don't expect you remember?'

She dealt with the winking lights, confirming children dropped off at home, directing cabs to pick up those coming off the afternoon shift, and those coming in.

'Of course I remember. Do you think there's anything else to talk about in a place like Jude's Ferry? But then it was our business in a way, our community. And it's not your business, is it, Mr Dryden?'

The room was silent then and Dryden thought that there was nothing that caught a sense of not going anywhere more precisely than a taxi office. Everything moved, but nothing changed.

'Mrs Cobley,' Dryden looked down, reluctant to turn the knife, guessing that Sam Cobley had never been reconciled to his son's sexuality. 'I don't believe the police took your word for the fact Paul's still alive. Perhaps your husband knows where he is . . . I could wait?' He turned his back and looked out over the sunlit fen.

She took her time making a cup of tea without offering him one. Dryden took a seat opposite the counter and watched her setting down her cup and then opening the office's one battered filing cabinet. She retrieved a cheap plastic wallet and put the picture within, a coloured snap-shot, on the counter. Dryden stood and touched it, setting it straight; a man leaning on a gate with a pair of cottages in the background – the kind of isolated semis they built all over the fens in the fifties for tenant workers. It was Paul Cobley, mid-thirties perhaps, a red setter at his heels, the hair still extravagant.

'Sam doesn't know. He stayed local for me, you see, so I can pop over when Sam's fishing or on a long trip. That's helped me forgive him.' Her eyes moved to the window where the sugar beet factory was belching white smoke into the evening sky. 'But Sam doesn't know and I'd ask you to keep it that way,' she said, lighting up another Silk Cut.

'Sure,' said Dryden, studying the picture. 'I only want a word.'

'I'll ask, but there's no promises. Leave your number. I'd like you to go now, I don't want this opened up again. So go. Please.'

Dryden nodded, studying the picture one last time. The house had been modernized with PVC windows and a conservatory latched on the side, but its twin next door was dilapidated and a For Sale sign had been nailed across the front door. Dryden noted the name of the estate agent: Foster & Co., Land Agents.

'Did he have much to tell the police?' asked Dryden, pushing the snapshot over the counter.

'He was there that last night – in the New Ferry Inn.'

The radio crackled and Sam said he was on his way home.

Dryden took his last chance. 'This was a lynching – they turned on someone, didn't they, Mrs Cobley. Why would they do that?'

She looked at him then, the small dark eyes set deeply in the flesh. 'Paul wouldn't do that. He knows what it's like to be a victim.'

Dryden noted the present tense. 'The landlord, Ken Woodruffe, says there was a brawl, about money apparently. The Smith twins?'

She laughed. 'Mark was a nasty bit of work.'

'And Matthew?'

She shrugged, her eyes watching the road outside for signs

of her husband's return. 'Gentler, smarter. They might have been identical to look at but in here . . .' She tapped a finger to her temple. 'Chalk and cheese.'

'And your son saw them fight?'

She shook her head. 'No, that was later. He got home about eleven, I was still up in case we got any calls.'

'Right. So Paul got home and then what?'

'We broke open a bottle of whisky. His dad was already in bed. Took it out in the garden and toasted the old place. By midnight we were all in bed. Dead to the world.'

Dryden said goodbye, knowing that wasn't the only lie she'd told.

23

By the time they reached Ten Mile Bank the moon was up, reflected in the broad sweep of the river as it turned north towards the sea. A swan flew upstream, black against the silver of the water. Humph parked up beneath the high bank next to the church, killing the lights. A cypress tree obscured the church clock but Dryden's watch read 9.30pm. A flood bank ran across the fen from beside the graveyard carrying the village's only street, two lines of houses clinging to the high ground. Three street lights out of a dozen were working, and somewhere a dog barked as the first stars appeared low to the east.

Dryden got out quickly before fear paralysed his legs as well as his brain. He cursed Shaw and the deal he'd struck, but knew now there was no way of going back which didn't brand him a coward. Standing by the Capri in the gloom he knew he was being watched, but by whom? The DI and his team should be in place, a surveillance boat on the river, and the helicopter standing by upstream. But who else was lost in the night? Would they meet him on the bridge or did they suspect a trap and have other plans?

In the dyke below, the mist was beginning to form, a weaving white sheet of vapour spilling out to claw at the cab's tyres. Dryden walloped the car roof. 'Right. If I'm not back in twenty minutes ring Shaw on the number I gave you. If you feel like it you can come looking for me as well . . .'

He set off up the bank and stopped at the top to look upriver. Two pleasure boats were moored on the far side, smoke snaking up from the stovepipe of one. Downriver, half a mile into the growing dusk, he could see the ugly iron girders of the bridge. Again, he started walking briskly before he could lose his nerve, trying not to imagine the face, edged in the balaclava, waiting in the shadows.

Thieves Bridge had been built by the army in the Second World War to help get food out of the fen fields and down to London quickly. It was a giant piece of Meccano, crossing the Ouse in a single span, held together with rivets and rust. Traffic was single track, with priority to the east, but most nights nothing crossed it, for now the route was faster using bridges to the north.

When he reached it Dryden climbed up to the road and looked east, then west. Nothing moved on the arrow-straight tarmac, which stretched out of sight like a runway. Dryden saw a holdall lying on the raised footpath which took pedestrians over the water, so he walked towards it, painfully aware of the sharp tap of his footsteps in the night.

The voice, when it came, was above him. 'You don't need to check it.'

He'd climbed up one of the girders and was sitting in the superstructure, ten feet off the ground, his back against the studded steel. His body was crooked, bent to blend with the metalwork, and Dryden wondered if Shaw's team had spotted him at all. No balaclava, just a black woollen hat pulled down low and something rubbed into his skin so that it was dark and blotched.

'We didn't think you'd come – alone.' Dryden didn't speak, and in the silence heard the knocking of a light boat against the bridge support below.

'Got a tongue?' He thought he recognized the voice from the phone but couldn't be certain.

'Sure. What d'you want me to say?'

Dryden leant against the steelwork looking upstream where, across the moonlit water, he could see one of the pleasure boats edging out, letting the current take it down-river.

He was down quickly, and Dryden didn't have the nerve to back off as he came forward and grabbed him by the shirt front. Up close he could see the eyes now, and where they caught the moonlight Dryden could see how scared he was. He stuffed a piece of paper into one of Dryden's pockets. 'That's a statement. We want that in the story too – along with something from Peyton saying he's packing the business up. We'll watch developments and keep the dogs, just for insurance. When Sealodes closes down he gets 'em back.'

Up close Dryden could actually smell the fear, laced with nicotine. He was just a few feet away now and Dryden tried to memorize the face: an oversized jaw, and small, flattened nose which looked broken.

'Let's go,' a second voice, this time from below, where an outboard motor suddenly burst into life. 'There's a boat coming.'

The grip tightened at Dryden's neck and the face came closer. 'I hope that's nothing we should be worried about, Dryden. Betrayal is a very ugly word – disfiguring.'

The engine below screamed and at the same moment a searchlight thudded into life from the deck of the pleasure boat upstream, blinding Dryden, so that he didn't see the punch coming, the knuckles cracking against the orbital bone above his eye. He went down on the tarmac, his cheekbone hitting the ground with a thud which made him lose consciousness. But as he drifted into an internal silence he heard a loud hailer, although the words made no sense, each unrelated, evading meaning.

When he came to he didn't know how long he'd been

down, but the side of his skull was numb and pitted with grit. In the distance he could see headlights approaching along the drove, a blue flashing light above. Overhead the thwup-thwup of helicopter blades was close enough to move the night air, while a spotlight burned down, illuminating the bridge around him. In the silvery light he saw a rat panic, zigzagging over the tarmac.

They'd left the holdall, just a few feet away. So he crept towards it, the pain in his head oddly distant. He was kneeling when he got the zip down and the helicopter was making a second run, the blazing halogen-white light suddenly electrifying the scene like a flashbulb. Inside there was some heavy material, like rotted carpet, which he prised apart to reveal bones and a skull. He took the head out and held it level with his own, and looking into that lifeless face he could see the glitter of a single metal filling, so that he knew one thing only as he heard footsteps running towards him – that these were not old bones.

*So now I know. I have a life, complete of itself. A name, a wife, a gift —
apparently — to write. She came with the policeman this morning while
I worked in the gym. Elizabeth. I call her Liz, that's what she told me. I
always have. She's beautiful, and I can see why I might have loved her. But
she's a stranger to me now, and I wonder if I'll ever remember what it was
we had together.*

 *Because I don't have to remember. That's how it works. The doctors
have set the same prognosis, that the past will return but from the
earliest memories first, rolling forward to the present. Flashes out of
sync perhaps, no more. But there are no guarantees the process will
ever be complete. It's started already, my childhood unfurling. But it
might just stop: stop short — so that I'll never know about Kathryn,
and I'll never know why I was on that bridge. And who did I meet?
And will they come for me again?*

 *I know more about you, Laura, than I know about my wife. At
least you and I have a past, however brief it's been.*

 *Liz told me what my life was like. I think she knew I couldn't
remember, and she wants me to remember, so that we can have something to share. But it's like sharing ashes, and there's not even a
memory of the fire.*

 *And then there's what I do remember, the past revealing itself. It's
an odd feeling, not so much remembering as uncovering. I don't recall
the past with any sense of triumph or discovery, it just appears, fully
made, already stale somehow, tarnished by a thousand other remem-
berings I've forgotten.*

 The present is the only reality in which I feel alive.

My life so far then, in a few paragraphs, as I've actually remembered it. Yes, I was born in Jude's Ferry. In Orchard House, where the garden ran down to the river. I only have the one memory before we started moving — hiding amongst the box hedges and watching a car crackle past on the gravel drive. Why that memory? I doubt I'll ever know. My father, a diplomat, took us away. The house, mothballed, we said was home. And we did come back for the summers, and a single Christmas.

But my life was somewhere else. To Singapore — where the wonderful gardens ran down to the harbour — to Belize, to Washington. A life oddly untroubled by all that movement. English schools in exotic climates, and the poor glimpsed through the windows of the polished cars that always whisked us from the airport. And then mother died — while I was at Coniston. I was ten and a boarder and father was in Saudi Arabia where we couldn't go. I can remember being told. I was out on the rugby pitches, the snow on the hills. I was called to a cold room, lined with books, and there was a slab of sunshine on the floor which edged away from me as the headmaster talked. University. English at Oxford. Keble, the rain running down those depressing red bricks.

Summers at Jude's Ferry. Always an outsider however hard I tried. Dad didn't tell me he'd sold up to the MoD. I found a letter, about the rent. He said it was a nest egg for me, but he'd sold the only home we'd ever had. And then a heart attack at Sunningdale lecturing to a room full of bored civil servants on a pale afternoon. I scattered his ashes on the beach at Holkham, trying to recall even then what he looked like.

I was alone, so I came back for that last summer to Orchard House. There was nothing else, just a bank account, blinking black on the screen. I was owed it — a year of my own, at home, at last, even if the family had gone.

And I felt a sense of liberation too. So I thought I'd teach. Whittlesea. A new scheme, for graduates, learning on the job. A windswept comprehensive built of concrete and glass with a playground like a supermarket car park. But I loved it; so different from my life until then, chaotic, raw, on the edge. And that's where I met her, Laura. Something's stopping me crossing that line, to what happened next, because there's something there I don't want to remember. But I know the emotions that match the missing pictures: passion first, then guilt. And then anger at last. I'm clinging to these because all I feel today is fear. Which is why it's so important that I know you're there.

Thursday, 19 July

24

'Imber,' said Garry, covering the mouthpiece. 'Jason Imber. He writes scripts for TV – comedy, radio, he's sort of half-famous really. Won a Bafta in '99. Wife turned up this morning – saw his face on the TV. She'd been away, seeing friends, and he'd said he might go to London, so she hadn't missed him till yesterday. House out at Upwell by the Old Course.'

'Imber?' repeated Dryden, knowing instantly where he'd seen the name. But he double-checked the notes he'd made from the TA records Broderick had let him see and there it was: Jason Imber, Orchard House, Jude's Ferry. He wrestled with the chances of a coincidence, but only briefly. Jason Imber had been fished out of the river less than forty-eight hours after the accidental shelling of St Swithun's and the outbuildings by the New Ferry Inn. There had to be a link.

Dryden checked the clock: 10.30am.

DI Shaw was due to ring on the hour with the latest on the animal rights activists. Dryden stood at the coffee machine studying his face in the chrome as the mechanical innards churned. He'd cracked a cheekbone and severely bruised his skull in the scuffle on Thieves Bridge – a set of injuries which had kept him in A&E overnight while they X-rayed his head. Shaw had come to see him in hospital during the night, but would say only that they'd caught one of the men who had met him at the bridge – the one in the boat.

'One?' Dryden had said. 'Oh great. Well, that's a result.

So now the other one is out there telling his mates I doubled-crossed them. Well done, well done. I can look forward to some mindless act of cruelty, can I?'

And there was more bad news. Shaw would now be certain to want him to hold the story for at least a week while they tracked down the second suspect. Dryden closed his eyes as a wave of sleepless nausea swept over him. His skull was numb but a single source of pain hovered behind his left eye. He'd only been home briefly to check Laura was OK and help her into the cab for her session at the unit; he hadn't trusted himself to lie down for half an hour in case sleep engulfed him, and he'd brushed aside her questions about his wound. He'd told Charlie, the news editor, that he'd fallen on the boat, cracking his head on a beam. Garry, predictably, had sneered at this version of events, suspecting alcohol had led to a fight, or at the very least an undignified fall down the wooden gangway of *PK 129*.

Dryden opened his eyes, refocused on the PC screen and began checking the newslist for that week's edition of *The Crow*, rereading the stories on the schedule that had his name on them. He was laboriously running through a 500-word screed about local planning decisions when the phone rang. It was Shaw, on the handsfree, his breathing matching a fast walking pace.

'Hi. Hi. I promised, sorry I'm early. We camped out here at Jude's Ferry overnight to get through the rest of the forensics, we've been up since dawn. Is this OK for you?'

'Yup. Bad news, right? I'm guessing I have to hold?'

'Indeed.' Dryden heard a door shut and the sound of the wind disappeared. He imagined him standing in front of the trestle table in the makeshift office at the New Ferry Inn, mapping out exactly what he was going to say. 'We haven't charged the man we arrested at Thieves Bridge – we're still playing him out for information. He's talking. He's not saying a lot, but he's talking. The other one's on the run, but we know the route – he may even take us where we want to go – a safe house in the Midlands. The unit here has located some activists who meet on an airfield, renting one of the old sheds. If we can catch our runaway suspect trying to make contact at the airfield we've hit the jackpot. The unit's guess is they're using the sheds to store the stuff they use for raids – spray cans, wire cutters, shotguns. They may even have some "liberated" animals on the site. So yes, we'd all appreciate a bit more time. We don't know if the leadership knows the drop-off was a set-up last night. We don't know if they know we've got someone in custody. Just a few days, Dryden.'

'An airfield?' said Dryden, ignoring the question, recognizing its inherently rhetorical nature. Instead he remembered the background sounds to the call he'd taken on the mobile from the local activists, a plane wheeling in the sky, then returning.

Before Shaw could answer Dryden told him his plans for the Skeleton Man story in that week's *Crow*, plans he did not intend to alter. 'You know what I've got on the body in the cellar. I'm using the lot today. Plus I've been working on the ID. According to my calculations there were eight possible victims – given that our man is not from out of town. I've talked to one – Jimmy Neate. You've talked to Mark Smith – what about the other brother?'

'No go. Part of the problem is that there are, naturally, a lot of Matthew Smiths in the world. And the one we're looking for might be in the morgue. So there's no point throwing manpower at it until we've got the DNA results.'

'Sure. So he's still your best guess for our friend in the cellar then?'

'Yes. But don't quote me, please. You're going to be a mile ahead of the rest of the pack on this story and I'd like them to think you got at least some of it from your other sources.'

'Right – but I can use the fight in the pub, the argument over money?' Dryden took silence for assent. 'Then today . . .'

'Indeed. Ely's been in touch, an ID on the man fished out of the river. Someone smart spotted the name on the list of possible victims we'd circulated to local stations. Plus he'd mentioned Jude's Ferry, of course; apparently he thinks he was born there.'

It was Dryden's turn to take refuge in silence.

'So we can take Jason Imber off the list as well,' said Shaw.

'How about putting him on another list instead – the list of suspects?'

Shaw hesitated, but Dryden knew the detective owed him a brace of favours after the failure to secure his safety on the previous night's exercise. Not only had he played a key part in getting the police operation an arrest, he'd taken a beating on their behalf.

'Possibly,' said Shaw. 'We're interviewing him now. My DS has gone out to the unit. There might be a link – it could have pushed him over the edge, literally. If he was involved he must have thought the crime was long forgotten. So perhaps it was a suicide attempt. But like I said, this isn't down to one man. There's got to be a conspiracy, and he can only be part of that. But we're interviewing him, you can report that.'

'Perhaps he met someone out at the bridge.'

Dryden heard pages turning. 'Maybe. A woman did come forward, a birdwatcher. She'd been up by the bridge the day before and said there was a car parked up off the road with a man in the passenger seat.'

'Passenger seat?' said Dryden.

'That's what she said. Said he gave her a filthy look so she didn't hang about. Description roughly fits Imber, but then it would fit half the population of East Anglia. But the car was a 4x4, black. Imber drives a red Audi.'

'Passenger seat,' said Dryden, thinking about it. 'What about the bones from Peyton's tomb? Tell us anything?'

'A woman. Pathologist says death occurred less than thirty years ago, but at the moment we can't say how old she was when she died. Teeth aren't great but that could just be poor dental care. The lot was wrapped up in a piece of carpet, pretty much rotten but design and threads point to 1950s. Cause of death is conjecture at this point, and possibly all points in the future too. There's not a lot left to examine. But we can get some DNA from the bones. And there are two chips to consecutive ribs on the left side, a sharp metal object had been thrust between them causing small fractures in both.'

'A knife wound?'

'Yeah. Or an accident. Could have been inflicted long before death of course, that's the problem. We need to talk to the vicar and to Peyton, find out if there were any later burials from the Peyton family. If not we've got another puzzle on our hands.'

Shaw rang off while Dryden checked the clock: he had half an hour to write up the story on Jude's Ferry for the front page.

But an image hung before him – those metal fillings catching the floodlight on Thieves Bridge. A woman's bones? Magda Hollingsworth perhaps? But hardly a suicide in that case – unless it was a very tidy suicide. Murder? Had someone decided Magda knew more than she should – and that she'd written it all down in her diary? He glugged some coffee, focusing instead on the blinking cursor of the computer screen, and attacked the keyboard . . .

EXCLUSIVE

By Philip Dryden

Detectives were yesterday (Thursday) interviewing a 41-year-old man in connection with the discovery of the so-called 'Skeleton Man' found hanging in a cellar in the abandoned village of Jude's Ferry.

'We are hoping this man may be able to give us information which will help us identify the victim quickly, and even give us a lead to the identity of his killer, or killers,' said a detective helping to lead the inquiry.

Mr Jason Imber, a TV scriptwriter from Upwell, will be questioned by detectives from the inquiry team now based in the village of Jude's Ferry, which was evacuated in 1990 to make way for military exercises.

Mr Imber was rescued from the River Ouse two days after the Skeleton Man's remains were revealed in a cellar in the village following a live artillery firing exercise involving Ely TA soldiers.

He was taken to the Oliver Zangwill Centre at Ely's Princess of Wales Hospital where he is being treated for amnesia under police protection. A hospital spokesman said his memory was slowly returning.

Mrs Elizabeth Imber identified her husband after the police released pictures taken at the unit to the media. She travelled to Ely yesterday to visit her husband but was not available for comment.

Mr Imber lost fingers from his right hand during his ordeal and it is believed he may have become entangled with a boat propeller after falling from Cuckoo Bridge, north of the city.

Mr Imber was a teacher at Whittlesea High School before becoming a TV scriptwriter.

Meanwhile police are keen to talk to Matthew Smith, a former builder and decorator who was involved in a violent argument in Jude's Ferry on the night before the final evacuation.

'Mr Smith was seen leaving the village pub that last evening and we are very keen to contact him so that we can eliminate him from our inquiries,' said the detective.

Police have released a picture of his brother – Mark – in the hope that he still bears a strong likeness to his twin. It is understood the brothers were involved in an argument over setting up a new business. It is possible that Matthew Smith is now known by a different name.

Detectives based at King's Lynn are working on the hypothesis that the victim, a man aged 20–35, was murdered by a lynch mob in the final days before the village's evacuation in 1990.

A thorough examination of the cellar in which the Skeleton Man was found has revealed another bizarre twist – an empty grave, dug and refilled.

'Perhaps it was designed for the victim,' said the detective, who declined to be named. 'But instead it was neatly filled in. It is a bizarre development in a difficult case.'

Forensic scientists are examining a cigarette butt found in the refilled grave. It is of a common Spanish brand, another example of which was found in the cellar itself. Samples have been sent for DNA analysis.

Several other items found at the scene, including a twist of fibreglass and some ornamental gravel, are being examined further.

Police are working on the initial premise that the victim is a former resident of Jude's Ferry. They are trying to contact men of the right age to eliminate them from their inquiries.

Any reader who might be able to help them should ring Freephone 0700 800 600.

Dryden pressed his fists into his eye sockets and thought about the rope tightening around the Skeleton Man's neck. He tried to imagine the years passing, the body rotting in its undisturbed tomb. Why had the cellar lain undiscovered for those years?

'Flanders May,' he said out loud, remembering the 'perfectionist' Major Broderick had said oversaw the survey of the village in the months after the evacuation. He Googled the name and found two references, the first to the regimental history and his role in mapping several British military installations in India in the months before independence, and the second to the Royal Society of Cartographers. Colonel Flanders May DSO had been president in 2003 and an e-mail address was provided. Dryden jotted down two questions and sent the message, betting himself he'd never get an answer.

He picked up a photocopy of the picture of Mark Smith that DI Shaw had released. They were not, apparently, identical twins but there was enough in the face to help prompt an ID: the narrow skull, the heavy jaw which seemed to throw the whole off balance, the weak fleshy nose. Dryden reread his story and filed it.

Then he added an extra paragraph:

Police have said that their inquiries at the scene will be completed by Saturday morning. The range will reopen for live firing on Sunday. All roads into the range area are already closed to traffic. A maroon will sound at 9.30am and 9.55am from the firing range HQ at Whittlesea Lane End. Artillery will begin live shelling at 10.00am. A combined forces exercise will follow involving units from the TA and US forces based at nearby RAF Lakenheath. Live ammunition and artillery will be used.

25

Humph and Dryden headed north through a curtain of St Swithun's rain towards Jason Imber's home at Upwell. The village was deserted except for a murder of crows tearing at the squashed flesh of a large rat in a gutter. The house lay along a drove by the church behind an ugly high wall and a protective ring of pines. At the gate an expensive, polished intercom panel appeared to work, but there was no answer.

'Scriptwriting pays then,' said Dryden, flopping back into the passenger seat after briefly inspecting the gates. 'There's a car in the drive that looks like a Porsche.'

'What else do we know?' asked Humph, a single yawn threatening to suck all the air out of the cab's damp interior.

'Well – back in 1990 he was twenty-four. He lived at Orchard House – which sounds posh I guess. That's it. His wife's called Elizabeth, there're no kids. He says he remembers nothing. He's got four fingers missing from his right hand.'

Humph nodded, looking at his watch. 'I gotta give blood,' he said, giving the large ham that was his upper arm a pre-emptive massage.

The cabbie was proud of his charitable donation of red corpuscles, a selfless act only partly inspired by the free chocolate biscuits.

Dryden took some pictures at the gate and chatted to the shopkeeper at the post office. Imber was known locally, gave to charity, walked a dog, but in the phrase dreaded by all reporters otherwise 'kept himself to himself'. His wife, it was thought, was in publishing and worked in London, travelling up at weekends.

Dryden reflected that Imber had one of those lives which become more elusive as you add detail.

'You can drop me at the unit. Laura's in the gym and we might as well see how chummy's doing. My guess is the police have some tricky questions for Jason Imber and that amnesia is no longer an acceptable answer to any of them.'

Dryden tried to sleep on the journey back but the injured cheekbone throbbed and his head ached behind his eyes. By the time they got back to Ely a summer mist had descended, cloaking teeming rain, wet and enveloping, the water running in broad streams down the 1930s stucco façade of the Oliver Zangwill Centre.

Dryden kept his head down as he ran from the cab to the automatic doors and was still shaking the water from his thick black hair when he saw that the reception area was empty except for one figure: Major John Broderick. He was in uniform, back straight, hands held clasped on his lap, holding the peak of his cap.

The soldier's back stiffened as Dryden took the seat on his other side.

'Hi,' said Dryden, having little option than to try a jovial tone. 'That legend about St Swithun's Day – forty days and forty nights – that's just an old wives' tale, right?'

Broderick laughed. 'There's a long way to go,' he said, shaking some droplets of water from the cap.

'Visiting?' said Dryden, aware that the question veered dangerously towards the obvious.

Broderick nodded, leaning forward and moving some tattered magazines around a tabletop like chess pieces.

'My wife's a patient,' said Dryden, trying for empathy if not sympathy.

Still nothing. Dryden stretched out his overlong legs. 'You never said what business you were in.'

Broderick ran a finger along the peak of the cap. 'Wholesale flowers. We import exotics, distribute within eastern England from local growers.'

Dryden nodded. 'So it runs in the family – or is it the same business? Blooms Nursery, if I recall correctly. You didn't mention your father's business in Jude's Ferry,' he said. 'Which was odd, wasn't it?'

Broderick turned slightly in his chair so that he could look Dryden in the eyes. The reporter didn't like what he saw. Nor did Broderick. 'You been in a fight?' he asked.

'Fell downstairs,' said Dryden. 'So what's so secret about you and Jude's Ferry?'

'Sorry, but you don't really have a right to ask these questions.'

'Really? It was a free country when I got up this morning – did I miss the coup? I think you'll find I can ask what questions I like – and you have the right not to answer them. Subtle difference, often lost on the military mind, if that isn't an oxymoron.'

Open hostilities were interrupted by the nurse at the desk. Cupping a hand over a phone she tried to catch Broderick's attention. 'Mr Imber will be free in about ten minutes, Major.'

Broderick nodded, blushing.

'He's still with the police,' she added, replacing the receiver soundlessly.

Dryden let the silence lengthen, sensing Broderick's acute discomfort.

The major stood abruptly. 'I'll take a walk,' he said, heading for the doors.

Dryden joined him uninvited, the rain covering his face in a refreshing layer of cool water almost instantly. The 1930s design of the hospital included a covered walkway which skirted the building at ground level. Broderick took refuge there, and Dryden followed, matching the immediate brisk pace.

'So . . .' he said.

'I visited,' said Broderick.

Dryden had lost the thread. 'Sorry?'

'I didn't live in Jude's Ferry. I visited. Although, as I have said, it is none of your business. I was brought up near Stamford, my mother's house. She runs a garden centre, flowers again – it was what they had in common; as it turns out about the only thing they had in common. My parents were separated. I was in the TA at university – Cambridge – and as I said we dealt with the transport for the evacuation. But that was in Ely. Father left home when I was three and moved, took half the business with him, and again in '90, but he'd really lost interest by then – he couldn't do the heavy work at all and he didn't really like relying on other people. He spent a lot of his time in a wheelchair. He died in '96. I inherited the business, diversified, merged it with Mum's. We don't grow ourselves any more.'

They stopped where the building came to an end, with a view out over a soaking field of carrot tops across which tiptoed a black cat with a tail like a question mark.

'He must have missed you, when you were away. I've spoken to a few of the villagers and they said he liked having . . . you know . . . a boy around.'

It wasn't very subtle and Dryden had the good grace to blush. Broderick laughed. 'Village gossip, Dryden. Father's weaknesses were far more conventional – which is why my mother threw him out. She threw him out several times in fact, and each time it was over a different woman. So your thinly veiled aspersion is wide of the mark.

'He liked having young people around – although I can't say that was ever that obvious when his only son visited.'

Broderick looked away, embarrassed by the sudden intimacy.

'My visits were pretty stilted affairs, I'm afraid. I tried to make him happy.' Broderick's hand wandered to the sharp edge of the military cap. 'He seemed to find happiness in other people. It's as simple as that, sometimes life is, although people like you might find it hard to believe.'

Dryden didn't bite, he'd been equally judgemental about soldiers.

'And Jason Imber? What did you have in common?' He looked up at the curving façade of the unit. 'What do you have in common?'

'Father knew the Imbers. They had the big house – Orchard House. It was what passed for a social set in Jude's Ferry; that, the doctor and her husband, and a couple of old biddies out on the Whittlesea Road, and that was polite society. Jane Austen would have struggled.'

They laughed, walking round the end of the old hospital block and into the lee side out of the rain. Through the plate glass window they looked into one of the lounges set aside for patients. Several sat reading, but few turned any pages.

'You've kept in touch?' prompted Dryden.

'Yes. When I did go to Jude's Ferry it was often university vacation and Jason would be at home too, and that last year he was teaching in Whittlesea, up the road. We hung out together a bit. Jason's funny – that's why he writes comedy so well. The village wasn't a very welcoming place for us, well, for anyone who hadn't been born there. Being the son of a retired colonel and a Cambridge undergraduate didn't seem to help – odd, eh?'

Dryden smiled, wondering how bitter he really was.

'So Jason and I had that in common: being newcomers. We'd stick together, go down the inn, see if they could ignore us all night. Things were better that last summer because Jason was teaching at the college, so he did know some of them, even if it was just to shout at them. He said the place was pretty rough, real blackboard jungle. Loved it for some reason,' he added, shaking his head.

Broderick looked up at the clouds. 'We lost contact in the nineties, but I saw his name often enough: in those lists at the end of comedy shows, the writers. Then I got an invite to the wedding, so we've kept in touch since. He moved out to Upwell, I live at Guyhirn, so by Fen standards we're neighbours.'

'And the wife – Elizabeth?'

'Yes. I've met her a few times, wedding obviously, and she came to the regimental fundraiser with Jason. Yeah – the wives got on, she was a nice woman, smart too.'

'Why'd you think he chucked himself off a bridge then?'

Broderick couldn't stop a hand wandering towards his throat. 'God knows.'

'Ever go back to the old house, your father's?'

'Occasionally. The exercises utilize all the properties.'

It was an oddly cold remark, Dryden thought.

'What about the last night?'

Broderick looked through him. 'I visited in the morning, I think, then got back to Ely. I was on the transport, like I said – a big job.'

They had their backs to the windows and they both turned as the wind, picking up suddenly, rustled the pines ahead of them and threw rain in their faces. They found themselves looking in on a long room. At one end there was a TV showing horse racing, and at a table four men played cards. In one corner there was a patient in a wheelchair. It was Jason Imber, the neatly cut hair framing the handsome face and the well-bred jawline. Laura Dryden was in her wheelchair too, holding his hand, watching tears run freely over the expensively tanned skin.

26

Humph was waiting for him in the Capri, a piece of surgical gauze held to his arm by a small plaster. The cabbie was listening to his language tape but still managed to exude a sense of painful self-sacrifice, one hand fluttering, but never quite touching, the wound.

Dryden got in and kicked out his long legs.

Humph disconnected the earphones and flipped down the glove compartment, retrieving two bottles of sambuca, cracking the tops of both and offering one to the reporter.

'Lunch,' he said, adding a packet of BBQ-flavoured crisps. 'How's Laura?' he asked.

Dryden flipped down the vanity mirror and looked at his bottle-green eyes. How was Laura? It was a question he seemed, suddenly, least qualified to answer. He'd seen her briefly while Major Broderick had visited Jason Imber. She'd asked him then, again, about the bruising on his face, holding his head in her hands, and he'd told her about Thieves Bridge, the animal rights activists and the woman's bones recovered from the Peyton grave, the ribs chipped by a blade. He talked about being afraid, and about not showing it.

'You should tell me about these things,' she said, her lips touching his ear. 'We talk about what you do, but we don't talk about you and how you feel.'

Dryden knew she was right, but he went on talking about what he did.

'There's this copper on the case, called Shaw, Peter Shaw. He's kind of weird really. Young, driven, knows his stuff on

217

the science, a real high flyer too, but then his dad was a DCI so everyone probably thinks he's had it easy. But I don't think so – Dad got chucked off the force a decade ago for fabricating evidence. I think it's chewing him up, driving him on. It's frightening you know, being around someone that focused.'

They'd laughed then and he'd taken the opportunity to tell her what he really feared. 'Don't get too close to Jason Imber, Laura – we don't know what happened to him. Help, there's nothing wrong with that. But remember he can't – he doesn't know what he did, who he was. That could be a shock when he does find out.'

She shrugged, but Dryden could sense the irritation. 'I just listen. I read the messages he sends,' she said, touching her laptop. 'He reads mine. I tell him about us, about your stories. It helps. He's got nothing else to think about but missing memories, Philip.'

She closed her eyes, seeing that Dryden's antagonism was undiminished. 'Please, my neck.'

He'd massaged her shoulders then, knowing the long silence was a reproach.

Dryden rummaged in the glove compartment for a refill. Laura's relationship with a man who might be a murderer disturbed him. What he couldn't admit was that what really troubled him was that she had a relationship with someone else at all.

He rang DI Shaw on the mobile.

'Tell me you've caught the other one,' said Dryden before the detective could speak.

'We still think he's on his way to Coventry. He got the National Coach out of Cambridge yesterday for Nottingham, he's on the CCTV. We've lost him at the other end, but he's getting close. We know where he's going, we just have to wait.'

Dryden inhaled some more alcohol. 'Anything breaking I need to know about on the Skeleton Man?'

'We've got a match on the gravel we found in the cellar . . .'

'Orchard House, right?' said Dryden. 'Jason Imber's home.'

'Indeed. But it isn't good enough for a courtroom – we'd be laughed out. It just helps if we get something else that puts him at the scene. And we'll be interviewing Imber again once he's recovered from the wounds to his hand. Forty-eight hours, perhaps a bit longer. He's not going anywhere in the meantime.'

'Charges?'

Shaw laughed and Dryden could hear him tapping a computer screen. 'Imber's keeping a secret. But the doctors say he's genuine about the memory loss. We can't push it, not now. Even if he did it we're still short of a few crucial elements in our case, don't you think – like a motive, the identity of the victim, the names of his accomplices, and any rationale at all which puts him in the river.'

'Anything else on forensics?'

But Shaw did not intend to be pushed any further. Dryden's deadline had gone, and with it some of his purchasing power. 'I'm not aware I have a duty to update you in real time, Dryden – let's have a chat after the weekend, OK?'

Dryden cut him off, angry that their deal had left him with one story he couldn't print and another which made little sense. But the anger worked, as it often did, fusing two images in his memory – the gently turning bones of the Skeleton Man on his hook in the cellar and Humph, running a finger around the patch on his arm where the blood had been taken.

Dryden snapped his fingers, knowing just how much it annoyed the cabbie.

'Surgical gauze,' he said. 'The Skeleton Man had a patch of surgical gauze on his arm.'

'So – that's narrowed it down, has it?' asked Humph. 'We're looking for a blood donor. Is Tony Hancock the victim?'

'Jabs,' said Dryden. 'When are you likely to need an injection as an adult?'

Humph tipped a packet of crisps back so that the last grains of monosodium glutamate could trickle down his throat.

'Inoculation – a trip abroad?'

'Correct. George Tudor was about to emigrate to Australia, so was Peter Tholy.' Dryden recalled the tape they'd listened to on the riverside. Tudor had said he'd got a reference from the vicar of St Swithun's – Fred Lake.

Dryden fished out the telephone number he'd dug from Crockford's directory and rang on the mobile, letting a minute pass as he imagined the phone echoing in an empty house. Then a child answered, confident and clear, running to fetch Fred Lake. While he waited Dryden thought of the voice on the tape he'd played on the riverbank, and the more distant memory of meeting him on that final day. He recalled a disdain for tradition and the fabric of the old church, and a mildly trendy upbeat emphasis on community, and the treacly remains of that South African accent.

Dryden tried to conjure up his face from that last day in Jude's Ferry, but the image was elusive, overshadowed by more potent images – an old woman crying on her doorstep, the men on the bench outside the almshouses watching the army clear the cottages along The Dring.

Footsteps clipped across an institutional floor. 'Sorry,' said Lake quickly, out of breath. 'Summer holidays. We run a club. I shouldn't say it, but it's hell. Believe me, I should know, it's my job.'

They both laughed. The accent was flatter, less distinct after seventeen years, diluted by the estuary English of King's

Lynn's overspill estates. Dryden did his pitch, nearly perfect. He was writing a feature to run with the latest news on the body found at Jude's Ferry. He needed a ten-minute chat, nothing personal, just a feel for the place and those last few hours in the life of a community. Community: the key word.

'Sure. The police have called too – I'm seeing a detective in the morning at St Bartholomew's – perhaps they're expecting a confession.' Dryden didn't know if he was joking so he said nothing. 'But like I said, we've got forty kids here and we're off to the beach . . . packed lunches, I'm afraid, no room for a proper Cape barbie.'

Dryden let the silence deepen a few more seconds. 'Just ten minutes.'

'Well, all right, all right. Let's say the pier at Hunstanton, at three. We'll eat on the grass opposite the entrance. There's a big pub there and they let us use the loos. Know where we are?'

Dryden knew it, had spent a childhood's worth of summers on the wide expanse of sand, and a small fortune in pocket money in the jangling arcades. Humph drove north and they stopped for chips at a roadside van where the owner brought the food out to the cab.

'I rang ahead,' said Humph, by way of explanation, passing on a polystyrene plate layered with fish, chips and processed peas. Dryden got out to put his food on the Capri's roof, a hotplate of peeling paint. They were in the shadow of an oak tree by the old A10. Looking west Dryden could see the grey-blue sweep of The Wash, waves of brilliant white surf marking the incoming tide, a distant charcoal line the coast of Lincolnshire. He dragged in a lungful of air and despite the carbon monoxide caught the exhilarating whiff of ozone.

By the time they reached Hunstanton the car reeked of

lost holidays; over-heated plastic tussling with vinegar and petrol. On the green above the pier a few couples lay, entwined listlessly in the sun. By an ice-cream hut a group of children sat on the ground eviscerating plastic lunchboxes with manic concentration. Lake stood, cradling a half-pint glass of beer, and Dryden knew him then, remembering the anonymous face, the defeated shoulders. His hair had thinned and was now stretched in individual strands across his skull, a touch of vanity which robbed a still-young face of what youth was left. He wore a white shirt, the neck open, the collar frayed, and his narrow limbs, folded now to sit on the grass, seemed to bulge at the joints.

Dryden was just a few feet away when Lake smiled, clearing a space on a dusty Greek beach mat. 'I thought so,' said Lake. 'I told my wife I'd met you before. That last day at the Ferry, yes? I'm right, aren't I?'

Dryden smiled a reply and took a plastic cup of orange squash from a small diligent girl who offered it, remembering for the first time that he'd liked Fred Lake when he'd met him, liked the irrational high spirits and the absence of personal vanity, the frankness, despite the weight of responsibility which seemed to crush him.

'I wanted to ask a few questions about Jude's Ferry. The police are trying to identify the skeleton they found in the cellar. There was an audio tape made before the final evacuation . . .'

Lake stood, touching a teenage boy on the shoulder as he passed out of the group. 'If – no, when – they threaten to riot, buy them ice creams. I'll just be ten . . .' he said, putting a twenty-pound note into his empty half-pint and pressing it into the boy's hand. 'My son,' said Lake, by way of explanation, as they walked down onto the hot, crowded sands. They retreated into the shadows beneath the pier, where the light shone in stripes through the decking above, creating a world lit through a venetian blind. Lake sat on damp pebbles and, producing a small tin of tobacco, began to roll a cigarette. 'My secret, when I can get away,' he said, lighting up and letting the smoke caress his face. 'And I promised I'd keep out of the sun.'

They sat on a steep bank which dipped down to the sand. 'George Tudor,' said Dryden. 'He said on the tape that you'd acted as a character reference, I think, for his application to emigrate. I thought you might have kept in touch?'

A skidoo whined out at sea, and Lake watched as a kite surfer rose out of the sea, twisted, and splashed back into a wave.

'Not a word from George, I'm afraid. I think it was Perth in the end, that's what he said anyway. But no, nothing, I contacted the church there as well to provide some help when he arrived but they never saw him. Still, we don't do these things to be thanked. It's just nice when it happens.'

Dryden didn't laugh. Lake passed a hand over his eyes and took a quick drag on the cigarette butt before drilling it down into the sand. 'You don't think it's George in the cellar?'

Dryden shrugged. 'Seventeen years is a long time. The police'll check him out. When was the last time you saw him?'

'Oh, I remember that all too well. It was in the church, that last night at a burial service.'

Dryden tried not to react, sitting back instead and using his elbows to angle his face into the slated sun.

'A burial? Who?' he asked, his eyes closed.

'Well. Er, where to start?' Lake closed his eyes. 'Jude's Ferry had its own special problems, but it had all the normal ones too. Like teenage pregnancies. That last summer there was a kid – just fifteen – who fell pregnant. That's very English, isn't it – that "fell" – makes it sound as if she could make herself pregnant. Anyway, this girl – Kathryn Neate – gave birth to a baby boy just before the final evacuation of the village. The doctor asked some questions, as did social services, but Kathryn wasn't telling who the father was and, frankly, it was her life. She'd kept it secret as long as she could and it was too late to get rid of the child. And she was torn anyway, between hating it and wanting someone to love. She was a lonely kid and sometimes people get confused about what love is. Anyway, when it all came out the family reacted badly. Especially her father.'

'He ran the garage on Church Street?' prompted Dryden, but he was thinking of something else; Magda Hollingsworth labouring over her diary, struggling with her conscience over the death of a child, before deciding to confront the mother over the rumour that she had killed her son. And the diary code entry for the child's mother L.O. – each letter one place on in the alphabet from K.N.

Lake didn't hear the question, wrapped now in his own memory. 'Walter, the father, odd bloke – I guess aloof is being kind. He loved Kathryn, but it was sadly not the unqualified love that kids really need. Walter's wife had died fairly young and I think he saw Kathryn as a kind of reincarnation – a symbol that she wasn't gone completely from his life. Weird, but then the Ferry wasn't a living example of robust mental health at the best of times. Anyway, it's pretty clear Kathryn's unwanted pregnancy didn't fit Walter's vision of his daughter, let's put it like that.'

Lake turned his head up to catch the thin slats of sunshine. 'Sadly the boy didn't survive. The delivery was at home and premature. There were complications – jaundice, I think – and he died less than forty-eight hours after the birth from heart failure. Kathryn, a child really, was in bits, not surprisingly, but that lack of maturity made it worse, if that's possible

224

to imagine. She came to me, alone, and asked if the baby could be buried at St Swithun's. I've often thought what a clever idea that was. She could visit him then, but only once a year when the villagers were allowed back for the annual service. It was a way of limiting her grief, I think, but still honouring her son.'

Lake was rolling up a fresh cigarette, agitated by the story he was telling. A wave broke out on the sand, the white water catching the sun.

'So, did you bury her son?'

'Yes. It was the last burial at St Swithun's. But it wasn't easy – there were two hurdles to jump. First, we had to rush through the paperwork and get the coroner to issue the death certificate. But we were lucky – I had contacts, and even in bureaucracies people can sometimes let kindness bend the rules. But the real problem was where to bury the child. Legally we'd been banned from burials in the graveyard from the point at which the MoD served its notice. They did not, and never have, guaranteed that the churchyard will not be damaged, you see – it's technically part of the range. But the church is listed so they had at least to give an undertaking that they would seek to preserve it – especially as they'd told many of the villagers that they'd all be back within the year. But obviously a burial in the church is very difficult. Happily, there was a solution.'

He turned to Dryden, the stripes of shadow shifting over his soft features. 'You know of the Peyton family?' he asked, and Dryden felt the hairs on his neck rise.

'Sure. There's a tomb in the nave. It was damaged in the bombardment that went astray.'

Lake nodded vigorously. 'Quite. Well, they were the patrons of the church – the Peytons – and we used to get visitors from the US on a very regular basis. It's a very distinguished family, Founding Fathers and such. There's actually a family association – in Baltimore – which made regular and substantial donations to the cost of the upkeep of the church and the tomb. Crucially, they similarly fund a church in Lincolnshire which holds the family vault of the other senior branch of the original family. They clearly had to be informed about the MoD's plans for Jude's Ferry, and they were pretty upset.

'The long and the short of it is that they paid to have the vault emptied at St Swithun's, and the remains transferred to Lincolnshire. I did try to argue for a year's grace to see if the MoD would let the residents back but their view, an understandable one, was that they needed prompt and reliable access for their members. Their solution means visitors can pay their respects in one spot. There was also talk of moving the funeral casket and its statuary but I'm afraid English Heritage put their foot down there. Perhaps not the best decision, considering what's happened.'

Lake stopped, and seemed to have lost his thread.

'So, when Kathryn Neate's baby . . .'

'Indeed. Technically the Peyton tomb had been handed back to the parish and because the army had suggested the villagers might soon be returned to Jude's Ferry the church remained consecrated – as it still is, by the way, although I suspect not for long. So St Swithun's was available for burials. Kathryn Neate's baby won't be the first cuckoo in the nest in St Swithun's – over the years I'm sure many of the vaults were reused. The bones were often dug up and put in the ossuary – the bone room, it's just off the nave and a very fine, and rare, example in England. They're much more common on the continent of course, where graves are reused all the time to save space.'

Dryden nodded, recalling the small Gothic doorway in St

Swithun's he'd tried on the morning of the bombardment.

'We held the service on that last night, at dusk. It's bizarre but it was also very beautiful. Colonel Broderick had heard about the service and had sent up flowers from his fields – lilies mainly, I mean hundreds of them, beautifully arranged. It was quite sensational actually, the smell was just astonishing, and I'm not a big fan of that kind of thing, but even I thought it made the service special. I think Kathryn was overwhelmed.

'The brother, James, dug the grave with his father. Walter had been the sexton for twenty years, he seemed determined to carry on despite the fact it was his own grandson. The service was not well attended. They were ashamed of Kathryn and angry too, so the rest of the village kept its distance. Exactly what they shouldn't have done, but there it was. It was really difficult. All those emotions, bottled up.'

Dryden searched his face where the shadows fell.

'We were stood around the tomb, I remember, and we'd lowered the small casket down. Walter had made it with as much love as he could muster – but there was no name, no mark at all. It was St Swithun's Day of course, and the sun had shone. The village was quiet. There were events planned for later – a dance at the Methodist Hall, games at the inn, and fireworks for after dark – but just then, around five, it was very quiet. And then the door opened and in came George Tudor. He walked up the aisle and found Kathryn, and he took her hand. And they stood there, together, as we covered the child's coffin over with earth. I always thought it was the bravest thing, what George did. He knew Walter and James and I think he knew they didn't have it in them to comfort Kathryn, not in public. George was a bachelor, childless, and I think he felt she should have someone with her, that it was wrong just to let a child bury a child alone.

And he was a cousin too, on the mother's side, I think. No doubt the tongues wagged, of course. And who knows, perhaps he was the father. I left them then, when the service was over, but I heard voices later from the vicarage – they were still in the church. Angry voices.'

Dryden nodded, pressing on. 'So. If someone opened that grave now, today, they'd find a small casket and the bones of a newborn child?'

'That's right. The paperwork was all in order. The death was properly registered. And there he lies, Mr Dryden, just two days old, and nothing to take with him but his name – Jude.'

Dryden tried to picture the scene. Dusk falling over the village, and the Neate family making its way home down Church Hill.

'So the service was at five – what time did they go home? Did George go with them?'

Lake looked up at the sky through the gaps in the wood above. 'It was all over in twenty minutes. I went back to the vicarage and I saw them leave about half past five – I know it was then because we had a little party planned at the vicarage and that's when people started arriving. And yes, I think George Tudor went back with them.'

'Did you see Kathryn again?'

'No. But I went down to Neate's Garage later – about eight.'

'Why?'

'Before the burial service Kathryn had asked a favour. She wanted to get into Peterborough the next morning and asked if we'd give her a lift. She didn't say but I know her social worker was there and she'd been in before, when she was pregnant. As I say, I didn't ask, but the fact that she didn't explain suggests that was where she was going. I don't think the family approved of the social worker, of any outsider really, getting involved in the family's business. The Neates were going straight to the new garage the next morning, so she was stuck.'

'So you gave her a lift?'

'I said yes at the time but then we decided, later on, that we'd drive up that night and leave the removal men to load up in peace the following morning. So I went down to say that perhaps they would take her if I had a word – but she'd have to get up to the vicarage by nine or they'd probably be off – we'd packed all the crates, you see, and we didn't have a lot of furniture of our own. A lot of the church's stuff had been sold at an auction in the village the week before – that's what a lot of people did.

'Anyway, I had to let her know that the arrangements had changed and she'd have to try her luck.'

'And?'

'Nothing. She wasn't in. Jimmy answered the door and we went into the kitchen. George was still there and they'd been drinking, there was a half-drunk bottle of whisky on the table. Walter was upstairs, they said, sleeping it off. I just told them to give her the message, that I couldn't help with the lift.'

'What was the atmosphere like? You said they'd argued in the church.'

Lake shrugged. 'Like I said, George was family really so I guess they'd cleared the air.'

'And that was it?'

'That was it. I thought about going into the village to try and find her but it was late by then and dusk was falling. I could see lights down on The Dring where the dance was on, people out in the street, music. The last thing young people want to see when they're enjoying themselves is a dog collar.'

Dryden nodded. 'Did you see anyone else that night, before you left?'

'A few. As I said, we had this little party, well a few drinks, for the sidesmen, the organist, the women who helped with the old people's club, and the ringers, of course – those that were left and still sober. And my wife went down to the almshouses to bring Joyce Crane up – she was ninety then. We would have brought the others up, the men, but they were already in the inn. Free beer, you see. Our invitation was not the first on the list of attractions.'

Dryden nodded.

Lake raised a finger to his lips. 'And Magda.'

'Magda Hollingsworth?' Dryden could see her now, bent over her diary, setting down the story of the girl who'd threatened to kill her baby.

'Yes. I remember because I told the police, when they got in contact later after they found she was missing. I said she'd had problems with depression and suchlike but that I never thought she'd harm herself. But I saw her that last night, yes, walking out along Church Street, out of the village, towards Telegraph Hill. That was later – just before eight, just before I went down to the garage.'

'Was that unusual, to see her out there?'

'No. Magda was a great walker, which caused a bit of a scandal – I mean talk about narrow-minded. They said it was gypsy blood, that she couldn't bear to be inside a house for long. Rubbish! That woman loved her home. I think it was losing it that broke her. She'd often go up there and sit by the water tower with a book – another dangerous eccentricity in Fen eyes, I'm afraid. My wife liked her, said she really cared about the place, the village community. But she was a bit much for most people – ankle bracelets, that kind of thing. They thought of her as a gypsy. And you couldn't say a lot worse than that in Jude's Ferry.'

Lake held up a hand, aware he'd gone too far. 'She had friends in the village, good friends. Not everyone tried to cast her out. Bob Steward – one of our churchwardens – used to work for the water board, it was his job to check the tower every week and the water quality. He'd often find her up there on the grass, enjoying the solitude. I told her once that if she really wanted peace and serenity she could always sit in the church.' He laughed. 'Didn't work.'

Suddenly there was a wave of screaming from the surf and they both stirred, as if wakened from a sleep. Dryden switched tack. 'And Peter Tholy – he was a friend of George, wasn't he? Did you help him with his immigration request?'

'Yes. I was amazed he did that, a lot of people were.'

'Why?'

'Just so timid. He was eighteen then, perhaps nineteen, and I really don't think he'd been out of the village but to go to school. But I guess he trusted George, and there was nothing for him here. I did warn him, you know. I said I was an immigrant too and it wasn't all bold new horizons.'

Dryden nodded. 'Nobody else in his life?'

Lake shook his head. 'I knew the family actually, going back a couple of years – his mother went out first to Australia after she remarried. Callous woman, she wanted a new life and I don't think she was particularly bothered if Peter followed her out or not. And there was Broderick, Colonel Broderick, he'd given Peter work and was genuinely concerned for his future I think. A glowing testimonial and references certainly – even if he was a bitter man.'

'Bitter?'

'I don't know much – they were Methodists and

231

worshipped in Whittlesea. But the marriage had failed and the son, the only child, had very much sided with the mother over the years. He visited, in fact he was often here in the holidays, but you could tell they didn't hit it off. So I guess Peter helped fill the gap.'

'So Peter's father, then? Dead?'

'Yes, that's right. Many years before, long before I came to the Ferry in '82. Farm labourer like his son. They were poor, genuinely poor. Those houses along the far side of The Dring were slums. The father had been married before and there were children from that marriage, I think. Anyway, complicated, if not by Fen standards. So plenty of mouths to feed and not much by way of a wage. Incredible, isn't it? People used to stop and take pictures of those cottages, Americans mainly, come to see the church. That's the problem with rural poverty, of course, it's invisible. But it's just as nasty as any ghetto. A little Soweto on Whittlesea Mere.'

'Did you hear from him, from Peter?'

Lake leant back on his elbows. 'Yup. I got cards from Peter and he made contact with the church in, er ... now, where was it? Fremantle, I think. Yes, he was studious at keeping in touch, Christmas cards, that kind of thing. At least for the first few years.'

Dryden nodded.

'But he never mentions George, which is odd now I think of it.'

'Not so odd if George's skeleton was hanging in Jude's Ferry all the time,' said Dryden.

A cloud crossed the coast, the temperature dropping suddenly, and as the rain began to fall the screams of little children filled the afternoon air.

27

They drove back south in silence, Humph lost in the vocabulary of a Faroese banquet, Dryden massaging his battered skull. As they reached Ely the sun finally broke through the mist and lit the cathedral's lantern tower, the damp lead of the vast roof steaming in the sudden warmth. Dryden leant his forehead against the cool glass of the passenger-side window. Fred Lake had complicated the mystery of Jude's Ferry to the point where Dryden found it hard to see any truth clearly. Where were the remains of Kathryn Neate's child? Had she killed him in a bout of depression after the birth? Whose bones had been robbed from the Peyton tomb? And what of the empty grave in the cellar? Had George Tudor's act of compassion in comforting his cousin cost him his life?

Dryden checked his watch: 5.20pm. The early editions of *The Crow* would be printed by now and sometimes the delivery vans dropped some off in the Market Square, offering the paper's loyal readers the chance to read tomorrow's newspaper. The square was still crowded with market stalls, and a children's roundabout played an annoying tune at the wrong speed. Skeg's trestle table was on his pitch beside the Big Business tea bar, but there was no newspaper seller and no *Crow*, just a pile of *Cambridge Evening News'* and an honesty box, although his dog lay tethered to one of the tea-bar tables. Dryden walked briskly to *The Crow*'s offices but there was no sign of any papers there either, and Jean was placating a gaggle of keen customers who'd turned up to get first look at that week's small ads.

Dryden jumped the stairs to the empty newsroom and logged on to check his e-mails. The US Peytons had been in touch.

Dear Mr Dryden,

Thank you for your e-mail – yes, we had been informed, but nevertheless what distressing news! As you may know, the society paid for the removal of the family remains in 1990 but we were unable to transfer the memorial and statuary due to the intervention of English Heritage. In retrospect we consider this decision was short sighted and ill advised. I thought you might like to know that we are reapplying to have the monument moved now – I attach the documentation – and have instigated legal proceedings against the Ministry of Defence for compensation. We hope to have the tomb fully restored in its new position at St John's, Boston, Lincolnshire. Our own architect and restorer, who visited the original site in 1989, estimates the costs of removal and restoration at $360,000. We are reconstructing our website on St Swithun's to accommodate an appeal form and this will be up and running by the end of the month. We hope your readers will be generous in their support.

Yours faithfully

John Peyton Speed

PS. I can't resist a bit of personal history, if you'll forgive me, Mr Dryden. My mother was a Peyton and was able to trace her lineage back to Sir Philip Peyton, one of the part owners of the *Providence*, the ship which made a landfall in Virginia in the third season after the arrival of the

234

Mayflower. Sir Philip's branch of the family had several manors in eastern England – including Nornea Hall at Jude's Ferry – now lost of course but which stood on the site of Orchard House in the village. If you look carefully at the gardens you can still see the ditch which formed the moat. My wife and I had a most wonderful visit to the site in 1985. One of the truly memorable moments of our lives.

PPS. And if you do get the chance to visit the church ask for the key to the ossuary – an extraordinary room which gave us a real sense of all those past generations stretching back into history. Totally unique!

Dryden winced at the tautology in the last line, then sent himself an e-mail reminder to follow up the message on the legal action for compensation with the MoD.

Splash, the office cat, appeared and sat on his keyboard, a line of question marks appearing on screen. The touch of the fur brought back an image, the teenage Martyn Armstrong lobbing a petrol bomb through a pet-shop owner's window.

He went online to find the archive for the *Cambridge Evening News.* Thankful for the slightly eccentric spelling of Martyn he quickly found eight articles stretching from January 1995 to November 2004. All were court cases involving animal rights demonstrations outside research companies in the Home Counties which experimented on live animals. The charges ranged from breach of the peace to assault, and most had resulted in short jail terms.

Armstrong's address was different in each article, but all were in or around Ely, except the last, which was listed as no fixed abode.

'Animal rights,' said Dryden, shutting down the screen

and running a finger along the still-tender wound round his eye.

Downstairs copies of *The Crow* had still not arrived so he cut down High Street Passage and into Butcher's Row, stopping outside the display window of Foster & Co., Land Agents. There were fifty properties in the window, none of them matching the cottage next door to Paul Cobley's he'd seen in the snapshot his mother had shown Dryden. He went in and a yob-in-a-suit, who was about to shut up shop, gave him an oily smile. Dryden liked estate agents, largely because they saved journalists from being listed as the country's most despised professionals.

'I was looking for a property someone said you had for sale – a cottage, one of a pair out on the fen. Victorian, I guess, red-brick, in need of work.'

The smile never faltered. 'Right. You know, that's so unlucky. I think we've just taken an offer on that and the vendor has accepted – so we've had to take it off the market.'

Dryden shrugged and headed for the door, wondering how long it would take for the prospect of a bigger commission to bend the rules.

'But ... you know. If you're interested, I can ring the vendor now because nothing's been signed.'

Dryden nodded. 'Bit of gazumping eh? Can I see the details?'

He got the file from a pile by a cappuccino machine.

Albert Cottage was on Sedge Fen, a bleak farming district close to the edge of Thetford Forest, about ten miles from Ely. Dryden read the details and noticed the broadband internet link, the double garage and the access to the A12. Then he memorized the address and tossed the file back.

'Actually I'll give it a miss – a deal's a deal after all, and if I offer more you'd probably stitch me up too, eh?'

He didn't deny it, and Dryden left him fluttering around a new customer.

Back on Market Square Skeg was now at his pitch by the mobile tea stall, a fresh pile of papers on his trestle table. He pasted on a smile for Dryden but couldn't hide the anxiety which made his narrow, childish body shake slightly as he handed Dryden a copy of *The Crow*.

Dryden looked into the wide brown eyes and guessed he was a few shillings short of a fix.

"Nother good week,' said Skeg, dipping the waxed hair like a cap, forcing a smile beyond its natural life. He cradled a plastic cup of weak tea and a toasted cheese sandwich lay beside the papers, oozing grease. As well as the pile of first editions of *The Crow* there was also the *Cambridge Evening News*. Dryden read the banner headline and froze:

ARREST IN HUNT FOR VILLAGE KILLER

He grabbed a copy, threw some coins in Skeg's tray, and read the first paragraphs, scanning the lines in a few seconds . . .

By Nikki Reynolds

Detectives have made an arrest in the hunt for the killer of the 'Skeleton Man' found hanged in a cellar in the abandoned Fen village of Jude's Ferry.

The 37-year-old was taken to Midsummer Common police station, Cambridge in the early hours of this morning.

The man, who is understood to live in the Cambridgeshire area, had been interviewed on three occasions before being arrested at his home. It is understood no charges have as yet been made.

'We are close to identifying the victim in this case, who we now believe may have been murdered by a lynch mob,' said one detective close to the case.

Dryden scanned down the rest of the story and found nothing else that was new – and none of the details in his story.

But it was still a better story than the one he'd run. 'Shit,' he said, walking quickly away from the market-day crowd around to the back of the fish stall, where he stood amongst the discarded plastic crates still half full of crushed ice. He hit the automatic dial for the detective's mobile.

Two rings. 'Shaw,' said the DI.

'Dryden. *Cambridge Evening News* – front-page splash. They say you've made an arrest on the Skeleton Man case, which makes me look like a tosser. Anything you'd like to say?'

DI Shaw's voice was low, and Dryden could hear the crackle of police radios in the background. He guessed he was still in the incident room at the New Ferry Inn.

Again, the maddening pause, time to work out exactly what he wanted to say.

'It's Mark Smith and he is under arrest for obstructing our inquiries, OK? That's it. He has not been charged with murder and there is no intention to charge him with murder. His version of events on the last evening, when the brothers fought, is full of holes. We've interviewed him three times and got a different story each time. I think the fight was about something else, something a lot more important than money, but he won't give an inch. This might convince him we are serious about finding out the truth.'

But Dryden wasn't giving up. 'And what if it turns out it was his brother on the end of that rope in the cellar? What if the *News* has called it right? You don't know for sure, do you – unless the DNA analysis is back?'

'The lab has not got the results yet, that's true. But I do know it wasn't Matthew Smith in the cellar.'

'You do? You going to share that information?'

'Sure. But I don't want it in the paper.'

A shower of rain had begun to fall and Dryden edged under a shop awning, watching the crowd run for cover. 'OK,' he said, realizing he had little choice.

'Jennifer Smith, the sister, backs up her brother's story for that night, as far as she can. She says they got home together before midnight and drank in the front room. I believe her about as much as I believe her brother, but there it is. I went to see her again this morning to run through it again and told her Mark was under arrest. This produced a remarkable return of memory. Apparently, a year after her mother's death, she got a letter from Matthew. Nothing specific, just saying he was OK, and not to worry. She didn't keep it. There was a snapshot inside of him kneeling by their mother's grave. She kept that. She said she'd never shown it to Mark. She showed it to me. They're not identical twins – so there's no doubt.'

Dryden let it sink in. 'You might have mentioned the arrest.'

'I didn't mention it because I didn't want some idiot running a story like this. It leaked from Cambridge. The *News* read me the story and I told them not to print it – it's misleading at best. We have absolutely no evidence he's a killer, and pretty good evidence he didn't kill his brother as he was alive and well several years after the evacuation. If Mark starts talking, and more to the point tells the truth, he'll be out by teatime. If he gets himself a decent lawyer he'll be out anyway. So the *News* will look pretty stupid tomorrow.'

239

Dryden held out the paper at arm's length. He didn't care about tomorrow, journalism was about today. The story made him look like an amateur from the sticks. His stuff on Jason Imber was all over the front of *The Crow* while the *News* implied the police had already got their man.

'A heads-up would have been nice,' he said lamely, and cut the line. Dryden had thought about telling him what he'd learned from Fred Lake but calculated he could wait until after Shaw had interviewed the vicar the following morning.

Then his phone went. He checked the incoming number. It was Charlie Bracken, *The Crow*'s news editor. Looking down Market Street Dryden could see him, standing outside The Fenman in the rain, a pint in one hand and a thin wisp of smoke rising from the other. Dryden guessed he'd just read the front of the *Cambridge Evening News* as well and wanted to know if they were going to look second-best all week. Dryden took the call, calmed him down, and told him to wait twenty-four hours. In the distance he watched as Charlie walked happily back into the bar.

Dryden set off for the riverside and found Humph asleep in the cab by the slipway. Dryden thought again about that last night in Jude's Ferry. The funeral of Jude Neate was the central event, and he felt convinced it was linked to the fate of both the Skeleton Man and the bones in Peyton's tomb. He needed to know more about Kathryn Neate and the men in her life.

He pulled open the passenger-side door, the rusted hinges squealing. 'The Stopover, Duckett's Cross,' he said, viewing Humph's collection of airport miniatures in the glove compartment. The cabbie stretched out, his finger joints cracking. 'Duty Free's open,' said Dryden. 'Now, what am I having?'

28

Jimmy Neate's girlfriend was at the pumps, splayed in a deckchair set out in the late-afternoon sun, her T-shirt rolled up from her waist to reveal the pale shadows beneath her breasts. She didn't move as Humph parked the Capri. The stand of dusty pines around the Stopover Garage shimmered in a light breeze, and a single HGV rumbled into the distance down the long stretch of featureless tarmac. When it had gone there was silence, except for the hum of flies from a manure bin by the BBQ coal.

Julie Watts stood to meet him, her eyes running over him from the ground up. 'Jimmy about?' said Dryden, trying not to do the same.

'Thought you might have come to see me,' she said, and Dryden heard Humph snort as he made a fuss putting on his headphones.

'Not unless you can tell me where Kathryn Neate is,' said Dryden.

She shrugged, and Dryden saw that she couldn't help her hands taking refuge in the pockets of her jeans.

'She left, years ago. I never saw her after we left the Ferry.'

'You must remember her though; look like her brother?'

She shook her head. 'Quiet kid. Her body grew up before she did, that happens to us all, but Kathy didn't have a chance. So she got knocked up. She was proud of it in an odd way. Like it proved someone loved her, which it didn't, did it?' She laughed again. 'She didn't deserve that, I guess.'

'Didn't Jimmy help – her dad?'

She laughed. 'They loved her all right – but with them it's the kind of love you don't do anything about. It's just there, and everyone's supposed to know without anyone saying anything. That wasn't what she needed. Adolescence is a mess, they just waited for her to survive it. She didn't.'

They walked towards the bungalow as Dryden recalled the desperate plight of the girl described in Magda Hollingsworth's diary – pregnant, frightened, alone.

'What about the father? Gossip says it was George Tudor.'

'Maybe. He loved her, you could see that, but then Marion – their mum – was his aunt. I think he felt protective, especially after Marion died, and that's not the same thing, is it? Although at the Ferry they got these things mixed up. That was always the joke they made at school in town – that the Ferry kids had family trees all right, they just didn't have any branches on them.'

Dryden laughed, closing his eyes and enjoying the sunshine. 'Kathryn's mother died young, didn't she?'

She nodded, not really interested. 'Did for the family,' she added, watching Jimmy Neate cross from the garage over to the bungalow in the trees. 'You could tell something was missing; something they couldn't put back. And Walter changed, he'd always been the jovial uncle type, but after that he just went into a shell. Kathryn looked like Marion too, so he found that painful, having her around. All he had was Jimmy really, and Jimmy doesn't like being the centre of attention, not for anyone.'

'They fight?'

'That would have been healthy. So no, they didn't. The old man's just kinda had Jimmy where he wanted him. He lived – lives – his life through Jimmy, even when he's stuck in some wing-backed armchair in a godforsaken old people's home.'

'Jimmy visit?'

'Sure. Most days when he can get the cover or I can do the pumps.'

Dryden could feel the heat radiating from the metal canopy. 'They must have found it hard to cope when the kid arrived?'

She slid a hand inside her jeans, stretching the belt out to reveal more skin, but didn't answer.

'D'you see him? Jude, wasn't it?'

She turned back to the road as a people carrier swept in, mangling gravel.

She shook her head. 'I never saw him, I don't know anyone that did outside the Neates, and George Tudor I guess, and the doctor. He didn't live two days, did he?' She ran a rag through her hands. 'Two days in summer.'

'So if it wasn't George Tudor, who was the father?'

Jimmy Neate walked quickly out to talk to the driver of the people carrier which had parked near the bungalow.

Julie turned to Dryden, dropping her voice just slightly. 'Kathryn needed to know someone loved her, and there were plenty of people prepared to say they did. Don't get me wrong, she was no angel, she learnt pretty quick how to use her body to get what she wanted. Ask me, I'd say she enjoyed the sex, it's just it wasn't what she was after, not in the end, and there was no one around to tell her that what she wanted didn't just follow on from the sex. So who's the father? How much gossip can you take? You could ask Jimmy – but don't expect an answer. Losing that kid hurt them all. They protect the memory, in fact they've put more effort into that than they did trying to help her when she was here.'

The people carrier swept out onto the open road and Jimmy Neate retreated into the bungalow. Dryden found him eating one of his pre-wrapped sandwiches in the kitchen of the bungalow. The room was in a time warp: a Rayburn range stood in one corner, a wooden pine table grey with age filled most of the space that was left, at its centre a clean ashtray. The lino on the floor was scrubbed but cracked. A portable TV was on the draining board showing the horse racing from Lingfield without sound.

Neate let his eyes linger on the final furlong before turning to Dryden.

'You're back,' he said, massaging his neck, the shoulders slumping down with fatigue.

He leant back and Dryden saw that he'd been reading the *Daily Mail*.

'Guess there's no chance you've seen *The Crow* yet?' he said, holding up a copy.

Neate shook his head. 'We get it delivered – mid-morning tomorrow out here. Welcome to the boondocks.'

Dryden nodded, calculating. 'They're making some progress on the skeleton in the cellar. Forensic science is a wonderful thing.'

Neate went to the fridge and pulled it open, taking out a can of beer. 'Want one?' he said, holding up the label so that Dryden could see.

'Sure. Thanks.'

They took the first couple of inches off the top of the cans in companionable silence. Dryden watched Neate's hands, shuffling the can, picking at the grain of the old table. Outside they could hear Julie serving a customer, the radio blurting out the local station. It was a news bulletin, replete with details of the *Cambridge Evening News*'s front-page story about the Skeleton Man. Even the boondocks get radio, thought Dryden, the insecurity of being scooped making him angry again.

'It was your sister I was interested in,' he said. 'Kathryn. She had a baby, didn't she?'

'Yeah. Yeah. So?' But Dryden had seen the glance, out of the door into the bungalow's gloomy hallway. There was a hardwood chest of drawers there in the shadows, the top crowded with framed photos.

Dryden took a chair. 'Picture?'

Neate ran a hand through thick unwashed black hair and then stood, coming back with a small snapshot in an older wooden frame.

Despite the studied air of indifference Dryden could sense the pride Neate felt.

'She's beautiful – when was this taken?'

'At the Ferry, before the end,' said Neate. She was by a hedgerow, a summer's view behind her of the allotments running down to The Dring, the ditch clogged with reed heads.

She had her brother's hair, but the face was softer, an oval, the forehead high and pale, the hands long and white. An uncertain smile seemed to emphasize the fleeting nature of the moment in which she'd been captured, a single summer between childhood and the rest of her life.

'You in touch?'

He shook his head. 'She didn't come when Dad fell ill. I couldn't forgive her for that. She took a car in '92 – said she'd send us the money. That was the last time I saw her – she was standing right there,' he said, nodding at Dryden. 'She said she wanted a new life. So that's fifteen years ago, the November. We asked her what her plans were, who she knew, but she just went. I got a letter from Dorset, a farm down there. Married and that, but no kids. Well, no more.'

'And George Tudor?'

He laughed. 'George wasn't the father if that's what you're thinking. George thought he knew what was best for Kath – which didn't go down too well in our house. Family feuds,

Dryden – Mum was a Tudor, and they always thought they were better than us. Ellen Woodruffe was Mum's sister, another Tudor. It's like the Mafia, only nastier. So George just tried to take over, said he wanted to take Kath with him to Australia, start a new life. Perth I think. Along with little Peter Tholy, just the three of them.' Dryden sensed the ritual denigration of the runt, the village scapegoat. 'Dad nearly killed him when he asked. Like we couldn't look after our own.'

Dryden let that hang in the air.

Neate shrugged, taking the picture from Dryden and, replacing it in the hall, he brought back another – a large black and white picture of a man standing in front of the old garage at Jude's Ferry.

'Dad,' said Jimmy simply.

Dryden nodded, taking the picture, sensing it was an icon. 'You're gonna look like him,' he said, knowing it would work.

Jimmy smiled. 'I miss her. Dad missed her – but it's too late for all of us now.'

Dryden thought he was trying to reassemble a memory, studying the picture himself as if it was new to him, but then he asked, 'Forensics, you said?'

'Yeah. It's all in the paper. They've found a grave.'

Neate picked up the beer can in a single fluid movement. 'Where?'

'In the cellar, where we found the Skeleton Man,' said Dryden, taking a last gulp of beer.

Neate leant forward, elbows on the newspaper. 'And I bet I know what they found in the grave,' he said.

'Go on.'

Dryden could see he wanted to say it but that the calculation was complex, and for a moment he hesitated. 'Bones,' he said, finally. 'Old bones.'

'And whose old bones would they be?'

246

'Ask Ken Woodruffe, it was his cellar.'

A woman's bones. Dryden recalled the picture behind the bar at The Five Miles from Anywhere, the oval face at the upstairs window.

Neate licked his lips. 'Ellen Woodruffe, Aunt Ellen, was dying – she'd had a couple of strokes and her heart was failing. Ellen begged Ken, begged everyone, to end it. She wanted to die in her own home. I know for a fact she asked Dad to do it – give her some pills or something. Ken told everyone there was no way she'd leave, he reckoned they'd have to drag her out, or she'd do it herself. And there was the pain. You could hear her some nights, upstairs at the inn, trying to stop herself crying out. It tore Ken up because he wanted her to die then, but the doctors said it could go on for years. She was a strong woman, Ellen, and it was like her body wouldn't give up, even when she wanted it to. So I wouldn't blame him if he did it for her, I'd have done it. After we got fixed up in business here Dad rang the home Ken said he'd put her in – out on the coast – but she wasn't there.'

Neate leant back in his chair, tilting it on to two legs. 'But like I say, good luck to him . . .'

Dryden finished the can. 'Actually, there was nothing in the grave. It had been dug, then filled in. Not a chicken bone, nothing.'

Neate didn't miss a beat. 'So where did Ellen go?'

In his mind Dryden was back on Thieves Bridge, cradling the skull in his hands again, the dark sockets lightless.

29

The North Sea was a grey slate, ruffled only by a squall of rain moving in from the east. The cab had cruised the front twice already but still they'd failed to see the sign. Perhaps it had long closed, perhaps it had been renamed, perhaps the picture had been a fake all along.

'Remind me,' said Humph, winding down the driver's side window to clear it of the droplets which obscured the view.

'The Royal Esplanade,' said Dryden.

It was dusk and the promenade lights flickered once then came on, somehow adding to the gloom. At sea a single trawler headed in, its green and red lights hinting at a subtle swell.

They reached the miniature clock tower by the marine gardens which was the centrepiece of Lowestoft's sea front.

'One more time,' said Dryden, wishing he'd done some research before they'd undertaken the trip.

Humph swung the cab in a circle and headed south.

Dryden was looking at the double-bayed fronts of the B&Bs with their winking 'Vacancy' signs when they came opposite a small park set back from the prom. Trees, heavy with summer leaves, obscured the buildings beyond.

'Take the next right,' he said. 'Let's go round the square.'

And there it was, behind elegant Edwardian railings – the Esplanade.

Dryden fished a tie out of the glove compartment and ran a hand through his hair, examining his face in the vanity mirror.

'I need to look like an accountant,' he said.

Humph was biting the top off a pork pie. 'Thank God you've failed,' he said, wriggling his backside down into the seat.

'Thanks for the support.'

A female nurse in uniform answered the door, ushering him inside beneath a chandelier which failed to provide enough light. A long corridor led off into the heart of the building, the lino reflecting institutional lights, a distant wheelchair being pushed across from one room to another.

The nurse left him in an office by the door, a room which had once been elegant, but was now disfigured by an electronic intercom board and a semi-circle of high-backed chairs.

A tall man in a suit appeared through a connecting door, his hand already raised in welcome. 'Mr Dryden? Dr McNally – I'm the head of care strategy here at the Esplanade – and at our other two establishments along the coast. I understand . . . please take a seat.'

Dryden nodded. They both sat, a coffee table between them covered in old editions of *Country Life*.

'It's my aunt. She's eighty-four. I'm thinking of suggesting she should . . . well, be looked after. She's had several strokes and she's now confined to a wheelchair. There are complications – mainly circulation. She needs a lot of looking after.'

Dr McNally's eyes flickered down to a notepad on the tabletop where his silver pen skated smoothly.

'There've been a few accidents. It's upset her, just the thought she's a burden on anyone. And even with a couple of care visits a day I think she's beginning to get frightened – worried that something will happen and there'll be no one there. So we've talked about it – which is when she mentioned the Esplanade.'

McNally nodded, letting him go on.

'She had a friend who came here I think – back in the nineties. Ellen Woodruffe? She always spoke very highly of the quality of the care so I think Miriam – that's my aunt – would be happy to at least consider a move. But she wasn't quite sure this was the right place. She seemed to think it was near the pier – which doesn't sound right.'

Dryden looked out of the window on to the dripping leaves of a plane tree.

McNally nodded, stood, and went behind the desk, tapping the keyboard on an AppleMac. 'Woodruffe, you said?'

'Right. With a final "e". She would have arrived in June 1990, I think.'

'Let's see . . .'

'Miriam said she had a wonderful room, with a balcony. If there was any chance we could offer her something similar . . .'

'Indeed, indeed. Have you seen our charges, by the way – there's a schedule in this leaflet.'

He pushed a brochure across the leather desktop. Dryden opened it, breathing in the mildly hypnotic whiff of freshly printed paper. The annual charges were listed in a small box and Dryden surreptitiously tried to hide his battered shoes by pushing his heels back under the chair.

'Here she is,' said McNally, and Dryden fought to hide his disappointment. 'Let's look at her file.'

Dryden nodded. 'Thanks. These charges seem very reasonable,' he lied.

McNally left the room, returning quickly with a box file.

'Yes. Ellen Woodruffe. She came to us much later than that actually – 1992 – in the December. She was in Rosemary, that's one of our best suites, looking out to sea. That's a sitting room with en suite facilities and a bedroom.'

Dryden rubbed his hands together. 'Right – now I need to tell her all of this if we're going to get her out to visit. Would that be OK?'

Dryden took out his wallet, making sure McNally could see the chequebook. 'It's odd though,' he said, letting his pencil hover over a scrap of paper he'd got out of the wallet. 'She's got such a great memory Miriam – and that's certainly not fading. She was sure she came here in '90. That's the year Uncle Bernard died.'

McNally nodded as if he knew who the fictional Bernard really was, while he flicked nervously through the box file.

'Yes. Well it does look like she was meant to be with us then. According to the file she was booked in for that year, and she was examined by the medical staff here and assessed for her needs. But there was a late change of plans. The contract was cancelled in May 1990. Looks like she went abroad with her son – Kenneth. Spain – Sitges on the Costa Dorada. They reapplied from there, that was in '92, and we undertook a fresh medical examination on her arrival. Her condition had deteriorated further. Stomach ulcers, and some early signs of diabetes setting in, alongside the chronic heart condition.'

He nodded, closing the file.

Dryden looked out of the window. 'We stopped getting Christmas cards in – what was it? Late nineties?'

McNally held his eyes for just a second beyond the point of politeness. 'Ninety-seven. She died here, in fact – I recall her now actually. Wonderful woman, terrible illness, but bravely borne.'

Dryden guessed he'd been sussed but went through the charade of fixing up a visit. Miriam would have been proud of him. McNally left him in the office while some forms were printed out off the computer in a side room.

He was looking out the window watching Humph complete his daily exercise by walking round the Capri when he saw a woman reflected in the glass. Dryden thought she was in her seventies, small sparrow-like frame, but her movements were quick and fluid. She edged in through the door clutching her hands together and Dryden guessed she'd been listening outside.

He turned to face her. 'I'm sorry,' she said. 'Rosa, the nurse – said someone had called asking about Ellen. It's nearly ten years, isn't it? I just can't believe the time has gone so quickly. I miss her terribly. We were in cahoots, Mr Dryden: partners. I'm Joyce, Joyce Cummings.'

Dryden took the paper-dry hand. 'Cahoots about what?' he asked, smiling, but she didn't seem to hear. 'My aunt was an old friend of Ellen's. They'd lost touch. She's hoping to come here too – Ellen recommended it.'

'I don't think so,' she said, the hand vanishing back into the folds of her dress. 'I'd very much doubt that. Ellen hated it here, every moment, so I can't imagine where you got that idea. We both hated it but, well, you know, we were dumped here so that was that. It's like the old joke – the food's dreadful here, but the real problem is that you get such small portions.'

She laughed, her eyes dancing around the room, and Dryden tried not to think what it took to keep a sense of humour alive for a decade in a place like the Esplanade. He could hear the printer still clattering in the back office. 'Did you meet Kenneth too – her son?' asked Dryden

'He more or less ran the pub, didn't he?' Dryden nodded. 'Never. She didn't want to see him. She always said that he'd let her down very badly. That he'd promised she'd never come to a place like this, that she'd never leave her home, that she could die in her own bed. But people break promises when you're old – that's something you'll discover for yourself.'

McNally came back in the room with a plastic folder, his irritation at the intrusion palpable.

Joyce Cummings put a finger to her lips, smiled beautifully at the doctor and fled.

30

By the time they got to the edge of the Fens night had fallen
and a full moon was climbing into the sky behind the distant
cathedral tower. They stopped for tea at a mobile café in a
lay-by. Humph swung his door open to take in the night air,
but Dryden sat on a plastic chair set up on the verge, watching the car lights strung out across the landscape. The tea
was acrid and stewed, the taste further marred by the stringent smell of exhaust gas in the air.

He thought about St Swithun's, its tower silhouetted
against the setting sun that last night. In the New Ferry Inn
the free beer was flowing, while in the nave of the church
Kathryn Neate struggled with her grief. And George Tudor,
leaving home in St Swithun's Cottages below the allotments,
climbing the hill to take his place beside the child's grave.
He was Kathryn's cousin after all, nobody could have
disputed his right to be at Jude's funeral. But why had he
not been there at the start? Why the theatrical entry, the
pointed solidarity?

What had really happened when they all got back to
Neate's Garage? Had they turned on George Tudor then
and made him pay with his life for giving Kathryn a son?
But the scene Fred Lake had described in the Neates' kitchen
that evening didn't sound like the prelude to murder.
Something else had happened to prompt the killing and he
needed a clear view of that evening from outside the family
ring to see what it was.

He walked to the cab and got the OS map for the eastern

fens, tracking a route across country to Sedge Fen and Paul Cobley's cottage. Fortified by a double hot dog, Humph agreed to the diversion, leaving the main road at Mildenhall and skirting the floodlit runways of the US base before the cab emerged into open country beyond, the distant lights of cottages and farmhouses studding the night, lightless now that the moon had risen to be obscured by rain clouds.

Sedge Fen was a hamlet flung across both banks of the Little Ouse. At its heart was a now abandoned industrial site, a miniature Manhattan of silos and storage warehouses which had once provided grain, potatoes and salad crops for the London market. A grubbed-up railway line ran across the open fields. A signpost directed Humph to Sedge Fen Methodist Church, a wooden ark next to a modern bungalow from which light flooded out onto a large American car. Dryden knocked and a woman with perfect teeth and big hair knew the way. 'End of the lane, turn right – 'bout a mile. There's just two cottages. They're in the one with the new windows. They've got a flashy BMW, and a van, but we've seen neither for a week. They go on holiday a lot – for the tan. You a friend?' she asked, and Dryden, who didn't bother to answer, could see that she was trying to stop the smile turning into a sneer.

The drove ended at the cottages: the deadest of dead ends. The houses stood in darkness but as Dryden got out of the cab the downstairs lights in one came on. He walked up the short drive, stamping on the gravel, trying to flush out any dogs, but nothing moved. The lights were on in the modernized house so he went to the door and knocked loudly, listening to the echo bounce back off a brick barn half a mile away. A dog barked then, but to the north, where a security light lit the foot of a pylon.

He stepped to the side and looked in at the front room.

The overhead light was on and so was the TV, although the sound was down. He worked his way down the side of the house through a gate to the kitchen door. Inside he could hear a radio playing and the light over the hob was on.

There was a custom-built wooden studio in the garden, beside the double garage, and through the window Dryden could see two computer workstations with flat screens big enough for design and make-up. The lights, which had been on, flicked off. On the door was a company logo and sign: DesignSolutions.

The studio lights flicked back on. 'Time switches,' said Dryden, and went back to the car. 'Looks like they're away, like the woman said,' he told Humph as the cab trundled a three-point turn. Dryden watched the lights in the rear-view mirror, so that he almost missed the post box a hundred yards down the lane where there was a lay-by for the van to park up.

'Hold on,' he jumped out and flipped up the unlocked cover to reveal a bundle of letters which he took back to the cab and examined by the vanity light.

'That's nice,' said Humph. 'And you reckon estate agents have no moral compass?'

There were some utility bills marked for Mr P. R. Cobley and Mr M. James, and what felt like some brochures and freesheets for the 'occupiers'. But there was one package, in a jiffy bag, marked for Cobley & James and stamped PHOTO POST.

'Look the other way,' he said to Humph, and ripped it open. It was a set of holiday snaps, Dryden guessed Greece. Paul Cobley was in most, pictured in cafés, bars and neck deep in a blue pool. But there was one of them both, slightly off-kilter so Dryden guessed it had been taken with a timer, kneeling in the sand. Dryden recognized Cobley's partner immediately and there were several things he didn't know about him: he didn't know what he'd been doing with his life for the seventeen years since he'd left Jude's Ferry, he didn't know how he'd earned his living, he didn't know how many times he'd been in love. But he knew one thing. He had a twin brother.

31

They saw the fairy lights on the pub as soon as they turned off the main road half an hour later – shuffling white and red bulbs neatly outlining the building. But the car park was nearly empty now that darkness had driven the evening trade home, or back to the boats. When Humph killed the engine they could hear a party somewhere out on the water amongst the floating gin palaces, the clash of glasses punctuated by overloud voices.

Dryden left Humph enjoying a nightcap from the glove compartment and found Woodruffe in the bar reading the *Licensed Victualler*. A barmaid moved to serve Dryden but Woodruffe waved her back, pulling the reporter a pint and then helping himself to a large whisky delivered direct into the pottery mug.

Dryden looked around. There were half a dozen customers at one table and two teenagers at the bar talking about *Top Gear*. Woodruffe's hands, trained by a lifetime behind the bar, effortlessly rearranged the bar towels and respaced a row of glass ashtrays.

'I've just been out to Lowestoft for the day,' said Dryden, dropping his voice to conspiratorial. 'Had a chat with one of your mother's old friends; a close friend actually. That's the thing about old age, it loosens the tongue, sweeps away inhibitions.'

Woodruffe walked to the barmaid, slipping a hand around her narrow waist, whispering in her ear. It was an intimate gesture and Dryden looked away. The publican flipped up the bar top and led the way to the patio doors which opened onto the riverside. There was a short jetty here for cruisers to use during the day. They walked to the end and Woodruffe stood at the rail, sipping his drink, his back to the water. The night was silent but for the ducks in the reeds and the rumble of generators from the cruisers moored on the bank.

'You dug the grave for her, didn't you?' said Dryden, looking downriver towards the cathedral. 'In the cellar.'

'Don't know what you're talking about.' A denial without enthusiasm, Dryden sensed that Woodruffe was already aware how weak it sounded.

'Right. Spain always a favourite holiday spot, was it? That's when you started smoking Ducados? When'd you give up? The day you read about the forensic evidence they'd found in the cellar?'

Woodruffe shook his head. 'This is crap.' He turned round, looking out into the night. On the far side of the river a flock of birds rose off the distant fen and crossed the moon.

'But they've asked for a DNA check, haven't they – so they'll know soon. They'll match you with the stub. That puts you in the cellar digging the grave. What was it going to be: pills? A pillow over the face?'

Woodruffe looked away but in the darkness Dryden could see the moonlight reflecting off the tears.

'You'd promised her, promised that if it came to it you'd end her life there, in Jude's Ferry, to save her the pain, and to give her the peace she wanted. So you got it all ready – the grave in the cellar, the concealed trapdoor, the booking at the Esplanade in case anyone asked where Ellen was going. You'd always planned to cancel it. But then you lost your nerve. What was Spain – a holiday to buy her off?'

He tried to gulp the whisky but fumbled with the mug so that it fell into the river without a splash.

'I bought a bar, back in the eighties. Sitges, down the coast. I'd always planned a long break and I said she should come too. I'd arranged nursing care, everything. If we liked it we could stay, flog the licence on this place.'

He bowed his head. 'But she wanted me to end it for her, then, at the Ferry. Her whole life had been in that village, she was born down along The Dring, moved to the pub when she married Dad, I was born there. It's like the place was part of her, like a limb. She used to say she could close her eyes and see it all, every door, every tree, and all the people who'd been there, even the ones who were dead.

'But I couldn't kill her. That's what it is, even if she said it wasn't. When I told her about Spain she cried all night, begged me to end it. She said that Dad would have done it for her, which I guess was true. Next day she started packing, and we never mentioned it again.'

He held a hand wet with sweat to his forehead. 'And it was a new life, a new life for me. Mum had her own flat and everything, a balcony, the sea near by, the nurse was good, the doctors. I said she could stay and I'd come out every month, see her, check on the bar. Winters it wasn't too hot, I said she'd get used to it; she said she couldn't take the pain, that she was just sick of living really and why didn't she just go home, see England again. She said if I wanted a new life why didn't I just stay in Spain.'

He knelt on the boards, fishing with his right hand in the dark green water for the mug. Then he stood, black strands of weed curled round his elbow.

'So you came back,' echoed Dryden. 'And the years went by and nobody found the Skeleton Man. But the police aren't going to stop asking questions, are they? Not if it is your DNA on that butt. And they're gonna keep asking you. They need to find out who killed George Tudor.

Perhaps they think you helped. Kathryn was your cousin, if the family turned on George they'd expect you to back them up, right?'

Woodruffe wiped his mouth with the back of his sleeve, his eyes on Dryden. 'Paper said they think Mark Smith killed his brother. They fought that night, we saw them out in the yard at the Ferry. It's Matthew in the cellar – got to be.'

'Bad news,' said Dryden. 'Matthew James Smith is alive and well and living with Paul Cobley – he's changed his name – fixed himself up with a new life. They run a business out on the Fen – by the looks of it pretty successfully. One Greek holiday this year already – my guess is they're just on another. To use a quaint term, they're an item. But my guess is you knew that. That was what that argument was really about, wasn't it? Mark wanted to set up a business with his brother but his brother had a better offer. Dirty linen in public, never a pretty sight.'

Dryden could see Woodruffe calculating. 'It's not George Tudor,' he said. 'I talked to Georgie by phone three days ago. He's running a smallholding in the Swan Valley near Perth, Western Australia. Three hundred sheep, a grove of olive trees and a vineyard. Sounds like paradise.'

Dryden was thinking fast. 'Why'd you ring him?'

'We kept in touch.'

'You told him what we'd found in the cellar, didn't you? Why did he need to know that, Ken? There was a murder in that cellar and you're shaping up as one of the main suspects. You need to tell the truth, and you need to tell it quickly. The police are gonna put you in that cellar – your cellar. And they're going to ask questions, questions like did you provide the rope as well.'

Woodruffe's head jerked up and Dryden saw for the first time the desperation he'd been hiding. The publican sank down to the wooden planking and sat, cradling his knees. 'I didn't go down. The others did but I didn't.'

Dryden fished in his pockets for a packet of Gauloise and offered one. Woodruffe took it with a steady hand, the prospect of confession calming his nerves.

'They're not George Tudor's bones,' he said, his throat full of fluid. 'They're Peter Tholy's. George was six foot, a carthorse. That sound right to you?'

Dryden tried to put the jigsaw back together, trying to picture the frail boy with learning difficulties Elizabeth Drew had described. 'But Peter Tholy went to Australia – Fremantle,' he said. 'He sends cards back to Fred Lake, he visits his local church. Why would he end up on the end of that rope – he wasn't a danger to anyone.'

Dryden took a step closer and saw that Woodruffe was still sweating in the moonlight. Under the jetty the river glugged and the cool stench of rotting weed was heady.

Woodruffe put the cigarette between his lips and hid his hands. 'Peter Tholy killed Kathryn Neate because she wouldn't go with him to Australia.'

Dryden sucked in some night air. 'You're saying Kathryn Neate was murdered?'

Woodruffe nodded, chin down.

'Hold on, hold on,' interrupted Dryden, struggling to take it in. 'It was George Tudor who wanted Kathryn to go with him to Australia. Peter Tholy just made up the party – because George looked after him.'

Woodruffe shook his head, exasperated. 'Sure, George wanted Kathryn to go with him, because he wanted her to have a life away from the Neates. But it was Peter that wanted to love her, wanted her as a wife. George went back to Neate's Garage that night to plead for Peter. George was like a big brother to that kid, always had been since school.

262

George likes to protect people – he tried to protect Kathryn, for her mother's sake. Christ, she needed it. She'd never really grown up. After Marion died she went back in her shell and Walter didn't help, couldn't help. He couldn't look at her sometimes, it was like Marion had come back to life.' Woodruffe raked in some more night air. 'And Jimmy isn't the type to give someone a shoulder to cry on. So she didn't really have anyone. But she was beautiful, and I don't think she understood, you know . . .' He looked at Dryden. 'What they were after. She was too lonely to keep them away.'

He rubbed fingers into his eye socket, trying to clear an image. 'George only turned up at the funeral because Tholy had promised Kathryn that he'd be there, because he was the father, because he loved her. But he didn't have the guts to show his face. Someone else letting her down, see? It was little Peter's child, and little Peter wanted to take Kathryn to Australia: the three of them, escaping. But Jimmy and Walter wouldn't have it.'

'And how do you know all this?' asked Dryden.

Woodruffe looked away. 'George and Jimmy told us – all of us – the next day. We met at Imber's house. And I knew about Kath, through the family.'

Dryden remembered the open window, the sunlight on the orchard below.

'They weren't lying, Dryden, believe me. It was little Peter that loved Kathryn Neate.'

Dryden closed his eyes, trying to imagine night falling on Jude's Ferry.

'When the family got back to the garage that night, after the funeral, Walter told Kathryn she had to be straight with Peter, tell him to go without her. Jimmy said later she set off down to The Dring towards Tholy's cottage, about six thirty. That was the last time any of us saw her alive.'

On the horizon the floodlights on the cathedral's Octagon Tower blanked out.

'Jimmy said it was late – nearly ten thirty – by the time they got worried enough to organize a search. He went down to Tholy's cottage, tracing her steps, and George checked out around the Methodist Hall – the dance was over but there were still kids about. Anyway, Jimmy found her soon enough, behind Tholy's cottage on the riverbank. He reckoned they'd met on the path where it cuts behind Orchard House. She'd been strangled and the prints were black round her neck – the fingers, where he'd pressed into the flesh. Jimmy said that as he'd come along the river he'd seen someone by her body, but they'd heard the footsteps and run for it back to the house, Tholy's house.

'Jimmy took her body along the river path back to the garage and then he found George by The Dring and they knocked on Tholy's door, forced it off its hinges. He was alone, packing, and he said he'd been alone all night, that he'd gone to say goodbye to old Broderick, but he hadn't seen Kathryn. That's when Jimmy said he knew he'd done it because he'd been down by the body. So they dragged him out in the street and down to the inn.

'We were all out in the back yard watching the Smiths fight. It was sport, really; everyone was drunk, and if they'd finished we'd have turned on Cobley next. We knew about them, see, knew what they were. They couldn't hide it that night, couldn't say it wasn't true.'

He laughed, brushing the back of his hand over his lips. 'There was gonna be blood spilt. Something about the drink, and leaving, it seemed to make everyone crazy for a night. And there was this bloodlust, you just knew it would end in blood.'

A pike surfaced on the river and then dropped out of sight with a plop.

'Anyway, we was all watching the fight but John Boyle – he's long dead – was out on the front step throwing up and he looked up the street and saw them coming. George had him round the throat so we knew then that he'd done something terrible because nobody stood up for Peter more than George. They said he'd killed Kathryn, strangled her down by the reeds because she wouldn't go with him.

'Everyone looked at Walter, of course. He'd doted on her all her life, since the mother died. He just crumbled at first, then turned on Jimmy, saying it wasn't true, that it couldn't be true. He felt guilty anyway, about the kid, we all knew he'd never wanted it. We were all looking at him, waiting for a lead I guess. So he went for Peter, like he'd kill him there, so we dragged him back – told him we hadn't heard Peter speak, that he had to have the chance.'

Dryden shivered, the sweat beginning to cool on his forehead. 'So what did Peter say?'

Woodruffe shrugged. 'He said he didn't do it, said he hadn't seen her that day at all. But Jimmy cut in, asked him if he was the father of her kid, and you could see he was because he couldn't think of an answer. So Jimmy said there was a place they could find out the truth. The cellar.'

'How'd Jimmy know about that?'

Woodruffe looked at his hands. 'Like I said, family. Jimmy said he'd help, when Mum said she wanted to die, he said it was what his mum would have wanted. I couldn't do it alone so we dug the grave.'

'Did anyone think of phoning the police?' asked Dryden. 'What about the army, didn't they have anyone in the village that night?'

Woodruffe shook his head. 'She was dead, they weren't gonna bring her back, were they?' He paused, deciding. 'I didn't go down. But they said – later – said they'd snapped his neck. Snapped the runt's neck.'

'And Kathryn?' asked Dryden, but he knew already. He'd held her skull that night on Thieves Bridge, the searchlight driving the shadows into the eye sockets.

'They'd sobered up by the time they came back up,' said Woodruffe, ignoring the question. 'When they realized what they'd done. Walter was kind of pumped up, like he'd enjoyed the revenge, as if he'd left his own guilt down in that cellar.'

'This was in the bar?'

Woodruffe nodded. 'Walter said that justice had been done and that now we had to keep Tholy's crime a secret, between us, for ever. They left him hanging in the cellar – I said the army'd find him but they said the trapdoor was good enough and they'd covered it up. Besides, Jimmy knew I'd left it off the plans the army made us fill in, so it wasn't like they'd look for it.

'It was Kathryn that was the problem. They had to hide the body. Walter and Jimmy hadn't finished with the child's grave up at the church, they were gonna do the rest in the morning. So that's where they took her. Walter wanted that, insisted, even when Jimmy said they should bury her out on the mere. But Walter said she deserved more than an unmarked grave.

'We worked the rest out next day at Orchard House. George said he'd cover Tholy's tracks – made sure no one was ever suspicious about where he'd gone. Tholy had told him about his mother out in Perth, so George said he'd fix that when he got out there. He went and saw her and said Peter had changed his mind, that he'd gone to the Midlands somewhere on a big farm. That he didn't want to be a burden.'

'And he sent cards back to Fred Lake,' said Dryden.

'Look.' Woodruffe held out his hands, and Dryden could hear the stress in his voice now, serrating the words. 'I didn't go down. He'd squeezed the life out of her. Jesus, she was sixteen, Dryden.'

Dryden thought about the chipped ribs amongst the bones he'd collected on Thieves Bridge. 'You knew Kathryn well, all her life. Any accidents, violence at home, fights?'

Woodruffe shook his head, confused. 'Childhood stuff – chicken pox, the usual. She was a quiet kid, she wouldn't fight. And her dad and brother made sure she didn't get picked on.'

Dryden stood, hugging himself against the sudden cold. 'So who did go down into that cellar?'

Woodruffe shook his head violently, tears flowing now, but Dryden guessed that it was self-pity.

'They'll want names,' said Dryden. 'I'd be prepared for that. If they don't get names they'll put you down there – with the mob. So think about it – my guess is George Tudor, Jimmy, Walter.'

Woodruffe shook his head, but it didn't stop him talking. 'Walter. Yeah, Walter. You couldn't stop Walter that night. But Jimmy didn't – Walter told him to stay in the bar and keep a lookout with George, that it was his job to deal with Peter. We all just sat tight.'

'So who?'

Woodruffe closed his eyes. 'Johnny Boyle, Jack Forde, Reg Bright – I think. They were from the almshouses and they'd been drinking all night. The rest, who knows? Some went home when they saw what was up. How many does it take?'

Dryden memorized the names. 'So – Boyle, Forde and Bright. How many are still alive?'

Woodruffe shrugged. 'Reg died last year – they always read out any deaths when we have the annual service back at St Swithun's. Johnny's dead too, like I said. Jack – I don't know.'

267

And Walter Neate's in a geriatric unit, thought Dryden. He suspected that, given time, Woodruffe would use the ranks of the dead and infirm to people the cellar that night. 'And Paul Cobley? That was it, wasn't it . . .' Dryden could see it then. The scene in the bar that night as the clock ticked towards midnight. They'd closed ranks, all of them, putting aside prejudices, and so Paul Cobley and Matthew Smith had escaped what had been coming to them – a beating, perhaps more.

Woodruffe didn't answer. Dryden saw him in his memory again on the sunlit doorstep of the New Ferry Inn.

'And Jill, was she there?'

Woodruffe covered his eyes. 'I sent her upstairs. She didn't see anything.'

Dryden wondered how true that was. 'But that's why she left you? Because of what you did that night? Because you let it happen. That was the end of it for her, wasn't it?'

Woodruffe ignored the question, looking out into the dark. 'How long have I got before you go to the police?'

'I'll ring DI Shaw first thing. Take my advice – drive up yourself, to Lynn. Tell him you want him to know the truth – and don't leave anything out. Tell him everything you've told me.'

Woodruffe knelt again and splashed some of the river water in his face.

Dryden looked up at the moon and thought of the cool light falling onto Laura's bunk on the boat.

'And what about Jason Imber? If you met at Orchard House the next day he must have been there. Did he go down into the cellar? And who else, Ken? Who else?'

He looked up but Woodruffe had gone, fleeing along the riverbank, away from the lights, the people, and the questions.

32

Dryden strolled to the bar of The Five Miles From Anywhere and got himself a pint and Humph a fresh hamper of bar snacks and two pickled eggs. The cabbie had swung the cab round so that he could sit in the driver's seat while, with the door open, he had an uninterrupted view of the river running north towards the silhouette of the cathedral. Suddenly, flying into the halo of light above the town, a fat-bodied military jet appeared heading east towards the runway at Mildenhall. As they watched another took its place, the beginning of a necklace of flights completing their transatlantic crossing.

On the river a pair of black swans glided past on the current, their wings cupped behind them like hands in prayer. Humph threw them a handful of crisps and their red beaks riddled the water.

Dryden sat on the bank, the grass already damp with dew. 'So. I think I know what happened,' he said, sucking two inches out of his pint.

Humph stretched his legs out into the night air and a spring in the driver's seat flexed. 'I'm listening.'

'With three blinding exceptions.'

'Ah,' said the cabbie, exuding happiness.

Dryden was surprised to find that he hesitated, aware that the mysteries of Jude's Ferry were intensely personal. 'The person I feel sorry for is Kathryn Neate.' He pitched a peanut at the nearest black swan, and from the reeds on the far bank a pair of Barbary ducks joined the food queue.

'She's sixteen, she's beautiful – well, on the edge of beauty perhaps. But it's there, in the willowy figure, the angel's face that's growing into something else – a woman's face. Men circle her, all of them for different reasons. Her father and brother, cousins, lovers, protectors, gossips, and the legions of the jealous. Her mum, possibly the only person who ever put her best interests first, is dead a decade. And now the men in uniform have arrived to take her home away. More men, circling.'

Humph hit the cab horn once to scare the ducks away and let Boudicca out from the back seat to sit on the grass. The greyhound edged forward until she could rest her large bony head on Dryden's shoe.

'Then – disaster. She gets pregnant. I thought George Tudor was the father. But now it looks like it's Peter Tholy, a friend of George's off the farm. A frail, vulnerable boy whose only other friends were girls. Peter and George have put their names down for emigration, and the Reverend Fred Lake has vouched for both. Either way, no one seems too eager to step forward and help Kathryn get through the birth. Peter wants to do the right thing but lacks the courage. There's a discreet silence for nine months and then the boy is born. He lives two days. According to Lake the child died of heart failure, brought on by acute jaundice.

'The funeral is the last in Jude's Ferry – at least it should have been. Jimmy and Walter Neate dig the boy's grave – in the old Peyton tomb inside St Swithun's. George Tudor turns up to give Kathryn support – moral and physical – which was either brave or stupid, or possibly both. The Reverend Lake certainly thought Tudor was the father, but nobody thought the police should know, and given that she was over-age by the time of the birth and wouldn't name the father that's not a great surprise. When they all get back to Neate's Garage that evening Tudor's got news for them – the father is Peter Tholy, and he wants to take Kathryn with him to Australia. Walter is against, Jimmy is against. They make Kathryn end it then, make her go and tell Tholy the family's decision. She walks out that last summer's evening and never returns.'

Dryden bent his neck back, looking straight up into the stars. 'Why didn't she want to leave, Humph? Australia must have seemed like a perfect escape.'

On the river a cruiser appeared around the bend, the cockpit lit, a couple standing enjoying the night, glasses full of wine the colour of pear drops.

'She was escaping from the Ferry, anyway,' said Humph. 'Perhaps she didn't love Peter Tholy, perhaps she never had,' he added, thinking of another girl.

Dryden got a fresh round of drinks, the last-orders bell ringing out as he stepped into the cool night.

'According to Fred Lake the funeral was at 5.00pm. The next thing we know for sure is when Jimmy Neate and George Tudor turn up at the New Ferry Inn with Peter Tholy – that's sometime after the Smiths begin brawling in the yard of the inn around eleven. They drag Tholy into the bar and break the news – that Kathryn's dead, that Jimmy saw Tholy fleeing the scene, even though he claims he's been alone all night except for a visit to old Broderick. Don't forget Walter's there by now and this was the daughter he loved too much, the one who always reminded him of the wife he'd lost.

'It's a tinderbox. Everyone's popped up with the beer and God knows what else. The Smith brothers have been trying to tear each other apart in the yard, with Paul Cobley the next bout on the bill. Blood's been spilt already and there's all kinds of emotions rising to the surface. It's the last night for this community; in a few hours they'll all be gone, scattered to new lives. There's plenty of anger, and suddenly they've got the ideal target – stumbling, half-witted Peter.

'And there's another strong emotion, Humph, they want to close ranks. This is something they want to deal with themselves, especially in those dying hours in the life of the village. They've lost one of their own, and the killer is one of their own. Tholy was never going to survive the night unharmed, but it turned out worse than that. How do ordinary people commit murder, Humph?'

'They don't,' said the cabbie, watching some swifts play in the floodlight mounted on the side of the pub.

'George Tudor is the key to this,' said Dryden. 'If there'd been any doubts about Kathryn's death then they'd have knocked Peter about, then got the police. But there are no doubts because George is convinced Peter's a killer and that's good enough for everyone, good enough for any sceptics, because George is his true friend, perhaps his only friend, and they all know that.

'And even then they don't tear him apart. They take him down into the cellar to try and make him confess. To hear it from Peter's own lips. And that's another step towards the grave for Peter, down the cellar steps, out of the light, away from the lives they've all led. Once that trapdoor closes he's never going to see the stars again.'

Dryden drained his pint. 'When he's dead they leave him there. That's the first bit that doesn't make sense. How could they be so sure nobody would find the body in the days after the evacuation? – the engineers were coming in to survey the place. OK, Woodruffe hadn't marked the cellar on the questionnaire – but the whole point of the survey was to double check.'

Humph shrugged, thinking about breakfast.

'Meanwhile Jimmy and Walter bury Kathryn with her son beside the Peyton tomb,' said Dryden.

Humph cracked his knuckles, a series of delicate pops. The

dog eyed the black swans, gliding past again without a sound. 'So where's the kid's bones?' asked the cabbie.

Dryden shrugged. 'Precisely. Question number two. Perhaps the animal rights people found them but discarded them.' But even he didn't believe that: if they'd found the delicate skeleton of a two-day-old child they'd have tried to screw Peyton even tighter. 'But I doubt it. If you're playing emotional blackmail you don't chuck in an ace.'

Humph struggled to his feet. 'Refill? I could run to the bar, there's just time. I might kip in the cab – you'll have to walk.'

Dryden nodded and watched as the cabbie headed for the bar, not so much a run as a lope. It was two miles along the riverbank to *PK 129* and he texted Laura to tell her where he was and that he'd walk home. Humph would curl up with the greyhound on his lap, and any car park was home for them.

Dryden turned to look back at the pub. A single bedroom light shone out, the curtains open to let the breeze through. Woodruffe appeared at the sill, a phone to his ear, but turned quickly and retreated beyond sight. A memory surfaced to match it, a figure, seen briefly at the window of Orchard House on the day of the evacuation.

Dryden heard the strangled cry of something being killed followed by the ghostly flight of an owl over the river.

Humph tottered back with the drinks and a question. 'And Imber?'

'I think he was down in the cellar too, but God knows why. He didn't really know these kids, but I think he wanted to be part of the village – that's why he'd stayed. But he was a posh kid in the wrong place that night. I think he got swept along and couldn't get out once things got really serious – and once Tholy was dead there was no going back. Did he try to stop them? Like I say, he'd be a brave man. A place like the Ferry, it's all about belonging – there's no half-way house. I think

273

when it was over he played a part in covering it all up. He got them to agree to meet next day at Orchard House, to double check their stories, make sure it all added up. And that's why Ken Woodruffe calmed the crowd down in The Dring. He didn't want the army moving in before they'd got the whole thing sorted. It was their last chance to make sure nobody ever knew Peter Tholy died at the end of a rope.'

They heard the bolts being shot on the doors of the pub, but the bedroom window remained open above, the light still burning.

Now that the pub was shut Dryden took his time, sipping the cool beer which caught the moonlight in its amber heart.

'When that stray shell uncovered Tholy's skeleton I think Imber cracked up, he knew the police would be on to them all and I reckon he doubted everyone would keep quiet. It only takes one to blow the whole thing apart, to name names. Seventeen years is a long time; just imagine how shocked they'd all be that their crime had been uncovered. They weren't a bunch of teenagers any more: they had their own lives, careers, families, perhaps children. I think Imber met one of the others at Cuckoo Bridge to tell them what he was gonna do, which has to mean the police. And that's how he ended up in the river.'

Humph drained his glass and swung his feet back in the cab.

'You said there were two things you didn't understand.'

Dryden stood, cold for the first time. 'Woodruffe was clear – Peter Tholy strangled Kathryn Neate. Squeezed the life out of her. But if the bones in the Peyton tomb are Kathryn's she died from a knife wound – the blade thrust between her ribs and into her heart.'

Friday, 20 July

33

With the dawn came the question: what should Dryden do next? He lay beside Laura in the silver light, feeling her warmth and the still thrilling movement of her fingers, stretching and gripping under the influence of a dream. He put his hand on her neck below the ear and stroked her hair, trying to soothe the anxiety which made an eyelid vibrate.

The luminous face of his watch read 5.13am. Would Ken Woodruffe be setting out soon to find DI Shaw? Dryden would give him until mid-morning before ringing the detective to check. The publican wouldn't tell the whole truth but enough of it to identify both victims: the skeleton of Peter Tholy in the cellar of the New Ferry Inn and Kathryn Neate's bones in the Peyton grave at St Swithun's.

Dryden rubbed a knuckle into his eye socket. Shaw's job would be to prove that Tholy died at the hands of the lynch mob and to find some suspects whose mutually supportive alibis didn't put them in the bar of the New Ferry Inn while the murder was taking place in the cellar. Dryden guessed that Ken Woodruffe's late-night calls had been to secure that ring of alibis, to provide the common song sheet from which they could all sing.

At least DI Shaw had his forensics – the DNA traces could be enough to put Ken Woodruffe in the cellar and digging the grave, although not necessarily when Tholy died, while the single helix coil of fibreglass was, Dryden guessed, a possible link to Walter Neate's garage. But the intervening years had almost certainly destroyed any chance of making a match with the original workshop. The gravel from Orchard House was an even more tenuous link to Jason Imber. Anyone could have trudged up the drive and got the stones in the tread of their shoe – anyone, including the village postman. Even with the link it was circumstantial evidence at best, and any decent lawyer would undermine its significance in front of a jury.

Without a break, or a witness outside the tight circle of village life, Shaw might never get his case to court. Unless, of course, Jason Imber's memory returned, and he was prepared to tell the truth, risking retribution.

Dryden gently eased himself over to his left side so that he could see out of the porthole. A white mist threaded its way past the glass, the only things visible the ferns and grass of the bank and the edge of the old wooden landing stage. He could feel the world pressing in, creating pressure in the boat like that in an aircraft cabin. The silence was profound, and he searched it until he located the reassuring hum of the generator below the deck. Then, on the edge of hearing, tyres screeched, and his heartbeat picked up as a car rumbled over the cattle grid up by Barham's Farm, prompting a rhythmic guttural bark from the guard dog.

He dropped a naked foot to the cool boards of the deck and dressed quickly. By the time he had unpopped the tarpaulin cover to the cockpit Humph's Capri was trundling to a halt, emerging from the mist like a ghost ship.

The interior was hot from the heater and laced with petrol fumes and the heady aroma of two fried-egg sandwiches. 'Sorry,' said Humph, as Dryden noticed the dog had been promoted to the passenger seat. 'Couldn't sleep – I went to the truck stop and the radio says there's been a fire at that garage – the Stopover, Duckett's Cross. Early hours – 4.00am. Sounds nasty, but they got someone out.'

Which meant they didn't get everyone out.

Dryden went back on board and whispered into Laura's ear that he'd send Humph at 9.00am to run her to the unit. Then he grabbed a coat and the office digital camera and they split the mist, the Capri wafting the white threads up and over the bonnet to trail like ribbons from the rear bumper.

By the time they reached the cathedral they were navigating through a fog, with a hint of the dark phlegm of carbon monoxide, but as they drove north the air cleared and they could see the watery blue of the river and reflected on its ruffled surface a first sight of the pale disc of the sun.

A mile short of the Stopover they joined a snaking line of commuter traffic headed for Peterborough, and Dryden noted that nothing was coming the other way. A hundred yards further on a police car was parked up across both carriageways, nose to tail with a Fire Brigade control car. There was a junction here and a yellow diversion board sent traffic off across Farcet Fen – a ten-mile loop down single-carriageway droves. Dryden got Humph to swing off the road and park up in the entrance to a field, then strolled forward, trying to rearrange his sheaf of dark hair.

He knew both the uniformed PC by the squad car, a special constable he'd interviewed when covering an anti-graffiti project on Ely's Jubilee Estate, and the fireman – an Assistant Divisional Officer from Cambridge who talked to the press on issues to do with safety each year ahead of Bonfire Night.

'Dryden,' said the fireman.

'Mr Walker,' said Dryden, then nodded to the copper. He was trying to recall just how critical the piece about anti-graffiti had been, but didn't like the scowl which had disfigured the young policeman's face. 'What's up?' said Dryden, unbuttoning his jacket to reveal the camera. 'Thought I'd get some pix for the *Express* – nationals maybe?'

Dryden knew that if they didn't turn him away in the first few seconds it was because they had a story to tell, a story they wanted in the papers.

The PC turned his back as a radio began to crackle.

Walker nodded. 'Who thumped you?' he asked. Dryden's broken cheekbone had spawned a black bruise, now turning purple.

'Fell downstairs,' said Dryden, not caring that he wouldn't be believed.

Walker smiled. 'Come on – your luck's in. Only one resident listed on the electoral roll – James Neate. No sign of him. But there was a girlfriend. We got her out of the bungalow when it went up, we've got video – unbelievable she's alive. She's at Ely now, the burns unit.'

Dryden nodded: a good story but bad news, if the brigade had a film they'd pass it on to the networks and it would be all over the teatime TV screens.

'And Neate?'

'Still looking – but he wasn't in the house, and he certainly isn't in the garage.'

Dryden didn't react, letting the information appear to slip by. 'But the girl – bad?' he said, changing tack.

'Well, she's out cold. The smoke got her down on the floor, which was lucky, as she could have passed out in the bed and then it would have killed her. There's some burns on her hands, but first degree, they'll heal. Face too.'

Dryden tried not to imagine it. 'Stay here while I square this off,' said Walker.

Smoke, lazy and thin, rose from the charred roof of the bungalow. Behind it the stand of pine trees still smouldered too, several blackened and stunted by fire. Dryden knew the stench well, not so much the burnt wood and the incinerated plastic, but the sodden carpets and the stagnant black water. The house was a shell, but the main shed of the garage appeared untouched, although he could see within a tape had been strung across the vehicle bay and a man in a white forensic suit was working in the office behind a glass partition. Out on the forecourt the covers to the underground petrol tanks had been raised while Neate's car was being hauled off on its front wheels by a pick-up truck.

'OK.' The fire officer was back. 'You can come with me; got a notebook?'

They stood in the small weedy garden in front of the house.

'The name you want is Firefighter Jo Campbell. When the first pump got here at 4.30am the house was well alight, and it was impossible to gain entry through either the front door or the kitchen. Jo smashed the windows to the lounge, got to the rear bedroom wearing a fire protection outfit and pulled the girl out. The first pump didn't have specialist breathing gear on board – so the rescue was completed unaided.'

'He'll get a medal?' asked Dryden.

Big smile. 'Yes. *She* will. Come on, I told you it was a decent story.'

The front door had been knocked off its hinges to reveal the hall within. All the walls were black, but splashed clean where the hoses had been at work. The sideboard which had held the family photos was charred, the pictures contorted, Walter Neate's face almost obscured by a smoky stain. The kitchen was blackened too, and Dryden noted two suitcases on the lino floor. He got a few snaps on the digital and then moved forward to the rear bedroom. The bed itself was just wire and metal, the mattress charred springs. A small bedside table had been reduced to a jet-black box of carbon, fragile and oddly beautiful, like an artefact in a museum. The curtains were wet and black, the window glass burnt bronze.

Dryden took his snaps, taking plenty and checking them out on the display screen. Then he moved back to the hall-way and out through the rear door to try to get a shot in through the bedroom window.

He stood in the cool early morning air, trying to imagine the flames. 'Can I speak to the heroine?' he said, using a word he hated.

'Sure, we've got a mobile canteen out down the road, she's just having some grub. You're in luck – she's a looker.'

They turned to go but stopped when they heard shout-ing from deep within the pines which shielded the house from the north. Dryden thought he heard a single word – 'medics' – then a dog barked once, the bark subsiding into whimpers. At the bottom of the bungalow's rough lawn there was a path into the woods and Dryden got there as two uniformed PCs began pushing aside the charred branches, trying to see ahead through the undergrowth, much of which still smouldered from the fire.

When he burst out of the trees behind the two police-men the landscape was transformed. Ahead lay the open fenland of Whittlesea Mere, low trees and a limitless stretch of water from which a flock of birds was now rising into sunlight. Between the wood and the firing range lay a wide drain – perhaps twenty feet across – a mathematically straight ditch brimming with stagnant green water.

But there was only one thing anyone was looking at. Access to the range was barred by a ten-foot-high wire fence with a curled razor-wire top. A man's body hung from the razor wire, his shredded mechanic's overalls snagged by several of the vicious teeth. The body was black and distorted, the limbs set in awkward ugly angles from the torso. The dog lay still now beneath, sniffing the air, while from the corpse a thin line of white smoke rose, caressing the charred skull, wisps of black hair whitened with ash.

Had he been trying to get to the water? Or had he been trying to get away?

And then Dryden noticed something else. Almost directly beneath the body a fresh gap had been made in the wire, cut methodically in a vertical line, opening the way towards Jude's Ferry.

34

They got Dryden off the site in five minutes, bundled into the cab with Humph, and as they drove away a line of squad cars passed them heading back into the Stopover. At the roadblock Walker had radioed ahead for the heroine firefighter and she posed while Dryden took some snaps, with the garage in the distance. Given the discovery of the body on the wire it was debatable whether Jo Campbell's heroism would get the treatment it deserved, but everyone went through the motions, striving for the upbeat.

Dryden swigged a vodka from the glove compartment, letting the antiseptic fluid scour the stench of burnt flesh from his nostrils and throat.

Humph leant forward over the wheel, looking up into the sky, from which a light rain had begun to fall. 'The big toys are out.' The beating heart of a helicopter was lost in the clouds, spiralling down towards the Stopover.

'Take me to *The Crow*,' said Dryden, closing his eyes and trying to think. Who would gain from Jimmy Neate's death? Had he decided to tell the police what had happened to his sister – and to hell with the consequences for the rest? Was he in contact with Jason Imber? Had they both posed a threat to the lynch mob, a threat which had to be removed? And why were there suitcases in Jimmy Neate's kitchen?

Dryden told Humph to pick Laura up and run her to the unit for her regular treatment. He'd join her later, and see if he could talk to Jason Imber.

The Crow's upstairs office was deserted, and he sat at his desk for a minute watching dust settle. It was still only 8.30am on the quietest day of the week – no paper for four days and everyone looking forward to the weekend. He rang police HQ at Cambridge for the latest from the Stopover. They were reporting a fire with one fatal casualty, male, and one woman rescued. Police units were in attendance and there was as yet no view on whether the incident was suspicious.

Dryden decided to get the heroine rescue story off his book as quickly as possible. He rang Mitch, *The Crow*'s photographer, and got an e-mail address to which he could send his pictures for the London agencies and the local evenings. He chose a set of six prints – putting the best aside for the *Express* and *The Crow* to use in the following week, then he bashed out a 400-word story on the heroine rescue, backed up with a few facts and figures he gleaned online. According to the press officer at the fire brigade HQ less than 2 per cent of firefighters are women, so the glory girl was a rare bird indeed.

Finished, he opened up his e-mail to send the copy to the same destinations as the pictures: again, he kept some of the best quotes and background for the *Express*. He deleted half a dozen junk mail messages and then clicked on one from FlandersMay@rsc.org.uk. The 'perfectionist' mapmaker of Jude's Ferry had taken the bait. The answers to Dryden's questions were detailed and frank.

'Well, well,' said Dryden, looking forward to his next conversation with Major John Broderick. He reread May's answers twice and then clicked on an e-mail from Laura.

He read the first paragraph and stopped, getting himself a coffee as he printed out the message. Then he sat in the light of the bay window and read it twice, slowly.

Philip

When I met Jason I agreed that he could send me these
e-mails about what he was remembering.

I want you to read them now because I think he's in
danger – from himself more than anything else. I got the
last one last night and I should have rung – I know that
– I should have texted. But he'd asked me to keep his
secrets and I wanted to keep my promise.

But this morning when I read them again I realized I
can't now – and you'll see why.

Philip, I want you to find him. Do this for me. Please
don't go to the police unless you feel you must.

My love

Laura

Dryden read the first three e-mails quickly, moving swiftly
through Imber's early life and the intimation that guilt lay
in the future and that the girl called Kathryn was the victim.
For Dryden the name Kathryn came ready laden with association, with the selfish manipulations of the men who had
surrounded her. Finally he reached the e-mail sent the previous night at 8.45.

When you read this, Laura, I'll be gone. There isn't much
time so I'll be brutal, because it was a brutal night, and
now I've remembered it all. Kathryn was in my class, one
of my pupils. I didn't want to sleep with her, although I'd
watched her, wondering what life would do to her face,
her body. But she got close to me, bringing me her
problems, because she was scared of something and I can
see now that she thought I would protect her.

And I can't hide it, once she was within reach I wanted
her.

286

So we met in the village at Orchard House that last summer. She'd come along the towpath and I'd lead her through the apple trees into the cool shadowy kitchen. We used the big bedroom overlooking the garden, and I can see her now at the window that last time, the time she told me there was going to be a baby.

I didn't want the child and I know she knew that. I made lots of excuses – that my career would be over, that the police would be involved. But the real reason was that I would have had to start a life I didn't want. That's selfish but it's what I felt. So I offered her the money to get rid of the child, but she said it was too late, that nothing could stop it now. And after that she never spoke a word to me again except on that last evening of her life.

She went away and made her plans. She found that boy – Peter – to cover up, to play the father. I didn't think she had that in her, to use him like that. I think he thought the baby – the boy – was his. I think she let him believe it. It took my breath away when I realized what she was doing, how she could manipulate anyone who loved her, anyone who cared.

And so Peter began to love the child that hadn't yet been born.

Jude. My son.

And then, unseen, at home, she became a mother. And what did I feel? I tried to ignore the sense of loss, the jealousy, the almost overwhelming physical need to hold him, to feel his weight, and the chaotic energy of his limbs. I went the first night after he'd been born into the water meadow opposite the old garage and watched the light burning at the upstairs window. And that's when I knew I'd lost the life that could have saved me, when I heard his crying from the half-opened sash window of the bedroom.

I knew he was ill, the village talked. But still the shock was visceral when it came. I was in the post office talking to Magda when her daughter came in with the news. Jude Neate was dead, dead in the night, and they wanted to bury him in Jude's Ferry. I don't know if I'd have been able to hide the way I felt if Magda hadn't cried. So we held her, comforting her, and I wondered why she'd cry for a child she'd never seen.

And so when the chance came, Laura, I tried to get Kathryn back, tried to redress the balance of right and wrong. I was standing at the bedroom window thinking about the past, about that last summer, drinking from a bottle of whisky I'd found in Dad's desk when we were clearing the house. I'd arranged to go down to the inn that last night but I still felt like such an outsider – so Dutch courage, I guess.

Then I saw Kathryn. She was coming along the towpath at the bottom of the garden in the dusk so I went out to meet her, as I'd always done. We could hear the crowd at the Methodist Hall, spilling out into the night. They put some fireworks up into the dusk and it seemed to make the shadows darker. I saw her face then, and realized what she'd been through alone.

I said I loved her, I said I should have been with her. I said I loved her again but I think it was grief talking, not love but loss, and I think she knew. She said I'd killed him, the baby, that he knew he wasn't wanted and that's why he hadn't fought. She said she was happy the boy was dead.

It was a cruel thing to say and I hit her. She went down in the dust, and I remember the fireworks exploding overhead, and I saw the colour of her face change. But she stood up and came towards me, her arms out to comfort me and then when our heads were together she whispered it in my ear.

'I hate you.' Just for me, like a blessing.

I don't know how long I had my hands round her neck. When I looked at her again, her eyes reflecting a bursting rocket in the sky, I think I knew she was dead. There's long grass by the towpath and I let her fall into it, and it closed over her, like water.

It's frightening how quickly we forget the dead; all I wanted to do was escape. No one had seen me, the path was deserted, and then the clock in the church chimed seven. So I ran quickly to The Dring, and then down to the New Ferry Inn. I bought people drinks and something clever in my brain cut out the memory of what I'd done. And I thought that if I stayed with them, part of the village that night, I'd be safe when they found her body. I'd be safe as long as I was one of them. And I wasn't alone, I wasn't the only outsider.

And then the hours passed, measured only by the fact that she wasn't there. I talked, shouting through the alcohol, trying to feel a part of what was happening, trying not to think of her lying in the dark now, growing cold.

There was a fight in the pub – the Smith brothers. Mark wanted to pool the money, set up a building firm in Peterborough. Matthew wanted to set up a business with Paul Cobley, the kid who ran the taxis with his parents. They'd always been friends. Mark said he knew why his brother wanted to be with Paul.

He let the accusation hang in the air. There were sniggers, a crowd forming, smelling blood. I didn't want to join in but I had to, I couldn't stand out, not then.

We spilled out into the back yard – Ken Woodruffe pushed us out – the fight whirling with Paul trying to keep the brothers apart. I don't know how it would have ended but it stopped when they dragged little Peter Tholy into the bar. When I saw Jimmy Neate's face I knew he'd found her, there was death in his face. And George Tudor had the boy's neck in the crook of his arm, twisting, smearing blood from cut lips over his skin.

'It's Tholy. Peter Tholy's killed Kathryn,' Jimmy said. And there he was Laura, pathetic Peter, his thin arms shaking with fear and yet proud, he said, to have been the father of her child.

'I've got money,' he said, trying to stop it happening. We laughed, enjoying the torment. Penniless Peter. He said he hadn't done it but we didn't listen, trusting George because he'd always been Peter's big brother, his champion when the bullies had circled.

So I said nothing. Nothing when we took him down into Woodruffe's cellar. Nothing when Jimmy kicked away the stool.

Next day we met at Orchard House, all of us, all twelve. We got our stories straight. Walter Neate said they'd buried Kathryn with her son and replaced the stone. George Tudor promised he'd cover Peter Tholy's tracks, make sure there were no questions. And we left the boy hanging, the cellar sealed up. Then we had a drink, swearing silence, and I felt ashamed that for the first time I felt part of it, Laura, part of Jude's Ferry.

And I thought that was the version of my life I'd have to live with until I died. A life in which I killed Kathryn Neate and let an innocent boy hang for the crime.

And then Jimmy Neate rang me. They'd found the body in the cellar, so he was making sure we were all going to toe the line. He had names, people we could put in the cellar; the guilty men, names plucked from tombstones. I met Jimmy on Cuckoo Bridge, because I said I thought it was time to tell the truth. And I was scared, scared that if they asked questions – the police – I'd let them all down. I just couldn't do it. And Elizabeth would know, she'd sense that I hadn't told her, hadn't told her why I didn't want children, which was the one thing she did want.

Jimmy hit me from behind, but I was conscious when I went into the water, and I saw him above as I floated away.

And then, at last, God did smile on me. Thank you Laura, for those e-mails. It's always the innocent detail that saves us. You were telling me about the Skeleton Man, telling me what Philip had told you, what the grave robbers had found in Peyton's tomb. The chipped ribs, the silent knife wound.

A wound to the heart of Kathryn Neate.

So there is someone I have to see before I die because there are two questions now. Why did he kill her, and why did he take Jude's bones away?

When I have answers I can die. I've remembered too much to think about a life now. So I won't see you again, and now, at the end of my life, that's the saddest thing.

I'm going to bury my son.

Jason

'There is someone I have to see before I die,' said Dryden. 'Because there are two questions now. Why did he kill her, and why did he take Jude's bones away?'

Dryden thought of the body hanging on the wire. Had Jason Imber taken his questions to Neate's garage?

He rang Humph and met him on Market Street. The cabbie was half out of the car, sweat in wide wet horse-shoes under his arms. 'There's something up at the unit – when I dropped Laura at the doors there were coppers everywhere. Security bloke says one of the patients has done a hop from a ground-floor room. Police are all over it like a horse blanket.'

Driving north out of the city Dryden could see a loose cordon of three policemen making their way across a field of lettuce towards the woodlands which skirted the bypass. Humph dropped Dryden on the main road by the gates to the unit and the reporter cut across the grounds through a boundary marked by leylandii. At reception he saw a squad car on the forecourt and a PC at the automatic doors.

Desmond Samjee was out in the hospital garden with a patient in a wheelchair, the swaddled figure hardly visible in a nest of blankets.

'I thought he was under police guard?'

Desmond fished in his pockets and began to assemble a roll-up. 'How'd you know it was Imber?'

'I didn't,' said Dryden, smiling. 'But it's a bloody good guess, right? You don't get this kind of operation if some-one discharges themselves. Imber wasn't meant to walk away from police protection. He was scared to death someone was after him. If they'd guessed he might do a runner they'd have had him in custody for an interview at least. He knows a lot more about that last night in Jude's Ferry than he's telling. So – how'd he get out?'

'Call of nature for the woman PC. She asked a nurse to keep an eye on him but she got distracted and our friend took his chance.'

'And they couldn't catch a man in pyjamas doing a runner across a floodlit car park?'

'It was midnight, and he had a car outside, plus one small technicality I guess – he wasn't under arrest. It was all supposed to be for his protection.'

'A car?' said Dryden. 'What, waiting?'

'No, no. His wife dropped off a people carrier the day before. The doctors told her to bring in his CD collection as it might jog the memory banks – he told her he wanted to listen in the car and chill out. She says she believed him, but she didn't mention it to the PC. So he had the keys, and he grabbed some clothes from a locker in the orderlies' room. Left his mobile by the bed. By the time they realized he'd got out through the window he was on the road – one of the nurses arriving for the shift saw him turning north on the A10. He could be anywhere.'

Desmond's face radiated his pleasure at the misfortunes of the Establishment. 'Perhaps he's gone home.'

Dryden thought about the automatic gates to Imber's house at Upwell. 'Maybe. But I'm not sure he knows where that is.'

35

Back in the cab Dryden tracked down his mobile under the passenger seat, wrapped in a greasy pork-pie wrapper. Humph said it had rung but he'd given up the search.

'You'd be amazed at what's under that seat,' said the cabbie, sniffing a mini Scotch egg he'd found amongst the debris.

Dryden scrolled down to find he'd got a text message:

MEET TEN POACHERS HIDE WICKEN FEN MATT SMITH

Dryden looked at the name long and hard. Matthew Smith, the missing brother and Paul Cobley's partner. The police had used the media to try to find him, including *The Crow*, but why had he used the media to get back in touch? What story did he have to tell? Had his mother persuaded him to talk to the reporter as Dryden had asked? Or was this an impostor, looking for a brief splash of the limelight?

He handed the phone to Humph, who read the message, nodded, and fired up the Capri.

They drove silently in the soft summer rain, the horizon never more than a sodden field away. Pickers out with the salad crops stooped amongst the vivid green heads of broccoli and lettuce.

Dryden hit the return call button on the mobile but got transferred to voicemail. He cut himself off and sent a text instead: WHY?

Wicken was a last precious corner of the old fenland, a maze of pools and rivers hidden in a wilderness of briar and reeds, the water mottled by surfacing fish and side-winding grass snakes. The National Trust had a lodge at the entrance, a bitumen black wooden teepee surrounded by a verandah. An elderly couple weighed down with binoculars and packs were setting out down one of the duckboarded pathways as they arrived but otherwise the fen was quiet: the small car park empty and the café closed. The dense fine rain had reduced the landscape to the ghosts of trees and reeds, and a single windmill. Dryden thought about ringing Shaw and telling him about the message, filling him in on the whereabouts of Matthew Smith. But what was the point before he found out what Smith wanted to say?

Dryden paid for a ticket at the counter and found a map mounted on a board showing the paths through the reserve. Poacher's Hide was the most distant of the many which dotted the winding waterways, a single cabin overlooking a wide lake marked as the habitat of migrating swans. Access was by the duckboard walkways maintained by the Trust, although there were plenty of other ways into the reserve for those who knew the lie of the land. Dryden trudged out into the fen, the visibility falling as he moved deeper into a world dominated by water. Twenty minutes later he was at the hide, deftly hidden in a thicket of thorns on the edge of the lake.

He paused for a few seconds, wondering if there was any danger, aware that he'd made himself come this far to prove to himself, yet again, that he wasn't a coward after all. He waited, listening, for ten minutes to make sure he'd got there first, then unlatched the door and slipped inside. There was a single bench up against a long observation hatch, its wooden shutter raised on the inside and suspended from hooks. Hanging from a string was a laminated pamphlet illustrating the birds commonly sighted from Poacher's Hide, as well as butterflies, moths, and insects. Dryden scratched himself uneasily and sat, acutely aware for the first time that there was only one door to the hide.

Outside the rain had intensified so that the dripping of water from the trees provided a soundtrack. A bird, dull and brown, alighted on the windowsill and looked at Dryden with one eye. Something large and covered in fur plopped into the water and left a trail like a speedboat through the weeds.

He smiled at the bird. 'Sod off,' he said, searching in his pocket for some wine gums he'd left there a week earlier.

The footsteps, when they came, were confident and multiple. Two people at least, perhaps more. He heard one set of feet circling the hide at his back while another approached the door. For the first time he thought of the hide as a trap, and fumbled with his mobile, trying to key in a text message for Humph to get help.

But too late. A man came in, keeping his eyes on the floor, and closed the door carefully behind him. He was thin, below average height, the face strangely oval and plump, like a child's. A face Dryden would never forget, but at that moment one he'd never seen before. The lips too, full in the middle, were pursed in a cupid's bow, out of place in the rough middle-aged stubble of the chin. Dryden didn't know who he was, but he knew who he wasn't. He wasn't Matthew Smith.

The man smiled just once, but Dryden knew then he had to get out.

'Questions, I know,' the man said, holding up his hands.

He walked forward confidently and took the mobile from Dryden's hands. Outside they heard a match strike, an inward breath, the smoke expelled.

'I thought you might respond to our text. How clever of

me. But that's journalists, I find: ever hopeful, even trust-ing. It's rather uplifting in its way, and everyone seems to think it's a cynical profession.'

Dryden considered the open hatch and what would happen if he jumped through.

'How can I help?' he said, surprised by how emotionless his voice was.

The man laughed. 'My name's Roland,' he said. 'Well, it's one of my names and will have to do for our purposes. How can you help me? Well, interesting question, Mr Dryden. Do I have a problem? Yes. I do. At this moment in time a plain-clothes police team is mounting a round-the-clock surveillance operation on my home, and my business, in Coventry. They are, I'm told, under the impression I am some kind of mastermind of crime. Ridiculous, but there it is. I apparently coordinate horrific attacks on innocent people engaged in the breeding and torture of animals.'

'And that's not true?' said Dryden, his jangling nerves making him dizzy.

'Well, I didn't say that. No. Oh no. My real problem is that the police – last night actually – arrested a colleague of ours. I use the term loosely; he was a member of our organ-ization, something we now regret. They are threatening to charge him in connection with a series of incidents involv-ing Sealodes Farm. This man will betray me. Because if he does not then he will go to jail, and that's something he fears very much. And he will go to jail because he was stupid enough not to wear a balaclava on Thieves Bridge.'

Dryden couldn't stop himself reacting.

'Indeed. And it will be your evidence of identification which will be crucial. And I've no doubt you will give it, Mr Dryden – after all, you've betrayed us once already. I need to persuade you to decline to give that evidence.'

The gun, when he took it out, was at first a comfort to Dryden. It was made of a dull smudged metal like pewter and he knew it wasn't designed to fire bullets. There was a large aperture in the side of the barrel for loading something, but something that wasn't lethal.

'So you're the man they're after?' said Dryden, only just succeeding in stilling the vibrato in his voice.

'Indeed.' The bird on the sill began to sing and the man stepped forward, genuinely captivated.

'Meadow pipit,' he said. 'What a gift to hear it call.'

'What's going to happen?' said Dryden, aware that the question betrayed his fear.

'Well – on a purely personal level, Mr Dryden, I'd like to see you suffer like some of the animals do: perhaps a few days of enforced smoking, or a quick course of detergents applied to the eyes? Revenge – an unsavoury human emotion, but what the hell, eh? And then we'd very much like to persuade you that giving evidence in the forthcoming legal process – which I think is now inevitable – is something we'd like to ask you to reconsider. But we'll ask nicely, when the time comes.'

That smile again, and laughter outside. He took out the bolt quickly, a small phial with a feathered tail, and slid it into the gun. 'We use these to upset our fox hunting friends,' he said. 'I've brought a horse down with this – very effective. The fall broke the rider's leg – an excellent outcome.'

From outside there was a low whistle. The man raised the gun and pulled the trigger. Dryden watched the bolt fly, in slow motion, turning like a winning dart from a TV replay. He felt the thud in his thigh and looked down to see the dart hanging out of his flesh. He lunged toward the open window and tried to raise his arm to the sill but found it disturbingly heavy, unresponsive to the repeated electrical orders he was frantically sending from his brain. He could see the pool outside, and the still reed heads, but they seemed to be at the end of a tunnel, drawing away from him, the sound of the dull bird singing beautifully fading quickly. His knees buckled and he slumped to the floor, his head thudding without pain against the bench on the way down. He could see a man's boot close up, and the small desiccated corpse of a mouse, and then nothing.

36

When Dryden awoke he thought at first he was still on the floor of the bird hide. Just a few inches from his face he could see another corpse – but it looked like a rat this time, the two incisors protruding over the dead black lips. His cheek lay on sawdust and bare boards and there was hardly any light, so if he was in the hide it was dusk. He closed his eyes tight and listened. It didn't sound like the reserve – that deep well of whispering silence was gone, replaced by the numbness of thick walls. Outside somewhere, he could hear something flapping, not a bird's wings, a sheet perhaps, out to dry on the line. And there was the rain, St Swithun's rain, clucking in drainpipes, trickling in a gutter.

And there – a seagull calling.

But otherwise the silence of being alone. At first he thought his arms were tied behind him but as he flexed the muscles he realized they had been starved of blood, folded under him where he'd been dumped on the floor. Slowly they came to life, and when he kicked out he found his feet were free too, and so the dark edge of the panic withdrew. He rolled over quickly and saw that the light was stronger and that he was in a room of whitewashed bricks, with heavy wooden-shuttered windows held fast by iron stays. His face, when he touched it, was cold and despite the addition of a fresh graze where his cheekbone had been broken there was no pain, so he wondered if he'd been drugged again.

And then he saw movement, in the corner where the deepest shadows had fled. Something moved on the floor there in a kind of random way, milling, but completely silently. He pressed his fingers into the corners of his eyes to clear them and looked again. This time the fur caught the light and he knew: rats, behind a crude little metal fence, swarming at a water bowl as if they were feasting on the innards of some unseen victim.

DI Shaw had said the animal rights people had a base, an old airfield near Coventry, a few buildings left over from the war. A place to keep their gear, and perhaps some of the animals they'd liberated. He heard the wind again outside and imagined it sweeping over the forgotten runway, buffeting the weeds between the cracks in the concrete. And the sheet in the wind, a windsock perhaps.

Dryden wanted to shout now, but decided to wait. Something about shouting might bring back the panic, so instead he put his head against the wall, brought his knees up under his chin and stood. Pain, like a dead-leg, ran down his right side, an electric current that made his knee give way. He slumped against the wall for support and took the time to breathe deeply and look around. He was in a brick-built hut, perhaps fifty feet by twenty. There was a rich smell of petrol and the concrete floor was stained black by decades of spills and leaks: a fuel store, perhaps. They'd left him a chair and, chillingly, an upturned feeding bottle at head height attached to the wall.

'I'm an animal now,' he said, out loud to calm himself. The thirst was desperate so he licked the aluminium tube, trying to get the water to run freely.

When he saw the door, he saw the blanket laid before it. The door was metal and Dryden noticed that the lock caught the light and was new, gold against the dull rust of the original. The blanket was gorse-green and rough and it had been laid carefully over something on the cool concrete floor.

Gently shuffling his feet to dispel the pins and needles in his legs, Dryden made his way forward. The light now was vibrant, almost sunshine despite the rain he could still hear, and it spilled in pools on the floor where it leaked through the high shuttered windows.

He stopped short of the blanket. The rats, unnerved by his movement, squealed in a knot of tails and teeth. There was a note, written neatly in an educated hand on a single piece of writing paper:

FOR YOU

He swung round quickly, thinking a shadow had moved beyond the metal shutters, but the room was still. Turning back he knew two things – that he would regret lifting the blanket aside and that if he delayed any longer he'd never lift it aside.

He took a corner with one hand, bending down, and as he did so caught the merest hint of a smell he could not place but which made his heart contract. Pulling the material back quickly he lost balance and he fell away. But he'd had enough time to see, enough time to understand what they'd planned for him. He felt his heartbeat begin to creak in his chest and a familiar sensation of panic seeped between the joints of his legs and arms, making them suddenly weak and uncertain.

Dogs. Three Alsatians, their eyes still dreamy with the drugs. Dryden, on his knees, watched as a pink tongue flopped out between the sticky teeth of the nearest animal, and a featureless white eyeball fluttered under a black lid. A small two-inch patch on its hind leg had been shaved to show where an injection had been given.

'Question,' he said, his eyes searching frantically for a way to climb up to the rafters above. 'How long have I got before they come round?'

A heartbeat before the panic had taken hold of his reason, he knew there was a hope. With a shaking hand he ran a finger along the dog's chin until he found a small copper disc, adjusting it in the light until he could read it clearly.

Smiling he said the single word out loud – 'Sealodes' – and plunging into his memory retrieved the name of a small village in Alsace.

37

He went back to his chair and tried to think clearly. The sun had broken through and sets of golden stripes inched their way along the rough whitewashed walls. So morning: but what day? If the dart had put him out overnight then it was Saturday.

If he was on the old airfield then the police must be close at hand. Shaw had said they had the area under surveillance, but then Dryden bitterly reflected, they'd had Thieves Bridge under surveillance as well. Could they know Dryden was a prisoner? It was possible, as Humph had dropped him at Wicken Fen and must have raised the alarm by now. But he'd probably been smuggled onto the airfield at night or in the boot of a car. So perhaps his best plan was to devise some sort of signal to say he was a prisoner.

Escape was improbable. His mobile had been taken, the windows were shuttered in iron, the door securely locked. There were no other doors and the roof rafters were too high to reach, even with the help of the chair. Roland, he sensed, was far away. But Dryden suspected someone was keeping watch. Roland had said they wanted to make him understand that he should not give evidence if the case came to court. They wanted simply to scare him, a task they had begun efficiently and would have accomplished triumphantly if his fear of the dogs was not mitigated by the knowledge that a single word *should* render them harmless. But he could act scared if needed: it hardly needed a leap of the imagination.

He laughed to himself, trying to drive away the fear. The sudden noise disturbed the dogs and one began whimpering in a tortured half-sleep. The rats, Peyton's rats he knew now, heaved in their pen. Dryden remained in his chair, hoping that it represented a position of authority. Remembering that dogs can smell fear he willed his nervous system into neutral, concentrating instead on how he could contrive to make a big enough noise to alert a police unit which must be within a few hundred yards of the building he was in.

He needed a tool of some sort, something he could rattle against the metal shutters. He was taking off his shoe when one of the dogs rose up suddenly and double-clamped its jaws with a hollow plastic 'dolck'. It stood, disorientated, trying to clear the grogginess by shaking its head. When it saw Dryden its lips rolled back in a snarl. It tried to jump but its legs failed to respond and it slumped instead. Then its aggression overcame its bewilderment with frightening speed, and scrambling to its legs, its nails clattering on the concrete floor, it edged down the room until it stood before him, swaying slightly, one of its back legs occasionally buckling.

All its teeth now showed, and it began to drop its shoulders preparatory to an attack. A second dog was standing, while the third whimpered and struggled to rise.

Dryden knew what he had to do and knew he had to do it with authority and timing. He crossed his legs, placed either hand on the arms of the chair, and said the word as calmly and clearly as he could.

'Saverne.'

The effect was miraculously instant. The dog's eyes left his and began to wander listlessly. Relieved of its duty it staggered to the edge of the floor and slumped down, its chin on its forepaws.

'Good dog,' said Dryden, and regretted it instantly as all three dogs barked, building on the noise level and until they were baying in time. Dryden sat still, hoping the police might hear, and noting that no other dog answered their call.

Outside the only noise was the snapping of the windsock and, a long way off, an aircraft, the engine note switching as it prepared for some distant landing. And then he heard the maroon and a second later felt a jolt through the earth. He imagined the purple smudge in the sky overhead.

Part of him knew then, but his conscious mind tried to hold on to the world he had constructed around himself since coming round. A signal flare on a commercial airfield? Why?

The answer was chillingly simple. Because it wasn't a commercial airfield. And it wasn't a windsock flapping in the wind, it was a target flag. And he wasn't near Coventry, he was in Jude's Ferry, in the heart of Whittlesea Mere. But if it was Saturday, why the warning? And then he re-membered something else, a fragment from the long drug-induced sleep. This room, half seen at night, moon-light at the shutters, a plate set down, an apple, some biscuits.

A voice: 'Eat.'

And then he knew. He'd slept for two days. Yes, he was in Jude's Ferry. But it wasn't Saturday, it was Sunday, the day the army was due to begin live shelling again.

Sunday, 22 July

38

What had the army statement said? That there would be
two signal maroons – one at 9.30am and one at 9.55am,
then the first bombardment of the chosen targets would
begin at 10.00am. He had thirty minutes. He checked his
watch: he had twenty-seven.

He walked to the iron door and taking off his heavy boot
crashed the heel into the unyielding metal – a stone stuck
in the tread producing a single spark which, together with
the noise, reignited the dogs' chorus. Dryden repeated the
blow ten times and then, his heart racing, returned to his
seat to listen for a response.

He searched the silence, finding again a distant aircraft,
and now perhaps the sound of other flags – signal flags for
the distant artillery, which he imagined flying over the village,
from the church, the factory chimney, and the roof of the
Methodist Hall. The flag that he could hear was close, very
close. Was the old fuel store a target? What if there was
another wayward shell?

Suddenly the bars of sunlight were gone, and the sound
of rain plashing on the sills filled the building. The light
dimmed and the dogs, still confused by the drugs in their
blood, flopped down together. He closed his eyes, trying to
bring relief to the tension in his shoulders, but the nerve
signals from his joints seemed to buzz in time with the ticking of his wristwatch.

'So this is their punishment,' he thought. 'My torture.'

When he heard the footsteps he thought he was hallucinating; they were at the door almost before he had accepted that they were real. But the clacking of the metal key in a heavy padlock was too crisp to be imaginary, and then the door swung in and he was blinded by the light around the silhouette – the figure short, stocky, with spiky hair making him look shorter still, and at his heels a wispy-haired terrier.

And before the Alsatians could react: 'Saverne.' He stepped in and closed the door. He looked at the docile dogs. 'You knew the command word? Lucky man. They'd have scared you to death otherwise. They don't bite, but you didn't know *that*, did you?'

Dryden recognized the cruelty more than the face. 'Skeg,' he said, suddenly seeing what he should have seen. The lapel badges, the maudlin affection for the thin-ribbed dog.

'I talked about my fear of dogs to you, didn't I? Shared the confidence. Thanks for passing that on to your friends.'

Skeg was nodding his head as the terrier whimpered and slunk behind his heels away from the silent Alsatians.

'Look. I do what I do because it's right. I need to do it.' The tight-wired frame was strangely animated, releasing emotion. 'And Skeg's not my name, all right? It's Martyn, Martyn Armstrong. I like to be called that now, now I know who I am.'

Dryden didn't move, sensing his position was no longer as precarious as it seemed. Why was he being rescued? The door was unlocked, why did he need anyone's help to escape? And the name hit a note which made him see Elizabeth Drew hunched over her desk in Goods In.

He had it. 'Armstrong – you were born here. Your father was the caretaker at the factory.' And then he understood him. 'And you didn't like seeing animals caged up, did you?'

'No. I didn't like that, I'm proud of what I did, what I do.'

He rounded up the dogs and carefully attached their collars to a set of leads.

Dryden knew then why he'd come for him.

'It's the dogs, isn't it? You thought they might get hurt.'

'We're supposed to be animal rights protesters. They made me shoot 'em up.' He laughed as if he couldn't believe anything that had happened. 'Bastards. And they think we're amateurs.'

'You're my guard?'

He nodded. 'I'm supposed to make sure you were in 'ere until the shelling started and then I'm to get out and let you sweat. I guess they didn't want you getting out and wandering into a shell. In here you're probably safe, I think the army'll be pretty careful for a while after the last fiasco. We're a hundred yards from any of the targets – more. I said the noise would freak out the dogs, but they didn't care. I don't know what they care about.'

Dryden brushed a line of sweat from his forehead and flexed his arms where the stress was making the joints ache. Carried on the wind they heard the sound of a vehicle, caterpillar tracks whirring as it climbed a dyke bank.

'We better go,' said Skeg, checking his watch. 'Twenty minutes – less – we need ten to get clear.'

'You think I'm just gonna forget it was you?' said Dryden.

'Christ no. I don't want anything to do with these people; they don't really care about the animals, it's a game for them, retribution. Like it's an excuse to be cruel, to damage people. I want out. And I don't fancy my chances with them when they find you got out. So I'm gonna do my own deal – I'd make a fucking good witness in this case they keep talking about. I got them into Sealodes in the first place, I worked there for a few months last year till old Peyton gave me the push. But he let me walk the dogs, see, that's how I knew.'

He sucked in air, trying to keep his courage alive. 'I'll do it too, but I want witness protection. I got a chance that way, but you get blown to pieces it's all over for me.'

He pulled the three dogs to their feet. 'So we're all going.'

They stepped outside and the soft rain was falling again in gentle folds like net curtains. The fuel store was on the very edge of the village, beyond the river, and so the cottages on The Dring and the New Ferry Inn were a distant jumble of grey shadows.

'Will they fire in this?' said Dryden, as Skeg tried to arrange the three dogs on the leads.

'Probably,' said Skeg. 'Now they can, they will. They're just more likely to miss.' He led the dogs down to the river and then down some stone steps. 'You're gonna get soaked, the water's up over the path, but just keep with me.'

They splashed in amongst the reeds, Skeg holding the terrier under one arm and the triple lead with the other. The water was at least six feet below the edge of the dyke so that their escape was covered from view, even without the comforting blanket of rain.

Dryden reckoned they were three hundred yards clear of the edge of the village when he felt the double percussion of the two maroons through his feet: a dull visceral thud followed by a rattling scream as the signal climbed; repeated again before the first echo had died. They scrambled to the top of the dyke and looked up into the grey sky. Above their heads the two signals exploded with a crackle like fireworks, the deep purple smudges seen for just a second through the cloud.

Skeg was beside him. 'That's the all-clear. They're gonna wait for the rain to stop.'

Dryden shrugged, watching a pale sun fade behind drifting cloud. 'I still don't understand why you came back,' he said, leaning against the damp grass of the steep bank. 'Why you're here.'

Skeg embraced the head of one of the dogs, squatting down. 'We took the rats two weeks ago, before Roland and his friends got involved. We needed somewhere to keep them. The range was closed then. I knew ways in, you can still get a boat to within half a mile – they never think of that, see; with a small boat you can almost get to the Ferry. Then you turned up those old bones in the cellar and the place was crawling with coppers. It didn't bother us – so what if they found 'em? But they didn't – they didn't even cross the river. I had the dogs in town so they made me bring them out for you. As a present.'

Skeg stood. 'We should take our chance, let's go.'

Dryden was about to scramble down when he saw across the fields that the rain was lifting and that the grey shadow of Neate's old garage could be seen on Church Street. The house was lifeless, the windows black, the glass long fallen from rotten frames. But there was an outhouse, a workshop, and through the windows of the double doors Dryden saw clearly the sudden flash of an orange-red torchlight, sweeping once, twice, in the shadows.

He watched, his eyes aching with the effort of seeing through the falling greyness of the morning.

But there: again, this time from an upstairs window, the sudden flash of electricity, as unmistakable as lightning.

Someone was searching Walter Neate's garage. He decided then, before he could assemble his fears. When he looked back Skeg's head was at the parapet, waving, but Dryden turned and ran on through the wet field, exhilarated by the sudden motion, the rain running down his face. Ahead of him the light had gone, but he didn't doubt what he had seen. Someone else had returned to Jude's Ferry.

39

Up close Neate's Garage was almost entirely obscured by ivy, the bole of which was as thick as a man's torso and had split the façade of the Edwardian house, bursting out to fill the eyeless windows. The rain had stopped suddenly and the landscape was still, trapped in a paperweight.

Dryden moved towards a downstairs window and looked in. The ceiling had collapsed and the floor was obscured by distended lumps of plaster, rotting timber and the remains of a dead sheep, the lines of the skull softened by alpine-green moss.

From the back of the house came the thin creak of a door, and boots on floorboards. Dryden circled the building and came to the corner around which lay the rear garden. A blackthorn bush had burst out of the concrete path and writhed against the brickwork. Through the black maze of the branches Dryden could see a man standing with his back to the house, his head turned up into the grey sky. In one hand he had a spade and the other a garden fork, both flaked with rust. He retrieved what looked like a quarter bottle of whisky from his coat and took a long drink, wiping his eyes and mouth afterwards with the back of his hand. He seemed to be orientating himself to the main features of the old garden – an oak tree in the far corner, a path made from circles of York stone and a trio of apple trees which had once been expertly intertwined but which were now suffocating each other, the stunted fruit diseased on the branch. And close to where he stood the frost-shattered remains of a stone bird table.

One of the blackthorn twigs broke and the man turned, giving Dryden a half second to duck back behind the corner of the house. There was a silence, punctuated by the sound of a match struck, then unmistakably the gritty slice of the spade cutting through the blue clay upon which the village lay, and the slight sucking sound of the clod being lifted from the wet earth. And another noise, less rhythmic, the sharp intake of breaths which accompany spasms of pain. The methodical work continued, and Dryden thought of the graves which had dominated the story of Jude's Ferry – from Peyton's tomb to the cellar itself in which Peter Tholy's frail body had been left to hang. And then there was another noise, unmistakable in that still air, the sound of metal on wood. Dryden peered round the corner and saw the man kneel, plunge his arms down into the trench that he'd dug and lift something free of the earth. He didn't stand but sank onto his heels, amongst the loose soil he'd turned out of the grave. Beside him on the ground he'd laid out a mildewed blanket which Dryden guessed he'd found in one of the old bedrooms, but he didn't place the object down. With his back to Dryden he rocked silently, cradling it to his chest, one hand rising to hold his head. Then he stood and turned and Dryden saw clearly what he held: a small wooden coffin caked in black earth, its white paint flaking. And Dryden saw the face of the man who'd reclaimed the body from the earth. The face was disfigured by dried blood, an ugly black wound cutting up between the forehead and the hairline. For a moment he thought it was indeed Jason Imber, returned to bury his son. But the skin was paler, the face dominated by the Celtic brow, the muscles knotted on the arms, the broken body seemingly supported by the blue mechanic's overalls. And so he saw the face before him for what it was – that of Kathryn Neate's brother, not hanging charred on the wire, but alive, a fresh gout of blood oozing from a wound on his head and trickling through his fingers.

40

In the silence a wood pigeon cooed and then footsteps sounded, leading away from the house, along the old road towards the village. Dryden crept from the ruins in time to see the grey silhouette fading into the mist, the angular coffin still held across Neate's chest, wrapped in the blanket, just visible from behind.

Dryden padded along the grass verge, keeping him within sight until he reached the allotments at the foot of Church Hill, where Neate turned off the road and out of sight. Dryden waited until he saw him reappear by the old church before following, threading his way uphill through the tangled berries and the ramshackle huts. Rain still trickled from the Victorian gutters of the church roof, and a rook cracked its wings between the battlements of the tower.

At the open doors of St Swithun's he stopped, aware now that he was close enough to be heard if he stumbled, and unable to push aside the image of what he now assumed was Jason Imber's corpse, the smoke still drifting from the charred clothes he had stolen from the orderlies' room at the hospital. He waited a full minute, listening, and then edged away into the churchyard. He moved from buttress to buttress until he was beside the window the army had blown out just a week earlier. The rain had already buckled the chipboard so that he could see through a gap into the church. Directly opposite in the far wall was the small Victorian door to the ossuary Fred Lake had described. From within came the sudden, violent sound of wood being wrenched, rusted nails finally breaking free. Dryden stood, waiting, compelling himself to remain still despite an over-whelming need to know why this small child's bones had meant so much.

Then the door swung open and he saw Jimmy Neate surrounded by bones, blood spattered on his overalls. At his feet the small coffin lay, shattered now. The far wall of the ossuary was covered in rough shelves, once white-washed, now grey with dust. Skulls filled them, and in the apex of the roof were stacked to the rafters. The floor, but for a narrow stone path, was made up of skeleton bones, thigh bones emerging from shattered ribs and a dusty weathered compost of medieval fingers.

Jimmy Neate looked about him, surveying his work. He picked up the shards of wood, stepped unsteadily outside and through the little Gothic door, and then closed it firmly. The sun, as pale as butter, glinted on the old key as he turned the lock, and Dryden remembered that Walter Neate had been sexton at St Swithun's for forty years. Neate didn't look back, walking quickly down the nave carrying the coffin and lid, awkwardly now, like lumber. Dryden waited until he'd left the graveyard and saw that he'd dumped the wood, probably amongst the rubble and burnt roof timbers the army had collected in a skip by the lychgate.

Then, overhead, in the blue sky, which was being stretched clear and pale as the mist fled, he saw the purple scar like a synapse, then heard the dull percussion of the maroon. A warning – the bombardment postponed was to begin at last. Dryden guessed they had five minutes, perhaps less. He saw Neate stop, watching the signal fade in the breeze, and then bow his head, holding the wound, before changing direc-tion, doubling back around the graveyard wall towards the old water tower on Telegraph Hill, keeping below the skyline.

Dryden gave him two minutes and followed, and as he ran across the open grass he looked up and saw the red target flag flying from the pole at the top of the tower, above the whitewashed wooden dovecote. The door of the three-storey brick tower stood open and stepping inside Dryden heard footsteps ascending a metal ladder somewhere above. The room he was in was twenty-five-feet square and had once held a diesel pump for the village's drinking water. A small modern electric pump stood in its place, dusty and unused now that the army had its own supply to tackle fires after each bombardment. In one corner pipes ran in and out of the brick walls, and then upwards to the tank above. Equipment, mothballed now, stood against one wall for test-ing water quality. Four large elegant windows flooded the room with light. Against one wall was an open metal stair-way with handrail, and Dryden climbed it, waiting for the moment when his eyes rose level with the second-storey room. This was empty too, littered with the tiny dry carcasses of thousands of greenfly born into the fetid, damp, atmos-phere of the enclosed tower. He climbed again, a shorter flight this time, to another empty room; but not quite: at its centre was a single metal twisting staircase rising, enclosed in circular safety bars, up through a circular shaft in the middle of the black metal tank above.

A footfall, perhaps above.

Dryden considered his options, sensing the weight and mass of the dark water above his head. He could slip away. He knew now where Jimmy Neate had hidden the bones of his sister's child. But why? Had he murdered Jason Imber? His own sister too? And why now was he seeking death, beneath the crimson red target flag?

How long since the maroon? Three minutes perhaps,

more. He took a step back, preparing to climb down to the safety of the earth.

But the voice was behind him, not above.

'Dryden.' Jimmy Neate stood by the top of the stairs, the light from one of the windows leaving half his face in shadow. The other half was caked in blood, and where the wound was deepest, the light glistened on exposed flesh and a hint of shattered bone beneath. Outside, through the frosted glass, they could just see the distant shape of the church.

'You followed me here?' said Neate, and the effort made his knees buckle so that he had to lean against the wall.

'Jason Imber said he was coming here to bury his son. I thought you were dead on the wire at the Stopover.'

Neate nodded. 'You followed me here,' he said again, and Dryden guessed that he wanted to know if he'd seen him slip into the ossuary.

'No. I saw you climbing the hill, I was down by The Dring looking for Jason.'

'You should go,' said Neate, standing aside, the tension ebbing from his body.

Dryden didn't move. 'This was Jason's plan,' said Neate. 'To kill me, and then kill himself. He should be standing here, but he's hanging on the wire.' He stopped and turned away, and Dryden wondered if he was crying.

'You tried to kill him at Cuckoo Bridge,' said Dryden. 'There was a witness who saw your car. They said there was something odd, that they thought there was just a passenger on board, parked up. But it was left-hand drive of course, one of the American cars from the garage. He wanted to go to the police, didn't he, to tell them he'd been there when Peter Tholy was lynched?'

'Yes. I couldn't let him do that. He said he'd take all the

blame, that he wouldn't name names. But they'd have got to him. We couldn't take the chance. And he'd promised to keep the secret, as we'd all promised that morning at Orchard House. When you found Peter's skeleton we checked around, making sure we'd got it straight; who went down, and who stayed up in the bar. Ken said if they identified Tholy then he'd go to the police, tell 'em our story, make sure we got in first. But he told you, which kinda worked better.'

He smiled, forgetting the pain.

Dryden cut in. 'So you threw him off the bridge. But he lived. As long as his amnesia lasted you were safe. But you couldn't bank on it, so you were going to make a run for it – the suitcases were ready. And you tried to send us off on a false trail, telling me all about Ken Woodruffe's plans for Ellen. But you ran out of time. Jason Imber did remember and he came looking for you. He didn't want revenge for himself, did he, Jimmy – he wanted it for Kathryn. Because he knew then that you'd killed her, that you'd let him think all those years that he'd been the one who'd snuffed her out that night. Laura told him we'd found Kathryn's bones and that she'd been stabbed, that the ribs were chipped by a blade to the heart. But if you'd found the body then you must have seen the knife wound. It didn't make any sense unless you'd been the one who'd killed her. And you'd taken the body away so that nobody could see, wound it in the carpet to hide the blood and got Walter to help bury her quickly. You didn't want to bury her in the tomb, did you, because that might draw attention one day to Jude's bones. You wanted to bury her out on the mere – but it was Walter's word that counted that night. So when you had the chance you took the child. And that's what Jason Imber couldn't understand, what he desperately needed to understand.'

'It's time,' said Neate. 'You should go, Dryden. Why bother with questions now.'

'Because I want an answer. An answer to the question Jason Imber came to ask: why hide Jude's bones? Well?'

They felt the explosion of the first shell before the searing sound shook the old water tower. Dust fell on them in a cloud and one of the windows imploded, a jagged pain registering in Dryden's ears.

When he lifted his head from the floor, where he'd fallen, Dryden saw that Neate was against the brick wall, his head cradled in his hands.

Then he looked up, the open wound now caked in dirt. 'You'll die here too if you stay. They've gone for the factory first, but they'll hit the tower. Go.'

Dryden knelt on the floorboards. 'The answer?' he said simply.

Neate smiled, deciding at last. 'Christ. He didn't like the answer,' he said. 'And neither will you. She killed him, Dryden. Kathryn killed him, with poison. Ethylene glycol – antifreeze. That's why I took the bones, took them that night down to the garage and buried them in the garden – it wasn't safe enough, but it was all I could do. I couldn't risk it, people were gossiping about Jude, saying Kathryn had wanted him dead. But Dad hadn't heard, no one had the guts to gossip to him, so I couldn't stop him burying Kathryn in the tomb.

'So I had to do it. I didn't want them to know, for Dad to know, what she'd done. And it would have been all right if you hadn't found Kathryn's bones. Jason found out about the chipped ribs, the knife that took her life. So I knew I had to move Jude again – that the police might come looking, so it had to be somewhere safer. They won't find them now. And that means they'll never be able to prove what she did.'

Dryden felt the truth had been twisted. 'You did all that for her? I don't think so.'

The pressure clicked in Dryden's ears and he threw himself to the floor as the second shell hit home down by the factory. Above them the old iron tank twisted, and a gush of water fell down one wall, swamping the floor. A wooden beam fell, bouncing once on its end, before crashing to the floor.

Dryden crawled towards the stairwell. 'I think it was you and Walter who didn't want the child,' he said, the room dense now with dust and debris. 'She might have given him the poison; did she? Perhaps. But you were holding her hand, because it's what you thought Walter wanted. And it's what she'd said she'd wanted, so she couldn't escape. But what I can't work out is why you wanted it, Jimmy? Why did you want Jude dead?'

The wind blew through the shattered window, and Dryden imagined the guns being reloaded, the hot shell cases smoking in the grass.

'And then, when the funeral was finally over, she'd made that appointment to see her social worker. You found out about that when Lake came to say she couldn't have a lift. She was going to tell them what you'd done, what you'd helped her do. Isn't that right, Jimmy?

'And Magda Hollingsworth had called as well. She knew about the rumours that the child had been killed. She'd put it in her diary and my guess is she was going to tell the police, to clear her conscience before she left the Ferry. And if they'd interviewed Kathryn she'd have told them the truth, that you and Walter had helped her kill the baby – to kill Jude.'

Neate stood, staggering to the blown-out window and looking out over the village.

'Magda,' he said, spitting the word out. 'We told her to go, to keep out of other people's lives, told her she didn't belong, that she'd never belonged. An outsider. A gyppo. A fucking pikey. She didn't like that, didn't like it one bit. Coming round sticking her nose in our business. We told her to go – she wouldn't be missed. She cried.' He laughed at the memory. 'Said she wanted to do right by the baby, said it over and over again. The police tracked me down after she went missing – they'd seen the diary and worked out it must be about Kathryn. I told them the truth – so did George – that we turfed her out and that was that.'

Suddenly blood trickled in a stream from the wound. He raised a hand but it had reached his eye, so he sank to his knees, cradling his skull.

'I found Kathryn on the towpath.' His voice thick with the phlegm and blood in his throat.

'We'd started searching when she didn't come back from Tholy's cottage. I took a knife, I knew there'd be trouble. She was sat on the bank, the bruises on her neck black in the moonlight. So I asked her who'd done it and she said it was Tholy. Another lie.'

'So it was a perfect opportunity to kill her,' said Dryden, knowing time was running out. 'But she had to die with Peter's hands round her neck, not from the knife. That's why you hid the truth about her wound. What you didn't know was that it wasn't Tholy at all – but Jason Imber.'

Neate blinked, and Dryden thought he was trying not to see something, something which had haunted him for seventeen years.

'She said I'd killed the child. That she'd been ill, depressed, and that we'd tricked her into it. She was going to tell – that she'd told Tholy already. It's true I showed her the stuff, the poison, that it was quick.'

Dryden risked the accusation again. 'So you killed her with the knife – and then led the mob to Tholy.'

'And Jason Imber stood by and watched,' he said, some spit showing white by the corner of his mouth. He touched the wound again. 'He was waiting for me, in the garage. I was packing the stuff. I'd fought with Julie so she'd taken some pills and gone to sleep. He hit me with a wrench before I'd realized it was him. But I got hold of his hand, then his arm. I dragged him to the vehicle well and got a tyre chain round his legs. He said I'd killed Kathryn, and stolen his son's bones. Said I'd stolen his life too, making him believe for all those years that he'd strangled the life out of her. He wanted to know why I did what I did. I told him, then I hit his head on the floor, against the concrete, hard until I heard the bone crack and then I poured petrol over him. It was a way out, the only one I could see – if the police found a body, burnt out, then they might not be sure it was me. I could have just faded away. So I lit it – but he wasn't dead.'

Matter-of-fact, devoid of emotion.

'He ran to the woods, blindly, and then he saw the water beyond the wire and tried to get to it. When I got there he'd stopped climbing and the body was still, so I let him burn.'

'And then you cut the wire,' said Dryden. 'Where did you go?'

Neate's hand returned to the wound on his head. 'I took some food and clothes. There's an old sheepfold out on the mere where we played as kids. I wanted this to heal, but it won't.' He dropped his hand and examined the blood on his palm.

Dryden nodded. 'What you didn't know was that he'd set light to the trees as he ran through, the fire spread to the bungalow.'

Dryden watched Neate's eyes; a single blink, a slight jerk of the chin.

'She'll live,' he said. 'But no thanks to you.'

Neate looked out again. 'Go, or you'll die,' he said, and Dryden knew then that he hadn't told the whole truth, that he was going to let that perish with him on Telegraph Hill. 'It might as well end here,' said Neate, not turning away from the light.

Dryden dropped swiftly down the flights of stairs out into the now brilliant sunshine.

He stood for a second considering his options. A thick pall of smoke rose from the old factory, drifting low over the village towards the church. He ran west and then down the hill to The Dring, turning north along the old Whittlesea Road. When he got to the cattery where the Smith girl had worked he cut off the road into the open fields, finding a low ditch to take cover. Looking back he was in time to see a gout of black earth springing up from a spark of red flame just thirty feet from the old water tower, then came the percussion, the thud felt through the earth. The second shell found its mark, punching a hole beside one of the windows on the second floor and exploding within the room. The blast blew all the remaining windows out and smoke, like milk, filled the interior. The third shell fell into the roof and Dryden heard the unmistakable scream of steel being twisted out of shape, and the hiss of water falling down through the burning rooms below.

Wednesday, 1 August

41

They let the villagers back one last time to bury the bones of Kathryn Neate and her son Jude. Crowded into St Swithun's they could hear the rain which still fell on the grey stones of the graveyard. At the lychgate a gaggle of press photographers held a line set down by the police, shutters whirring. And over Whittlesea Mere a single tenor bell rang out sixteen times for Kathryn, once for her son, the ringers struggling with the rotten ropes and the falling dust in the bell chamber.

Inside, the villagers edged forward down the nave, past the rows of plastic seats, seeing in each other's faces the joy and despair which had filled the years they'd been away from Jude's Ferry, the years in which Peter Tholy's bones had hung in the lightless cellar. Dryden sat on a stone bench by the ossuary watching them, Humph beside him, tiny hands held in a prayer over his stomach.

Matthew Smith and Paul Cobley stood together, pale beneath their summer tans, their shoulders close but never touching. Jan Cobley was with them, alone, trying to be proud of the son who had torn her family apart. Smith's twin, Mark, stood with his wife on the other side of the nave, a lifetime apart from his brother, his eyes set on the remains of the stained-glass figure of St Swithun above the altar in the east window. And Ken Woodruffe held back, in the side aisle near the Peyton tomb, an uncertain hand pushing his thin hair over his skull, nodding to those who were prepared to acknowledge him.

And then the Reverend Fred Lake climbed the charred pulpit and looked down on the two coffins set on trestles in the nave, below the patched hole in the roof punched out by the stray artillery shell.

'Let us pray,' he said, and what was left of Jude's Ferry fell to its knees.

Dryden, suddenly suffocated by a sense of being too close to a past he no longer wished to share, slipped out through the warped oak doors into the rain. The press had retreated beneath a sycamore where they huddled under umbrellas, waiting for the service to end. Laughter, barely suppressed, rippled through the group. Dryden recognized faces, a few from his Fleet Street past, and felt uneasy again, finding himself part of the story. The gruesome death of Jason Imber on the perimeter wire of the range, the identification of the bones of Kathryn Neate and the suicide of her brother had been enough to bring the Fleet Street pack to Whittlesea Mere; they had a few facts, but as yet no story to link them all together.

DI Shaw stood by his black Land Rover, a white shirt open at the neck, enjoying the cool rain. On the dashboard Dryden glimpsed a row of seashells and a package, rolled roughly in newspaper. A brace of sea rods was bound expertly to the roof rack, ready for a trip.

'The beach?' asked Dryden.

Shaw nodded. 'A few days off.' He looked towards the church. 'I came to talk to Ruth Lisle,' he said. They moved into the lee of the tower out of the wind, looking down on the village, monochrome in the flat afternoon light.

'They're all inside,' said Dryden. 'Why Ruth?'

DI Shaw looked towards Telegraph Hill. 'The shelling punctured the tank in the water tower. It took some time but the 600 gallons finally seeped out this morning. There were some bones at the bottom, human bones, weighted with stones in an overcoat pocket. It's difficult to say, but there was a silver anklet above the right foot.'

Dryden saw her again, walking along the road to Neate's Garage, relieved perhaps that she had finally taken the decision to unburden herself of her debt to Jude. And then the brutal rejection at the hands of Jimmy Neate and George Tudor – the final confirmation that she was still an outsider, would always be an outsider. So she'd run, suddenly overcome by the depression which had haunted her that summer, run up to Telegraph Hill where she had always found peace. She knew where Bob Steward kept the keys so she'd got them, climbed up as he had done through the empty brick rooms and then further, past the point where Dryden had stopped – up the spiral staircase to the platform above the black dripping water, below the dank wooden roof.

Then she'd let gravity take her life.

Dryden shivered. 'Magda called at Neate's Garage that last night to say there was a rumour in the village that Kathryn had poisoned the baby, and so she was going to go to the police, and that she wanted the family to be prepared for that. An honourable woman, foolish too. All she wanted was a home.'

Dryden leant back against the rough stone wall. 'They drove her out. A hundred years ago they'd have done it with clods of earth. But they knew her, they knew how to hurt her – with words. How to make her feel exactly what she didn't want to feel – rejected like an eternal outsider, carrying the stigma of the newcomer who doesn't belong. It was what she'd always feared. It was enough.'

They both looked towards the distant ruin of the water tower on Telegraph Hill, a grey silhouette in the rain.

'I doubt she ever suspected the truth; that Jimmy had

331

poisoned the child, or at least harried his sister into giving the child the dose,' said Dryden. 'God. Imagine it.'

Dryden looked into Shaw's water-blue eyes and saw the first hint that the truth was worse.

'Jude's bones,' said Shaw, looking down at the grass. There was a stone tomb chest behind him and for the first time since Dryden had met him he sat – a small act of respect.

Dryden felt the slight nausea which always told him he'd got something wrong, that some fundamental truth had eluded him. 'Jimmy said they'd used ethylene glycol – that there'd be traces,' he said.

Shaw returned his gaze. 'I don't want this used – not yet. You can have it first when we're ready. The forensics aren't signed off.'

Dryden stepped closer. 'Tell me.'

'We had a series of test results. The DNA on the Ducados in the grave matched up to Jimmy Neate.'

'What?'

Shaw shrugged. 'Real life's like that. Perhaps Ken Woodruffe offered him one while they dug the grave. It's a lucky break for Ken, although he neither deserves nor needs it. I wouldn't get a murder charge past a committal with the evidence we've got, and the alibis they've manufactured are pretty watertight. But a DNA match would at least have given us a chance of breaking him down, peeling him away from the rest. But no go, I'm afraid.'

Dryden nodded, knowing that wasn't the news Shaw had brought. 'What else?'

'Jude's bones. The toxicology is clean, which it wouldn't be with that kind of poison. It lodges in the bones, and it'd still be there if it had killed Jude Neate seventeen years ago.'

Dryden pushed himself away from the stone wall of the nave.

'And I checked with the death certificate,' said Shaw. 'The doctor who attended was a locum from Peterborough, near retirement, and now dead. But he kept decent notes. The baby had been born with severe jaundice and a blood transfusion had been recommended. There was a rapid deterioration, they tried to get him into hospital, but he died before leaving the house. Natural causes. There was a full post mortem, which wouldn't have detected the antifreeze, but then we now know he hadn't been dosed with that. I think he died of natural causes, Dryden.'

Dryden looked up into the sky, trying to work it out, to see what could have driven Jimmy Neate to hide his nephew's bones that night in 1990, and then to return to try and make sure they'd never be found.

'But the answer *was* in the bones,' said Shaw. 'I was unhappy with some of the assumptions we'd made about identity in this case so we set about cross-checking DNA samples. We needed to find Jude's skull in the ossuary – the child's other bones were probably dust, anyway – so we did some standard tests using material from Tholy's bones, and from Imber's corpse. Both candidates for the child's father. There were no matches at all.'

'There must be . . .' said Dryden.

Shaw held up a hand. 'We used Kathryn's DNA and found him quickly enough. But it was Jude's DNA which told the truth.'

'Meaning?'

'The science is a bit of a nightmare, but broadly we've found that it is probable, certainly beyond doubt in my mind, that Jude's birth was the result of an incestuous relationship – a very close incestuous relationship. Practically speaking, the father was one of two people – either Kathryn's brother or her father, Walter. So we matched up Jimmy and the child's

DNA and got the exact match we were looking for. There's little doubt, Dryden. Jimmy Neate was the father of his sister's child.'

Once he'd said it Dryden knew it was true, the extent of Kathryn Neate's nightmare life revealed at last.

'No chance it's Walter?' he asked.

Shaw shook his head.

'Surrounded by men,' said Dryden, watching a crow shuffle on the rim of a gravestone.

'I'm sorry,' said Shaw, as much to the gravestones as to Dryden.

Inside the church the congregation sang, Fred Lake's the only voice clear and strong.

Dryden shook his head. 'Jimmy couldn't risk a pathologist getting near the bones. Even in 1990 there'd have been enough genetic material to lead them back to the family. But with modern methods and technology Jimmy was right in the frame. With the police now in pursuit it would not take them long to search the old garage and garden. That's why he came back – he knew it was all over but he still couldn't die with the knowledge that his crime would finally be revealed. Above all that it would be revealed to Walter – probably the only human being Jimmy Neate actually ever cared about.'

A few villagers had left the church now and were standing in a group in the churchyard, cigarette smoke curling up above their heads, huddled close under umbrellas.

Dryden looked up, letting raindrops fall into his face. 'I think Kathryn threatened to expose him that night on the towpath. And to protect herself she told Jimmy that Tholy knew the truth, a little lie that cost Tholy his life as well. If she did tell Tholy, he took the secret to the grave with him. But no one would have believed him anyway.'

A crow cackled from a hawthorn tree and made Dryden

jump. The press was bunched at the gate again trying to entice comment from the mourners with little success.

They walked to Shaw's Land Rover and the detective reached inside and retrieved the newspaper package and gave it to Dryden.

'Sea trout,' he said. 'A brace. Caught just after dawn.'

Dryden could smell the ozone and the salt. 'They're all guilty,' he said. 'All of them in the cellar. The mob.'

Shaw laughed, shaking Dryden's hand. 'But no one was in the cellar – they all went home that night. Jan Cobley heard Paul coming in about 11.00 apparently. They shared a drink in the garden. The Smiths had their fight, made up, and split a bottle of whisky in the front room of the family council house. Their sister watched them from the stairs and remembers the clocks chiming midnight – a charming scene. Ken Woodruffe was in bed with Jill Palmer. We tracked her down in Sheffield – married with two kids. But still sticking to the story. You can't really blame her, it's a past she doesn't want to revisit.

'When he came to making a statement Woodruffe was a little more selective with the truth than he had been with you. Sure, he admits digging the grave for Ellen and conceal-ing the trapdoor, but he insists he stayed in the bar with the others when Jimmy and George Tudor dragged Peter Tholy into the yard. He claims he never knew what happened later, didn't want to know, and that he'd shut the pub when the mob left. He named those he claimed made up the gang – all of whom, except Walter Neate, are now dead.'

'And George Tudor?'

'Interviewed by police in Fremantle yesterday. He named Jimmy Neate as the ringleader who took Tholy down to the cellar – but by then he knew he was dead. Ken Woodruffe's made six calls to Australia in the last three days according to his BT records, so not surprisingly Tudor's story tallies beautifully with the others. He denies sending the postcards home impersonating Tholy, or ringing his mother. And, of course, he wasn't down in the cellar either. He says he walked home alone at midnight, had a sleepless night, but heard nothing.'

Shaw leant against the damp black bodywork of the car. 'So the only names I've got of those in the cellar are on stones like these,' he said, looking into the graveyard. 'Woodruffe now says Jimmy Neate and Jason Imber went down – along with three old boys from the almshouses. All dead. And Walter Neate of course, but he's never leaving the bed he took to when they told him his son had gone before him. The only person who was ready to tell us who was really in that cellar was Jason Imber, and he paid for that with his life.'

Dryden looked down at the crowd, dispersing now, climbing into an army coach parked up below the allotments. 'But Imber's e-mail to Laura said there were twelve of them that night. So there's six missing. My guess would be Woodruffe, Cobley, the Smiths, and Tudor. We're still one short.'

Shaw looked at his boots in the grass. 'My job's getting people into court, Dryden. If there's one missing, there's one missing. Fact is, I haven't enough evidence to issue a parking ticket to any of them when it comes to murder. My best bet was conspiracy to pervert, seeing as they do admit that they knew Kathryn had been killed, and that they failed to report that in 1990, and again when Peter Tholy's skeleton came to light. But conspiracy's a tough call – it only needs one of them to slip the charge and the whole lot walk. And do we really want a trial which highlights the fact we can't nail anyone for the murder? The file's with the CPS, but I wouldn't hold your breath.'

'So they got away with it, didn't they?' said Dryden.

'You think? You don't have to be behind bars to serve a sentence, Dryden. Jimmy Neate went gladly to his death, which tells you something about the life he had.'

The wind had picked up, and Dryden turned his face into it, closing his eyes.

'I'd like them to know that their guilt isn't a secret any more,' said Dryden.

Shaw climbed into the Land Rover. 'They know,' he said. 'Believe me, they all know. But if I can't get a conviction I need to move on. They'll just have to go on living with what they did. They hanged an innocent man, something they didn't know until a few days ago. So that's something Jason Imber would be proud of. The truth. It's justice of a sort.' Shaw edged the 4x4 forward, rolling up the side window, and joined the queue of vehicles edging its way down Church Hill.

The rain, heavier now, began to bounce off the gravestones.

Dryden found Major Broderick in the church standing before the wreaths arranged on the Peyton tomb.

'Spectacular,' said Broderick, nodding at a huge bouquet of lilies.

'Your father grew lilies, didn't he, when he was here at Jude's Ferry. It was a kind of brand almost, what he did best, right?'

Broderick nodded, sensitive enough to pick up the insistence in Dryden's voice, the edge of accusation.

'So when he offered to decorate the church for Jude Neate's funeral it had to be lilies. Lilies, Fred Lake said, hundreds of them beautifully arranged. And that must have been you. Your father was in a wheelchair by then and no one else had the skills, except perhaps for Peter Tholy and he said he spent all day packing in his cottage down on The

Dring – except for a brief visit to your father that evening. Did you meet him then?'

Broderick stepped forward and ran the petals of a rose through his fingers.

'Did you hate him?' asked Dryden, walking round the tomb, aware now that they were alone. 'I wouldn't blame you if you did. He'd taken your place in some ways, a son's place. And then he came that last evening and your father gave him something, didn't he, some money?'

Dryden nodded as if there had been an answer. 'He tried to buy his life with it later, in the inn, didn't he? He told them he had money but they all laughed. Did you laugh?'

Broderick looked around, checking they were still alone. 'Ten thousand pounds – unbelievable, really. Dad was rich, but still. It was an insult, an insult to me. Sometimes I think that if Peter had lived and stayed in England Dad would have left him the lot.' He took a deep breath. 'But I just took it, like I'd taken all the insults down the years. Peter took the cheque and went. It was never cashed, so I guess the rats had it.'

'And Tholy went back to pack and you went down to the New Ferry Inn to join your friend Jason Imber. He said he wasn't the only outsider there that night. That's you, isn't it? And you went down into the cellar.'

Broderick took a small knife from his pocket and cut the rose free, pushing it through his buttonhole.

'And that's what I couldn't work out. Why it was that nobody mentioned your name at all, why they'd all agreed to that. There was a deal, but what was in it for them?'

The Reverend Lake appeared from the vestry, and sensing the mood walked quickly past, his footsteps echoing down the nave until the door swung open and they saw the rain still falling outside.

'Then I got an e-mail from Colonel Flanders May, outlining how he'd undertaken the survey of Jude's Ferry in the days after the evacuation. Apparently there was this young TA cadet who volunteered. He knew your father, didn't he? So there was no problem getting a temporary posting. Terrific help apparently, lots of local knowledge, trawled through the questionnaires making sure nothing had been missed. It can't have been difficult I guess, steering them clear of the outbuildings. Woodruffe did a good job covering the trapdoor. But it must have been a comfort to them, to know you'd be there, that you'd always be there. And when the worst happened you made sure they all knew, and that they knew what the plan was, who they should blame when the police started asking questions. What you didn't know was that your friend was the real killer that night, and you'd snapped the neck of an innocent boy. But you know now. Did he tell you when you visited him at the hospital that day?'

Broderick's face froze, a vein on his forehead knotted with stress. 'If I'd known the truth I'd have stopped it then,' he said. 'You can't prove any of this.'

'I know that. You're quite safe. I'm just curious, you know, curious to know if you were glad to see Peter Tholy's head lolling on a broken neck.'

Broderick clipped his heels together. 'I must go.' He examined the braiding on his military cap. 'I felt lots of emotions that night,' he said. 'We made a mistake, many mistakes, but I'm going to have live with that.'

'Yes. I'm afraid you are, that's all the justice there is in Jude's Ferry.'

Postscript

Jimmy Neate was cremated in Peterborough. Julie Watts attended but, seeing a press photographer, fled before the brief ceremony began. Walter Neate was taken by ambulance to the chapel and was the only mourner. He refused to comment on the case. A statement was issued by the health authority which ran the home in which he was a resident pointing out that he wished to be left in peace to grieve for his children, and his grandson.

Magda Hollingsworth's bones were buried in Ely in the town cemetery, just a few minutes' walk from her daughter's house. Dryden attended a crowded funeral service. The lesson was read by a representative from the University of Surrey, and tribute was paid to Magda's years of sympathetic observation of her fellow villagers at Jude's Ferry.

Peter Tholy's bones remained in police custody for some time. Australian police officers finally contacted his mother to inform her of her son's death. She said she didn't care what happened to her son's remains as long as they didn't send her a bill. Major Broderick paid for cremation in lieu of the £10,000 cheque from his father Peter Tholy never cashed. The ashes are interred at Ely Crematorium and marked by a simple stone plaque.

The animal rights activist identified by Dryden at Thieves Bridge led DI Shaw's team to arrest and charge three senior members of the organization based in Coventry, including the man known as Roland. Forensic evidence for the case was collected from Coleshill Airfield near Rugby. The three are due to appear at Newark Crown Court on charges of conspiracy to cause grievous bodily harm, and attempted blackmail. Eighteen similar charges are to be put before the court. The

CPS is still considering DI Shaw's recommendation that seven men face charges of conspiracy to pervert the course of justice by withholding information about the murder of Kathryn Neate. Unofficially the detective has been advised the file is likely to remain open but that action is unlikely owing to the length of time that has passed since the original offence and the deaths of key witnesses.

Henry Peyton's business continues to flourish, security enhanced by the return of his wife's three pedigree Alsatians. Contracts with a group of overseas universities and research institutes have allowed Sealodes Farm to concentrate exclusively on providing animals for medical research. All supplies to cosmetic and other commercial companies have been terminated. The business won a Queen's Award for Enterprise.

Jason Imber's body was identified by dental records. He was buried privately in Upwell but a memorial service was held at All Souls' Church in London, beside Broadcasting House, attended by TV executives, actors and fellow writers.

Laura's performance in The Silent Daughter was widely praised. Her return to TV seven years after the accident which appeared to have ended her career prompted a series of tabloid newspaper stories. She made a string of brief appearances in Casualty. Further offers of work are being considered by her agent.

Major Broderick resigned his commission shortly after witnessing the bombardment which had killed Jimmy Neate. The family business – Blooms – continues to blossom, and the major has diversified further, returning to his father's first love – the breeding of roses. A deep red variety, with an almost black heart, sells extremely well and won a silver medal at the Chelsea Flower Show. It is called 'Jude's Ferry'.

The death of Jimmy Neate marked the end of any campaign to reclaim Jude's Ferry as a living village. The range at Whittlesea is now in use throughout the year, training soldiers for active service in the Middle East. Joint operations with the US army are a regular *feature of these exercises. The church has suffered no more wayward shells but dry rot has attacked the roof beams and a storm severely damaged the louvres surrounding the bell chamber. The church has been deconsecrated. There was no last service.*

The hunt for Philip Dryden after his disappearance from the hide at Wicken Fen, and the story he had to tell once he'd walked to safety out of Jude's Ferry two days later, made national news. But soon the media circus had rolled on and he returned to The Crow's *diet of petty crime and parish pump. But not all has remained the same: he now has a more flexible contract with the paper so that he can sometimes be with his wife during rehearsals and filming. Laura's speech has improved remarkably, although her doctors still consider a full recovery unlikely. She has, however, mastered crutches and the wheelchair has been stowed below decks.*

Ruth Lisle has written a book based on her mother's observations of life in Jude's Ferry. It has, as yet, failed to attract a publisher.

The Peyton Society of Pittsburgh paid $360,000 for the transfer and restoration of the family tomb to St John's Church, Boston, Lincs. An action for compensation against the MoD was settled out of court for a sum understood to be in the region of £60,000.

Humph enjoyed Christmas in the Faroe Islands and is now learning Sami, having booked Christmas 2008 in Lapland.

Dryden has built Boudicca a wooden kennel on the bank beside PK 129.

DI Peter Shaw sits beside his sea rod on the beach at Old Hunstanton, waiting for his next case.